Son of a Star

Andrew Meisels

SON OF
A STAR

G. P. Putnam's Sons
New York

Library of Congress Catalog
Card Number: 69-18189

For my father

D AVID B EN - M ORDECHAI M EISELS
of blessed memory,

who taught me that it was a hard thing to
be a Jew, but that there was pride in it

Son of a Star

Prologue

IT is told in the Talmud of Jerusalem that one day, some thirty years after the destruction of the Holy City by the Roman Titus Flavius, four of the foremost rabbis in Judea went up to the ruins of Jerusalem to sit and mourn.

And these are they: Rabbi Gamaliel, the son of Simeon; Rabbi Eleazar, the son of Azariah; Rabbi Judah, the son of Baba; and Rabbi Akiba, the son of Joseph.

And as they sat themselves down, rending their garments and bewailing the fate of that once great city, it happened that a fox darted out from the very spot where the Holy Temple's Holy of Holies had formerly stood.

Upon seeing this, three of the rabbis raised up their voices and wept. But Rabbi Akiba laughed.

Whereupon they said unto him, "How can you laugh at this great calamity? How can you laugh when animals of the forest make their home on the most sacred site in all the world?"

"I laugh," answered Rabbi Akiba, "for the very reason that you weep. For was it not prophesied that 'Jerusalem will be a desolation, and the Mount of Zion will be as a forest'?

"Now, therefore, I laugh, for if this prophecy of desolation has come to pass so literally and so exactly, surely all of the prophecies of redemption will also come to pass. And this Temple and this city and this nation shall rise from the dust to be greater even than before."

It was at about the time the foregoing episode took place that the hero of this narrative was born. Growing to manhood in a conquered country, among a people broken and divided, he took hold of a vision and pitted it against the mightiest empire on earth. The vision has survived; the empire has not.

The book opens in the Jewish year 3892—corresponding to the year 132 in the calendar of the Minaeans, who compute the years after the birth of Yeshu of Nazareth.

Book One
B'NEI B'RAK

Now it happened that Rabbi Eliezer and Rabbi Joshua and Rabbi Eleazar Ben-Azariah and Rabbi Akiba and Rabbi Tarphon celebrated the eve of the Passover in B'nei B'rak and spent that entire night discussing the Exodus from Egypt, until at last their disciples came and said to them, "Masters, it is time for the morning prayer."

—PASSOVER HAGGADAH

1

QUINTUS ARMINIUS CARO, tribune of the X Legion, rode his horse across the gentle slopes of Judea's coastal plain at full gallop. It was late winter, and the air still had a damp coolness which hit Quintus in the face with a soft slap, chilling his body and bringing to his nostrils the strangely sweet smell of his own sweat.

It was a good smell, an honest smell. And the feeling Quintus now had of weariness and muscle soreness was exhilarating. How long since he had felt tired—not the head tiredness that comes from lack of sleep and excess of wine, but the body tiredness, the pleasantly painful physical exhaustion that makes one feel mortal and yet so much alive?

Quintus admitted to himself that he did not remember. It was his thirty-fourth year; he was still young, but the essence of boyhood had passed. He had lost it, as all men must, along with that whole series of first thrills that only a boy can really feel. And the thrill of galloping through open country with a good horse under him and the wind in his face Quintus relegated to that magic time lost at the academies of philosophy and in the houses of love.

The tribune glanced about him at the ala of cavalry he was leading, and in the faces of the men in that contingent he saw none of the pleasure he now felt. Instead of exhilaration, he saw discomfort. Well, he thought, that was only natural. A steady gallop over a long period was nothing unusual for these men. It was work, and hard work at that.

For the first time since they had set out from Caesarea that morning Quintus took a close look at the men who had been temporarily placed under his command. That he had not done so before did not strike him as strange. They were legionaries, with nothing to distinguish them from other legionaries elsewhere. Quintus led them today. Tomorrow they would be somewhere else, and he would probably never see them again.

Yet he looked at them now from his vantage point on the horse, watching the sweat roll from their heavy plumed helmets down into their eyes, watching them wipe the sweat away with a disgusted gesture, hearing their curses spoken in Aramaic and in a bastardized Greek.

They were Syrians mostly, recruited from the neighboring province on the promise of Roman citizenship and riding beautiful mounts that had been purchased, or perhaps taken in taxes, from the Arabs in another neighboring province. The legionary who carried the purple banner was a Greek or, at any rate, one who had a few drops of Greek blood in him and who called himself a Greek.

Quintus looked closely at this man as he tried to hold the standard steady against the quivering flanks of his horse. Emblazoned on the banner were the letters *SPQR,* the emblem of Rome which stood for *Senatus Populusque Romanus.*

"The Senate and the Roman People," Quintus whispered to himself, and in that instant Quintus the boy was gone, and in his place was Quintus Arminius Caro the patrician; Quintus the cynic; Quintus the student of many philosophies; Quintus who believed in none of them.

The Senate and the Roman People:

The Senate of which his father was a member.

The Senate of which his grandfather had been a member.

The Senate which his ancestors had helped to found in that Ancient Rome of the Ancient Virtues.

The Senate, now a collection of doddering old cowards who had not dared oppose an emperor in a century, not even when the mad Caligula had made his horse a Senator.

The Senate, which would no more oppose the Emperor Hadrian now than it would dissolve its endless committees and fact-finding groups or cease from its daily useless debates on the future of the Roman state.

So much for the Senate, Quintus thought bitterly. And as for the Roman people, that polyglot mob which inhabited the Eternal City and crowded her arenas at the first smell of blood, that mass of freedmen and foreigners and illiterate plebeians which claimed descent from the Roman *coloni*— well, it was best not to think of them at all, for that way lay treason.

And yet, Quintus knew, these were the twin pillars he had sworn to uphold. And uphold them he would, even at the cost of his life.

It was what the philosophers would call a dichotomy. Or perhaps a paradox.

The Roman tribune reined up his horse at the crest of a hill. Below, nestled in a little valley, was a large white structure surrounded by several dozen smaller houses. The centurion rode up beside Quintus. "The place is called B'nei B'rak," he said, as if in answer to the unspoken question. "The entire area is the university of the Rabbi Akiba Ben-Joseph, and the big building is his house. His disciples lodge in the other houses."

"Do you think that we could impose upon the rabbi to provide us with hospitality?"

The centurion smiled at the tribune's formal speech. "With as much hospitality, certainly, as any other Jew. And perhaps with some information as well."

"We will go there," said Quintus, turning his horse toward the valley. The troop followed him, each rider picking his way down the rocky hillside and, as Quintus did, avoiding with care the large vegetable garden maintained by some of the university's students. Finally the Romans reined up beside the stables and dismounted.

The tribune turned to one of the grooms at the stable. "We would appreciate it," he said in Aramaic, "if you would care for our horses and give us some water to drink as well."

The groom seemed taken aback by the Roman's manner. "Surely," he said. "Surely," he repeated, taking Quintus' horse by the reins and leading it to a watering trough.

Without a word Quintus followed the groom to the trough. There, while his men watched him, he unstrapped his heavy armor, flexed his hard muscles and began washing his arms and face with water from the trough.

The groom stopped him. "It is not meet," he said in shocked tones, "that a man of your rank should wash in this place. Permit me to call the steward of the house."

The groom ran off and returned moments later with the steward. "In the name of the God of Abraham," said the steward to Quintus, "I beg your forgiveness. I pray you follow me into the house, and your men will be cared for also." He turned to the groom. "Wash down each horse, and give them provender." The groom nodded hastily.

The steward led the legionaries into a dining hall and urged them with some ceremony to sit and relax while their food was being prepared. Quintus he directed into the large house itself, into a room where servants brought fresh water and towels. Then all of them left quietly, and Quintus found himself alone.

He took off his tunic and sprayed some of the cold water on his chest. He washed the sweat from his face and the tiredness from his eyes. Standing in front of the polished mirror in the room, he brushed his thinning hair forward in the Roman manner with his hands and considered his face. It was still unlined. His hair—what was left of it—was still dark. His eyes still retained a certain look of boyish wonderment.

It was, all in all, the face of a Roman patrician, complete with its delicate brows and aquiline nose. It had looked better, but it had also looked worse, and vanity was not one of Quintus' faults.

In any case, he thought, testing the muscles of his arms and legs, he felt better than he had felt in some time. The exercise had done him good, and although Cornelia had been against this assignment, she would like him the better for it.

The steward returned just as Quintus was replacing his armor and ushered him into a large room where meat, bread and wine had been placed on a table. Quintus turned to the steward before sitting down. "I thank you," he said. "Now I wonder if I might impose upon you still further. I should like to speak to someone in authority regarding some information."

"Certainly," said the steward. He made a slight bow of his head and left the room.

Quintus sat down and began eating the lamb and the bread that had been set before him. He tasted the wine and decided it was rather good, far better than the sour wine the legionaries drank. He noticed the absence of any milk, butter or cheese from the table, and he recalled having once read somewhere that the Jews did not eat meat together with dairy products.

Quintus was wondering about the reason for this strange prohibition when an elderly man entered the room. The tribune made as if to rise.

"Please sit," said the man in perfect, only lightly accented Latin.

Quintus resumed his seat and considered the old man. He was in his nineties, the tribune estimated, yet he stood firm and erect. A small skullcap rested on his totally bald head, and a long gray beard hung down to his chest. He was dressed modestly in Judean fashion, like a thousand other old Jews, but Quintus sensed that there was something different here— so different that the Latin words coming from this old Jew's mouth did not seem especially strange. And then, suddenly, it came to Quintus what set this man apart. He looked into the old man's eyes and saw there the same sparkle of wondering, of searching, even of doubt that he had seen so many times in his own.

"I am Quintus Arminius Caro, a tribune of the legion," he said.

"Welcome to this house," said the old man. "I am Akiba Ben-Joseph."

Quintus was visibly embarrassed. "Forgive me," he said. "When I asked the steward for someone in authority, I did not think he would send you."

"I thank you for your concern," said the rabbi with good humor, "but we are not so formal here. What is it you require?"

"I seek," said the Roman, "the whereabouts of a bandit called Simon. We have been searching for him since early this morning but have found not a trace."

The flash of annoyance in Akiba's eyes turned at once to amusement. "I am not accustomed to dealing with bandits," he said softly.

Quintus realized that the question had been somewhat insulting. "I beg your pardon," he said hastily. "It was . . ."

Akiba cut him short with a little motion of his hand. "I am not offended," the rabbi said. "But I really cannot help you in this. I know nothing of the ways of bandits. We have been fortunate here, thank God. Bandits have not troubled us."

"No," Quintus smiled. "They wouldn't. You are not Romans."

Akiba returned the smile. "What has this Simon done?"

"He ambushed a caravan last night. It was on its way to Caesarea with a shipment of supplies for the garrison. Five legionaries were slain, and the entire shipment was taken. You may understand, therefore, that we are most anxious to find him."

"I understand and sympathize," said Akiba. "But from your description of the caravan raid this man Simon sounds more like a rebel than a bandit."

"And would that make his crime any the less?"

Akiba shrugged his shoulders. "In the eyes of some that would make a difference."

Quintus looked at the old man wonderingly. "I do not understand you," he said. "True, I have been in Judea only a month, yet I find that my understanding of your people does not increase but diminishes. Surely yours is not the only province governed by Rome, and I don't imagine the temper of the administration here is essentially different from anywhere else. Why then this unique hostility that you bear toward us?"

"A question for a question," said Akiba.

"What?" asked the Roman.

"It is a means of reasoning we use in our discussions. I will try to answer your question with one of my own."

"Ask," said Quintus.

"Why did you and your men so scrupulously avoid our vegetable garden when you rode in, and why did you ride to the stables instead of directly to the main gate?"

"It seemed like the correct thing to do, especially since we were imposing upon your hospitality."

"Agreed," said the rabbi. "So our Law teaches as well. Yet would it surprise you to know that you are the first Roman to show such consideration on coming here? That vegetable garden you saw has been trampled several times by troops of the legion."

"Would you rebel because of a few vegetables?" asked Quintus.

"No," said Akiba with a smile, "but in a sense all of Judea is a garden, and it has been trampled by Rome more than once."

"Has it been without provocation?" asked Quintus. "Have you not rebelled twice against Rome?"

"But was there no cause?" asked Akiba.

"But was the cause worth the cost?" asked Quintus.

Akiba laughed aloud. "Truly, you sound more like a Jew than a Roman. You are not new to the manner of philosophical discourse, I see."

"I have studied from many masters," said Quintus.

"As it is said, 'From all my teachers have I gained understanding.' "

The Roman was silent. He rose to go, and Akiba accompanied him to the door of the house. "I should like to speak with you some more," said the rabbi. "Please consider that you have been invited to return to this house at any time. We will talk again, and you can reacquaint me with that noble Rome I once saw but which, alas, has begun to fade from memory. For myself, perhaps I can help you to understand us a little better."

"Agreed," said Quintus with a smile. "I shall look forward to our next meeting." He raised his hand in salute. "Shalom, Rabbi."

Akiba reached for the Roman's hand and shook it. *"Ave atque vale,"* he said.

2

From the chronicle of Mariamne:

I said good-bye to Philip today. It was easier than I had expected. You build up to these things for weeks and months, worrying; but if I will be honest with myself, I must admit that the one overriding feeling I had when it was over was relief: I was free.

But is one ever free? Ah, these endless questions!

Why didn't I love Philip? Surely there was every reason to do so. He is intelligent and from one of the best Jewish families in Alexandria. Any matchmaker would have put us together. But we don't go to matchmakers anymore these days (thank goodness!), and the fact is that I did not love him. Worse, he bored me.

I sometimes think that I shall never marry, and this distresses me, though I don't know why. If, as some of the philosophers think, everything is predestined, then it will all work out as it should. But what if we are free—truly free—to work out our own destinies? How frightening is the thought of such freedom, where every small decision could enslave you.

Perhaps the old ways were better. Then my father would have given me to some man years ago, and by now I would have a house full of children and no time for such worries.

Philip took it very well, as I would have expected. Right afterward, I went out and booked my passage before I could think too much about it and change my mind. In fact, there is not a great deal of sense to what I am doing, so perhaps it's best I not think about it. But I have to get away for a while from this wonderful, magnificent city with its so many questions and so few answers.

Is it the memories I am fleeing? I think not, for the memories are in me, not in Alexandria. And I have been happy here, as happy as I have been unhappy. And why to Judea? I don't know, except that there was my beginning.

I tried to pray today for the first time since father's . . . death. (How strange! It is still hard for me to write or say the word.) I said *"Modah Ani"* as father had taught me, but I felt nothing. They were just words.

Well, in three days I sail to Judea. What will I find there, I wonder? Change your place, change your luck, goes the old Hebrew maxim. But Horace thought differently: "They change their clime, not their disposition, who flee beyond the sea." Alas, I fear Horace was right. We shall soon see.

3

In the wilderness of Judah, far from the cities and farms, a series of dead cliffs rise steeply from a dead sea like gnarled stone fingers clawing their way to the sky. The sea sits in the deepest valley on earth, and on a summer's day, when the heat in that valley is punishingly oppressive, the calm waters seem to beckon the weary traveler. But the invitation is a false one, for the waters are exceedingly bitter and they contain more salt than any other waters in the world, and should even a drop find its way into a man's eye it will be felt for days. The Hebrews named the sea Yam Hamelah—the Sea of Salt. Others call it the Dead Sea, and in a sense this is the more fitting name, for nothing lives in the water, nor can most creatures of flesh long survive in the desolate area around it, nor can any but the most rugged of strange growths cling to life in the dead soil of its plain.

Once, in ancient days—so the legend runs—before the Lord rained down His wrath upon the wicked cities of Sodom and Gomorrah that had stood here, this place was green and well-watered, a fertile plain in which Lot grazed his sheep and kings went forth to battle. Perhaps the story is true, or perhaps the awesome sight of the cloudless sky and the barren cliffs and the grassless plain and the unmoving water gave rise to the legend. For if ever an area looked accursed by God, this one does.

And once having cursed the spot, God left it, so that even some of the common laws of nature do not apply here. So dry and lifeless is the air that even the small form of life which men call decay thrives but slowly, and a thing can die here and long remain unchanged, while objects of human manufacture can, if kept out of the sun, be preserved indefinitely.

Still, in the fullness of time, some small changes had come. Throughout the centuries the blazing desert sun and the brief but torrential rains had carved rough openings in the cliffs.

The ages had formed these into crevices, caves and passes through the lifeless rock.

It was through one of these narrow passes, high up on a cliff and invisible from below, that a small knot of men now rode.

They seemed a ragged bunch, some wearing old and battered armor and some no armor at all, armed with swords of various lengths or with spears or with woodsmen's axes. But in a small cart being pulled and pushed up the steep cliff lay several dozen pieces of new Roman armor and helmets and as many of the double-edged Roman short swords.

The two men riding side by side at the head of the slowly moving column wore such armor and such swords, but they were not Romans. They were Judeans. The name of one was Jonathan Bar Ba'ayah. The other was called Simon Bar Kosiba.

Upon close look at the two men as they carefully guided their horses upward around the rocks, nothing at first would distinguish either from most other Judeans. Both were dark and bearded, with unruly black hair beneath their plumed Roman helmets. Jonathan had a slightly hooked nose—a legacy from the Hittites who had converted to Judaism a thousand years before. Simon's was the more common sensitive nose of the Jews, and his eyes were a dark blue—a legacy from the Philistines conquered by David.

Both types were common enough in Judea. But a search of Simon's weather-beaten face, beyond the small scars and the premature wrinkles, would reveal a difference. A sadness born of old angers, an anger born of the sadness.

From somewhere now there came the almost imperceptible cry of an eagle. Simon and Jonathan reared up their horses as the group came to a halt.

"L'herut Yerushalayim," Simon shouted to the wind. "For the freedom of Jerusalem."

"L'herut Yisrael," came the answer from the unseen sentry. "For the freedom of Israel."

The group rode on, now moving single file through the narrowing pass. At length they came to a broad, rocky plain surrounded by a wall of cliffs dotted with caves. Here they dismounted as other men and some women emerged from the caves and ran to them.

"How went it?"

"Perfectly," answered Jonathan, pointing to the cart that bore the Roman weapons and armor. "There is enough here for all of us."

The women pressed forward and handed clay jugs to the weary men. They drank thirstily, some of them pausing first to say a simple blessing over the water.

Jonathan moved eagerly toward one of the women, and they embraced. Ruth was Jonathan's wife, a woman neither beautiful nor old but who looked at first glance hewn from the very rocks of this barren spot. The appearance was deceiving. Ruth was not hard, merely strong, and had once been beautiful.

A shadow of this former Ruth could be seen later in the day when she put their little boy to sleep with gentle coaxing and a lullaby. The boy, Emanuel, was only three, and he had known no home but the cliffs and the caves.

Later, as the small community gathered around campfires to eat the evening meal, Ruth and Jonathan sat, as was their custom, beside the leader, Simon Bar Kosiba. Jonathan told her of the raid, of how the Romans had been ambushed and slain before they could even draw their swords and of how the Jewish raiders had made their escape from the pursuing cavalry. Ruth hung on every word. Simon was silent.

At one point Ruth sought to question the silence, but Jonathan signaled her not to. He had witnessed it before, and he accepted it. He understood that for his friend Simon the successful little raid had been a painful symbol of failure.

Late that night Simon lay in his cave, his arms behind his head, and looked upward into the blackness, thinking. It was a grown man lying there, but there was a youth within the man and a boy within the youth and a child within the boy, and they were all there too, as they must be in every man. And as Simon lay with his eyes wide open, the youth and the boy and the child paraded before him.

He reviewed them all, the child sitting and eating his meal in the hall of the children of the congregation of Kosiba, the young apprentice learning to be a smith. But it was the boy on whom his inner gaze settled.

The boy Simon sat in the town square of Kosiba with his legs drawn up. It was summer, and the hot sun beat down on his naked legs and arms, but he was unaware of it now, for he sat with some of the other boys of the town listening to the old man, the Zealot.

It was nearing the ninth of Ab—the day of despair, the day of disaster—and with its approach came the old man, the Zealot, as he had every year. No one knew exactly where the old man lived, or where he was from, or how old he actually was, or even his name. He was simply the old man, the Zealot, and from year to year, at the beginning of the month of Tammuz, he would suddenly appear in the town.

The men of Kosiba would stop for a moment on their way to the field or to the market and would listen to the Zealot speak, then they would shake their heads and move on.

But not the boys. The old man had a way with children, and he would tell them stories. They were the same stories every year, but the boys who heard them three or four times never tired of them until, one summer, they would find they were no longer boys but men, and then, suddenly, the stories would seem silly and full of childish dreams. Or so it was with most of them.

Simon was not yet seven years old when he first heard the tales of the old man, the Zealot.

"He who has never seen Jerusalem in all her glory has never seen a beautiful city in the world," chanted the old man. "Happy are these eyes that beheld the Temple. Happy are these eyes that saw the high priest offer the sacrifice. But, alas, merely to hear of them grieves our soul."

Thus, with this formula, began the old man's tale, and although Simon by now knew the words well, he sat enthralled.

"Ten measures of beauty came into the world, and of these nine were taken by Jerusalem."

It was of this great city that the Zealot first spoke, telling of the magnificence of its palaces and public buildings and of the glory of its Temple. Then, taking up his tale, he would tell of the last Judean kings who had held court in Jerusalem—men not entitled to the throne of David by birth or deeds and who did evil in the sight of the Lord.

"I will tell you now of Herod—cursed be the villain's name," the old man would say, "for it was in Herod's bloody reign more than a hundred years ago that there began that unfolding of events which led to our disaster.

"Now this wicked Herod was not of noble birth, nor even an Israelite by blood, but he coveted the throne and conspired without scruple to gain it. It was Herod who, in usurping the kingdom, first brought the Romans to the land that their legions might put down his enemies.

"Woe unto us on that day," the old man would wail. "Woe unto the generation that bore Herod's yoke. Woe unto the babes as yet unborn."

He would tell of Herod's excesses and his murderous fury; how, seized by an insane and groundless jealousy, he had put his beautiful wife to death and then, in the madness of his uncontrollable grief, had had the effrontery to name a tower of the Holy City in memory of his slain beloved. He told how the king, seeing plots everywhere, had murdered three of his own sons and had butchered hosts of true Judean princes because he feared their popularity with the people. At last he would tell of Herod's slow and painful death from an abominable disease.

And then the old man would begin to tell of the Romans, for what had started out as a friendly hand of aid to Herod became an undisguised occupation soon after the king's death.

"Now the Romans were worse unto us even than Herod, for they oppressed the people sore and took away what little remained of our ancient liberties. The Sanhedrin, our highest court and lawmaking council from of old, was stripped of all its power, and the Romans dispensed their own justice for a price. Now in those days, remember, the land was rich and fruitful, and men came from all over the earth to see the wonders of Jerusalem. But there seemed no end to the greed of the officials sent here by the imperial power, nor was anything held sacred by them. They stole from rich and poor alike and openly looted even the Temple treasury. Ignoring our holy rites, they sold the office of the high priesthood to the highest bidder. In the villages, when small farmers taxed beyond endurance could not pay, the Romans took their land away and then had these same farmers work the land of their fathers as tenants. Those who had neither land nor money were enslaved, contrary to our Law. Those who dared protest were nailed up on crosses by the roadside like so much meat as an example to others.

"And so it came to pass," intoned the Zealot, "that certain men arose in Judea who sought to free the land from the oppressor, even as their forefathers, the Maccabees, had freed the land from former tyrants. There were many heroes among these men. There was a John"—and here the old man would point to one of the boys—"just like you. His name was John of Gush Halav." Then he would turn to Simon. "And there was a Simon, too. The great leader, Simon Bar Giora, a mighty man of battle.

"There were many groups of these brave men seeking to free the land—alas, too many—but by far the largest and most powerful of these were the Zealots, each of whom had sworn to die before surrendering to Rome."

And so the tale would continue, a tale of glorious rebellion, of victory after victory gained by the valiant Jews, of the liberation of the Holy City, of Roman retreat. But then the old man would tell of terrible division among the rebels, of battles among the various factions within Jerusalem, of the dread crime of fratricide—the very sin the sages had warned would bring about the destruction of the Holy City.

And so the tale would begin to be one of Roman gains, of the return of the legions to the walls of the Holy City, of the horrid months of siege and, finally, of disaster—of the heroic fight for Jerusalem and of her mighty fall.

All of these stories were not told on one day, of course, but on many days, and the old man would stretch them out, keeping them familiar yet adding one or two different episodes each year to keep the older boys interested.

The final part of the tragedy always would be saved for the ninth of Ab—the day of mourning—the anniversary of the destruction of the city and the Temple. The old man would tell it while sitting on the ground with his robe rent. He would tell it with groans and in tears, and there was not a boy who did not weep with him.

"Some of the Zealots fled the city through sewers and tunnels," the old man would relate. "They made their way to Masada above the Sea of Salt and continued their fight against the Romans. Others escaped to Alexandria or to Cyrene in Africa and stirred up the flames of rebellion there. But most fell in Jerusalem, slain by the sword or else throwing themselves in their grief into the flames of the burning Temple. Those captured by the Romans were crucified.

"Few of the Zealots remain to this day," the old man would say, "and I am one of them. I saw with my own eyes the things I tell you, and I tell them to you that you may remember them and not forget. I seek out you, the children of Judea, for in you lies our hope. For even as we mourn the destruction on this day, so must we on this day lay the foundation for the rebuilding.

"Behold," the old man would say, "the time will come when you shall rise and cast the Romans from the land, even as your grandfathers tried to do."

"Amen," the children would reply.

"But first," the old man would continue, "you must listen and hear and learn. For your grandfathers—even my generation—perished in its iniquity and fell in its division. Fratricide doomed us and delivered up the Holy City to destruction.

"Learn, then, from our sin and our disaster. And when your day comes, unite as one, rise as one and strike as one for the freedom of Israel."

And again the children would shout, "Amen."

So, year after year, Simon would listen to the old man, the Zealot, and dream about him. And sometimes—since he did not know his own parents—the boy would wonder if perhaps the old man might not be his own grandfather. For Simon loved the old man, and the tales he told would remain in the boy's mind from summer to summer.

And then, one year, as the old man told his tales, there was a Roman centurion in the crowd of older people. He listened for only a few minutes and then stepped forward and grabbed the old man roughly and ordered his men to seize him.

The Romans stripped the old man and tied him to a stake in the town square and flogged him without mercy. The old man uttered not a sound until the end. Then he turned to the centurion and told him, "You have waited a long time." And then he said the Shema—the final prayer required of all Jews before they die: "Hear, O Israel, the Lord is our God, the Lord is One." And then the old man died, under the lash. And from that day forward, all of the men in the village agreed that he must indeed have been a Zealot, for he had died like one.

Simon had witnessed it all—the flogging and the old man's death—and he had watched it without any show of emotion. But shortly after this, he disappeared from the village for a few days.

Simon ran to the hills, as he would again many times in the years ahead, but it would never again be like this first time. For the boy spent the next several days lying on the ground and weeping and tearing the grass and rending his clothes and heaping dirt on his head in mourning for the old man, the Zealot, his grandfather.

And in between his tears, he thought. He wondered about such things as justice and right. He thought about God, and when he tried to picture Him Simon saw the old man, the Zealot. Indeed, he thought, God must look like the old man, must feel as the old man felt. But then why had God permitted the old man to die so horribly?

How does one serve God? the boy wondered. And how does God repay this service? Was the old man's ignominious death just payment for his many years of fidelity? Simon began to doubt. Lying there on the dew-soaked grass, he began to wonder if there really was a God. And since it had never occurred to the boy before, he thought it was a new idea and he dwelt on it.

But although Simon could and did and would sometimes doubt, he found it impossible to reject God. For to reject God was to reject everything. It was to reject Israel's sole reason for being. It was to reject all hope for justice in the face of might. Simon would as soon reject these as life itself. So in the end he decided that perhaps the old man, the Zealot, had died for a reason, and he suspected that the reason was himself and the other boys, that they might not forget, that they might perhaps carry on the fight for justice in their own day.

And having decided this, Simon Bar Kosiba left the hills and returned to his village. But it was not the same Simon who had left. For the Simon who returned would never be a boy again. He was a man, and a man with a purpose.

Simon the rebel threw his arm across his face and lay in the dark cave and wondered again how he had failed himself and his cause and the old man. How does a group of outlaws become an army? How does a series of raids become a rebellion?

How had David managed to unite this freethinking, highly individualistic people in his own day? What was it that had unified the people so firmly under the Maccabees that they were able to sustain a thirty-year war against the Greeks?

For the thousandth time Simon had to admit to himself that he did not know. He sensed that he was overlooking something, some unifying principle, some spark; and thus blaming himself for not recognizing it, Simon fell asleep.

The sound of the sentry's horn awakened him. He poured water from the clay jug in the cave and washed his hands and face. Then, together with the other men of the small outlaw community, Simon went outside to say the morning prayers.

The men put on their tephillin, small wooden boxes containing words of the Law. They fastened these to their left arms —near the heart—and to their foreheads by means of leather thongs, in literal obedience to the Biblical injunction to bind the words of the Law "upon your hand" and "between your eyes." The custom was ancient and symbolized the unity of might and mind in God's service.

The men stood before the caves, and the reader began intoning the first of the morning prayers: "How goodly are your tents, O Jacob, your tabernacles, O Israel." The congregation repeated the prayers after him.

The service continued, and the reader began reciting the age-old blessings:

"Blessed are You, O Lord our God, King of the universe, Who has not made me a heathen."

And the congregation answered, "Amen."

"Blessed are You, O Lord our God, King of the universe, Who has not made me a slave."

And the congregation answered, "Amen."

And suddenly, Simon knew.

In that instant, in the repetition of the simple prayers he had been saying all of his adult life, he saw the unifying principle that had been eluding him.

David had said these prayers. The prophets had said them. The sons of Mattathias, the Maccabees, had said them. Jews said them today all over the world. Daily they equated freedom with the service of the only God, affirming that one was impossible without the other.

Only with the greatest difficulty could Simon control his excitement and complete his prayers. Then, after removing the tephillin, he approached his friend Jonathan.

"I am leaving for a few days, perhaps a week," he said. "Alone. You will be in command."

"Where are you going?" Jonathan asked.

"I am going to see the great rabbi Akiba Ben-Joseph."

"There is great risk now," Jonathan said. "Why not wait a few weeks? What is the urgency?"

"I wish to go now," said Simon simply. "I wish to see the great rabbi and to ask him what it means to be a Jew."

4

Cornelia was preparing her toilet when Quintus burst into her chamber with such suddenness that the slave girl arranging the lady's long hair jumped back in alarm. Quintus, spotting the girl, halted in the entrance and uttered a formal greeting.

"My respects to the Lady Cornelia, daughter of the late Senator Publius Caecilius, wife of the Procurator Tinius Rufus," he said.

Regarding the tribune through a hand mirror while busily straightening a few locks of hair, Cornelia casually returned the salutation. "Greetings to the Tribune Quintus Arminius Caro, son of the Senator Marcus Arminius."

Then, just as casually, she dismissed the slave girl.

The instant the girl was gone, the two ran together and embraced. Quintus lifted the beautiful woman and carried her to the bed. With a few deft motions he removed his tunic and threw it on the floor. Cornelia, breathing heavily, drew up her simple gown, and without preliminaries they came together with an urgent violence.   .

There was a knock on the door, and Cornelia had great difficulty making her voice sound as casual as before. But she managed.

"What is it?"

"The Governor Rufus requests your presence," said the slave on the other side of the door. "He requests also the company of the tribune Quintus Arminius."

So Rufus knew they were together, Quintus thought. Interesting. Interesting but not surprising. Interesting that he shouldn't care. Interesting that he should choose to inform them in this way that he knew. But not surprising. It was Rufus' way.

"I shall be there shortly," he heard Cornelia say. "And if I see the tribune, I shall ask him to come also."

Cornelia jumped out of bed and began fixing her hair. "You'd better go," she told Quintus. "It won't do for us to arrive together."

"Rufus knows."

"Perhaps he does, but it still won't do. You know how he is."

"Yes," said Quintus. "It's his way of toying with us. That's why he's sent me off on one fool's errand after another, chasing bandits and supervising tax collections—all tasks that could have been handled by any centurion. But don't worry." He kissed her. "Rufus won't try to harm either one of us. It would remove a major source of his amusement."

Cornelia accepted the kiss coldly. She had her mind on other things now. "Please hurry," she pleaded.

Quintus replaced his tunic and went downstairs to the large room where Rufus took his meals and received guests and petitioners. There, to his surprise, seated beside the procurator was Rabbi Akiba.

"Hail Rufus," said Quintus on entering.

"Hail Quintus," said Rufus with a tired salute. "It is good to see you back in Caesarea. I trust your missions have not been too arduous." He motioned toward Rabbi Akiba. "I understand you have already met our distinguished guest."

"Yes," said Quintus with a slight bow which the rabbi returned.

Rufus pointed to a chair for the tribune, then turned to Akiba. "It was fortunate for me that Quintus was able to have himself sent here. We had been friends in Rome, or, rather, Quintus had been a good friend of my wife Cornelia. My wife, as you know, arrived here only a few months ago. And then, shortly thereafter, Quintus arrived. What good fortune to have one's wife and a friend arrive so soon one after the other, don't you agree, Rabbi?"

"The friendship of men is second in importance only to a happy marriage," said the rabbi sagely.

Quintus was furious. Private jests were one thing, but to make such pointed remarks before an outsider was inexcusable. He looked straight at Rufus now, considering the gross head, the puffed face, the fat, shapeless body—just like the lowborn pig he was.

Cornelia entered the room, and the men rose. As she moved gracefully toward a seat, Quintus considered her, her long auburn hair piled high on her head in the fashion of the day, her skin without a blemish, her lips the full lips of a beautiful child, her well-formed body capable of giving and taking so much pleasure, and he wondered again how such a woman could ever—under any conditions—lie in bed with a Rufus.

Of course, she rarely did now. Rufus called her to him now only when he was exceedingly bored or made love to her when he wanted to punish her, because he knew she detested him.

It had been a marriage of convenience from the first, convenient for everyone, that is, except Cornelia. Like Quintus', her family was patrician, and although this no longer meant what it once had, the family was of Senatorial rank; it was old and venerable with roots in Rome's dim and glorious past as a republic before the first emperor had proclaimed himself *princeps* —chief and first citizen. The patrician status also implied that the family was wealthy, but old Senator Caecilius had been anything but a shrewd businessman.

The new times had produced a new aristocracy, and Rufus was one of these—men who had been able to amass fortunes partly through cleverness and luck, and mostly through ignoring every scruple that noble Romans held sacred. The two classes despised each other. But they envied each other, too, so now and again a marriage between aristocracy and money was quietly arranged.

Senator Caecilius had had little trouble convincing himself that his sixteen-year-old daughter was smitten with love for the wealthy commoner, although Rufus was already forty at the time. And Quintus knew that Cornelia had brought to the conjugal bed all the wonder and enthusiasm of a young girl. She had told him as much.

But Rufus had no sooner awakened the girl than he had returned to his more pleasurable premarital pursuits. As had been the gossip in Rome for years, he much preferred to share his bed with young boys. Not that he had no use for women. He enjoyed having them trussed up and whipping their naked bodies with rods and lashes until they sank into insensibility. While this type of activity could be freely pursued with slave girls, clearly it was impossible with the daughter of a Roman patrician, and so Rufus soon lost interest in his young wife.

But Rufus was the only man Cornelia had ever lain with, and she desired him and for a long while even thought that she loved him. In time, of course, she came to hate him, but that was later, much later, after she had shared the embraces of a succession of lovers far more satisfying than her husband. Quintus was the latest in this line and—he hopefully told himself—the last.

But if the mating of the two families had been less than ideal for Cornelia, it had not been such a good bargain for Rufus either. He had had high hopes when he first entered government service after the marriage, for although proconsulships were still reserved for men of Senatorial rank, there remained the possibility of an eventual imperial commission as a *legatus,* a governor of an important province with legions under his command.

Instead, Rufus had had to content himself with this post of procurator of a minor province, and while people in Judea called him governor out of courtesy, he was actually little more than a caretaker. Even this was a rather high position for a man who did not know who his grandfather was, Quintus thought, but in these modern times a man's station at birth tended to count less and less in his career. What did count were the steps a man took on his way, and, of course, Rufus had taken a bad step.

To become procurator of Judea was hardly a step upward. The post had proved a dead end for every one of Rufus' predecessors, even those who had held the office in the old days when Judea was still a power to be reckoned with in the East. Yet even then, Judea had broken the men who had tried to gov-

ern her for the simple reason that the province was impossible
to govern. Now, since the destruction of Jerusalem and the last
vestige of Judean independence, what little prestige there had
been to the post of procurator had disappeared, leaving only
the problems behind.

These problems, Quintus knew, were considerable and re-
volved around two hopeless tasks. The first was to get revenue
out of a country whose natural wealth—hardly great to begin with—had been ravaged by more than half a century of warfare and strife. The other was to keep the peace in Judea with
the help of the two legions assigned to the small province—
the VI Ferrata in Galilee, and the X Fretensis, partly in Caesarea but headquartered in the Judean hill country. Should
the procurator ever need reinforcements, he would have to ask
for them from the Legatus of Syria or from Egypt, and such a
move, especially for an ambitious man, would hardly be wise
politically.

Nor was this all, Quintus reflected. Throughout the rest of
the empire, throughout the entire civilized world, men had
learned to subordinate their adoration of the gods to the more
pressing needs of everyday life; indeed, as every cultured Roman knew, this was a necessity that even the gods themselves—
if they existed—must recognize. Only here in Judea was the
arrangement turned upside down, so that the strange religion
of the Jews was more important to them than practical matters,
more important than progress, more important than life itself.

Where else in all the empire would a people willingly leave
their fields and shops every seventh day, regardless of how important it might be to work on that day? Not that the Jews were
lazy. If anything, they were perhaps too energetic for the taste
of some of their neighbors. Yet they would waste this seventh
day religiously, along with a host of holidays on which they also
refused to work.

And to complicate matters still further, the Jews were split
into all sorts of religious factions, each of which had to be
placated in its own way and all of them united on only one point
—hatred of Rome.

Despite what Quintus thought of Rufus, he could not help
but sympathize with him. Eclipsed by the Legatus of Syria on
the one hand and by the Legatus of Egypt on the other, he had a

Herculean task which—even if he could perform it—would probably gain him nothing.

All of these random thoughts swirled through Quintus' mind in the brief moments that Cornelia took her seat beside the procurator.

"This is my wife," said Rufus.

Akiba made a slight bow of his head.

Rufus turned to Cornelia. "Permit me to introduce Rabbi Akiba Ben-Joseph, a leader of the grand council of the Jews, a most learned and scholarly man."

Cornelia smiled graciously. Quintus couldn't help noticing how calm she looked.

"Rabbi Akiba," Rufus continued, "has no doubt come to us with some sort of petition, since that is usually the reason for his all too infrequent visits. Is that not so, Rabbi?"

"The governor is a busy man," said Akiba, "and I would not think of disturbing him unless the reason were pressing."

"The rabbi is also a great diplomat," Rufus said. "Well, what problem have you brought me this time?"

Akiba looked about the room uncomfortably.

"Do not be concerned about my wife and my friend," said Rufus. "It would be well for them to hear some of our problems, to become better acquainted with the country."

"Certainly," said the rabbi. "I bring you two petitions to-day. The first concerns a certain Mordechai the son of Joshua, who is also called Marcus and who is a leader of the Minaean community. This Mordechai has brought to the council several complaints about the treatment of Minaeans by the Roman authorities. He contends that their synagogues have been summarily closed, many of their leaders scourged and imprisoned. I ask your intercession in this matter."

Rufus looked honestly bewildered. "No matter how long I am in Judea your people never cease to amaze me. Why would a representative of the grand council be petitioning for aid to the Minaeans, whom you detest?"

"We do not detest them," said Akiba. "We differ with them. We believe they are in error in thinking that the Messiah has already come, so we discourage the acceptance of their ideas."

"Well, in any case," said Rufus, "it seems to me we are doing you a favor by suppressing these wrong ideas."

"We do not see it thus," said the rabbi, "for we learned long ago that the surest way to perpetuate an idea—right or wrong —is to suppress it. But beyond that, these Minaeans are Judeans and entitled to the intercession of the grand council and"—he added ominously—"to the protection of Rome."

"I will thank you to permit me to decide who is to be protected," Rufus snapped.

Akiba nodded courteously.

"Perhaps you are not aware of the special problem these Minaeans pose to Rome," the procurator continued. "Whatever I may be able to say against the rest of you Jews, I must concede that at least you keep your strange ideas to yourselves and do not try to impose your ways upon others. With these Minaeans it is quite different. They have literally infested the city of Rome with their missionaries, proclaiming that the Kingdom of God is at hand, turning people's minds to devious paths and finding converts among the more gullible. The order to suppress this disease at its source comes from Rome itself, and my hands are tied."

"I do not ask you to disobey the order," said Akiba, "merely to temper it with mercy."

"Mercy is expensive," said Rufus curtly.

Quintus was shocked at the procurator's bluntness. Did Rufus have no concept of shame?

Yet Akiba remained unruffled. "I think you have found we are not niggardly when it comes to acquiring mercy."

"Very well," Rufus said. "I will do what I can, but I expect you to understand it will not be easy."

"We understand perfectly," Akiba said.

"What is the second problem?" asked Rufus.

"The second problem is one that I have brought you before, but it grows in urgency. As you know, several years ago your great emperor, Publius Aelius Hadrianus—may he live and prosper—visited this land. At that time he graciously indicated that we might soon be permitted to rebuild our Holy Temple on its ancient site, and Jews throughout the earth began to bless his name. We raised money for the rebuilding; we drew up plans; we reorganized our priesthood. Yet now, after more than five years, we have still not received the required permission. Not only has the rebuilding not yet begun, but Jews are still forbidden even to go up to the Temple Mount save by official permit. I ask your intercession in this matter, and let me make clear that if this one petition is granted, you will find us Jews transformed into perhaps the most loyal subjects in the empire."

Rufus stood up and paced about the room for several minutes before answering what to Quintus had seemed a reasonable request. Finally, he turned to Akiba.

"You seek a direct petition to the emperor, is that it?"

"Exactly," said the rabbi.

"I can make such a petition for you, but you know of course there is no guarantee it will be honored."

"Certainly, but if the governor will but use his good office to intercede for us, to recommend to the emperor . . ."

Rufus cut him short. "There is great danger in that to me."

"That the petition will be refused?"

"That it will be granted."

"And why would that be dangerous?"

"I don't trust you Jews."

"We have not earned your mistrust."

"Ha! You have earned the mistrust of every Roman, you who are the most contrary, the most rebellious people in the empire."

The procurator began pacing about the room. "Permit me to review some recent history for you. About sixty years ago you had your beloved Temple and your Holy City and a senate of sorts that was supreme in your own affairs. You had all these things that you now seek so desperately, and what did you do with them? Your leaders declared themselves in rebellion against Rome. Your Holy City was turned into a stronghold and your Temple into a fortress. Years it took to overcome you and thousands of Roman lives. Shall I personally advise the emperor to risk this again? What sort of fool do you think I am?"

"I do not think you are a fool," said Akiba quietly. "I think you are a man of reason, and, therefore, let me appeal to your reason. The conflict between us was not as simple as you have just stated it, as I'm sure you know. You Romans had entered this country as guests, invited here by King Herod to help him fight his wars. Then you remained. Gradually, you assumed suzerainty, yet even this did not disturb us, for the common people had no great love for the House of Herod, and the mode of government was of no importance to them. I am old enough to remember this; in those days I was not yet learned or a rabbi but a simple farmer in the hut of my father, and I well remember what led up to that unfortunate revolt. Day by day, more and more, the Roman administration infringed upon our most elemental rights. Summary executions became commonplace, and the horrible sight of a human being dangling from a cross was known throughout Judea. Scourgings no longer attracted attention. Forcible seizures of land and property were daily occurrences. I do not blame any of this on Rome herself but, rather, on a succession of the most corrupt officials whom she sent here—greedy men, men who sought to drain the land not merely of money but of hope, men to whom our most sacred laws were objects of derision. What choice had we but to rebel?"

Rufus dismissed the rabbi's statement with a wave of his hand. "That's neither here nor there," he said. "That's ancient history now. But what guarantee have I you won't do it again if given the opportunity of a rallying point like the Temple?"

"You have the guarantee of reason," Akiba said. "We are an old people, and we have a long memory, and much foreknowledge can be gained merely by looking at our history. Cyrus the Persian permitted us to rebuild our Temple here hundreds of years ago, and we still honor his memory. I beg you to remember that we accepted Persian rule without rebellion and without incident for a very long time. When the Greeks prevailed over the Persians and inherited their empire, we submitted to them without protest. We named thousands of our children Alexander merely for a small kindness on the part of Alexander the Great, merely for a passive favor, because he did not ask us to change our ancient ways. It was only after Alexander, when the Greeks had corrupted themselves in every way and began to oppress us and force us to desecrate our Law that we rebelled under the Maccabees and drove them from the land. But the lesson of our history is this: Permit us to practice our Law fully; grant us our basic rights. Do this, and we will gladly submit to Rome's government; we will obey your civil laws diligently and will ourselves punish those who transgress them;

we will pay our just taxes without complaint; we will pray
daily for the welfare of Rome."

Akiba paused, then added one thing more. "You could
achieve all of this, you yourself, single-handedly, by using your
influence to have the emperor grant our request. You could
make the name of Tinius Rufus immortal among our people
—and extremely valuable in the eyes of Rome."

How clever, Quintus thought. The old man had struck home.

Rufus was silent for a long moment. Then he smiled at Akiba,
and it was truly a benevolent smile. "I will do what I can," he
said. "I can promise nothing, but tell your people I will try."

Akiba inclined his head. "I will surely tell them of the governor's graciousness."

"Very well," said Rufus. "Now that we have spoken, let us
have some wine together."

The rabbi demurred, as of course Rufus knew he would.

"Oh, I'm sorry," said the procurator with undisguised malice.
"I forgot that you do not drink our wine."

"If I might instead have some milk," said Akiba.

"Certainly, certainly," said Rufus. He clapped his hands,
and a few moments later a slave brought the wine and then a
goblet of milk.

It was while they sat drinking that Cornelia spoke for the
first time. "This thing with the wine," she said to Akiba, "is
this a religious matter with you?"

"Yes," said the rabbi with obvious discomfort. "It is not that
we think your wine to be impure. It is only that we know it is
sometimes used in connection with . . . for certain purposes
that are against our religion."

"You mean for the gods," said Cornelia. "You mean the liba-
tions."

"Exactly," said Akiba.

Cornelia smiled, happy as a child who had guessed a riddle.
"I had heard that," she said, as if to show that she was not uninformed. "I had heard that you Jews believe in no gods but
your own. How strange."

"Strange?" Akiba said. "I don't think so. How many emperors of Rome are there?"

"Only one," said Cornelia, "but he has governors and tributary princes and servants."

"That is only because your emperor, for all his might, cannot be everywhere at once. Our God can."

Quintus smiled. It was a good answer.

"You say your God is everywhere," Cornelia said, "but I have heard that, in truth, he is nowhere, that he cannot even be seen."

"The sun is everywhere," said Akiba, "yet you cannot look upon it without going blind. And the sun is but one of our God's many creations."

"And that's all there is to it?" asked Cornelia. "I mean, you believe in an invisible God who is everywhere, and that is what sets you Jews apart from every other people? Is that all?"

Akiba smiled. "There is more to it than that, far, far more. But that is a good starting point if you wish to understand us."

"I do wish to understand you," Cornelia said. "Very much."

"It is a hopeless task," Rufus interjected.

"No," said Akiba. "It is not even hard. If one tries."

"I should like to try," said Cornelia.

"Permit me to invite you to my home in B'nei B'rak," said the rabbi. "My door will be open to you at any time."

"He seeks a convert," said Rufus.

"No," Akiba said. "Our Law does not permit us to seek out converts. But if one desires to know the Way, we show it openly."

Rufus turned to his wife. "It would be easy for you to convert. You wouldn't even have to be circumcised."

Quintus spoke to break the uneasy silence after the vulgar jest. "I am interested in these Minaeans. I had a servant in Rome who called himself, I believe, a Nazarene, but it sounds like much the same sect."

"It is much the same," said Akiba, "except that the Minaeans —or *Minim,* as we call them—are Jews who keep our laws as well as the special rules of their sect, while the Nazarenes are Gentiles who consider themselves unbound by the Judaic Law."

"This is all very complicated," said Cornelia. "Do these people believe in your invisible God, too?"

"Yes," said Akiba, "but they also believe in a man who lived about a hundred years ago. I call him a man, but actually they believe he was more than a man. His name was Yeshu, and he was a man from Nazareth, and he went about urging people to keep the Law, much as other Jewish teachers do and have done. In any case, this particular teacher ran afoul of the Roman authorities—as so many did in those terrible days leading up to our revolt—and he was crucified."

"Well," said Quintus, "that sounds like the end of the story."

"Hardly," Akiba said. "Remember what I told you about the impossibility of suppressing ideas? The disciples of this Yeshu, both here and abroad, believe that he was the Messiah—the Saviour for whom we have waited for centuries. They believe he will return soon."

"Saviour," Quintus snapped in spite of himself. "He couldn't even save himself."

"But how can anybody believe this?" asked Cornelia. "It's so absurd."

Akiba smiled. "I am not a Minaean, but there is more to this also than I have been able to tell you in these few words." He rose to go. "I thank the governor for his hospitality."

Rufus nodded.

"As for the Lady Cornelia," Akiba continued, "I ask her only to consider that often the simplest ideas are really the most complex, while ideas that sound terribly complicated are sometimes, really, quite simple."

Cornelia smiled.

"Please do come to B'nei B'rak," the rabbi said, "and I will tell you whatever you seek to know."

"I will come," said Cornelia.

5

The steward met Rabbi Akiba at the entrance to his house in B'nei B'rak. "There is a young man waiting for you. He has been here since early this morning."

"What does he want?" Akiba asked.

"I do not know. He refuses to say. He would not even give us his name but insisted he would speak only to you."

"I will see him now," said the rabbi. He moved into the large chamber of the house to find his visitor pacing about the room.

"Peace be with you," said the rabbi. "I am Akiba Ben-Joseph."

"And with you, peace. I am Simon Bar Kosiba."

Akiba removed his traveling cloak and sat down, motioning Simon into a chair opposite him. "How may I serve you?" he asked.

"I have come," Simon said, "to learn what it means to be a Jew."

"You seek to become a student?"

"No. I seek to apply the teachings of the sages."

"Your meaning escapes me," said Akiba.

"What does it mean to be a Jew?" asked Simon.

Akiba looked at his visitor for a moment. From a Gentile the question would be a comparatively simple one. But this Simon appeared to be a Jew, and he spoke the High Tongue. Coming from a Jew, the question was complex and required a studied answer.

" 'You shall love your neighbor as yourself,' " Akiba quoted. "I teach that this is the greatest and most basic principle of the Torah."

"And what if your neighbor is in need?" Simon asked.

"Then you must help him."

"And what if your neighbor is hurt?"

"Then you must heal him."

"And what if your neighbor is oppressed, even enslaved?"

"Then you must free him," Akiba answered.

"What of the cost?" Simon asked.

"Reckon not the cost," Akiba said. "There is no cost too great for this, seeing that the Lord Himself has commanded us to serve no human masters, for we are His servants alone."

Simon nodded his head. "I had hoped the great Rabbi would answer thus, for I seek his help in freeing all of my oppressed and enslaved neighbors in Judea."

Akiba wrinkled his brows, and a look of sudden understanding came into his eyes. "You are Simon the rebel," he said.

"You have heard of me?" asked Simon, not without a touch of pride.

"I had heard of you as Simon the bandit," Akiba said. "A Roman tribune came by here some days ago seeking you. From his description I suspected you were one of the rebels. You were rash to come here. Roman cavalry patrol these roads regularly. If you were found, it would mean your death."

"There are things more important than life," Simon said. "I took the risk because I desperately need your help."

Akiba looked puzzled. "But how can I help you? I am an old man, and my concern for many years has been primarily with the Law."

"Yet time and again you have interceded with the Roman authorities on a variety of secular matters."

"I see," said Akiba. "You wish me to intercede for you, is that it? To ask for an amnesty?"

"I do not seek forgiveness from the oppressor," he said shortly. "I do not regret what I have done to them. I regret only that I have been unable to do more, and that is why I now seek your help."

"I do not understand," Akiba said.

"Then let me come to the point. I seek the freedom of Judea. I seek the expulsion of the Romans from this land. I seek the rebuilding of Jerusalem and of the Temple. Yet," he added bitterly, "for all of this I have forty-one men under my command."

"Continue," said Akiba.

"This is my dream and the dream of many others. Yet it remains only a dream, aimless, a hope without direction. Throughout Judea the dreamers are numbered in the hundreds of thousands, yet they do not act because they do not know what to do or how to do it. I have pondered this problem for many years, and then I thought to myself, I will go to the man who has helped to fashion the dream. I will go to him, and I will ask him what does it mean to be a Jew?"

Simon paused. "Continue," Akiba urged him. "Say what you will, all that you will, without fear."

"If I understand your answer correctly," Simon said, "then to be a Jew means more than to pray in a certain way. It means to act as a Jew, to love right and hate wickedness, to heal sickness and to relieve oppression."

"You have understood correctly," the rabbi said. "But again I must ask, how can I help you?"

"There are in Judea fifty or more chieftains such as I, men who dream and who have translated their dream into some sort of action. They head bands much like mine, and they seek the same things I seek, but among us there is no organization nor any regular contact. I would bring these men here, to B'nei B'rak, and have you, Rabbi Akiba, choose a leader from among us so that we might all unite under a single banner."

"You would still have only about two thousand men. There are six thousand in a single legion."

"True," said Simon, "but from this small seed a mighty army could grow, an army such as the world has never seen because it would be made up of a united people determined to be free. Such a people could form an army that even the legions could not withstand—an army not only of warriors but of men and women who would continue to work the land even as we fought for it, of builders who would continue to build and teachers who would continue to instruct. Plant this seed, Rabbi, and it will grow into an army of liberation that will encompass all of Judea."

"Such an army could also lead to the destruction of all of Judea," Akiba said.

"Reckon not the cost," said Simon. "I believe those were your words."

Akiba arose and walked slowly to a window of the large room. "Why have you come to me?" he asked. "Judea is no poorer in rabbis than in rebel chieftains. Several of them are known to favor some sort of action. On the other hand, my own pacifist views are well known. I have long felt that our salvation can best come through the study of the Law of our fathers and the transmission of this Law to future generations."

"Among rabbis as among rebels there must be one leader," Simon answered. "You are the logical one because all factions respect you—those who openly hate Rome as well as those who seek to conciliate it, Jews in exile as well as those living here, the extreme pietists as well as those who have let slide the practice of our religion."

Akiba took a deep breath and looked silently out the window to the garden beyond before speaking. "All that you say only makes my responsibility that much more grave." He turned to his visitor and considered him, the young man's tall, erect bearing, the skin browned deep by the desert sun, the simple merchant's robe he had put on for his journey.

"I have no reason to doubt your sincerity, Simon, my son," said the rabbi with genuine warmth. "I too seek what you seek. I share the same dream of a reborn Israel and a restored Jerusalem. But there are many roads to this end, and I, as a rabbi and a teacher of the Law, cannot urge a path of violence unless I should become convinced that this is the only path, that there is no choice, that we must fight or lose even what little we have. I am not convinced of anything like that at this time."

"In other words," Simon said, "your answer is no."

"In other words," said Akiba, "my answer is let us wait and see. There is a strong possibility at this moment that the Romans will soon give us permission to rebuild the Temple, that they will in time permit our grand council to become a true Sanhedrin again and give us a measure of autonomy. If we could achieve all this through peace, I would much prefer it, even to total independence, if such independence had to come through bloodshed."

Simon arose. "I would not," he said and made as if to go.

"Please sit," Akiba said in a tone of command. "There is no reason for us to part in anger. I pray you, break some bread with me."

Simon sat down. The rules of civility, he knew, demanded as much.

A servant set a table with bread and vegetables, a variety of cheeses and a large pitcher of cool milk. He brought water in a basin and towels and two cups for washing. As the ritual law required, each of the two men took cupfuls of water and poured them first over the one hand, then over the other, making sure that their hands were absolutely clean before the meal would begin. Then Akiba moved to the table, broke off a piece of bread, sprinkled some salt on it and recited the required blessing: "Blessed are You, O Lord our God, King of the universe, Who brings forth bread from the earth." He ate the piece of bread, then broke off another and handed it to his guest. Simon also recited the blessing and ate the bread. The men then sat down and began to eat, Simon in depressed silence.

Akiba caught the young man's mood, and it pained him. He thought for a flashing moment of his own youth, of the intensity of its passions, of its hates and of its loves. He thought of his dead wife, Rachel, of the lovely woman who, long ago, had urged the peasant that had been Akiba to leave his father's field and enter the house of study to become a rabbi, a master of the Law. Many times had Akiba told his disciples that the honor they paid to him should instead be paid to his wife, for it was she who had inspired him, who had encouraged and given him the strength to make the first beginnings in his studies, as a child might, when Akiba was already in full maturity. Her passing had pained him deeply, and it had required all of Akiba's faith to end his mourning, for the Law insisted that a man could not spend his life in mourning for one who had passed on to the world to come. Yet, from time to time, may the Lord forgive him, Akiba grieved for her still.

The rabbi wondered if Simon had a wife, and he asked him. The young man said he did not, and Akiba was not surprised. A man happily married could not have hated with such intensity.

"You are an orphan?" asked Akiba.

"Yes," said Simon. "But how did you know?"

"Your name. I take it the name derives from the town of Kosiba in the region of Judah."

"That is so," said Simon. "The men of the town found me by the wayside one day when I was still an infant. I had been circumcised, and so they knew I was a Jew, but they never learned who my parents were or where they had come from or what had been their fate. It was assumed they had been taken by the Romans for some offense and slain."

"Alas," said Akiba, "such cases are today not uncommon in Judea. And this is why you hate the Romans so?"

"No," Simon shook his head. "I do not hate them for this. I cannot remember my parents, nor do I know the manner of their death, so in truth I have no feeling in this matter."

Akiba nodded in approval. It was an honest answer.

"Though I was an orphan," Simon continued, "my childhood was a happy one. The orphans of Kosiba lacked nothing. The citizens of the town, poor as they were, treated us as well as their own children; sometimes, out of tenderness, even better. No, this is not my reason for hating the Romans."

"May I ask," said Akiba, "what then is your reason?"

Simon sighed. "There are so many reasons. So many." He closed his eyes and spoke softly. "There is an old man flogged to death. There are dreams destroyed. There are houses burning and men crucified. There are so many reasons." Simon opened his eyes suddenly and looked at the rabbi. "But let me tell you two of them. Two reasons named Jonathan and Ruth, who are my friends."

"Say on," said Akiba.

Simon began. "Jonathan Bar Ba'ayah and I grew to manhood together in the town of Kosiba. He was my friend from boyhood, my companion with whom I learned the shape of the characters in which the Law is written. Unlike me, Jonathan was not an orphan, and his parents—may they be at peace—treated me like another son. Every holiday of my boyhood was spent at their home, and Jonathan's mother more often than not would save for me the best part of the roast or of the fowl in preference to her own son. As for his father, he made no distinction between us whatever. He was the blacksmith of Kosiba—a big, muscular figure of a man—and as he taught Jonathan how to heat the forge and temper the metal, so also he taught it to me. He would listen to us reciting our lessons, and if we did well, he would reward us both equally. And if we did something bad, as boys do sometimes, he would punish us both equally, but this was a rare thing, for he was a most gentle man for all of his great strength. So you see, he was in a way like my own father, yet even more than a father, for he treated me like a son although he didn't have to.

"It went on like this until shortly after Jonathan and I had marked our *Bar Mitzvah* and had come of age. It was at about that time that the troubles began, when the Jews rose up again here and in Alexandria and in Cyprus. We were divided, of course, as always, and so the Emperor Trajan had little trouble putting the revolt down. And afterward, although Judea had had but a minor part in this revolt, there came the bloody repressions under the Governor Quietus—may his name be blotted out—whose single purpose seemed at the time to be to cause as much grief to the Jews as possible. Kosiba had been practically untouched by the revolt, being a poor community and an unwalled town off the main trade routes of no particular use to anybody. Until one day a Roman cohort came to the town, and the centurion in command announced to the council of the elders that the Governor had placed a fine of fifty thousand dinars on the town for having aided the rebellion.

"None of this, you understand, was true. Not that Kosiba had not sympathized with the revolt, but no one in the town had done anything to aid it for the simple reason that no one was able to, since none of the fighting had taken place anywhere nearby. As for the fifty thousand dinars, the whole town could not have been sold for such a sum, and the Romans must have known it. Obviously the elders could not produce the fine. But the centurion became furious, accusing the Jews of hiding their wealth, and he put the elders to the torture. Several of them died, but none revealed the treasure's hiding place, for, of course, there was nothing to reveal.

"At this point the centurion lost all reason, and he turned his men loose on the town to pillage and rape and destroy at will. It was only a cohort—six hundred men at the most—and I suppose we could have overcome them. But, you see, the men of Kosiba were men of reason, as you are, Rabbi, and they had therefore never taught themselves to fight, nor had they ever organized for a struggle. They just prayed and assured themselves that the horror would pass, and meanwhile the Romans killed and robbed.

"At last they came to the house of the blacksmith, and they accused him of having made arms for the rebels. Poor Ba'ayah protested that he didn't even know how to make a sword, but it didn't matter. His wife begged the decurion to let him go, and the soldier cut her down with one stroke right in front of Jonathan's eyes. As for Ba'ayah, the Romans put up a rough cross near his forge, and they nailed him to it. He was a strong man, and it took him three full days and two nights to die. Jonathan and I watched him die. We stood there, helpless, watching his agony, unable even to give him a drink of water. The Romans guarding the crucified man were much amused by us, but they left us alone. Apparently even they had grown tired of the easy slaughter.

"And then, toward the end of the third day, we could hear Ba'ayah whispering the Shema as he hung there, and we knew that he was readying himself to die, so we drew close and wept at his feet, praying silently for him to live and also praying for him to die, for it is no easy thing to live on the cross. He said only one thing to us just before he died. Gently he said, 'Remember what I taught you.'

"It took awhile for the Romans to realize that the blacksmith was no longer alive, and when they did realize it, they made ready to depart, leaving the body on the cross. Jonathan ran after them, crying 'kill me too, kill me too,' but the Romans just laughed and rode off. Afterward some of the men in the town reappeared and took Ba'ayah down and buried him next to his wife. Jonathan said not a word during the entire service, nor did he cry. He had cried that once when he had begged the Romans to kill him, and he didn't cry again for a long time after that.

"When it was all over, Jonathan and I left Kosiba. There was nothing to keep us there anymore. We were both orphans now. We wandered about from town to town, not really knowing what we were looking for, doing odd jobs here and there, taking whatever hospitality was offered us. Everywhere we went we saw the burned houses and ravaged fields, and we heard the laments of the widows and orphans. Eventually we went to the mountains and gathered about us a band of young men like ourselves, men with no place to go and nothing to do. What we needed we took from the oppressor, and whenever possible we took their lives as well. This is the band I was telling you about."

Akiba shook his head. "Terrible. Terrible," he said, and there were tears in his eyes.

"You have heard only half the tale," said Simon. "The story of Ruth has yet to be told."

"Please go on," said Akiba.

"Some years ago we were riding in the Judean desert when we saw a group of Roman legionaries—perhaps five of them—and gave chase. The Romans fled from us, but our horses were rested and theirs were not, so we began to gain on them. In a move to slow us down one of them cut loose a horse that had been tethered to the others. On approaching it, we saw that there was a body tied across that horse, the naked body of what had once been a young woman. I say once because the body was covered from the neck down with welts and bruises the like of which I had never seen.

"The woman was still alive, though only barely. We took her back to the camp with us, and Artemon—a physician who is a member of our band—dressed her wounds as best he could. Several of the men in our group had taken wives by this time, and the women helped also to care for her. But it was Jonathan who stayed with this injured woman day and night, changing her bandages and caring for her in every way until she finally regained consciousness after many days.

"I was there when she awakened and like the rest was most curious to learn what had happened to her. But at first she could tell us nothing and was able to do little more than mumble her gratitude to Jonathan for nursing her. In time, however, under Jonathan's care, she did come to remember many things, although it might have been better for her had she not done so.

"She remembered being in Caesarea, having apparently been abducted there by the Romans and taken to the palace of the Governor Rufus. She was, you understand, an extremely attractive woman—or had been—and no older than about nineteen or twenty. She had been placed in a cell in Rufus' basement and had spent several days there before the governor finally came for her. When he did, he ravished the woman repeatedly while some soldiers held her. Then he had the soldiers tie her up, and then and for days afterward he would whip the bound girl mercilessly and perform other unspeakable atrocities on her body to satisfy his twisted desires.

"The whippings were the last thing the woman remembered before awakening in the cave where we had taken her. Jonathan heard this story from her lips when I did, and a strange thing happened. He wept bitterly, and this was the first time any of us had seen him weep since that day many years before when his father had died. In time he married her, and they now have a son who, I pray to God, will have a better life than his parents have had."

"May it be His will," Akiba whispered.

"In any case," Simon continued, "the woman never remembered more than this, and perhaps that is a blessing. She does not know where she came from, or who her parents were or are, or even her own name. Her memory begins with her rape by Rufus, and her life begins with Jonathan. It was he who gave her the name Ruth, and she accepted it along with his love."

Simon had finished, but Akiba remained silent for a long while afterward. "I think I understand you now," he said at last. "Yes, I understand you now and your hatred of the Romans."

Akiba arose and placed a hand on Simon's shoulder. "You have taught me much this day, young man. Now permit me to try to teach you something."

"As you wish, Rabbi," said Simon.

"Hatred can be understood," Akiba said, "even justified, but it can never take the place of reason. Not that I worship reason, as the Greeks do, nor am I among those sectarians who believe that everything under the sun can be proved by logic. Yet the fact remains that reason alone lifts man above the beasts, and its application in questions of morality of action—regardless of how cowardly it may have seemed to you at times— is one of the elements that lift Israel above the nations."

"What is your meaning?" asked Simon.

"My meaning is that our decision on whether to fight the Romans or not—whatever it may be and whenever it may come —must be guided by more than a desire for vengeance, no matter how righteous such a desire may be."

Simon remained silent.

Akiba continued. "Let us, for a test, apply reason to what you have just told me. The Romans, in their inexcusable cruelty on towns like Kosiba some fifteen years ago, were but taking vengeance on the Jews who had rebelled against the Emperor Trajan. Those rebels, in turn, had been seeking to avenge the destruction of Jerusalem and the Temple some forty-five years before. Now I concede that the Romans were the first to move against us, but does not reason dictate that at some point this hatred must end?"

"Why must we always end it?" Simon asked.

Akiba shrugged his shoulders. "Perhaps this is part of our mission. The great sage Hillel himself taught that we must love our enemies."

Simon arose and faced Akiba. "I am sorry, Rabbi," he said,

"but I am not a sage. I am only a man. I still seek what I sought when I came here."

"I would speak with you again," Akiba said. "Is your face known?"

"No Roman who has crossed swords with me has lived to identify my face."

"I would have you come here for the feast of the Passover. That will give us two months to see what reason can accomplish. There will be many here for the celebration that night, and you will not even be noticed. I will speak to you then."

"Very well," said Simon.

Akiba escorted him to the door. "And remember, my young friend," he said, "hatred can blind one's eyes to the truth."

"And what is the truth?" asked Simon.

"I am not here to plead the cause of the Roman Empire," said the rabbi, "but try to keep in mind that when you speak of what the Romans did to you and your friends, you are not speaking of the best of Rome. I have been to the city of Rome, and I found there many highly civilized men, poets and philosophers and builders, some of whom openly sympathized with our cause. Whatever we may or may not do, these men and their works will surely outlive all of the scum of whom we have spoken, from Rufus on down."

"Perhaps," said Simon, "and perhaps not. Perhaps the scum will inherit the earth."

"I do not really think so," Akiba said.

6

Shortly after Simon left, Rabbi Akiba received another visitor—a beautiful young woman named Miriam Bath-Menashe Ben-David. She was the daughter of a distinguished Jewish family that traced its ancestry back to King David, but she now spoke her native Hebrew and Aramaic with the faint trace of a

Greek accent, and the name by which she called herself was, in the Greek fashion, Mariamne.

Akiba was delighted to see her and remarked good-humoredly how much she had grown.

Mariamne laughed. "The last time I was here, Rabbi, was more than fifteen years ago. Somehow, everything in this room seemed so much larger."

"Yes," Akiba nodded, "that is how it is. As children we do not think of ourselves as small, only of the world as large. When we grow up, we still see things only through our own eyes. For instance, I look at you and see a beautiful young woman. But, forgive me, I also see that I am growing very old."

Mariamne sat down at the large table, then looked beneath it, her dark eyes sparkling. "I used to play underneath this very table. I remember I would crouch there and watch your feet and my father's feet as you sat and talked. I often made as if I were going to touch your feet, but I always stopped at the last moment. I think I was dreadfully afraid of what would happen if I did."

"Little Miriam," Akiba smiled. "I remember your playing there as if it were yesterday. And your father winking at me to pretend we didn't notice." The old man sighed. "Your father —may he be at peace—he loved you very much. When your mother passed away giving birth to you, he lavished on you all his love. I don't think he could have given more love to ten children."

"I know," Mariamne said softly.

Akiba silently rebuked himself. Old age was time enough for reverie. "You are now—what—twenty-one?"

"Nearly twenty-two," said Mariamne.

"If you will forgive an old man an impertinent question, how is it no man has yet betrothed you to himself? Surely the young Jews of Alexandria must be blind."

"I've had a few suitors," Mariamne said with a faint bow of her head. "But, well, I didn't feel love for any of them. That must sound silly to you."

"Not at all," said Akiba. "I teach that it is wrong to marry without love. And you still have time."

"What is life like here?" asked Mariamne. "I've been gone from Judea so long that I feel like a stranger."

"You'll see for yourself soon enough," said Akiba. "There are problems here. We are not as well off as the Jews in Alexandria. Life is hard sometimes, especially for the poorer people. But this is our home, and for a Jew there is meaning here."

"Meaning," said Mariamne. "The Alexandrians would give much for that."

"Ah, yes," said Akiba. "The modern sickness. The endless questioning and wondering and doubting instead of doing. I understand it is becoming quite prevalent in the world around us."

"And here?"

"That is one trouble we have been spared. Alas, we have too many real problems, the problems your father sought to avoid for you by moving his business to Alexandria when you were still a child. Judeans are too busy fearing death to fear life. And, of course, there is the matter of faith in something beyond ourselves."

Mariamne nodded absently. "I suppose that's the main reason I came back, to see what it was like. My father's business is being managed by men he appointed for the task, and I have no worries about money. So I thought I'd return to the land of my birth to look for what we probably lose forever by just growing up, anywhere."

Akiba arose. "I beg you to remain here as my guest."

"I do not wish to impose," Mariamne protested.

"You will not impose. There are many here, students and frequent visitors. I ask you to indulge an old man in this, for I counted your father among my true friends."

"I will be honored to stay," said Mariamne.

When Mariamne had been shown to her quarters, Akiba sat himself down in his garden and watched the setting sun. And he thought. He thought about the stories Simon had told him and about the problem the young man's visit had raised.

"Whosoever sheds human blood may be described as having diminished the image of God." This had long been Akiba's teaching, for was not every man—Roman as well as Jew—fashioned in the image of the One God? From this belief in the inherent wrongness of killing had sprung Akiba's pacifism, a pacifism that was not moved by the greatness of causes or the purity of motives. For Akiba also taught that there is no distress save that which affects individuals.

But these arguments which had satisfied so many of his colleagues failed to satisfy Akiba himself now. For this rebel Simon had not spoken of national pride or dreams of glory but of the present and very pressing distress of individuals; he had spoken not of abstract causes but of a fight for freedom against the wrong, of a fight for the kind of Judea the Law required.

"Hatred can blind one's eyes to the truth," Akiba had told the rebel. That was true enough, but what of justice? The truth required justice. Yet in urging conciliation, Akiba asked himself, was he not really urging a compromise without justice? Had he become more of a political realist than a teacher of the Law?

Rabbi Akiba the son of Joseph sat alone in the twilight and felt himself inadequate to the task. Who was he—a peasant turned latter-day scholar—to make decisions that might affect the destiny of Israel for centuries? To the world at large he appeared a venerable sage, but in his own eyes Akiba saw himself as only an aged man of the fields who had, through the virtue of a good wife, managed to acquire some learning.

That he was now—like it or not—accepted by all of the other rabbis as the successor to great masters like Hillel and Yohannan Ben-Zakkai did not cease to amaze him. Nor to frighten him as well.

And so he sought now to guess at what his predecessors of blessed memory would have advised Simon. The gentle Hillel and the learned Yohannan, Akiba felt sure, would have said that the Law had to be preserved at all costs. For the Law— the Torah, the Revealed Will, the Covenant—this was Israel's key to immortality. And, conversely, the Law could not survive without Israel. "My lover is mine, and I am his," said the Song of Songs, and Akiba saw this as an allegory: the Eternal Covenant was also an Eternal Embrace.

And that, Akiba realized, was his answer. He would go along with a policy of peace and conciliation—leaving justice to the Almighty—so long as the basic tenets of the Jews could flourish. If these were threatened, well . . .

Well what? Akiba asked himself.

"You shall love the Lord your God with all your heart and with all your soul and with all your might," taught the Law, and Akiba had interpreted this Biblical verse to mean that a Jew must love God without restraints, at all costs, even though his own life be required of him.

But if it came to a fight with Rome, what could all the dying accomplish? What chance was there of defeating a Roman army? Reason told him there was no chance. And reason, he had told Simon, was the one element that raised man above the beasts.

But did Akiba really believe this? He had heard the words come from his mouth, but were they really his words, the words of a man who had ultimate faith in One whose presence could neither be seen nor proved by reason? Or were they, rather, sentiments more fitting for Elisha Ben-Abuyah, the apostate, the one they called *aher,* a rabbi who had followed reason so devoutly that it had led him to atheism?

It was a question he would have occasion to resolve in person, for shortly after Simon's visit Elisha himself—the Jewish apostle of reason—arrived at the university in B'nei B'rak to pay a call on his old friend and colleague, Rabbi Akiba.

This Elisha had once been among the greatest rabbis in Judea, a leading member of the grand council whose opinions on various points of Law were widely respected and had been set down for all time in that still unfinished collection of opinions, judgments, sayings and parables that went under the general heading of Talmud—"Learning."

And then one day Rabbi Elisha had lost his faith.

Many and varied were the stories about what had led to this cataclysmic personal decision, but they all agreed on one point —that one day Elisha had come to the blasphemous conclusion that God does not exist.

From that time on the rabbis would refer to him as *aher,* which is Hebrew for "another." They would still invite him to their homes and councils, of course, for they still respected his judgment and his vast storehouse of learning, and some secretly harbored the hope of bringing him back to the faith. But even if they did not harbor this hope, the devout rabbis were quite fond of Elisha and saw no reason for casting off his friendship merely because of a difference of opinion.

Furthermore, Elisha had not lost his knowledge, only his faith. And so to preserve his learned judgments, yet in token consideration of his eternal damnation, Elisha was no longer quoted by name. Instead it would simply be noted that "Another said . . ." or "it was pointed out by another . . ." and so forth.

Elisha himself didn't mind his enforced latter-day anonymity. As a matter of fact, he rather enjoyed his pseudonym of *aher* and would make pointed jests about it, much to the embarrassment of the devout rabbis. Since Elisha believed no more in his own survival after death than anyone else's, he could not bring himself to care very much whether future ages remembered his name or not.

Akiba met his old friend at the entrance to his home, and they broke bread together. After Akiba had said the grace alone, the two of them went for a leisurely stroll through the garden.

"You seem troubled," said Elisha. "Is there something I might do to help?"

Akiba stopped short and looked at his visitor. "I would ask your opinion on a certain matter," he said, continuing the stroll. "But before I do, tell me, can I trust you to keep secret both the question and the answer?"

"Have I ever been known to betray a confidence?" asked Elisha.

"No, you have not. And therefore I will tell you that some days ago there came to me a man who called himself a rebel against Rome and who asked my help in uniting various rebel factions for a full-scale revolt against the imperial power."

"And you told him?"

"I put him off. I told him that at present we were negotiating for certain concessions from Rome, which is true, and I suggested that he return here at a future date."

"You did wrong to raise his hopes," said Elisha. "That in itself is dangerous. You should have told him no from the start."

"But will the answer surely be no?" Akiba asked. "In your

opinion what would the Law require of a Jew if the Romans
were to make it impossible for us to follow the ways of our fathers?"

"The Romans are civilized men," Elisha said. "They are
not likely to do that."

"Granted," Akiba said. "But still, what if they did?"

Elisha was silent for a moment before answering. "Do you
wish me to answer that as a scholar of the Law," he asked, "or
as a man of reason?"

"As both."

"As a scholar of the Law, I would say that the Law requires
rebellion before submission to idolatry or before submission
to a tyranny that would ultimately cause our descendants to
submit to idolatry. But as a man of reason, I would say that
some other way must be found."

"Supposing there were no other way?"

"There must be another way, for the way of rebellion is
madness." Elisha sighed. "Akiba, it pains me to see your customary devotion to peace weakening. It pains me, and it
frightens me, for you are today the most dangerous man in Judea."

"I?" Akiba exclaimed. "Come now."

"Yes," Elisha nodded, "you. I believe firmly that you are the
only man in all of Judea who could spark another revolt. And
I believe just as firmly that such a revolt would end in the ab-
solute destruction of Judea."

Akiba smiled. "You must admit that your view is somewhat
prejudiced. After all, you have no faith."

"Indeed I have not," Elisha declared, "and therefore I believe my way to be the last hope of the Jews, while your way
could well lead to a fresh disaster.

"My way," Elisha went on, "makes it possible for me to see
things as they are, instead of as I might wish them to be. I know
that there is no One up there, and so I can see clearly what is
down here—and that, my dear Rabbi Akiba, is an empire of
unprecedented size and power backed by the best trained,
best outfitted and best organized army the world has ever
known. This massive army has defeated every single nation that
has ever risen against it, including our own. To oppose it, your
rebel would place into the field a few thousand ill-trained and

poorly armed Jewish soldiers, each ten of them following a different leader with a different plan. The result would not be hard to predict."

The two old men walked on for a time in silence. "You see," Elisha said at last, "how clear these things are when you take your idea of God out of the picture?"

"One can never take God out of the picture," Akiba said.

There were other visitors to B'nei B'rak in those weeks preceding the festival of the Passover. Students came and members of the grand council and even the wife of the procurator of Judea.

Cornelia came in response to Rabbi Akiba's invitation, and she asked him simply, "What does it mean to be a Jew?" Akiba couldn't help noting that the question was the same Simon had asked. But the differences were equally noteworthy, for this was a Gentile woman, the governor's wife, and all her inbred sense of manners could not quite manage to stifle the faint trace of a mocking smile.

But no matter. Akiba didn't mind indulging her idle curiosity, and he began at the beginning. "Once, long ago, my people were slaves . . ."

Cornelia listened, and in time the smile faded.

Thus for Rabbi Akiba passed the final days of winter. Until one day he received an urgent summons to appear before the procurator in Caesarea.

7

It was the month of Nisan, the first month, "the beginning of months," the month of the Exodus from Egypt, the month of spring when the land of Judea began to come to life. On the fourth day of the month, less than two weeks before the festival of the Passover, Rabbi Akiba arrived in the Roman city of Caesarea on the Judean coast.

He found Rufus in the large chamber of the palace; the governor was pacing the floor. "You are late," he said.

"I beg your pardon," said the rabbi. "I was delayed at the last moment."

Rufus waved his hands. "No matter. I have some news for you regarding your petitions. There are three matters," the governor said. "I want you to know and appreciate I did what I could."

"We know and shall surely appreciate," Akiba said.

"Regarding the Minaeans," Rufus began, "your petition is granted. Rome reserves her freedom of action toward this noxious sect in the city itself, but here in Judea the persecutions will cease and the fate of the Minaeans will be left in the hands of the grand council."

"A wise decision, a noble act," Akiba said.

"There is a second matter," Rufus continued. "In consideration of the spread of alien doctrines within Rome, the emperor has decided to reactivate a long-dormant law forbidding mutilations of the body."

Akiba grew tense. The antimutilation law, while broad in terms and humane-sounding, was a piece of vicious legislation directed specifically against the Jews. The law appeared reasonable enough, since it merely prohibited a man from mutilating his own body. However, the Romans considered circumcision mutilation, and the Law of Moses required circumcision of all Jewish males. If the Romans forbade this ancient practice, the point of no compromise would be reached.

Rufus had paused after making his statement to let its full effect sink in. "However," he continued now, "the emperor has decided to be especially gracious to the Jews. In consideration of your primitive custom of circumcision, an exception will be made in the case of the Jews, and the law will not apply to those born of Jewish marriages. It will, though, apply in full force to those not born Jews."

Akiba felt relieved. The antimutilation law was being revived, then, to deal with the increasing number of conversions. The law would be burdensome, of course. It would be difficult for the rabbis to turn away those Gentile men who earnestly sought to enter the fold of Judaism, and equally difficult for the Minaeans—who also required circumcision. Still, the law of Rome would have to be obeyed. It would be a compromise, a hard one, but still preferable to war.

Yet Akiba still sensed danger; there was something ominous in Rufus' manner this day. His entire approach suggested that he had been building up to something that would be especially hard for the Jews to take.

"You spoke of a third matter," Akiba said.

"The third matter," Rufus said calmly, "is that you will be permitted to rebuild your Temple."

Akiba grasped the arms of the chair. This news was good almost beyond belief. "I thank the emperor," he said in a voice throbbing with emotion. "And the governor I thank for his gracious intercession. We shall not forget this, I assure you. Jews will bless both your names until the end of time."

Rufus smiled benignly. "You may, as far as we are concerned, begin choice of site and construction as soon as is practicable. Naturally we shall expect to see the plans in advance to make certain your Temple cannot again be turned into a fortress."

"Choice of site?" Akiba asked in sudden concern. "I do not understand."

"Well," said Rufus casually, "of course you will not be able to build it in Jerusalem. I thought that was clear."

All at once Akiba understood everything. Yet his mind would not accept the comprehension and so he continued hopefully, in a voice nearly indistinct. "But it must be Jerusalem. It must be on the same site as the first two Temples, on Mount Moriah, on the spot where Abraham offered up his son Isaac for a sacrifice. Please try to understand, and try to make your emperor understand. Our synagogues and houses of study can be built anywhere, but for our Holy Temple, the repository of the Holy of Holies, there can be only one site in the whole world, and this is the site chosen by God himself. I beg you, I plead with you to understand. This is not merely a matter of sentiment with us. Our tradition requires it. Our history requires it. Our Law requires it."

"Then change your Law," said Rufus, "for the emperor will not change his mind."

"Perhaps if you intercede for us only once again," the rabbi pleaded. "We will do anything to gain your help."

"Impossible," Rufus snapped. "I have already done all that I can, and it is out of the question."

Akiba sighed. Well, then, he thought, it would have to mean more waiting. The rebuilding of the Temple would have to wait. The restoration of Jerusalem would have to wait. The realization of the dream would have to wait. It would be unpleasant but necessary. And the Jews were good at waiting. They had outwaited more than one enemy.

"Please tell your emperor that we are not ungrateful," said the rabbi solemnly, "but that if Jerusalem is to continue to lie fallow, our Temple cannot be built anywhere else. We thank him for his offer, but our Law forbids us to accept it."

"Jerusalem will not lie fallow," said Rufus quickly, as if in afterthought. "The emperor has plans for it."

"I do not understand," Akiba said.

"For some reason I cannot divine," said the governor drily, "the emperor has decided to honor this land by building a great city on the site of your former capital. He will name it Aelia Capitolina, after his own family name of Aelius, and he will make it the greatest city in the East."

Akiba remained silent, forcing himself to absorb all that he heard.

"So that you do not harbor any false hopes," Rufus continued, "I might as well tell you that the preliminary plans for this city have already been drawn in Rome and that these plans include a great temple to Jupiter on the mount of which you earlier spoke. So you see, you might as well go ahead and build your own Temple elsewhere, because the former spot will soon be occupied."

Akiba was thunderstruck. Was Rome insane? Had she decided to drive the people to revolt? No, Akiba knew, it was far from being a calculated move. It was just a ruler's vanity, compounded perhaps by bad advice and certainly by sheer stupidity.

The rabbi sat there numbly. He felt a fleeting sensation of utter grief. But then the emotion changed to hatred, a hatred so vast that Akiba felt sure it passed even Simon's hatred in its intensity. It was a hatred the rabbi had never before permitted himself, for it was personal: It was directed not at Rome nor at the Romans nor at the emperor himself; it was directed at

Rufus. The emperor could have been ill-advised, Akiba knew. His counselors may be uninformed or even fools. But Rufus was no fool. Rufus could have given different advice, and the words of the procurator of Judea would have had great weight in such a matter. But Rufus had not chosen to give such informed advice—perhaps for the very purpose of accomplishing what he had just done, of ruining hopes and dashing dreams.

Well, Akiba thought, he shall have his reward.

A sudden calm descended upon the old man, a calm born of decision, a calm born of the knowledge that there would be no more tortuous thinking and sleepless nights wondering which course was preferable. There was now only one course left open.

The rabbi rose from the chair and with a deliberate gesture took hold of the collar of his robe and pulled downward hard, tearing it.

"What are you doing?" asked Rufus, shocked. "Have you gone mad?"

"It is not I who have gone mad," said Akiba. "What I have just done is a sign of mourning. It is also a sign of rending that which has been to make way for that which shall be."

"I do not like your tone," said the governor. "You would do better not to rend your clothes but to go to your grand council and tell them what I have just told you. Urge them to stop exciting the people with their foolish dreams. Urge them to cease their endless prayers for the restoration of Jerusalem—prayers that now could be considered even treasonable. Urge them to make peace with Rome and Rome's will and thereby to make peace for themselves."

Akiba looked straight at Rufus. "We will do what we must," he said.

The old man moved toward the door, the torn part of his robe flapping at his side, exposing his chest like that of any beggar on the highway. But Akiba did not look like a beggar, and he turned at the doorway majestically.

"Farewell," said Rufus in a manner which, for all that had transpired, was friendly enough.

Akiba's face showed no emotion. "I wonder," he said simply, "if you know what you have done."

8

The festival of the Passover, commemorating the deliverance of the Israelites from Egyptian bondage, began with the sundown on the fourteenth of Nisan.

Throughout the land of Judea and wherever else the descendants of the generation of the Exodus were now settled, Jews gathered together with their families for a great feast to celebrate their liberation 1,500 years before from all masters save One.

The feast itself was a religious obligation, and if any house in Israel was too poor to afford the best food or the required amount of wine or festive clothing, the elders of the community would see to it that the family was provided out of the common funds. For even the poorest Jew had been delivered by God from slavery, and therefore even the poorest Jew now had the right to celebrate with the mighty.

And if by chance a Jewish man or woman should find himself alone in the season of the Passover in a strange town or even a foreign land, it was incumbent on the Jews of that place to invite him to their homes—indeed, to give him a choice of homes and feasts.

And if there was a Gentile stranger in the town, the invitation was extended to him as well, even as the Law taught, "You shall love the stranger, for you were strangers in the land of Egypt."

That is how it happened that the houses of Judea were filled that night with guests—foreigners and strangers among them—and that Rabbi Akiba himself had stood before the gates of his house immediately following the evening prayer and, holding some flat unleavened cakes of matzoth in his hand, had intoned, "Behold, this is the bread of affliction which our ancestors ate in the land of Egypt. Let all who are hungry come in and eat; let all who are in need come in and celebrate the Passover with us."

The invitation, spoken in the common Aramaic rather than the High Hebrew, was but a formula; by this time all the invitations had already been extended to the stranger, and provisions made for the poor. Still the master of each house repeated the invitation, just in case some lately arrived traveler or beggar should pass by.

Only after making this customary public invitation did Akiba go inside to the large dining hall of his house to greet the many guests who had journeyed to B'nei B'rak to celebrate the eve of the Passover with him.

Several members of the grand council were there, along with Another—*aher*—Elisha Ben-Abuyah.

And Mariamne was there.

And Quintus Arminius Caro was there.

And Cornelia, the wife of the governor, was there, although without her husband. She was seated next to Quintus.

Very near them, not particularly noticed by either the tribune or by the governor's wife, was a bearded young Jew who looked like dozens of other young Jews, whose face and manner did not especially command attention and whose name was Simon.

For this one night the chairs and normal-sized tables had been removed from the large hall and replaced by low couches or cushions and a series of low tables. On this night the Jews and their guests reclined as they ate—in the manner of freemen throughout the Roman world—for this was, above all, the Festival of Freedom.

After opening the feast by saying the blessing over the first cup of wine, Akiba reclined on a couch at the head of the room flanked by his guests of honor—the venerable Rabbi Eliezer, the simple and saintly Rabbi Joshua, the polished Rabbi Eleazar Ben-Azariah, the good-humored Rabbi Tarphon, and Another.

In former days, while the Temple still stood, the sacrifice of a paschal lamb had been a key feature in the celebration of the Passover. But with the sudden end of the sacrificial service, other, more symbolic ways of marking the holiday began to be emphasized. Many of these customs dated back to the Exodus; some had grown up gradually over the centuries, and some had been devised and solemnized only in the six decades since the destruction of the Temple.

Together these formal and informal customs—like the public invitation to the poor—now formed the Seder, Hebrew for "order" or "program" of the feast.

Akiba, who had already added more than one feature to this Seder, now hewed to it in great detail. After he and the guests had washed their hands, he dipped bitter herbs in salt water —symbolizing the bitterness and tears of Egyptian bondage— and passed them around. Then the seven-year-old grandson of one of the rabbis arose to ask the customary questions about this strange order.

"Why is this night different from all other nights?" asked the boy. Why were only matzoth eaten instead of bread, why the procedure of dipping the bitter herbs in salt water, why recline instead of sitting on chairs?

Akiba began the age-old answer.

"We were slaves unto Pharaoh in the land of Egypt, and the Lord our God brought us out from there with a strong hand and with an outstretched arm . . ."

It did not matter that most of the people in the room knew the story well and that, indeed, even the child who had asked the questions knew their answers, for as Akiba reminded them all, "Even though we may all be wise men, all of us learned men, all of us venerable men, all of us well versed in the Law, yet it is incumbent upon us to tell again the story of the Exodus from Egypt."

And of course not everyone in the room fit Akiba's highly flattering description. Quintus, for one, had never heard the reading of the Haggadah—or "retelling"—and he was fascinated by it. He had found the little boy and his questions most charming, and the answer now being given impressed him more than anything he had ever before heard of or from the Jews.

On the other hand, Quintus was less than pleased when, at one point in the retelling, Akiba raised his cup of wine and intoned, "And what happened to our fathers happened to us as

well—not only in one instance—but in every age and generation; whenever tyrants rose up against us to destroy us, the
Holy One, blessed be He, saved us from their hands."

It was but an allegory, Quintus told himself, merely a
means of bringing the past to life again for this one night.
Still he could not quite hide from himself the suspicion that
when the rabbi said "tyrants," he meant Romans; nor could
the tribune suppress a certain annoyance that these people
should consider themselves specially singled out by Providence
for immortality. Then the annoyance passed as swiftly as it
had come and was replaced by Quintus' knowing, calm cyni-
cism: Every nation died in its time; Rome too would die in its
time. This was the only eternal truth, and the rest was a tale
fit only for a child like the one who had asked the questions.

Cornelia was touched by the ceremony, although she understood little of what was being said. Her knowledge of the
Aramaic spoken throughout the East was rudimentary at best,
and the Hebrew of the retelling—while closely related to Aramaic—was too much for her. But she contented herself with
the beauty of the symbolism.

Mariamne could not control her emotions as she recalled the
Seders her father had conducted.

Simon, directly opposite, could not take his eyes off her, and
he wondered now why those lovely eyes of hers were welling
up with tears.

The other rabbis joined Akiba in a discussion of the miracle
of the Exodus. Rabbi Eliezer suggested that each of the ten
plagues visited on the Egyptians had been composed of four
basic plagues, thereby adding up to forty plagues. Rabbi Akiba
went beyond this and suggested that up to the time the Israelites finally crossed the Sea of Reeds the Egyptians suffered a total
of 300 plagues.

As the discussion came down to these purely Talmudic
points, Simon's mind began to wander. He wondered who
the girl opposite him was and toyed with the idea of asking her.
But of course that would be inexcusably bad taste during the
Seder; besides, he would be gone from B'nei B'rak by tomorrow
night and would probably never see her again.

His thoughts went to the task Rabbi Akiba had set for him.
Without explanations, the rabbi had instructed him to gather

together the various rebel chieftains in Judea and to conduct them to B'nei B'rak two weeks hence.

"The time is too short," Simon had protested. "I will have to locate these men, and that will not be easy."

"The time is shorter than you know," Akiba had answered. "Do what you can, and bring them here as soon as possible."

Simon was frankly puzzled. He had considered not even coming to B'nei B'rak tonight, so clearly against any action had the rabbi seemed. Had he changed his mind? And if so, what had caused him to change his mind? And why did he want to see all the rebel leaders so soon?

As Simon thought, he stared unconsciously at the girl opposite him. He caught himself suddenly and looked away but continued stealing glances at her from time to time. She was, he observed, the most beautiful girl he had ever seen. And it was exactly that: an observation, the noting of a fact. Her hair and eyes were black, setting off delicately light skin; she had high cheekbones, a small nose, and a sensitive mouth—her beauty did not startle but impressed itself with the quiet force of truth.

Mariamne, of course, was not unaware that the young man was looking at her, and she too wondered. She wondered who he was and why, though obviously a Jew, he should seem so out of place at the gathering.

The retelling of the ancient tale and the discussion of its finer points came to an end, and the servants once more brought bowls and pitchers of water for a second hand-washing before the feast itself. Then other servants followed carrying trays of fish, meat and vegetable dishes, along with ample selections of the best Judean wine.

Simon continued glancing at Mariamne during the meal. He noted that she ate and drank with a certain elegance, and he became suddenly conscious of his own simple manners, his limited formal learning. No, he would make a fool of himself if he so much as spoke to this girl. His place was among his own kind.

But what were his own kind? Simon wondered, and a melancholy descended on him.

From the time he and Jonathan had left Kosiba to wander among the towns and villages of Judea, he had known many women—slave girls and peasants, middle-aged widows who had taught him much, harlots by the wayside, even one or two women who had professed great love for him. Yet he had never been able to feel close to any of them. He had not even spoken to them, really, but had merely repeated the same formulas of flattery and simple charm that he knew would bring the same reaction from this woman as from the last. They had never disappointed him in this nor in satisfying the needs of his body. But as for the needs of his soul, no woman had been able to fill them.

Not far from Simon, Quintus was also thinking of love, and he squeezed Cornelia's hand several times during the meal and whispered in her ear. But Cornelia was cold to him now, and Quintus could not understand why. The truth was she was seized with a strange embarrassment, a fear that Rabbi Akiba would notice the relationship between them, though why she should care one way or the other she did not know.

A dessert of fruit and nuts ended the sumptuous meal, and the rabbis said grace and recited a series of prayers that concluded the Seder. But then, when the prayers were finished and the required number of cups drained, when some of the guests had begun making ready to leave the large hall, Akiba filled his cup again and rose.

"The order of the Passover ceremonies is now complete," he announced, "in accordance with the prescribed rules and customs."

Akiba's searching eyes looked across the room, scanning the faces of his varied guests. And then he lifted his glass in a toast.

"This year here; next year in Jerusalem. This year slaves; next year freemen."

After a moment, most of the guests joined the rabbi in his toast. Quintus Arminius Caro did not. He was shocked. This, he knew for certain, was treason.

Only one other person in the room understood Akiba's toast. Simon knew now that the rabbi had made up his mind.

None of the guests left B'nei B'rak that night, for the Law forbade travel on the first day of the week-long Passover, and even those who did not normally observe the Jewish tradition observed it now in deference to their host.

Most of the guests, wearied by their journey, or by the un-accustomed late hour, or by the cups of wine, retired to their rooms soon after the conclusion of the Seder. Those more used to wine and late hours wandered into the university's lovely garden.

Beneath the trees in the cool night air Quintus renewed his efforts at exciting Cornelia. But Cornelia would not be excited.

Mariamne strolled lazily through the garden, remembering it from her childhood. About ten paces behind her, trying to look equally casual and cursing himself for a fool, was Simon.

Finally she halted in the midst of the large garden and sat down beneath an olive tree, her knees drawn up with her arms across them in the manner of a little girl. Simon, still behind her, also halted and wondered for several agonizing moments what to do. In the end he decided to walk by as if coming upon her by chance.

"Good evening," he said.

"Good evening," said Mariamne.

Simon looked up at the stars. "It is a clear and lovely night."

"Indeed," said Mariamne.

With a sinking sensation, Simon realized that he was run-ning out of things to say. Then, just as suddenly, the sensation gave way to one of wry amusement: He was acting like a boy; he felt ridiculous. Simon, whatever his doubts, did not normally think of himself as ridiculous, and he resented the feeling now. So he became direct, a tactic far more to his liking.

"I couldn't help noticing you at the Seder," he said. "I am Simon Bar Kosiba. May I ask your name?"

"Mariamne Bath-Menashe Ben-David."

Simon sat down on the grass facing the girl. "You are not from here," he said, and it was a statement, not a question.

Mariamne smiled. "Is my Hebrew that bad?"

"No, no," Simon said. "Not at all. It's just that, well, if you'll forgive my saying so, you slur the gutturals."

"I grew up in Alexandria," Mariamne said good-humoredly, "and I'm afraid some of the subtle shadings of pronunciation were lost in the process."

"There are many Jews in Alexandria, are there not?"

"Yes. A great many. About a hundred thousand."

"I don't understand that," Simon said. "Why don't they come home?"

"But they are home," said Mariamne. "Most of them have lived there for generations."

"Yet they are Jews."

"Yes, but not Judeans."

Simon shook his head. "I don't believe in it," he said.

Mariamne laughed.

"I mean it," he said. "Jews are Judeans."

"But there is so much more to it than that," said Mariamne. "It is not the land that keeps us together but our ideas. And those ideas can thrive outside the land as well. Indeed, they have thrived in Alexandria."

Simon shrugged. "I am a simple man," he said. "To me the Jews are a people, not a collection of ideas. And a people needs its own land, its own government, its own army."

"But you don't have those things now."

"We will have them again. The Romans won't be here forever."

"Don't speak so loudly," said Mariamne. "They haven't left yet."

"One day the Jews outside will see that I am right."

Mariamne smiled. "And then you'll have hundreds of thousands of them here slurring their gutturals."

Simon smiled back. "If they look like you, it is a risk worth taking."

"What do you do?" asked Mariamne. "Are you a disciple of Rabbi Akiba?"

"No," said Simon. "I am merely a visitor here."

"From?"

"I live in the south now. But my business often takes me around the country."

"You are a merchant, then."

"Do I look like a merchant?"

"No. Nor like a Talmudic scholar."

"Well," said Simon, continuing the game, "what do you think?"

Mariamne considered him with an amused and long look. "I couldn't say precisely," she said at last, "but whatever it is that

you do, I don't think you are as casual about it as your manner
would suggest. Your eyes betray you. There is an intensity in
them that says you are seeking something, and a sadness that
shows you have not yet attained it."

Simon was flattered and frankly astonished. "You have come
very close to the mark," he said.

"And just what is the mark?"

Simon thought for a moment. "I suppose you might say I
seek justice."

"No wonder you are sad."

"And what of you?" asked Simon, changing the subject. "I
take it by the Ben-David in your name that you are a descendant of the royal house."

Mariamne made a motion with her hand. "Ah, yes, the royal
house, a house that has not ruled in Israel for seven hundred
years. I was much impressed by it all as a child. I'm afraid I'm
not so impressed now."

"But I am," said Simon earnestly. "It is no small honor to
be a descendant of David. In all our history we have not had a
greater hero nor a greater ruler. And surely you are aware of
the tradition that the Messiah will be of the seed of David. Possibly one of your own descendants."

"Possibly," Mariamne said, "but I don't even know if I will
have any descendants. And to tell the truth I have my doubts
about these Messianic hopes. Too many have died for them already."

"One must have faith," Simon said.

Mariamne smiled. "So everyone here tells me." She stood
up. "I take some things on faith, too. I believe firmly that the
sun will rise before much longer, and I think it is time for me
to retire."

Simon also rose. "Perhaps I will see you again."

"Perhaps," said Mariamne.

Now it happened that Rabbi Eliezer and Rabbi Joshua and
Rabbi Eleazar Ben-Azariah and Rabbi Akiba and Rabbi Tarphon celebrated the eve of the Passover in B'nei B'rak and spent
that entire night discussing the Exodus from Egypt.

And with them was Another. And discussed by them were
other things as well.

Now for the first time did Akiba tell the rabbis of the emperor's decision to build a Roman city and a pagan temple on the site of Jerusalem. And he told them of his own decision to oppose the move with all his might, even to the point of supporting a rebellion against the Roman empire.

It was Rabbi Joshua who first found his voice. He counseled restraint. "We shall outlive the Romans," he said. "Let them build their city with its temple. It cannot prosper but will surely die, and we shall rebuild Jerusalem upon its forgotten ruins. That is the only true victory, Akiba—survival."

"It is our survival of which I am thinking," said Akiba.

"We have survived for sixty years without the Temple," observed Rabbi Tarphon.

"Yes," said Akiba, "without the Temple but with the hope. And with the Idea which our forefathers handed down to us. But what the Romans now propose would be worse than the original destruction. It would in one move both destroy the hope and thereby undermine the Idea possibly beyond repair."

"But could such a revolt succeed?" asked Rabbi Eleazar Ben-Azariah.

"I have discussed this with one of the rebel chieftains," said Akiba, "and I believe there is a chance for at least partial success, so that if we do not free ourselves from Rome completely we might at least gain some concessions through a show of force."

"Akiba," said Rabbi Eliezer soberly, "have you thought about what would happen if we fought and lost?"

Akiba sighed. "I have thought about it," he said. "It would be the end of Judea in our time."

Eliezer looked at Akiba, studying the familiar, wizened face. "My old friend, is it worth the risk? The terrible risk?"

"Do we have any choice?" asked Akiba. "Consider this: If the Romans build their pagan city and if our people, though capable of action, stand idly by while our most holy ground and cherished hope is desecrated, what will remain to us?"

"What will remain to us if we lose?" asked Another.

"The Idea," said Akiba. "Whatever the outcome, the Idea would survive all the more strongly because we had fought for it; yes, and the hope would survive as well and would in time be realized."

"Here is our point of difference," said Another. "I would sooner let Judea survive and let the Idea die."

"Without the Idea," said Akiba, "we are nothing. We are then only a small and miserable nation inhabiting a poor land. Without the Idea, my friend Elisha, Judea would not long survive in any case."

Thus, with a discussion no more heated than had it been on a small point of Talmudic Law, did the rabbis pass the first night of the last Passover of peace in Judea; until at last their disciples came and said to them, "Masters, it is time for the morning prayer."

9

On the twenty-eighth of Nisan, two weeks to the day after the Passover Seder, a strange group of men rode into the university area at B'nei B'rak. By the cut of their clothes one could see that they were not students; and by their bearing and their weather-beaten faces one could see they were not merchants, either.

There were fifty-six of them in all, including Simon Bar Kosiba, and together with a total of not quite 2,000 men under their commands they represented the core of what Judean resistance there was to the Roman power. There was Nathan Bar Deroma, a big, muscular man who looked like the horse breeder he had once been; there was Amram Ben-David, who claimed descent from the great king; there was Judah Ha-Cohen, whose grandfather had been a priest ministering at the altar in the Temple; there was Samuel of Ashkelon, an aristocrat whose father's wide land holdings had been confiscated by the Romans; there were several men who called themselves by the popular rebel pseudonym of Bar Abba—freeman—or, as it was transliterated into the Greek, Barabbas. And there were many more.

Among the chieftains were a few pietists, so religious that they would not move out of their hiding places on the Sabbath or fight on the holy day except to defend their lives. By contrast, there were one or two who had thoroughly lost their faith in God. Some had grandiose plans for a Judean empire, others for a strict theocracy, while still others dreamed of a simple communal kind of life once the Romans had been expelled from the land.

They had in common only two things: their desire for Judea's liberation from Rome, a desire for which they had each proved ready to die if necessary; and a deep respect for the great Rabbi Akiba Ben-Joseph. They had been separately approached by Simon in their caves and mountain hideouts. Each had agreed to let the rabbi choose a leader from among them.

The men were given lodgings on the university grounds, and Akiba himself saw to their personal comfort. Then, beginning on that very day and continuing for two days thereafter, the rabbi held individual meetings with the rebel chieftains, talking to each man privately, questioning, probing.

Akiba was painstakingly thorough in these discussions, seeking to learn as much about each man as he could, seeking to learn his past, his present and his plans for the future, seeking to picture him as the leader and to guess at the kind of leadership he would provide.

And as the discussions came to their end, the conviction grew within Akiba that one of the rebel chieftains had long ago been fated to lead. For there was an ancient prophetic passage in the Book of Numbers that seemed increasingly to the rabbi to have been meant for this time and this man.

The passage, recorded during the wanderings of the Children of Israel toward the Promised Land, spoke of the distant future, saying, "And there shall come a star out of Jacob, and a meteor shall rise out of Israel and shall smite the brow of Moab and crush all the children of Seth. And Edom shall be a possession; yea, Seir shall be a possession for its enemies, and Israel shall do valiantly."

The ancient names of ancient peoples were not to be taken

literally, Akiba knew. The reference was to Israel's enemies far and near.

"And there shall come a star out of Jacob . . ."

This had to be his choice, Akiba felt sure. Not merely a leader who had the right qualifications, but a Bar Kochba—a "Son of a Star" whose light could be sensed by all, as Akiba had sensed it, and whose fire would bind all Israel together.

Now it came to pass on the first day of the second month, which is Iyyar, in the year 3892—corresponding to the year 132 in the calendar of the Minaeans—that Rabbi Akiba Ben-Joseph rose up on a hillock in the plain of assembly at his university in B'nei B'rak.

To emphasize the solemnity of the occasion, the great rabbi wore a white robe usually reserved for the High Holy Days. Before him in the natural amphitheater stood the fifty-six rebel chieftains, and gathered around them were the thousands of the university's students, straining to hear the words the rabbi would speak. Also there were various selected guests, members of the grand council, as well as Mariamne Bath-Menashe Ben-David, who now understood what it was Simon sought.

Rabbi Akiba spoke thus to the assembled multitude:

"It is written in the Book of Koheleth that to everything there is a season, and a time for every purpose under the heavens: a time to keep silent and a time to speak; a time of war and a time of peace.

"The rabbis of Israel have kept silent for a long time. Even when our people first rose against the Romans in the horrible war that resulted in the destruction of our Sanctuary, the greatest of our sages held their peace. For, my brethren, I ask you, how can a teacher of the Law urge men to fight and kill and perhaps die when he knows that all human life is sacred unto the Lord our God, the lives of Romans as well as the lives of Jews?

"Yet there is a time to speak, and that time has come.

"To my disciples now gathered here, I say this: To kill is wrong and a sin in the eyes of God. But are there not things worse than physical death? Is not bodily death—even killing —preferable to death of the soul in a man or in a nation? This is, for each of you, a moral question which you must each decide. My own view is that it is incumbent upon a man to take up arms as a last resort when the personal sanctity given to him by God is threatened. I feel that sanctity is threatened now. Thus I have elected to lend my efforts to the first step toward rebellion—the selection of a national leader. I am aware that such a step, once taken, cannot be retraced. I am aware that war with the mighty Roman Empire can bring disaster upon us. But inaction is also an irrevocable step, and I am of the opinion that this step would lead to even greater disaster.

"To the rebels standing before me, I say this: You are all good men, all worthy men, all dedicated men who have thus far fought a lonely struggle. Choosing a leader from among you has not been an easy task, and in making my decision I have been guided by the Biblical passage that prophesies, 'And there shall come a star out of Jacob.'

"I believe I have seen this 'star' among you. He is not the most distinguished of you by birth or even by deeds. Yet I sense in him a certain dedication stronger than I have ever seen in any other man, a dedication that has consumed him and has directed his entire life and which shines from him—though he may not know it—like light from a star.

"Before I name this man," Akiba continued, "I wish each of you to swear before me and this multitude that you will respect my choice, that you will give your loyalty to this leader without question or reservation, that you will—by standing together behind him—remove the curse of disunity which doomed your fathers."

The rebels smote their breastplates with their swords and, as one man, shouted, "We swear."

Akiba looked out across the plain. His eyes moved past Judah Ha-Cohen, past Nathan Bar Deroma, past Amram Ben-David, and they settled at last on a broad-shouldered, dark young man in the midst of the group. And Akiba intoned, "Arise Simon, Prince of Israel, Son of a Star."

Pushed to the forefront by the others, Simon made his way unsteadily to the hillock and stood before Akiba. The rabbi placed his hands upon the young man's head and blessed him in the sight of the people. Then, speaking so that all could hear,

Akiba said, "From this day forth you shall no longer be called Bar Kosiba, but your name shall be Bar Kochba, for as a star have you risen in our midst."

And the multitude answered, "Long live Simon, Prince of Israel, Son of a Star."

Book Two
TUR MALKA

Soon, O Lord our God, may there be heard in the cities of Judah and in the streets of Jerusalem the voice of joy and the voice of happiness, the voice of bridegroom and the voice of bride, the jubilant voice of bridegrooms from their marriage canopies and of youths from their feasts of song. . . .

—JEWISH MARRIAGE SERVICE

10

SLAVERY. Death in the arena. Crucifixion.

From all that was Rome in all her greatness—the builders who established her, the leaders who ruled her, the poets who sang of her, the thinkers who molded her and spread her ways—the mind of man is often distracted by three unhappy memories: Slavery. Death in the arena. Crucifixion.

Like all evil in a society, these three were not isolated from one another. Connected from the first, they joined in time to form an encircling embrace that affected, overwhelmed and ultimately smothered a once noble civilization. Yet, curiously, none was essentially a Roman evil. Not until the end approached.

Long before Quintus Arminius Caro was born, there were few slaves in Italy. That fertile land was worked by freemen whose simple and hardy lives exemplified all the traits that were to pass on to future generations of Romans as *virtutes:* They worked hard and said little. They revered the gods. They raised families to go on after them in the same fashion. They gave to the state its just due, for it was a state they owned as a *res publica*—a thing of the people. In time of war they would leave their farms and go out to battle by lot—or *legiones* —forming the legions, a new kind of citizen army that fought with a firm dedication because it fought for its own land and its own rights.

Here and there a farmer with more land and fewer sons than his neighbors would purchase a slave. But such a slave would live in the master's house and would by and large be treated as a member of his family. The slave would have a chance for

eventual freedom and even perhaps for a share in the inheritance on the master's death.

Italy's society might have remained this way indefinitely had
it not been for the increasing overseas trade carried on by the
queen city on the peninsula—Rome. In exchange for the wine
and oil grown on the simple farms, Rome brought to Italy its
first taste of an older and more luxurious East.

But the Republic of Rome was not alone in seeking this
profitable trade. Carthage, herself a mighty power on the
northern coast of Africa, presented strong competition to the
fledgling Roman commerce. And Carthage, governed as it was
by a select ruling class of landed aristocrats, had a more efficient
if somewhat unequal economy. Her produce was grown on
large plantations owned by a handful of rich men and worked
by a multitude of slaves. And to defend this way of life, she
had a formidable army, even though it was made up largely
of mercenaries who fought for profit.

The Senate and the Roman People found it increasingly
difficult to compete with this more ordered society. Senators
began denouncing Carthage as imperialistic, hungry for power,
unscrupulous. Carthaginians were pictured as corrupted by
slavery, softened by the luxuries of the East, decadent. Inevitably, war followed—a struggle between East and West that
was longer and more bitter than either side had imagined
possible.

History records that there were three wars between Rome
and Carthage, but really it was all one war, drawn out for more
than half a century and interspersed with periods of uneasy
truce. At one point in the long struggle the Carthaginian Hannibal managed to cross the Alps and menace the very city of
Rome. For fifteen years Hannibal held sway over a large part
of Italy, and it was something the Romans would never forget.

The disaster that Rome had so narrowly escaped left her
people with an obsessive fear, a fear for her security that would
for all time affect the course not only of Rome but of mankind.
"Delenda est Carthago," insisted the Roman censor Cato again
and again. "Carthage must be destroyed."

Ultimately, at the end of the struggle begun by their grandfathers, the victorious legions carried out Cato's harsh sentence: They burned the city of Carthage to the ground, drove

the plow over it, sowed salt into the earth so nothing could grow there again, had their priests pronounce a curse over the site and sold the surviving Carthaginians into slavery. The destruction of Carthage was so complete that not a trace of her civilization remained. Not a trace, that is, except among the victors.

For Rome looked with growing interest on what she had destroyed.

The plantation system with its accompanying mass slavery may have had its faults, but many Romans could not help note that it had resulted in greater production than Italy's traditional system of small landowners. And greater profits.

Quietly at first, then more openly, Romans who had profited from the wars with Carthage began buying land in Italy and forming large holdings. Those small farmers who hesitated to leave their ancestral soil soon found they could not compete with the plantations and their slave labor. So in time they sold out as well and joined the mass of unemployed who thronged into the city of Rome and became the *plebs*—the common people, or the mob—depending on where one stood to look at them.

An increasing number of these men could not find gainful work in the city, for they could no more compete with slave labor there than on the farms. Some became merchants, some artisans, while others swelled the ranks of the legions, now made up mostly of professional soldiers whose numbers grew steadily as the borders they had to guard expanded. A few plebeians managed to get into the Roman civil service, and a handful even achieved wealth and position. But the mass had nothing but the clothes on their backs and the vote that was theirs by ancient right. It was for them that politicians organized circuses where entertainment progressively more bloody was provided—along with bread.

But if the plebeians could be satisfied with bread and circuses, this still left the problem of the slaves, who now outnumbered the free citizens of the republic. Treated as impersonally as animals at best, and with cruelty at worst, these slaves posed a very real danger. They had to be kept subjugated somehow, and there was no better force for this than fear. But with what could Rome threaten a slave, a creature who was born without hope and would surely die as miserably as he had lived? Death to a slave held not much more terror than life, and pain was as much a part of that life as breathing.

To find an effective threat, Rome turned again to the decadent culture of Carthage to see how it had maintained control over its armies of slaves and found a means of execution so horrible that even a slave feared it. It was death through exposure, starvation and agony, and it was brought about by nailing the offending slave onto a crossbeam of wood.

Rome adopted this punishment for rebellious slaves. Later, when she became master of the earth and had already discarded the hobbling outward trappings of a republic, she applied the punishment to all whom she considered rebels against the authority of the empire.

And so, the figure of a man nailed to a cross with his life ebbing out in pain and delirium became well known throughout much of the world. But few in Quintus Arminius Caro's time would have believed that as a universal symbol it would long outlive the Roman fasces.

One of those few who did believe it was a Jew named Mordechai Ben-Joshua. . . .

On a spring day early in the month of Sivan, this Mordechai rode his donkey through the hills of Judah until at length he came to a certain small town where he sought out the local blacksmith and inquired of him where he might procure a sword with its hilt in the shape of a star.

"We are forbidden to make swords," said the blacksmith. "Would you have the Romans put me to death?"

"Rome need not know everything," said Mordechai Ben-Joshua.

"The arm of Rome is long," said the blacksmith.

"The sword I seek would be longer by many lengths."

"Perhaps I might interest you in a sickle."

"The weeds must be cut before the grass will grow," said Mordechai Ben-Joshua.

Without another word the blacksmith left his customer standing there and withdrew to the rear of the shop. In a few moments he returned with a young man, perhaps his son or an apprentice.

"There are no stars by day," said the young man.

"He who would seek light must wait," said Mordechai Ben-Joshua.

"At midnight," said the young man, "on yonder hill over-looking the town, one can often see the stars most clearly."

"Perhaps I shall look," said the stranger. Then he turned and left the shop.

In the middle of the night Mordechai Ben-Joshua was indeed standing on the rocky hill and looking up at the stars when many hands seized him. Hands placed a blindfold over his eyes and bound his own arms behind his back. Rough hands attempting gentleness lifted him up onto his donkey. A hand slapped the donkey's rear, and another hand directed the animal into motion. Throughout it all, not a word was spoken.

For what seemed like a long time, Mordechai Ben-Joshua weaved about on the moving donkey, trying to steady himself by holding his bound hands on the animal's shanks. And then there was heard the cry of an eagle, and the group halted.

"*L'herut Yerushalayim,*" one of them shouted.

And from somewhere ahead there came another voice that answered, "*L'herut Yisrael.*"

The donkey was slapped into motion again, and it moved again up and down and around winding paths before it halted, and hands once again lifted Mordechai Ben-Joshua and directed him stumbling across a rock-strewn way.

He continued in this blind fashion until he sensed a sudden stillness and a damp that told him he had entered some closed shelter in the hills. And then the blindfold was whipped away, and Mordechai Ben-Joshua stood in the flickering light of oil lamps before two men. One of them rose and approached him.

"Speak," said the man in Latin.

"I am not a Roman," Mordechai answered in Aramaic.

"Who are you?" asked the man in Hebrew, "and what is your house?"

Mordechai spoke his answer in the High Tongue. "I am called Mordechai, the son of Joshua, may he be at peace, of the city of Bethar in the region of Judah. I am a follower of the Nazarene, Yeshu Ben-Joseph."

"By what gate do you seek entrance?" asked the man.

"By the gate of your captain, Joseph Ben-Zadok, who is my close kinsman."

"Joseph is no Minaean."

" 'The house of my Father has many mansions.' "

"What proof do you have of your good faith?"

"I am here," said Mordechai Ben-Joshua.

"Enough," said the big, dark man sitting in the rear of the cave. He rose and approached the newcomer. "You could have entered our brotherhood through your kinsman or through another captain. Yet your passwords asked to see me. Why?"

The Minaean bowed his head slightly and said, "Peace be with you, Simon Bar Kochba."

"And with you, peace," said Simon, thinking to himself how strange the ancient civilities sounded here and under these circumstances.

"I lead the sect of the Minaeans in the region of Judah," said Mordechai. "We are few, but our hearts are with you. I have come as their representative to seek you out and to learn what it is you would do with us if God should favor your cause."

"Why," said Simon, "I had not thought to do anything with you, unless, of course, you should join our enemies."

Mordechai was silent for a time. "There are among us many who would join your army," he said. "But they seek assurances that victory would not bring new persecutions to those who believe the Messiah has come."

"That seems reasonable," Simon said. "But we too seek assurances. Ours is no band of rabble but a society of men dedicated to freedom or death—with no compromise. Those who seek entrance must prove themselves worthy, and once admitted they are our brothers in all ways. There is no turning back."

"So be it," said Mordechai. "What do you seek?"

"I seek to know why a group which believes the Messiah has already come would want to make common cause with us, who strive for the redemption of Israel through our own efforts."

Mordechai answered without hesitation. "We are Judeans and Jews even as you are. Your blood flows in our veins. We follow the dictates that your fathers—our fathers—handed down to us. Why should your cause not be our cause as well? We believe that the Messiah has come and will come again—

but surely He will come here, to us, as He came before. Shall
He find an Israel enslaved, or free and ready for full redemption? If we seek His speedy return, we cannot stand aside in an
honest struggle against evil."

"You have answered well," Simon said. "How many men do
you represent?"

"Two hundred and seventy-nine fighting men and their families in Bethar and the surrounding area. There are several
thousand more throughout the country. Shall I summon them
here?"

"No," said Simon. "Stay in your homes unless you receive
word to leave them. We shall start with the Bethar community
and go on from there. I will send an officer with you to super-
vise your training and to test you and gauge your loyalty. You
will obey him, and you will keep silent."

"Agreed," said Mordechai.

"I do not ask you to change your ways or beliefs," Simon said,
"but you must refrain from attempting to proselytize others.
This is a strict rule in our brotherhood, and it applies to all.
We cannot afford to be divided one against the other in any
way. For our part, we will not try to sway you from your belief
in Yeshu. Until final victory is ours, these differences must be
forgotten."

"You have spoken well, and we shall surely honor your
words."

"Beyond that," Simon continued, "we swear to you that if
the Lord brings us victory, all men in Judea will be free to seek
Him in peace and in their own way."

"So be it," said Mordechai, and he rose to go. "Peace be with
you."

"And with you," said Simon, "peace."

When the Minaean had left, the other man in the cave, Jonathan Bar Ba'ayah, turned to the leader and asked, "Now, was
that wise?"

"Two hundred and seventy-nine men in and around Bethar
able to draw the sword. Perhaps thousands more to come. Our
ranks swell daily."

"You know very well what I meant," said Jonathan impa-
tiently. "When you first took the Samaritans into our army,
some of the rabbis made no secret of their displeasure. Now

we will have Minaeans preaching their stupid Gospel in our brotherhood. Just what kind of movement is this to be?"

"It will be a unified rising of all Judea," answered Simon, "just as I said it would be."

11

It was the Lady Cornelia who first asked Rabbi Akiba where the bulk of his students had gone, but when the rabbi told her they had returned to their homes to celebrate the Feast of Weeks, she seemed satisfied and went on to ask what the Feast of Weeks was. Akiba told her.

Later Cornelia asked the question again in her casual fashion, and the rabbi told her many of the disciples had to earn their livelihood in the fields, and he pointed out that the first grape harvest was in progress, which indeed it was. So, again, Cornelia went on to a multitude of questions about all sorts of matters. What was the Jewish concept of justice? Where was God, and what was He supposed to be like? What had they done in the Temple? Why were some things ritually clean and others unclean? What were the rights and duties of marriage in Jewish law? Why all this stress on learning? Why did God permit evil to exist? The questions seemed endless and without connection, and they were often asked in such a way that it was hard to tell if Cornelia was really listening to the answer or if the question had just popped out of her head. But Akiba answered the questions as best he could, and if he was ever impatient with the governor's wife, he didn't show it.

Cornelia herself asked about this once. "Don't you ever get impatient with me?"

Akiba shook his head.

"I mean," she continued, "I know I'm childish sometimes."

"You are never childish," said Akiba. "You are always quite serious and intent. The childishness is only a pose." It was the closest he had ever come to a rebuke.

Cornelia grew sullen. "But if you know that," she said, "if you've known it all these months, why have you put up with me?"

Akiba smiled. "Well, what could I do? I couldn't very well turn the governor's wife across my knee, even if I am old enough to be her grandfather."

"Then it's true what my friend Quintus says. You only tolerate me because of Rufus."

"Come now, don't be foolish. It was but a jest. I do not tolerate you at all. You have been most welcome here as often as you have come, and you will continue to be so."

"But why?" Cornelia persisted. "You have told me that your Law forbids you to seek converts. Why, then, if it is not because I am Rufus' wife, do you put up with the idle questions of a foolish young woman?"

"Do you really want me to tell you?"

"Yes."

"Because I feel that somewhere, deep down, covered up by your pose of childishness and flightiness and the casual air you try so hard to cultivate, you really want to know. And I have no right not to tell you—even if you are Rufus' wife."

Cornelia was silent for a time, and when she spoke again the pose, at least for the moment, was gone. "Tell me, Rabbi, how does your God feel about love? I don't mean the love of a man for a god or brotherly love. I mean real love, the kind of passion felt between a man and a woman."

"It is one of the holiest things on earth," said Akiba.

"Then why does God make it so hard?" asked Cornelia bitterly.

"To love?" Akiba seemed surprised.

"No," said Cornelia with a wave of her hand. "To love is easy. I mean to make anything come of it, anything lasting?"

"I don't understand your question."

"Never mind," said Cornelia, and her smile returned. "Tell me again about your festivals. . . ."

When Cornelia returned to Caesarea that evening, she had a frightful headache. She left her litter near the entrance to the Roman capital and walked through the streets unrecognized and alone. She walked past the governor's palace, her home, past the garrison where Caesarea's two cohorts were quartered, past the grand temple to Jupiter that Herod had erected in honor of Augustus and despite the laws of his own faith, and she came at last to the sea, and she stood there and let the cool ocean breeze fan her. She began removing the multitude of pins that kept her hair in place and shook her head to let the hair run free in the breeze. There was only one ship in the harbor, a beaten old vessel that helped to maintain regular communications between the capitals of the East and the city of Rome. Cornelia looked at it, framed against the sky with the blinding setting sun cutting through its sails, and she averted her eyes. She looked down at the beach and spied there the last remaining young couples, oblivious in their loving to the speedy approach of night, and she wept for them and for herself and for her lost youth, and her headache grew worse.

The Lady Cornelia, daughter of the Senator Marcus Caecilius, wife of the procurator of Judea Tinius Rufus, returned to the palace, told her personal servant that she would not be down for dinner and promptly went to sleep. It was her birthday, and she was twenty-five years old. . . .

Cornelia awoke hours later to the presence of a naked man in her bed. He kissed her on the eyelids, then on the lips. "Happy birthday," said Quintus.

"Go away," said Cornelia angrily. "Leave me alone."

"Why so angry?" Quintus asked, running his hand up and down the inside of her thigh. "You knew I'd be here."

"Not tonight. I have a dreadful headache tonight, and I'm tired."

"But you promised," said Quintus, a hint of fury in his voice. "Night after night you've put me off, and then you said 'on my birthday' "—he mimicked her voice.

"Can't you understand that I don't feel well? Am I not human? Must I always be radiant and ready for you?"

Quintus ignored the rebuke and began rubbing her flat stomach. But it was a frenzied act and no good, and Cornelia resented it. She took his hand off and rolled over to go to sleep.

Quintus sat up on the edge of the bed. "I just don't understand," he said. "Have you lost interest in me already or is it that damned rabbi and his ideas that's making you this way?"

"He has nothing to do with it," said Cornelia, the sound of her voice muffled in the pillow.

"Then what?" demanded Quintus. "Don't you care for me at all? Aren't you interested in how I feel? How about me, aren't I human?"

Cornelia sighed and turned and moved toward Quintus and kissed him on the back of the neck. He reached for her body, and she let him. And she let him excite her, and he did. They made love, and Cornelia enjoyed it as much as she ever had. And she hated herself for it.

It was morning by the time Mordechai Ben-Joshua had concluded his meeting with the rebel leader, and he no sooner left the cave and sighted the rising sun than he was blindfolded again and once again placed on his donkey. Later, when the blindfold was removed, he was on the familiar mountain road to Bethar and his home, and he found himself accompanied by a young man on horseback who identified himself only as Samuel.

Mordechai sensed at once that this Samuel hated him and what he stood for, but it was a measure of the man that he did not return the hatred. He forgave it, for had not his Master forgiven even the Romans who crucified Him? And, indeed, Mordechai, as one who had been raised in the ancient tradition, could easily appreciate the young man's feelings. He was well aware that the teachings of the Minaeans, on the surface, would seem repulsive to a traditional Jew. He regretted now that he could not at least make himself and his beliefs less repulsive to this Samuel, who would, after all, be the rebel officer in charge of the Minaean group. Even after a full explanation, Samuel might not believe as they did. Many, like the great Akiba, understood but did not believe. Yet he wished that he could make the young man understand that his people were not pagans and not heretics. But Mordechai had given the leader his word.

And so, bound to silence, Mordechai whiled away the ride through the mountains of Judah by reviewing in his own mind what he believed and why and how he had come to where he was.

Mordechai Ben-Joshua was born nearly twenty years after

the great revolt against the Romans was crushed, into a family of Sadducees strict in the law and zealous in its observance.

He had never seen the Temple, nor had he ever witnessed the age-old sacrificial service of which his father spoke so reverently and so often. Young Mordechai could not understand why God had permitted these beautiful things to cease, and when he asked his father, Joshua would answer that it was because of the sins of the Jews which they had committed through fraternal strife, even as their forefathers had sinned with the Baalim and the Ashtaroth. When the Jews had atoned for their sins, they would be freed from the Roman yoke and the Temple would be speedily rebuilt in our days, amen.

It was a typical Sadducean answer, all of it stated in concrete, straightforward terms, and all of it based on observable reality. The Jews had sinned and had been punished; if they did well, they would be rewarded. The balance was just, and God did not hide the weights from man.

Unlike the more liberal Pharisees, who sought meaning in the Bible beyond the literal statement of the words themselves and who made long commentaries and deductions and interpretations of various passages, the Sadducees believed the Bible meant exactly what it said, no more and no less. They discounted the Pharisaic belief in a world to come and rejected explanations based on the idea that God's purpose was sometimes too vast to be observable at all in a single lifetime or generation or even longer. Where in the Bible did it speak of a future life? Joshua would demand to know. And where could one find support for all this mystical thinking? Every man would get his just desserts in this life, so that all might know that God was just and God was One, amen.

Mordechai listened and believed and waited with perfect faith for the Romans to get their just desserts, but somehow they never seemed to. And yet it seemed to him that they were sinning far more than the Jews ever had. He once asked his father about this, and Joshua had told him to be quiet and be patient.

Mordechai was quiet and patient until his twenty-third year when the second revolt against the Romans broke out. Most of the fighting was centered in Egypt, but there was some minor rebel activity in Judea, and Mordechai and his three best friends joined in it. He saw one of them slain on the first day with an arrow through the throat. Another disappeared. The third was captured by the Romans and crucified. Mordechai alone escaped to return home from the battle.

His father still spoke to him of the justice that was to come, but from that time on Mordechai believed none of it. He would nod his head in dumb acquiescence at the old man's words, but, in truth, the faith based on observable reality was dead. If there was a God at all, Mordechai thought to himself, there had to be more to it than that, or there was no God at all.

The Pharisees, of course, had another answer, and it was the answer accepted by the great bulk of the Jews. Their faith, too, was based on reality, but that reality was not bound by time and space as the reality of the Sadducees was. They saw reality from many vantage points, and they looked at it across ages, past and future.

But it would have been too late, in any case, for Mordechai to accept the teachings of the Pharisees. He knew too well the arguments against them. And besides, any philosopher could have told him that a man very rarely goes from an extreme to a middle path. He will more generally go to another extreme.

But for a long time Mordechai went nowhere at all. He worked the land with his father, and he buried his father in it. He took a wife. On the Sabbaths and festivals he went to the synagogue and sat where his father had sat and said the prayers he had said.

And then, one day, a wandering preacher came through the town and told anyone who would listen that the Messiah had come, had been crucified by the Romans but would return from the dead and come again. The story made no sense to Mordechai at all, and he scoffed at it just as most of the other men in the town did. But he was strangely drawn to it as well, perhaps because it made no sense, because it was not tied at all to sense or observable reality. Whatever the reason, he sought the preacher out and listened again to what he had to say, and he asked questions, and he even went once to a synagogue service of the Minaeans.

It was only curiosity at first, but during a period of months it grew into something more. And then, all of a sudden, Mordechai realized one certain moment that the teachings of the

Minaeans, in their own irrational way, made a great deal of sense to him. Once one accepted the basic premises, one could easily explain everything that had happened.

Israel was God's light to the nations, even as Yeshu was God's light to Israel. Israel was the spotless lamb delivered up to the power of evil, but by her sacrifice she would be redeemed in the Kingdom, while evil would perish. And to prove this very point, God had delivered up His Chosen to the power of evil as God's own sacrifice. But this triumph of evil was only temporary, and the Messiah would return at any time now to found the Kingdom of God on earth, with Israel at its head.

Mordechai felt instinctively that this must be the truth. Indeed, had the Messiah died a less ignominious death, he might have doubted the validity of the entire teaching. But specifically because Yeshu had died the most painful, the most horrible and the most shameful of all deaths was Mordechai convinced that He was not dead at all. And was not the parallel between Yeshu and Israel clear? The suffering of both was temporary, while their reward would be eternal.

Mordechai was thirty-three years old when he accepted the waters of baptism, and for him the step entailed immediate suffering. But Mordechai saw that this too was just. His wife demanded a bill of divorcement, which he granted her, along with the custody of their two daughters. They left him soon thereafter and went to the woman's family in the north. Mordechai forgave them, and he understood them, and he prayed for them daily, even as he now prayed for the young man riding beside him.

The past seven years had been hard, he reflected, but the small Minaean community had survived and had even grown. The traditional Jews had ostracized the sect, but they tolerated it, being a people used to tolerating such divisions. The Romans, however, reacted most unfavorably, and many Minaeans in Galilee and elsewhere had been forced to flee the country. Indeed, only the intercession of such men as the great Akiba had saved the entire community from martyrdom. Consequently, when rumor came of preparations for a new rising, the sympathies of the Minaeans were with their fellow Jews. But they were divided on just what to do. Some argued that any overt act on their part would bring on fresh persecutions to believers throughout the world. But others, Mordechai among them, pointed out that the older loyalty was still valid. And they argued that it would be morally wrong to remain neutral when an oppressed people tried to throw off its oppressor—especially when that oppressor had crucified the Messiah and still persecuted His followers.

"We go this way," Mordechai said, pointing to a small branch of the main path. The young man, Samuel, followed him as he rode his donkey toward the meeting house of the Minaeans.

It was a day's ride from the coastal plain to the hills of Judah where Bar Kochba now made his headquarters, and with preparations for revolt going on amid the strictest secrecy, communications between the leader in the hills and the rabbis of the grand council in Lydda and B'nei B'rak were scant at best. From time to time the rabbis heard rumors, and several of these were most disquieting.

Akiba did his best to assure his colleagues that most of the disquieting rumors were false. In the case of one or two true ones, like the recruitment of the neopagan Samaritans for the struggle, Akiba tried to explain that such moves were militarily necessary.

But then another rumor came, one which persisted and gained wide circulation. The report had it that the leader was requiring each of his soldiers to prove his courage and strength by cutting off a thumb—an act of mutilation and therefore forbidden by Jewish law. The whole thing seemed unbelievable to Akiba, but because of the rumor's stubborn persistence he felt it necessary to have Bar Kochba himself deny that he had ordered any such savage trial.

The great bulk of Rabbi Akiba's disciples had joined the rebel forces, and there were not many at the university from whom he could choose a messenger to send to the leader. But a volunteer who stepped forward at once seemed ideal for the task. The volunteer did not look especially Jewish, spoke a perfect Latin and Greek and could easily pass through the country to the rebel hideout without being questioned.

12

Mariamne Bath-Menashe Ben-David entered the rebel head-quarters exactly as everyone else did, blindfolded. But in her case, the leader removed the blindfold himself. "It is a pity to cover such eyes," he said with a smile.

Mariamne blinked her eyes to see Simon standing before her, and she noted to herself that he looked about the same, although she had not really expected him to look any different, and so she wondered why she had thought of that at all. And then an unexplained annoyance came over her so suddenly that when she spoke, the sharpness of her voice surprised even her. "I have been sent by Rabbi Akiba to learn why you are making cripples of young Jews," she said.

Simon's brow wrinkled. "What are you talking about?"

"Word has come to the rabbis that you call upon each volunteer to prove his loyalty to your cause by cutting off a thumb."

"And you believe this?" asked Simon. "You believe this barbarism of me and of us and of our cause?"

Mariamne looked away from him. "What I believe is not important," she said. "Do you deny the report?"

"Yes, I deny it," he said in deliberate tones. "It is a lie, a lie spread by enemies of our movement or else made up out of the air by such idle men as delight in gossip."

"Might I see for myself?"

Bar Kochba motioned to one of his officers. "Take this girl through the camp," he ordered. Then he turned to Mariamne. "If you will find one man in this camp who has cut off his thumb, bring him to me and I will judge him for breaking the Jewish Law by desecrating his body. But if you do not—as you will not—then you will return here to me and apologize for having accepted this evil report against all these loyal men. For you did not come here to inquire, as I am sure Akiba asked you to do. You came to accuse." And Simon turned his back on the girl.

Mariamne followed Bar Kochba's officer from the cave and through the camp, and she saw preparations for war far more intensive than she had been able to imagine. She saw hundreds of men, then thousands, being trained in the use of the sword, the javelin and the bow. She saw warriors being taught how to ride and how to jump off a moving horse and jump back on again, how to climb and how to dodge, how to fight with broken weapons and with no weapons at all. She saw other men sitting calmly and drawing charts or taking notes or eating or reciting the afternoon prayer in small groups or listening to a lecture by an older man who appeared to be a rabbi.

Despite herself, Mariamne was impressed by all this seemingly disorganized activity. Here a group was running for cover from a flight of blunted arrows; there some men were standing around an officer who was explaining how to tie up a bleeding wound; on a cliff above them a group was learning the mechanics of setting up an ambush, while below some men were crouching in a dark cavern. There seemed no end to all of them, men of all ages and descriptions, even children being taught how to run messages and graybeards sitting and making arrowheads. Yet among the whole lot Mariamne did not see one without a thumb.

The officer escorted her back to the cave of the leader, then diplomatically withdrew. Mariamne entered haltingly. She knew what she had to do and was even anxious to get it over with, but a host of emotions was running through her, and she felt strangely confused. She came into the lamplight of the cave to see Simon sitting and looking at a chart. He must have heard her enter, but he didn't look up. Well, Mariamne reflected, she supposed he was entitled to his moment.

"I beg your pardon," she said stiffly. "I spoke hastily."

It was only then that Simon looked up, as he had planned it. But when he saw her, saw the crestfallen, childlike way she held her head as she uttered the apology, he felt his heart going out to her. And in that moment, he knew that he loved this girl and that he would always love her.

"Well," he muttered, "I suppose it was wrong of me to get so angry."

"No," Mariamne insisted. "You were quite right. I don't blame you." She wasn't making it any easier for him.

"Anyway," he said, "logic alone would have told you that the rumor must be false. A man without a thumb is no good with a sword."

"A man could have cut off his left thumb," Mariamne suggested.

"Sometimes a fighting man needs both thumbs," Simon said.

They looked at each other then and suddenly burst out laughing at the insane horror of it all. They laughed long and loud and hardly pausing for breath, so that in the end the man solemnly appointed Prince of Israel was holding his stomach, while the lovely Princess of the House of David had to sit down to keep herself from falling.

It was Mariamne who first caught her breath. "You know that we are both mad, don't you?"

"No," said Simon. "One must laugh to keep his senses."

"But here we are, at the beginning of the end of everything, and we laugh like children."

"I don't think we're at the beginning of the end at all," said Simon. "I'd like to think we're at the beginning of a new era."

The amusement left Mariamne's eyes, and she turned them away from Bar Kochba. "You are doomed," she said softly. "You and all those men and boys out there and Judea with you. I'm sorry, but that's the way I feel, and I suppose that's why I came here ready to believe anything about you, because I feel that what you are doing is wrong and will surely end in disaster."

Simon sighed. "I don't know, Mariamne," he said, the last trace of laughter gone now, "perhaps it will."

"But if you feel that way, then . . ."

"Then what? What would it change if I knew the outcome for certain, one way or the other?"

Mariamne shook her head. "I just don't understand you."

"But you should understand. You are a Jew like the rest of us."

"No," said Mariamne. "Not the way you are or Akiba is."

"And how not?"

"Because I don't join in this ancestor worship of yours or in this pathetic desire to perpetuate a way of life that might perhaps best be ended. And because I don't believe in the mystical fatalism that makes you stick to a path you are intelligent enough to know can lead to your doom. I believe in reason above these strange feelings of must and destiny, and in that, it appears, I am not a Jew."

"Then why did you return to Judea?"

Mariamne shrugged. "I don't really know. A foolish sentimentalism, I suppose. It wouldn't stand the test of reason, either."

Simon smiled.

"What's so funny now?" Mariamne demanded.

"Come with me. I want to show you through the camp."

"But I just saw the camp."

"I know. But I want you to see it again."

Simon took the girl's hand, and she went with him from the cave up rocky paths to the same scene of activity that she had observed before. "Do you see that man there?" he asked, pointing to a figure drilling a group in archery.

"Yes," said Mariamne.

"His name is . . . well, never mind his name. For a long time now, he has called himself Bar Abba, and it's as good a name as any. He can hardly read, and the only thing he knows outside of fighting are the simple prayers his father taught him before the Romans took him away one day and never brought him back."

Without another word Simon continued leading the girl. "That man there," he said, "the man making arrowheads. He is seventy-three years old, so old that he still remembers the Temple. For the past fifty years or so, he has been teaching little boys how to read and write. Now he is here. . . . And do you see that other old man, the one standing in the middle of that group and speaking?"

Mariamne nodded.

"That man's name is Eleazar Ha-Modai. He is, as his name suggests, from the town of Modin, and he is a Cohen, which makes it likely that he is related to the family of the Maccabees, who, as you know, were also from Modin and also of the priestly line. He is no great scholar like Akiba. Just a simple country rabbi. He turned up here one day and offered to help in any way he could. So now he performs weddings, answers questions on ritual and expounds the Law to anyone who will listen."

Simon took Mariamne's hand again. "I don't understand the point of all this," she said.

"That man there," Simon went on, indicating a figure on horseback. "He was born a rich man's son and spent much of his youth in travel. He speaks ten languages, they say, including a Latin so perfect that no Roman would suspect he was not one of their own."

He pointed to a young man wielding a sword, a youth still beardless but with the long earlocks that identified a rabbinical student. "He came to us from Akiba's university," Simon said. "He's very young, and he learns fast. He's quite good with that sword, but I don't know what will happen the first time he draws blood."

They were on their way back to the cave when Simon stopped again and indicated a man standing nearby. "That man," he said, "believes firmly that there is no God. He does not pray, nor does he keep a single positive commandment of the ritual law, thinking it all just so much superstition."

They stood at the entrance to the cave now, and Mariamne said, "I'm sorry, but I don't know what you're trying to prove."

"Just this," said Simon. "What do all of these men, the young and the old, the illiterate and the learned, the pious and the disbelieving, what do they all have that brings them here?"

"I suppose you'll say it's because they're Jews."

"Simply being born a Jew is nothing. What brings these people here to risk their lives is a certain feeling—mystical, if you will—that things are wrong and ought to be set right. It seems that Jews get this feeling more than others, though why that is I leave it to Akiba and the other thinkers to explain."

"But what you fail to see, Simon, is that reason dictates you must lose and that if war comes, all these people and all their feelings will die."

"And what you fail to see," Simon said, "is that there is more honest reason in a strong feeling than in all the cold logic you can muster. What is real in you, Mariamne, is what you call the foolish sentimentalism that brought you back to Judea. And all the rest, that's all just talk."

As they entered the cave again, Simon looked at Mariamne by the flickering light, saw the dark eyes return the look, and he kissed her, hard.

"Did you enjoy that?" he asked when their bodies had parted.

"Yes," she whispered.

"Why?" he asked.

13

It was an arduous ride back to B'nei B'rak, and Mariamne consented to remain at the camp overnight and rest before returning. The following day was Friday, and since the descent from the rebel hideout was safest under cover of darkness, she put off her departure until after the Sabbath. But on Saturday evening Simon invited her to stay another day, and she agreed. And then it was the first day of the week, and then the second, yet Mariamne stayed, and Simon, or so it was said, seemed to like it so.

Before long, the pretty young girl was a familiar figure in the rebel camp, a society to which new people came regularly and were quickly accepted. At first, she would spend her days just walking through the hills and talking to people. Then, after a few days, she began helping Ruth with the many children who had been brought to the camp. Mariamne had not been asked to do this, or in fact anything at all, but her help was quietly welcomed, and the children liked her, and it appeared somehow to everyone that she had always been there and always would be.

Simon sent word to Akiba that the girl was safe, along with a categorical denial of the thumb-cutting slander, and he, too, soon accepted her presence as quite natural. He would spend most of his evenings with her, sitting by the fire under the open

sky and talking with her about all sorts of things. They didn't
kiss again after that first time, and neither of them spoke of it,
nor of much else that seemed very important.

Simon asked what Mariamne had done at Rabbi Akiba's university, and she explained that she had tended the flowers and
had read and had done a lot of thinking and had set some of
her thoughts down in a chronicle she kept.

Another time Simon asked the girl about her father, and he
saw her eyes well up with tears as they had on that night of the
Passover Seder in B'nei B'rak.

"I'm sorry," he said.

"It's all right," said Mariamne. "But what can I tell you
about my father? He was a man like other men, I suppose, except to me. I never knew my mother. There were no other
children. But somehow, it was always enough just to have my
father. I remember when we left Judea to go to Alexandria.
All during the voyage he pretended we were pirates on our
way to dig up treasure, and the game was so good that I soon
forgot about the little playmates I was leaving behind. It was
like that most of my life. He was always there, helping or teaching or comforting or joking, changing subtly toward me as I
grew, so that when I was an adult, I still looked up to him but
could also regard him as an old friend. And then . . . well,
one day he got sick. The physicians wouldn't say anything one
way or the other, in that way they have of cruelty when they
want to be kind. I did what little I could. I nursed him. I called
in new physicians. I prayed. I made vows and begged God to
help." Mariamne shook her head. "He was sick for more than
a year, getting worse all the time. All that was left for me was
to try to cheer him. I would sit by his bed and read to him, as
he had once read to me, because toward the end he could
hardly see. And I would talk to him and tell him funny stories
while my heart was breaking, and . . ."

The girl's voice cracked, and she began to cry softly, and
Simon wanted to console her, but he didn't know how. Or to
say something, but he didn't know what. And so he just sat
there for a long time, watching her as she shook the tears out
of her eyes and sniffed in the cool night air, and he thought to
himself, There are so many kinds of pain.

*   *   *

Another time, as they were sitting by the campfire at the end of a day, Mariamne asked Simon, "What moves you?"

"What do you mean?" he asked.

"I mean, the others here, they follow you and your dream. But what moves you, and what is your dream?"

Simon lay back on the dew-wet grass and put his arms under his head. "I'd like everyone . . . to be happy," he said.

Mariamne chuckled. "But that's a child's answer."

"Perhaps. But when I think about it to the end, that's what I come up with. So I guess that's my dream."

"And you think through all the fighting and killing you're getting ready for that people will become happy?"

"No," he said, "not through the fighting but after, when the Romans are gone, when Judea is free, when her people are free."

"But specifically," Mariamne persisted, "if you should win this struggle . . ."

"Then you think it possible now that we might win?" Simon interjected.

"In this madhouse," Mariamne laughed, "with all these boys and old men gone mad, anything seems possible. And supposing, by some miracle, that it should happen that you should manage to drive out the Romans, together with all their administrative apparatus. What then? How do you propose to rule these people?"

"I don't propose to rule them at all," Simon said. "Let a sage rule them, or let the entire Sanhedrin rule them, or let them rule one another. For myself, I seek only to free the land and then to free myself. I want to get a farm somewhere, perhaps in Galilee. I want to work that farm and raise healthy children so they can work it for me while I grow fat."

Mariamne smiled. "You would look funny fat."

"What did you do with yourself in Alexandria?" Simon asked.

Mariamne drew up her legs and wrapped her arms around them in the little girl manner Simon loved. "Well," she began, "first I went to the Jewish school with other children. Later there were lessons in the womanly crafts and the social graces.

Then my father got me a tutor so that I could learn the classics and Latin and the sciences. I know so much learning would be strange for a girl here in Judea, but in Alexandria it is not uncommon. Even in the forum you can usually see a few girls sitting and listening to the philosophers. I sometimes went there. And then there were the theaters and poetry readings and gatherings among the Jewish community. There were always many things to do."

"No suitors?" Simon asked.

"Oh, thousands," said Mariamne with a sweep of her hand.

Simon smiled. "But not one, I see."

"No," said Mariamne. "Not one who could make me feel that I wanted to spend my life with him. And . . . well, how about you? How did you spend your boyhood?"

Simon rolled over on his stomach. "I didn't have much of a boyhood. I was a child, and then I was a man. Most of my youth I spent in hills like these or in the cliffs by the Sea of Salt, fighting the Romans and fleeing from them."

"How terrible."

"Not really. I and the others with me were young and free with no responsibilities to anyone but ourselves. We had our small triumphs and pleasures. And as for the danger, it became a way of life, and we grew accustomed to it."

"No women?" asked Mariamne.

"Thousands," said Simon, and they both laughed.

"I was speaking today to that old man, the teacher who spends his time here sharpening arrowheads," Mariamne said. "Did you know that in his youth he was a seaman and journeyed as far east as China?"

"Why, no," said Simon. "I didn't know that."

"He told me the most fascinating stories," Mariamne went on, "about the strange customs in the lands to the east. Did you know that in China the feet of women are bound in childhood so that they never grow but remain small even when the women are adults? It's a sign of beauty there."

"No, I didn't know."

"And in Parthia, selected young girls are taken from their homes to become brides of some god. And they're never heard of again. I never knew that. Did you?"

"No," Simon admitted. "I didn't."

"Well," said Mariamne with a certain tone of rebuke in her voice, "you really should. I mean, here you are, the leader of all these people, and you have a man like that in the camp, and you don't even know about it. Think how much help a man like that could be as a counselor. And you let him just sit there and sharpen arrowheads."

Simon smiled at the girl. "I will speak to him tomorrow," he promised.

Mariamne seemed quietly satisfied. Simon continued looking at her, an amused expression on his face.

"What's so funny?" she asked at last.

"Well, for one thing, there probably isn't another girl in all Israel who would speak to me like that."

"What would you have me do?" Mariamne asked. "Just flatter you?"

"No, no," Simon protested. "Please don't misunderstand me. I like it, and I like you just the way you are." He realized suddenly that it was the first time he had said it. "But it's strange. And it's strange that you came here a few weeks ago so very hostile to our cause, and now you know my men better than I do."

"I'm interested in the people," said Mariamne softly. "Not the cause."

"It comes to the same thing," said Simon.

And so, the days that Mariamne spent in the rebel camp grew into weeks, and the weeks into a month, and then more than a month. During the days, while Simon supervised the training of the tens of thousands who had joined the rebel brotherhood, she would be with Ruth and the children. And in the evenings, they would talk. And at night, before he fell asleep, Simon would think of Mariamne. More and more. And sometimes, he would catch himself thinking of her even during the day until at last he was somewhat stunned to realize that she occupied more of his thoughts even than the great mission he had undertaken. It was then he decided the time had come to do more than talk.

Simon thought about what he was going to do for days before he actually did it. He thought about the entire idea, and then he framed the words and rehearsed them in his mind, and then he waited for the appropriate moment. It came on an evening after the Sabbath in the month of Tammuz, when the uncomfortable heat of the day had broken.

"Smell that breeze," Mariamne had exclaimed, closing her eyes and lying back on the grass. Simon looked at her there, at the form of her body outlined against the simple shift she wore.

"Mariamne," he said, "do you ever think about the future?" She opened one eye to look at him. "I try not to."

"Well, I think of it a great deal," he said. "I've thought of it since I was a boy, but somehow I've always seen it as it would be for myself, by myself, and I never realized there was anything wrong in that, until now. Do you understand what I mean?"

"No," said Mariamne, sitting up.

Simon arose and began his accustomed pacing. "All my life," he said haltingly, "I've been alone. And . . . that seemed right, because it was never the kind of life a man could really share . . . I mean, the running and the hiding, the fighting, the risks. I've been surrounded by others all the time, and now there are so very many with me, and yet inside I'm still alone. Only, these past weeks . . ." He stopped and stood looking away from her. "There's so much I've got to do. So very much. And I don't want to do it alone. I know I'm not putting it very gracefully, Mariamne, but I've come to love you . . ."

"Please stop," Mariamne pleaded, and when Simon turned to look at her, there were tears in her eyes. "I beg you not to go on."

Simon looked at her for a long moment as she sat there. Then he nodded his head slowly and said, "I see."

"No," said Mariamne sadly, "you don't. You can't, because I don't. I should have realized that it was coming to this, yet I stayed on. Please forgive me."

"Of course," said Simon, his voice low. And with that, he left the girl and went to his bed.

Mariamne departed the following day. Simon made no move to stop her, nor to see her before she returned to B'nei B'rak. He sent with Jonathan his farewell to the girl and his respects to Rabbi Akiba.

14

Simon Bar Kochba, the Prince of Israel, stood on a mound overlooking a broad plain in the hills of Judah, his right hand on his hip and his left on the hilt of his sword, and he felt a deep sense of pride. Before him, standing stiffly in their tens and in their hundreds, were 5,000 chosen and trained men, comprising Judea's Third Battalion. Their new armor and weapons of iron, made in secret by hundreds of blacksmiths across the country, were Roman in design; the armor, while free of the traditional human and animal figures, was of the Roman type; the swords were short and light and double-edged, easy to wield quickly in hand-to-hand combat, and the lances were a good replica of the *pilum* used by the legions. But he saw nothing ironic in borrowing from Rome; he had borrowed from others as well, whatever he felt was worth borrowing.

From the old army of royal times he had borrowed the division of fighting men into tens, hundreds and thousands. From Judah the Maccabee he had borrowed the style of warfare he taught his men, to strike and disappear, to use the land as a shield for themselves and as a trap for the invader. From David he had borrowed the idea of using the hills of Judah as a place to hide and train while awaiting his moment. And to all of this he had added his own ideas, many of them.

Simon had given the matter much thought. He had been planning for this most of his life, and in the months since he had moved his headquarters from the remote Dead Sea cliffs to the region of Judah in the heart of the country he had sought to mold an army that could not only reclaim the land but keep it. He walked now past the men of the sword, past the archers with their bows of supple Judean wood, past the cavalry on their mounts, past the slingers, past the catapult men, past the fortifiers, and he felt that here was that kind of army.

There were now three such battalions in the camp, each of

5,000 men. Their training had been intensive and hurried, for who knew how much time there was left? Two more battalions were even now being readied. Together, the 25,000 men in their ranks would form the core of an army of liberation.

But they would still be only a core, for what Bar Kochba had had in mind from the first was, as he had told Akiba, more than a clash of armies. When these warriors took the field, they would find comrades all across Judea—tens of thousands who had been secretly organized and armed and who waited in their homes for the word to rise. And there were farmers ready to supply his army, and women ready to bake bread for it, and smiths ready to make more weapons, and an entire people ready for freedom.

It had all happened so quickly, more quickly even than Simon had hoped. If they could only have a little more time—a few more months and they would be ready for anything.

The prince stood before the men of the Third Battalion, drew his sword from its scabbard and raised it high in a signal of salute. In a single movement the 5,000 warriors returned the salute with sword and lance and bow and sling and hand. The inspection was over. Bar Kochba was satisfied.

Simon Bar Kosiba, the orphan and outlaw, returned to his quarters in a cave and to the unshakable melancholy that had plagued him in the weeks since Mariamne had left. He unbuckled his sword, took off his breastplate and lay down on the cot. He was tired, but there was no cause for his fatigue. He was depressed, but he reflected that there was no real cause. Everything that he had dreamed of and that had seemed a faraway vision only six months before was on its way to being realized. The land would soon be free again; Israel would be reborn, and he would be the architect of it. What could be weighed in the balance against all of this? Surely not a girl who seemed content to spend her time in idle talk.

For Bar Kochba, the Prince of Israel, no problem existed. Nothing that had happened had changed him. He worked and prepared and planned and dreamed with as much vigor as before, for he was not a man like other men.

But for Simon the man it was a different matter, and in the little time of each day that was his own, he dwelt on thoughts of Mariamne more than he considered wise or justified. He

wondered at these times if it was not only injured pride that
made him feel as he did. Clearly, his reason told him, there
was no sense to it. He pictured her, and by rationally considering her features, he proved to himself that she was not all
that beautiful. Certainly there were hundreds, perhaps even
thousands of young women in Judea more fair, and most of
these, he knew, would give anything to be his wife. And more
important than the matter of beauty, Simon reminded himself
that Mariamne's ideas were a world removed from his. Why,
she was hardly a Jew at all, and she seemed to scorn the cause
he was willing to die for. The girl was so obviously not for him,
nor could she ever be. There was not a single logical doubt in
Simon's mind. Why, then, did he feel so abandoned?

"The heart has a logic of its own," said Akiba gently. "The
mind cannot always follow it, but the feelings it gives us are
sometimes more correct than the conclusions of rational
thought."

"Then love is everything," said Cornelia eagerly. "Then
nothing should stand in the way of love, not reason or convention or anything."

Akiba shook his head slightly. "That is not exactly what I
meant. There are other considerations, such as honor and duty.
If these are nothing to us, then we are only animals."

"But that's all we are, only animals. And the rest is vanity.
Your own Koheleth said that."

"But we are higher animals bound by higher rules. What
Koheleth meant was that we should not consider ourselves
gods."

"You always have an answer, don't you?" said Cornelia without even trying to hide her annoyance. "That's all you Jews
seem to do. Sit around and make up answers."

Akiba smiled. "Somebody has to."

"But as far as love is concerned," Cornelia persisted, "didn't
you tell me that it is the highest emotion?"

The rabbi nodded.

"Then, in your religion, I take it that if a person feels love,
she should not be swayed from following her heart because,
well, let us say because of some marriage vow taken before a
pagan deity."

Akiba looked at her sadly. "I'm sorry, Cornelia," he said, "but our Law does not permit any honorable vow between two people to be tossed aside. It matters not if the vow is made before the One Living God or before Juno or Isis or any other false idol. The same Ear hears it."

Cornelia stood. "Oh," she said, "you are all the same, all of you. All of the religions seek only to keep things just the way they are."

Akiba rose to see the governor's wife out, and for a fleeting moment he wished he could tell her just how wrong she was. But of course he didn't.

Cornelia paused at the door. "I will come again next week," she said, "if I may."

"You know you need no invitation here," said Akiba with a small bow. "But I hope I have not upset you in any way."

"Certainly not," said Cornelia emphatically. "It was but a philosophical discussion." And she went out the door to her waiting carriage, passing on her way a woman about her own age who was walking toward the rabbi's house.

Mariamne knocked softly on the door to Rabbi Akiba's study and waited for the word to enter. When the old man saw her, his eyes expressed an undisguised pleasure, and he replaced the worn book he had just removed from the shelf.

"I trust I do not disturb you in your studies," said the girl.

"There is no end to my studies," Akiba said, "and therefore there is no great hurry. It is nice to see you, Miriam. I have hardly set eyes on you since your return from Bar Kochba's camp two weeks ago."

"Who was that woman who just left?" asked Mariamne.

"She is the governor's wife. She comes here often, and we talk. Mostly she asks about our religion, in a casual sort of way. Something was troubling her today, but I don't know what."

Mariamne smiled. "You have a strange congregation. In the time that I have been here, students of the Law have come to see you, and peasants, and warriors, and now the governor's wife. Don't you find it all a bit tiring?"

"At times, but not so much tiring as discouraging," Akiba said. "It is part of a rabbi's duty to advise people who seek help. The trouble is, I often feel I am no help at all, because the problems they bring me are either too real or too obscure."

"How so?"

"Well, when a peasant comes to me and complains bitterly that his land is being confiscated, there is little I can do about it. And when people come and tell me they are unhappy, there is equally little I can do. I feel quite useless sometimes, and so," he motioned toward his library, "I turn to my books."

"You helped Simon," Mariamne said. "You got him what he wanted."

"No," Akiba shook his head. "What I did was a comparatively small thing. Only God can really help Simon get what he wants."

"Maybe. But if you will excuse me for saying it, he doesn't seem to be waiting for God."

Akiba chuckled at the observation. "Tell me," he said, "what did you think of it all? I mean, after you had done what I asked and were there for a time, how did it strike you?"

"It is hard for me to say. I have no knowledge of military affairs, but as I told you on my return, the army seems numerous and dedicated. I suppose you might say I was quite impressed by it all despite my pessimism about a war with Rome, which you are aware of."

"And what of the man Simon?"

Mariamne turned away. "He is an excellent leader. The men respect him and obey him willingly. He is a man of honor whose own devotion is clearly evident and inspires others."

"So felt I," said Akiba, "and I am pleased that he impresses you thus. I think him to be a singular man, the like . . . But forgive me. You seem troubled."

"It is nothing. I have had difficulty sleeping of late."

"You do look somewhat pale," said Akiba with concern. "How thoughtless of me not to have noticed it at once. Shall I call a physician?"

Mariamne shook her head. "It is nothing. As I said, I have not slept well. Perhaps it is the warm weather. Do not trouble yourself about it. It will pass. We were speaking about the rebels. Tell me, Rabbi, what do you think will happen now?"

"Who can predict the course of events? Simon has promised to start nothing until I send word that all else has been definitely exhausted, but an unexpected incident could set off a war at any time now. And as for my own continuing attempts to find a peaceful solution, frankly, I don't even know where to begin anymore. Our messages to the emperor appear to have been ignored. Members of Rome's Jewish community have been trying to receive an audience with Hadrian for months without success. And here, the situation grows steadily worse. What little land remains in Jewish hands is being methodically confiscated on the slightest pretext. The Roman troops read the official attitude as a permit to license, and their outrages grow from day to day. Men are robbed and murdered; women are abducted. The legion commanders are decent enough, and when one of their men is found guilty of committing a crime against us, he is severely punished. But the perpetrators of some of the worst crimes are never found, and popular report lays the blame for many of these directly on Rufus. So whom can I turn to? Rufus?"

"What of Rufus' wife?" Mariamne suggested.

"She has no influence over him. No one seems able to sway Rufus at all. But the problem goes beyond him in any case to the very heart of Roman imperial policy. In practical terms, the entire situation leaves me very little power to stop a war nobody wants."

"Nobody wants it," said Mariamne bitterly, "yet daily we move closer to the edge of disaster. I don't understand any of you."

The old man looked at the girl for a long moment, and he sighed. "Miriam," he said softly, "we simply have no choice."

"There is always a choice. I do not believe that we are playthings of the fates. Nor, I am sure, do you."

"No, but sometimes an individual, or a people, can follow one path and one alone because honor demands it and because simple survival demands it. Didn't you sense this at the rebel camp? I have never been there, and so you have the advantage of me. Weren't you impressed with the fact that we are doing now the only thing we can?"

Mariamne rose and stood looking out the window of the study. "I saw very much that I admired. I saw men who believed in something very strongly and their wives and children with them. For a time, I thought even I might find a place there, might forget all I knew and all my reason and live with

them as intensely as they did. But then . . ." Her voice trailed
off.

"Then what?" Akiba asked.

"It's difficult to explain."

"What happened?" the rabbi persisted.

"Nothing happened," Mariamne said. "Nothing has ever
really happened to me."

Akiba stood facing the girl. "Well, what do you want to happen? You know, you must make plans, too. You cannot indefinitely stand by and observe."

"Do you want me to leave here?"

"Of course not. You know that's not what I meant. You are
a delight to have here at the university, especially now that it
is so empty, and you would always be more than welcome here
in any case. But . . . isn't there something more you would
like to do?"

"What?" Mariamne asked.

"Well, I don't know," said Akiba, "but surely there is something more for a girl of your upbringing and your intelligence
and your beauty than tending the flowers in my garden."

"What?" she repeated.

The rabbi was openly perplexed. "That depends on you.
What do you seek?"

Mariamne sighed. It was a deep, audible sigh. And then she
fainted.

Mariamne stood in the hills of Judah, on the site of the now
deserted rebel camp. She looked for Simon, but he was nowhere to be found. She looked for the old man who had been a
sailor, but he too was gone. So was Ruth, and so were the children.

Suddenly there came from below the sounds of battle—the
clashing of swords and the shouts of men, the whistle of arrows
and the shrill scream of chariot wheels. Mariamne could hear
the sounds clearly, but each time she ran to a crest of a hill she
saw nothing but a peaceful plain below. She ran from one such
crest to another, but the battle whose sounds blotted out everything else was nowhere in view. She was running in desperation to still another height when she awoke, out of breath. . . .

Mariamne opened her eyes to see a strange man bending over her and Rabbi Akiba standing in the background with a look of concern.

"You've been asleep for hours," said the stranger, apparently a physician. He motioned to the rabbi, who left the room while he examined the girl. The examination was short. The physician could find nothing wrong with her, and after prescribing the usual rest and healthful diet, he departed.

Akiba returned a short time later and sat by Mariamne's bed. "You gave me quite a scare," he said, "but the physician says it is nothing. He says you are only nervous."

"I'm sorry," Mariamne said. "In fact, I have always been somewhat nervous, but I can't imagine what made me faint like that."

"The blame is partly mine. I shouldn't have interrogated you the way I did." He rose to go.

"I beg you to stay," said the girl. "I would like very much to talk with you now."

Akiba resumed his seat.

"I have not been honest with you," Mariamne began, "not with you, nor with Simon, nor with anyone else."

"How not?"

"I fear there is something the matter with me, not something you could see or that the physician could find, but something inside. It is the way some people cannot walk or cannot see, only with me it is not that obvious. Rabbi, I . . . I do not feel."

"What do you mean?"

"I mean that things like love of a man or dedication to a cause, things that move other people so deeply, these things don't seem to move me at all. Not at all. That is why I could not answer you when you asked what I seek. The truth is, I don't really know."

Mariamne turned her head away and began crying softly. Akiba rose and put his hand on the girl's hair, stroking it as if she were still the child he remembered. "But if you do not feel," he said gently, "then why are you crying now?"

Mariamne looked up. "It is not the same," she said.

Akiba sat down again. "I knew a man once who was blind," he said. "He had not always been blind, but during the first

war against the Romans he had watched helpless while his wife
and children burned to death in their flaming home. He was
struck blind by the sight. For years he wandered about seeking
charity and begging men like me to ask God to restore his vision. And then, one day, as he was being helped along on the
road, he clasped his hand over his eyes and cried out. When he
took his hand away, he could see."

"But how?" Mariamne asked, sitting up in the bed. "I don't
understand."

"Who can explain the ways of God? I have observed similar
cases, and I think I may know what happened, although how it
happened I cannot say. I believe that when the man saw the
manner of his family's death, he could not bear it and wanted
to blot out the possibility of such a sight again forever. And so
God, in His mercy, granted the man's deepest wish. But as the
years passed, the terrible memory of what had happened began to fade, as it mercifully does with all men, and the man
wished once again to see. And so God, in His mercy, granted
the man's wish a second time and restored his vision—but not
immediately, only when he was ready once again to look out
upon the world of men."

Mariamne looked pensively at the rabbi. "It's a fascinating
story," she said, "but I don't know what it has to do with me."

"It was you who compared yourself to a blind man," Akiba
said. "But you see, the man was never really blind."

"He was blind if he thought he was."

"Until his desire to see overcame his fear of seeing."

Mariamne shook her head sadly. "You don't understand."

"Perhaps," said Akiba, "I understand more than you think.
I have been watching you here these past months, and you
don't act like a girl who cannot feel. Nor do you speak that way,
for instance, about your father."

"That was something completely different," said Mariamne.

Akiba stood up. "Rest now," he said. "We'll talk about it
again."

Cornelia lay back in her bed, feeling full and satisfied and
wondering what she should do. Her situation was extremely
difficult. Why couldn't Quintus see that? If only he didn't press
so, the problem might resolve itself somehow. But then Quin-

tus was . . . well, he was Quintus. One couldn't just have an
affair with him; he became too involved, too demanding.

But did she just want to have just an affair with Quintus?
Cornelia supposed not, or there would be no problem. Well,
then, what did she want? Cornelia thought about that a moment, then changed the question to ask: What way was open
to her?

The most direct way, of course, would be to ask Rufus for a
divorce. But Rufus would never go along with a quiet divorce,
not even at the risk of his precious career; the possibilities of
a juicy scandal were so rich that Cornelia felt certain her loving
husband would not resist the temptation; that meant her reputation would be ruined, along with that of Quintus, who de-
served better. Just running away with her lover would be im-
practicable, and besides, Quintus, with his patrician sense of
honor, would never agree to it. On the other hand, the present
arrangement could not be continued indefinitely, though Cornelia was unable to say at the moment why not. She rolled over
on her stomach to go to sleep. That left them in quite a quan-
dary. She would have to think about it some more.

Mariamne also slept, but it was a fitful slumber disturbed
by the kind of dreams she had been having continually for
weeks. She awoke in the middle of the night and remained
awake for what seemed like a timeless period in the company
of a strange feeling she could not quite bring herself to identify. She wept at the feeling, and it lingered until she finally
managed to go back to sleep. The feeling so strange to Mariamne Bath-Menashe Ben-David was loneliness.

15

Not far from the ruins of Jerusalem there was a hill with
terraced slopes and carefully tended vineyards that no conqueror had thought it prudent to destroy. Grapes grew on the

hillside, large eating grapes so fat and tasty that only the least choice were pressed into wine. And there were plums so sweet that a man could taste of them long after he had finished eating. And pomegranates. And figs. And dates. And other produce as well, all alike of surpassing quality. But the fruit prided most by the farmers on the hill was their children.

The hill, flourishing in the gleaming sunlight with destroyed Jerusalem on this side of it and a war-ravaged plain on that side, looked as if it had somehow been forgotten by brutal time and the vicious sword. But it had merely been spared.

The history of the fertile hill went far, far back to the time before men began recording their deeds. David had conquered it, along with the city of Jerusalem, from the Jebusites. The King of Jebus had owned the place outright, in the manner of the pharaohs of Egypt, so that its farmers worked the land for him. But David freed the hill, as he freed every territory that the Lord delivered into his hand, and he gave it as part of the inheritance of the Tribe of Judah. But the name of the place remained what it had been in olden times, Har Hamelech— the Hill of the King.

For a thousand years and more had the hill basked in the rich Judean sunshine, its fruit growing uninterrupted from season to season, like an oasis in the midst of desolation. The descendants of the settlers placed on the hill by David were still there, and although Herod had taken their land from them and the Romans had taken it from Herod's sons, they worked it still as tenant farmers. Because of their fortunate position, they had been unable to take part in the first rising against Rome; for they were far enough away from Jerusalem to be spared her fate, yet not so far as to become a stronghold for either side. And as for the second rising, this part of Judea had not been involved in that at all.

So nothing very much had changed on the hill from the beginning. Officially the name of it still remained Har Hamelech, although the residents had not called it that for some time—it sounded formal and dramatic and even a little harsh in Hebrew. And so they translated the name into the softer Aramaic that was spoken all across the East, and it came out Tur Malka. Which is what they called it.

Now there was a village on Tur Malka, but it had no spe-

cial name at all. It was simply "the village," and it consisted
of a synagogue and a market place and the shops of a few artisans. Nearby was the cemetery, and some of its tombstones
were so old that the elements had rubbed them smooth, so that
the writing on them was no longer legible.

The communal life of the people on the hill was centered in
the village. On Sabbaths and festivals the men would gather in
the ancient synagogue and pray in the same way and with the
same melodies that their grandfathers had used, and they
would gossip a bit with their neighbors during the reading of
the Torah, a practice which was regularly denounced by every
rabbi who had ever officiated in the place. And at other times
the residents would gather in the synagogue to discuss matters
affecting the common good of the people on the hill. And they
would go there for funerals and for weddings.

Weddings, as common an occurrence as they were on Tur
Malka, always occasioned great celebration. All the people on
the hill were related by this time, and so, on the day of a wedding they would leave their farms and shops and assemble in
the village to watch the ceremony and to wish the young couple *mazal tov* and to drink a glass of wine with the parents of
the bride and groom and to express the hope that the newly-
weds would "found a house in Israel."

And so it went on Tur Malka, as always. A man was born,
he married, he procreated and he died. Little that he might do
in between was taken very seriously by his kinfolk on the hill,
but his arrival on Tur Malka, his setting up of a family and his
departure—these were taken most seriously. And of course,
each of these significant events was surrounded by its own special ceremony peculiar to Tur Malka, the origins of which were
often lost in antiquity.

When it came to weddings, for instance, the family of the
bride would present a hen to the family of the bridegroom,
while his family presented a rooster to the family of the bride.
It was symbolic and had no religious significance whatsoever,
but the people of the hill hewed to the ceremony because of its
age, and no rabbi who had come to the little synagogue had
ever dared question it.

Weddings were always heralded well in advance, and if some
other young man in from the fields for the ceremony should

take note of some maiden whom he had known all his life but had never really seen before, well, who on Tur Malka would object to attending another wedding some months hence?

Which is how it happened that on the twenty-second day of the month of Tammuz, the following notice was posted on the door of the synagogue in the village on Tur Malka:

> Be it known to all men that Jacob the son of Eli has consented to give his daughter, Elisheva, in marriage to Aaron the son of Joseph the tanner, the son of Isaac. Let any who may object to this match come forward before the appointed day or for all time keep silent.
>
> For, in the absence of proof that the marriage would be a forbidden union, and the Lord willing, the ceremony will take place on the sixteenth day of the month of Ab— may it come to us all for good—in the fifteenth year of the reign of the emperor Caesar Publius Aelius Hadrianus.

The notice was the common one, and the wording traditional. The sixteenth of Ab would fall on the first day of the week, and there was nothing especially significant about that, except perhaps that it would correspond to the last day of July in the Roman calender, the day the monthly Roman patrol would arrive on Tur Malka preparatory to collecting Rome's due from the hill's farmers the following day. But this was a routine procedure.

"I have been thinking," said Mariamne, "that perhaps I should go back to Alexandria."

"Would you be content there?" asked Akiba.

"I don't know. But you said yourself that I am not doing anything here, and so I thought . . . Oh, Rabbi," she buried her face in her hands, "I'm so unhappy."

"But why?" asked Akiba. "You didn't seem particularly unhappy when you came here. What has changed?"

"Nothing, really," said Mariamne, wiping her eyes. "But I had hoped something would."

"Won't you tell me about these upsetting dreams of yours?"

"And what will you do," asked Mariamne with more arrogance than she had intended, "interpret them like Joseph?"

"I promise you nothing so grand," Akiba said. "But you have asked me for advice."

"I'm sorry," Mariamne said. "The dreams are usually more or less the same. I am in the rebel camp, alone, and I run frantically looking for the others or toward something which I cannot find. This disturbs me very much, and I wake up in bad spirits."

Akiba looked at the girl for a long moment. "What happened at the rebel camp?" he asked. He leaned forward and lowered his voice. "If it is something you are ashamed of, Miriam, I beg you to remember that I am a rabbi, and an old man, and your father's friend. You can tell me, and it may ease your mind."

"No," Mariamne shook her head, "it was nothing like that. Nothing like that at all. When I first went there, I thought to stay a day or two. But it was so interesting, so different from what I had known, that I stayed and stayed and stayed. I began helping with the children, and I enjoyed that. And Simon was so nice to me. We used to talk, every evening, and once he even kissed me, but just once. I liked being with him. It was pleasant and nice and easy, somehow. . . . Until one evening Simon asked me to marry him, or began to anyway, and then I knew that I had done a terrible thing by making him think I felt that way, and so I left."

"So you didn't feel that way about Simon?"

"No," said Mariamne. "I wish I had, but I didn't."

"Then, if I may ask, how did you feel toward him?"

"I . . ." Mariamne looked up. "Can we speak Greek?"

"Why? Your Hebrew is perfect."

"But Hebrew makes it so hard to explain something like this. In Greek there are different words for the feelings one has toward a parent, or toward a friend, or toward a lover, while in Hebrew there is simply the one word 'ohev' for them all."

"We can speak Greek," Akiba said, "yet I think the Hebrew tongue is wiser, for it does not suggest that love is some rare thing that comes only to a few. Look about you, Miriam or Mariamne or whatever you want to call yourself. Love is everywhere, and not nearly so complicated as the Greeks make out."

"I like Simon," Mariamne said in Greek. "I admire him. Certainly I find him interesting. But that is all."

"I take it you did not find him personally attractive," suggested Akiba.

"I wouldn't say that," said Mariamne. "But I didn't feel love for him."

"Supposing," said Akiba, "that you learned Simon needed help."

"I would do everything within my power to help him."

"Supposing you learned he had been captured by the Romans."

Mariamne closed her eyes. "That would be horrible. It would distress me greatly. I can't even tell you how much."

Akiba rose and stood by the window. "And all of these feelings put together—friendship, interest, admiration, physical attraction, concern for his well-being—these are not love?"

"No," said Mariamne.

"Then what is love, Mariamne? Tell me in any language that you like."

"I can't describe it."

"But you just have," said Akiba.

There was a long silence in the room as Mariamne sat there staring at the rabbi. "Supposing you were right," she said at last, "what reason would I have to hide this feeling from you?"

"From me, none," Akiba answered. "But it could be that you seek to hide it from yourself and that your soul won't let you, and therefore the dreams."

"But why would I want to hide it at all?"

Akiba shrugged. "The mind is the most wondrous of God's creations, and we will never understand it fully, any more than we can hope to understand God fully. But perhaps you seek to avoid pain."

"How?"

"By not seeking happiness at all. You yourself have made it clear that you loved once, deeply, and were terribly hurt."

"Who?"

"Your father."

"That was not the same kind of love," said Mariamne.

"Yes, of course," said Akiba. "All love is different. Yet all is basically the same. You loved your father with all the depth of feeling that you have—the depth you have tried so desperately to hide ever since you returned here. Perhaps you fear a repetition of the kind of pain his long illness and death caused, and so you strive to cut your feelings the way a man would cut off his arm. But you can't really."

"It seems a bit farfetched," said Mariamne.

"Not at all. There is nothing especially new in any of this. Our forefathers were well aware that this kind of thing could happen, particularly to a person of great sensitivity. Why do you suppose they prescribed such an extensive ritual of mourning, along with a definite time limit to that mourning? It was to insure that a mourner would get the pain out of his heart, so that he would go on living."

Akiba walked over to the girl. "That is what you must do now, Miriam. You must seek happiness even at the risk of finding pain, for that is living."

16

"I warn you, Rufus," said the tribune. "You can't go on ignoring this without imperiling Rome's position here."

Rufus reached a fat hand over to the great glass bowl, removed a ripe plum after squeezing a few, ate it, blew the pit into his cupped hand and tossed it onto a plate before speaking. "Do you know what the trouble with you is, Quintus?"

"No."

"You are much too serious. Mind you, if you were already a Senator—as you undoubtedly will be one day—it would be all right. Senators are expected to be pious upholders of the virtues, at least on the Capitoline. But a pompous hedonist!" Rufus made a face. "That will never do."

Quintus walked over to the chair where the procurator sat next to his young wife. "I'm not interested in what you think of me," he said. "I ask you only, for the sake of the empire and

of the troops here, to consider the danger signs. For years—
even decades—there has been minor but incessant rebel activity in this province. And then, almost immediately following
your announcement that their most holy place will be, in their
eyes, desecrated, suddenly all rebel activity stops—at least on
the surface. For months now not a single murder, not a single
act of violence, not a caravan ambushed, not one attempt at
seizing military supplies. Does this not strike you as strange?"

"Not particularly," said Rufus, starting on a cluster of grapes.
"Perhaps the Jews have finally decided to submit to Rome's
will."

Quintus watched a drop of grape juice roll down the procurator's jowls onto the napkin that covered the top of his toga.
"You are not that stupid," the tribune said. "Why do you
choose to ignore the obvious signs of a buildup?"

Rufus tossed the grapes aside. "You are right," he said. "I
am not stupid. Therefore, why do you persist in talking to me
as if I were? Do you think I am unaware of what your father
is doing in Rome in an attempt to undermine my authority
here? Your show of filial devotion is touching, Quintus, but it
does not move me."

The tribune paused for a split second. So Rufus knew about
his father's group and their moves to have the emperor recon-
sider his decision to build Aelia Capitolina. That was too bad,
but it was to have been expected. He'd have to try another
tack.

"Why must you assume there is something personal in this?
All I urge is that you prevent potential trouble. Double the
patrols. Triple them. Find out what is going on."

"I'm not that interested."

"Well, I just don't understand," said Quintus in exasperation. "Do you want another rising?"

"I'm not as terrified of it as you seem to be," snapped the
procurator. "Perhaps it might even be a good thing to give
these Jews a reminder of what Roman force is like. Perhaps it
would end the troubles here once and for all."

The tribune looked at Rufus in disbelief. "So that's it. You
actually want them to rebel. You calculate that an unsuccessful
Jewish rising would enhance your career. And, of course, I
suppose you could be right. But that's a dangerous game."

Rufus rose to his feet. "I don't play games," he said angrily. "I don't play guessing games, and I don't play hide-and-seek with rebels, and, frankly, your philosophical word games, Quintus, begin to bore me. So let us forget about the games and look at some realities." He strode across the room to a large map of the province hanging from a wall. "You speak to me in the kind of dramatic tones usually reserved for political speeches of great peril and threat to the empire. What, at most, could your threat consist of? A few thousand ragged Jews armed with clubs and scythes? The two cohorts in Caesarea alone would suffice against these. But they wouldn't have to. Here, in the area where the new capital will rise, we have the rest of Legion X Fretensis. Here, in the north, we have the VI Ferrata. That's about twelve thousand legionaries right there, all of them fully trained and armed and led—no offense—not by political appointees but by men hardened to battle and unafraid of it. And in addition to the crack troops of the line, there are the auxiliaries and cavalry, bringing the Roman commitment here to more than fifteen thousand men and making this the most strongly fortified province of its size in the empire." Rufus paused for a long moment to let that sink in. "Mind you," he added, "I don't see the threat of rebellion as clearly as you seem to. But if I did, I would say, let them rise. We will crush them so easily and so utterly that it will remain an object lesson for all time."

The procurator sat down. Quintus watched him, and the painful realization crossed his mind that he had made a tactical blunder. Rufus, by his very appearance and the air of moral decay that seemed to surround him, invited underestimation. But the mind in that jaded body was sharp. Clearly, the procurator had already noted and weighed all that Quintus had come to tell him. He had merely come up with a different conclusion, and that was only because they valued things differently. "Does it not occur to you," asked the tribune in a final attempt, "that if a rebellion should break out, lives will be lost—Roman as well as Jewish lives—that property will be destroyed, that the value of this already poor province to the Empire will be further reduced? Does this mean nothing to you?"

"Nothing," said Rufus. "The honor of the empire is of greater value than any one province, and I will not compromise it."

So Rufus would now pose as the guardian of Rome's honor, Quintus reflected. He realized that there was nothing further he could say to this man.

The tribune raised his right arm in salute, turned on his heel and walked from the room. The procurator's wife, in a show of hospitality, accompanied him.

When they were out of earshot, Quintus turned to the woman. "How can you stay with that pig?" he demanded. "How can you let him touch you, kiss you? How can you sleep in the same house with him?"

Cornelia smiled. "You'd be surprised at the things women can get used to."

"I'm serious," said Quintus in a whisper. "How long do you intend to let this little farce of yours continue? Can't you see how it hurts me? Or don't you care?"

A sudden show of concern came over Cornelia's face. "Soon," she said, squeezing the tribune's hand. "Truly, it will be soon. I have been thinking of it. Believe me, I await only the right moment to leave him, and it will be soon."

Quintus put on his helmet and turned to the woman as he walked out the door. "Shall I come to you tonight?"

"Yes," she said. "Tonight."

It was on the following day, the third day of the month of Ab, that Elisha Ben-Abuyah, called *aher*, journeyed to the university of Rabbi Akiba and asked his friend if he planned this year to keep the fast of the ninth of Ab commemorating the destruction of Jerusalem and the Temple.

"Of course I shall keep it," said Akiba as they took their customary walk in the garden.

"You know, of course, that the Romans have declared it an act of treason to keep the fast."

"Yes," said Akiba.

"Yet you will keep it?"

"Yes," said Akiba.

"And you will advise others to keep it?"

"I will tell them that they must keep it as a religious duty."

"You are a foolish old man," said Another.

"Perhaps," said Akiba. They walked on in silence.

"What do you hope to gain by all of this," asked Another, "except perhaps more deaths?"

"Our redemption," answered Akiba.

On Tuesday, the fourth of Ab, Simon Bar Kochba began the training of his Sixth Judean Battalion and, at the same time, opened communications with certain influential Jews in Alexandria who were sympathetic to his cause. The Jews in question were ship magnates who offered to place at Bar Kochba's disposal more than a score of vessels and their crews should these prove to be of need and value.

On Wednesday, the fifth of Ab, the mother of Aaron Ben-Joseph sent to her neighbors on Tur Malka, the family of Elisheva Bath-Jacob, a cake made with honey, while the girl's mother sent to Aaron's family a flagon of mead wine, the exchange of gifts symbolizing the mothers' hope that the marriage of their children would be a sweet one. The show of joy, however, was limited to this small exchange, in consideration of the approach of the day of mourning.

During the following night, being the sixth of Ab, Mariamne Bath-Menashe Ben-David dreamed she saw many things but was herself never seen.

The rebellion had broken out in Mariamne's dream, and although she had no part in it—was, indeed, separated from the entire scene—she could see clearly all that was happening. She saw Bar Kochba's troops marching from the hills to meet the Roman legions in the plain. From somewhere above the battle she could see all the fury of the clash, both as a whole and close up. For a long time neither side seemed to prevail, and then, as she watched horrified, the Jews began a slow retreat.

With cries of triumph the Roman troops followed them as they tried to make their way back up into the hills, while from another side fresh cavalry poured into the passes. There were many inconsistencies in Mariamne's dream, for she had never seen a battle and knew nothing of the ways of war. But what she saw now seemed very real and frightening.

The Roman swords slashed out without mercy, cutting here and severing there. Jonathan, Simon's friend, fell before them, and his wife Ruth. The old man was slain, and the boys, and the children Mariamne had helped to tend.

In the end they were all dead except for one man, the single man who by his vision had started it all. The Romans captured him alive, and dragging him to a nearby mound, they crucified him and left him there to die, in the now horribly quiet valley, alone but for the fallen comrades around him.

Mariamne wanted only to flee from the scene, to blot out its view and its memory forever. But instead she found herself drawing nearer and nearer to the crucified man, until at last she could see him close up, as if she were next to the cross. She looked into Simon's twisted face, but he did not seem to see her. There was no look of recognition in those familiar eyes—only pain and disappointment and approaching death. Mariamne looked again into the face and felt a surge of feeling go out to the dying man so powerful that she was sure she too would soon die. She turned away and tried with all her might to keep from looking again, but it was no use. Something moved her head back and forced her to look yet another time, and so she did. But now, suddenly, the crucified man was not Simon at all. It was her father.

Mariamne screamed and awoke trembling in a terror such as she had not known before.

The night of the eighth of Ab, when the Jews had already begun their twenty-four-hour fast, was warm and wet and without a breeze, as if the wind itself had left to join the Jews in their mourning. On that night Quintus Arminius Caro sat down and wrote the following letter to his father:

> To my Father, Senator Caius Arminius:
> Hail and greeting.
> I write you tonight more out of duty than desire, for in truth I have little of interest to relate, and the news I have is neither good nor pleasant. My service here grows more intolerable with each passing day, and especially as the novelty of it wears off, I find the military life at worst trying and at best a bore.
> To begin with, Rufus is intractable on the subject of the Jews, so that any and all hope for a bettering of conditions

here rests in Rome with you and your colleagues. I am personally convinced, both by what I have observed and by my instinct, that a fresh rebellion is brewing in this province. Yet, whether because he hates the Jews as a people or because he hopes to gain some personal advantage by his inaction, Rufus will not so much as lift a finger to avoid a clash.

What can I tell you? He will not try to find out what is behind the sudden lull in anti-Roman activity. He will not increase our patrols. He will not put the legions on alert. He will not in the slightest delay the plans for the new city. He will not make any attempt to soothe the feelings of the Jews. Nay, beyond that, he makes use of every opportunity to irritate their wounds.

If Rufus were purposely goading the Jews to some foolish and violent move, he could not do a more complete job of it. And, in very deed, I feel that this is precisely what he has in mind. Talk of honor and morality is useless with him, and if I tried to convince him that the task of a good administrator is to avoid wars rather than win them, I would only be wasting my time. Apparently Rufus envisions a quick and decisive victory over the Jews in the event of a revolt, with a proconsulship for himself as the outcome.

And the worst of it is that I fear he may be right. The Jews cannot indefinitely ignore these insults to their pride. They will surely do something in anger that will give Rufus the excuse of loosing the legions upon them. Undoubtedly the troops will have an easy time of it, dealing as they are with a people long broken. But that will not stop Rufus from making it an occasion for butchery—nor from proclaiming a triumph for himself. Alas, I see it all too clearly. Before the end, I fear, this son of a rug merchant will sit with you in the *curia,* having a voice equal to yours in the deliberations of the august Senate.

And one question keeps plaguing me: Whose fault will it be, Father? It is easy and convenient to blame a Rufus for injustice, but who has made him what he is, and who has placed the fasces of authority in his hands, and who

sustains him, and who permits him to rule this small corner
of the world like an Oriental despot? Strangely, this is what
disturbs me most of all. I do not believe in the inscrutable
workings of the gods any more than you do, and I cannot
believe that we are all victims of blind circumstance. Who,
then, is to blame? Surely it is not you or your distinguished
colleagues in the Senate. And Hadrian seems a fair, well
meaning man.

Am I growing too philosophical? Rufus said recently that
I was, and in this, perhaps, he was right. So I shall spare
you more of my tortured cogitations.

The weather here, at the moment, seems to be collaborat-
ing with the Jews to make life miserable for us. It can be
quite pleasant in the north of this country, and in the hills
around the old Jewish capital there is always a breeze. But
here, in the coastal plain where we are concentrated, the
air is sometimes so heavy that one can hardly breathe. Such
is the case tonight.

I ask you, while knowing how difficult it must be, to continue your efforts toward attaining a just and realistic
Judean policy so as to bring a long-awaited peace to this
troubled area.

Despite my current dispiritedness and the heat, I am in
all ways well. I hope you are the same.

Quintus

It was on the ninth of Ab, while the Jews sat in mourning for
their departed glory, that the Romans began laying the foundations of their new city, plowing under the ruins of what was
left of Jerusalem. They permitted one such ruin to remain
standing—a large charred segment of what had formerly been
the massive western wall of the great Temple's outer court-
yard. They left that as a wry memorial, that men might know
how mighty a city had once stood here before being reduced
by Roman arms.

According to the plans, the western wall would remain there
while the rest of the old Temple area would be occupied by
the new Roman temple to Jupiter. Some of the architects had
opposed this particular detail of the plans, suggesting that the

charred wreck be removed as an eyesore. In any case, they argued, the significance of the wall as a memorial would soon be forgotten. . . .

It was said that the ninth of Ab had been chosen as the date for the final leveling of Jerusalem by Tinius Rufus himself, who knew full well that the Jews were defying him and keeping the fast. The report had it that the procurator had said he wanted to give the Jews something to really wail about. Accordingly, while the Jews would continue to refer to the last remaining section of the Temple complex as simply the Western Wall, the Romans and others began referring to it as the Wailing Wall.

And it was at about this time that the rabbis began referring to the procurator as "Tyrannus" Rufus.

17

In the synagogue at his university in B'nei B'rak the great Rabbi Akiba Ben-Joseph sat upon the floor, his beard tousled and his robe rent, and in a voice trembling with grief he chanted the words of Lamentations:

"How does that once populous city now sit deserted; how is she become as a widow, she that was great among the nations and princess among the provinces, how is she become tributary!"

And across the world, wherever Jews lived, they mourned with him.

"Jerusalem has grievously sinned; therefore is she become an abomination," chanted the reader in Tur Malka's synagogue.

"All you that pass by, behold and see if there be any sorrow like my sorrow," intoned the reader in the great synagogue of Alexandria.

"How has the Lord covered the daughter of Zion with a cloud in his anger and cast down from heaven to the earth the beauty of Israel," lamented the faithful of Babylon.

In the synagogues of Greece, of Rome, of Persia and Yemen, of Hispania and Gaul, men who had never seen Jerusalem wept for her fall and spoke the words of Lamentations with their brethren:

"Remember, O Lord, what is come upon us; consider and behold our reproach.

"Our inheritance is turned to strangers, our houses to aliens.

"We are orphans and fatherless; our mothers are like widows.

"We have drunk our water for money; wood is sold to us.

"We are pursued with the yoke upon our necks; we are weary and have no rest. . . ."

In Judea, the cause for these lamentations was sometimes painfully obvious. But in the many other lands where Jews lived—and had been living for centuries—their inconsolable grief for a disaster in which they had had no part and their un-ending nostalgia for a place they had never been was a source of puzzlement to their Gentile neighbors.

Yet Jews everywhere wept as with one voice for the national tragedy, and as with one voice did they pray for redemption, and as with one voice did they utter the ancient vow:

"If I forget you, O Jerusalem, may my right hand forget her cunning.

"May my tongue cleave to the roof of my mouth if I remember you not, if I set not Jerusalem above my chief joy."

It was the ninth of Ab in the Hebrew year 3892, the year 885 since the founding of the city of Rome, the fifteenth year of the reign of the Emperor Publius Aelius Hadrianus, the year 132 in the calendar of the Minaeans. It was sixty-two years to the day that Jerusalem had been destroyed by the legions of Rome.

Rabbi Akiba spent the entire day in the synagogue, praying on behalf of his people. It was there that word came to him of what the Romans had begun on the site of the Temple. He said nothing in response to the shocking news, expressing his feelings only to One. He asked Him for mercy, for forgiveness, for aid. Most of all, Akiba asked Him for strength to do what had to be done.

At nightfall, when the fast was over, when the news had already moved across Judea with the speed with which such tidings always travel, when Akiba had washed and had refreshed himself with a glass of milk, he let it be known that he sought a messenger to send to Bar Kochba. The first to answer the call was Mariamne.

"I am not so sure it is wise for you to go again," said Akiba.

"Please," said Mariamne.

"Why?"

"I want a chance. A chance to find some meaning."

Akiba nodded. "I understand," he said. "Here is the message for Simon: Tell him that I confirm him in his title of prince. Tell him that henceforth he need not wait for instructions from me but is free to act as he sees fit. Tell him there is nothing further I can even begin to do now. Tell him . . . tell him to know before Whom he stands."

"Very well," said Mariamne, and, as the rabbi had clearly finished, she rose to go.

"May the Lord be with you," said Akiba as the girl stood at the door. "May He be with us all."

Mariamne's contact with the rebels was made at a different point this time, since these spots were periodically changed for reasons of security. But otherwise the procedure was much the same as before—the blindfold, the long, silent ride through the hills.

Akiba's messenger had much to think about as she rode toward the rebel camp. She wondered how Simon would react to her coming, whether he would be angry or glad or simply unmoved. It had been only a month since she had seen him, but it seemed like so much more, and besides, much could happen in a month. She wondered if his feelings toward her had changed, if he had perhaps fallen in love with someone else. Most of all, she wondered about herself, about what she would feel, about whether, in fact, she would feel anything at all.

The horse carrying Mariamne halted, and she was helped from it gently. She was guided on foot for a short distance, and then the blindfold was removed.

Mariamne saw Simon standing before her, trying without success to keep a look of puzzlement, and of hurt, from his face. She saw a man there—not the Prince of Israel whom the people respected and even revered, not the Son of a Star who knew no fear, not some fabled hero whose strength came from heaven. She saw a man with doubts and weaknesses and flaws and fears, a strong man whose real strength lay in having been able to put these things aside. And she understood how this strength had drawn the multitudes to him and had, at the same time, left him all alone. And in that instant of seeing Simon, Mariamne knew what her dreams had been trying to tell her. . . .

"I love you," she said as they sat before the campfire that evening, and she marveled at how easily the words came. And Simon embraced her, holding her to him and thus setting her free. And Mariamne cried, because she was happy.

The wedding of Mariamne Bath-Menashe Ben-David and Simon Bar Kosiba, Prince of Israel, called Bar Kochba, was held in the hills of Judah on the evening of the fifteenth day of the month of Ab, following the Sabbath. Jonathan Bar Ba'-ayah and Nathan Bar Deroma were the official witnesses who signed their names to the marriage contract; Rabbi Eleazar Ha-Modai performed the ceremony, which was attended by a congregation whose members—like the rabbi and the witnesses—were all liable to the death penalty for treason against the established government. Many women were there, including Ruth, who had presented her own wedding veil to Mariamne and who now wept silently as Simon took the ring from her husband and placed it on the bride's finger, saying, "Behold, you are sanctified to me with this ring, by the Law of Moses and of Israel."

Rabbi Eleazar Ha-Modai then pronounced the traditional seven benedictions:

"Blessed are You, O Lord our God, King of the universe, Who creates the fruit of the vine."

He handed a cup of wine to Simon, and both the groom and Mariamne took a sip from it. Then the rabbi continued:

"Blessed are You, O Lord our God, King of the universe, Who has created all things to His glory.

"Blessed are You, O Lord our God, King of the universe, Creator of Man.

"Blessed are You, O Lord our God, King of the universe,

Who has made Man in His image, after His likeness, and has prepared for him, out of his very self, a perpetual fabric. Blessed are You, O Lord, Creator of Man.

"May the barren one be exceedingly joyful and exult in the happy gathering of her children within her. Blessed are You, O Lord, Who makes Zion joyful through her children.

"Cause these loving companions to rejoice greatly, even as of old You gladdened Your creation in the Garden of Eden. Blessed are You, O Lord, Who causes bridegroom and bride to rejoice.

"Blessed are You, O Lord our God, King of the Universe, Who has created joy and gladness, bridegroom and bride, mirth and exultation, pleasure and delight, love, brotherhood, peace and fellowship."

To this was added the following, in accordance with the dictates of the sages:

"Soon, O Lord our God, may there be heard in the cities of Judah and in the streets of Jerusalem the voice of joy and the voice of happiness, the voice of bridegroom and the voice of bride, the jubilant voice of bridegrooms from their marriage canopies and of youths from their feasts of song. Blessed are You, O Lord, Who causes the bridegroom to rejoice with the bride."

And the congregation shouted, "Amen."

With that, Simon stepped forward and, with a stamp of his foot, smashed a jar that had been placed on the ground. This too was a new addition to the ceremony, a small reminder of destruction and mourning even amid great joy.

"Mazal tov," the group shouted. "Good luck."

It was a night of great rejoicing in the rebel camp, a night such as there had not been since they had first entered the hills. The men and women drank and sang lustily and laughed, as if they felt that they had to crowd as much normal living into this one night as they could because it might never recur.

The celebration continued till dawn, but the bride and groom slipped away long before that to the cave that was to be their home. And there Simon taught Mariamne how the force of love could satisfy the hunger of love.

Afterward, when he lay with his head on her breast, Mariamne asked him, "Will it always be like this?"

"It will be better," said Simon sleepily, "and I suppose it will also never be as good."

"Another paradox," said Mariamne, half to herself, and she laughed softly, and Simon laughed with her without knowing why.

There was a long silence after that, and when Mariamne spoke again it was in a small voice that she asked, "Simon, how does a rebellion begin?" But Simon had already fallen asleep.

Five of the members of the Roman patrol hiking up the road on Tur Malka had been this way before. The sixth had not. An eighteen-year-old recruit from Sicily, he was fresh to the Legion X Fretensis, fresh to the army, to Judea and to most everything else. And his older comrades on the patrol, all of them seasoned legionaries, wouldn't let him forget it.

"This is a rough job, this rent collecting," said one of them with a wink to his fellows. "I'm glad we have this sturdy lad with us in case there's trouble."

The boy walked on without speaking. He knew they were goading him, and he wasn't going to bite.

"The worst of it is," said another soldier, "this business of having to be circumcised before they'll let you pick up a payment. By the gods, I'll never forget my first time here. I thought I'd die of the pain."

"A young buck like this," exclaimed the third man, "he'll never miss a piece of it. He'll still have plenty left for the girls, though I'll wager he doesn't know what to do with it."

The baiting of the youth continued as the group rounded the bend and entered the village on Tur Malka. There was a large crowd in front of the synagogue, and the soldiers walked over to see what was happening. They stood at a distance and watched as young Aaron pronounced the oath taking Elisheva to wife.

"What a fine cut of meat," said one of the soldiers appraisingly, looking at the bride. "Jupiter himself wouldn't mind getting into that one."

"It's lucky we arrived today," said another of the older men, keeping a straight face. "Now we all get a chance to lie with her, in accordance with the custom."

"Really?" exclaimed the young recruit. He had bitten at last.

The older men laughed raucously at his gullibility. The youth flushed with embarrassment and rage, but he said nothing. He knew that anything he said would only make it worse. He knew the men would spread the story around the barracks and that for months he would be ridiculed and taunted unless, somehow, he could redeem himself in their eyes.

The soldiers continued watching the ceremony, and the boy listened to their banter but took no part in it. He felt a great anger grow in him, and as he watched the ceremony that anger was directed at the people there, those people who looked so strange and were taking part in that stupid service and who seemed so happy.

Some of the wedding guests noticed the legionaries, but they paid little heed. It was simply the time for the Romans to come and collect the rents. There was nothing in that to mar the celebration. Now the rabbi had concluded the seven benedictions, and a glass was placed on the ground in front of the groom. But before Aaron would smash it and solemnize the marriage, there was to be the traditional exchange of rooster and hen beneath the marriage canopy.

The eyes of the crowd now shifted to a stall not far from the synagogue, near where the legionaries stood, and they too looked that way. A woman, a friend of both families, had slipped into the stall and emerged with a live rooster in one hand and a live hen in the other. Holding the two apart amid loud cackling, she began making her way toward the marriage canopy to hand one of the birds to the father of the bride and the other to the father of the groom.

As the woman approached the place where the Romans were standing, one of the legionaries whispered to the young recruit, "Now, if you can grab one of those chickens, the Jews really will let you have the bride. That's the law." The men laughed. So it was starting already. Well, maybe he would show them just how much nerve he had.

Suddenly, the young legionary leaped forward and made a grab for the hen.

The woman was stunned, and she held on tight as the youth tried to wrest the bird from her. The crowd, equally stunned, did not move. "Let go," the boy shouted. But the woman held on, and now she screamed and the rooster crowed and the hen screeched in terror of being torn apart.

"Let go," the youth shouted again, this time through tears of rage as he realized he was being made to look even more of a fool. He smashed the woman across her mouth with his clenched fist, knocking her to the ground and, wrenching away the hen at last, ran with it in the direction of his comrades.

The soldiers looked pale, and one of them started to run away. "It was only a jest," said the legionary who had given the boy the idea. Those were the last words the boy would ever hear. . . .

It was to be noted later that the men of Tur Malka—normally the most gentle of people—had acted without thinking but in an instinctive fit of fury at a senseless desecration. It was all over in a moment, and five soldiers of the Roman Empire lay dead by the side of the road.

The sixth legionary, who had had the presence of mind to run, got away.

18

Simon slept late the morning following his wedding, and after he had finally gotten up to wash and pray, he rejoined his wife in their cave home for the morning meal, and they spoke in whispered tones of things that made no sense at all. Until a voice from outside the cave called for Bar Kochba, and he went to answer.

Tur Malka was not far from the rebel camp in the hills of Judah, and Jonathan was able to tell his friend all that had transpired that morning.

Simon shook his head dumbly. "What a thing," he said. "And in Tur Malka. We don't have a single man there."

"No," said Jonathan. "They never wanted to take part. Just like in Kosiba."

"What a thing," Simon repeated. "And over a hen."

"Well," Jonathan said, "you know what will happen now. The Romans will destroy the place and crucify the men and enslave the women and children. That's the usual punishment."

Simon looked up. "No," he said quietly. "This time it will not happen that way."

The soldier who had escaped from the crowd's wrath at Tur Malka brought his report directly to the commander of the Legion X Fretensis, which was encamped in the vicinity of what had formerly been Jerusalem. The commander's next move was clear, and he could have acted at once. But instead, being one of those military men who was not particularly anxious to act on his own authority, he dispatched a messenger to Caesarea with the news.

Rufus was furious. He sent the messenger back with orders that a full cohort of the X Legion be sent to Tur Malka to exact a collective retribution for the lives of the five Roman soldiers. . . .

Few of the 600 men who set forth from the garrison for Tur Malka two days after the incident of the hen could be said to be angry over the slayings of their five comrades. Close friendships within a legion were rare; the dead soldiers were not known to most of the 600 men, nor were they thirsting for vengeance or looking forward to their brutal task. Many secretly dreaded the horrible screams that attended a crucifixion.

No, if anything, most of the men in that fateful cohort felt only an annoyance at having to march in the hot Judean sun, coupled with a vague excitement at being able to escape for a day or two from the routine of garrison life. They marched now through the hills, upward over winding roads and tortuous paths, in a time-honored order, bearing their arms in a fashion long prescribed and with a discipline that had become legendary.

From a hill high above a distant pass that led directly to Tur Malka, Nathan Bar Deroma watched the legionaries approach. At first he could see only the glint of their armor in the noonday sun, and he thought to himself, with a mixture of eagerness and apprehension, that the Romans were indeed following their anticipated plan. There were no surprises so far. He glanced quickly about him at the surrounding heights and saw some of his own men waiting for his signal.

Bar Deroma looked again and saw the Roman column disappear around a bend. There was just the faintest possibility, he knew, that they would not come this way. There was another pass through the hills, a narrow one, but the chances were the Romans did not know about it and would not choose to go through it if they did. But in the event they did, Judah Ha-Cohen was stationed there with his men. Bar Kochba had decided to permit no chance for error.

The Romans came into view again, closer this time. Well, Bar Deroma thought, that was it. They were coming this way. He raised his right arm and let it drop. All around him, moving soundlessly, men who had been preparing for this moment took up their positions, their arms at the ready.

Bar Deroma had been waiting for this moment longer than most. He was no longer young, and he had seen much. He had buried his parents and his wife and their child. He had been a rebel in the Dead Sea cliffs. He had plundered, and he had slain, and he had long dreamed of just such a time as this. Strange now, as the time drew near, that he found no pleasure in it.

The drums of the legion could be clearly heard now, their dull booming resounding through the silence of the hills. The soldiers marched in cadence to the drums, which now beat a leisurely pace as the cohort approached the pass. The Romans were in no hurry. Boom, went the drums. Boom, left leg. Boom, right leg. Boom, to the glory of Roman arms. Boom, for the swordsmen. Boom, for the archers. Boom, for the men who would fashion the crosses.

The drums grew louder, and the rebels in the hills could make out the figures in the vanguard of the Roman column. Bar Deroma could see the faces of the drummers, could see the bored look on their countenances as they marched along, beating out the death knell of Tur Malka. Boom. Boom. Boom. Boom.

So many of the men in those hills felt hatred in that sight and in that sound, hatred for the calm way in which the Romans were moving forward, hatred for what they were planning to do, hatred for what had already been done, hatred for the very sound of those drums which had so often before heralded some disaster.

Boom. Boom. Boom. The drummers had entered the pass now. Boom. Boom. The cohort was following. Boom. Boom. Bar Deroma drew his sword out of its scabbard and held it aloft, poised. Boom. Boom. The drummers had passed beneath the spot where he stood and were followed by two Roman officers on horseback. Boom. Boom. Next came the swordsmen in close formation. Boom. Boom. The archers followed. Boom. Boom. The drummers at the head of the column approached the end of the pass. Boom. Boom. Boom, for the dead of Judea. Boom, for the ravaging of the land. Boom, for the Temple. Boom, for Jerusalem. Boom, for the crucified multitudes.

Bar Deroma brought down his sword with such violence that it smashed against a rock and sent up sparks.

"L'herut Yisrael," shouted a hundred voices in the hills as the Jews filled the air with their arrows. Arrows cut down the drummers in the midst of a beat. Arrows transfixed the Roman archers before they could begin to return the fire. An arrow through the throat brought a tribune of the legion from his horse.

"Withdraw," shouted a centurion, holding his own shield above his head and urging the other soldiers to do likewise.

"L'herut Yisrael," came the cry from angry voices as the rebels poured down from the hills into the pass, swinging their swords above their heads and bringing them crashing down on Roman helmets and Roman armor and Roman flesh. Jews with arms who knew how to use them, Jews with fire in their eyes filled the valley and blocked the pass, slashing and thrusting and cutting.

"For my father," screamed one warrior, tears streaming down his beardless face.

And others shouted likewise. "In the memory of ——." "For the village of ——."

When the cohort had failed to return by evening of the following day, the commander of Legion X Fretensis grew alarmed and sent out a patrol to Tur Malka to learn what had happened. The patrol also failed to return. But still the commander would not act on his own. He dispatched a messenger to Tinius Rufus for further instructions. . . .

Meanwhile, on the day after the slaughter in the pass leading to Tur Malka, Simon Bar Kochba caused the following letter, written in the High Tongue, to be sent to the officers of his men and the representatives of his sympathizers in 457 separate towns and villages throughout Judea:

> In the name of the Lord, God of Israel, written on the nineteenth day of the month of Ab.
>
> Brothers, the day of our redemption is at hand. Let each man prepare to serve the cause of the Lord, which is the cause of freedom and the cause of Judea. Remove your arms from their hiding places and gird up your loins that we may, together, cast the invader from our land.
>
> Take no direct action without orders, lest we be divided before the Romans as were our fathers, but be ready for the word to rise together as brothers. And cause our villages and our towns and our land to aid us in our struggle. Let the Romans find no peace in them. Let them find no food in our communities, nor water in our brooks, nor rest in our houses.
>
> Unite now as never before, for then nothing will be impossible for you. Let every man take the hand of his neighbor to oppose the oppressor. Stand together, and dare to be what you are. Keep your traditions. Follow your ancestral laws. Speak the language of your fathers, even the Hebrew which David spoke. And in all of this, be strong, for the Lord our God will surely be with us.

Simon had composed the letter with great care, and he had hesitated before signing it. The title "Bar Kochba" seemed much too pretentious for the orphan from Kosiba, and could he as yet call himself a prince? So, in the end, he had signed the letter simply "Simon."

It was on the next day, while the Romans were as yet unaware of what had happened in the hills of Judah, that Quintus received the following letter from his father:

To my son, Quintus Arminius Caro, Tribunus Legionis X Fretensis:

Warm greeting.

I hasten to answer your last letter, my son, for I found in it a spirit that is unlike you. You must remember who you are and what you are. I have no doubt that you find your military service trying at times, but surely this is a small price to pay for the privilege of Roman citizenship and the glory of serving Rome. And keep in mind, Quintus, that you are no ordinary Roman citizen, just as you are no ordinary foot soldier of the legion. If you have received special consideration in your appointment, you have also a special duty. You may not permit yourself the luxury of sulking in your tent like some Achilles.

Regarding Rufus, I know him most of all by reputation, and that reputation is not good. But the fact remains that he has managed to keep the province at peace and paying its taxes, and that, as far as the Senate and the Roman people are concerned, is the ultimate test of his ability.

You must know by now of the emperor's final decision to build Aelia Capitolina. There is nothing further we can do here on that score except perhaps try to give some other sop to the Jews. As I told a delegation of them here only recently, they would be wise to urge their coreligionists in Judea to consider the building of a great Roman city in their midst a source of some pride. And I suggested to them that, with a right word here and there, Rome might even help them to build a new Temple to their god somewhere else in the country, a Temple that would far outshine the former structure in its splendor.

While there was an understandable reluctance on their part to accept this, they agreed with me that any act of insurrection on the part of the Judeans would be most foolish. Indeed, should the Jews actually resort to arms, they would lose the respect and sympathy of many in the Roman world who, like myself, now find some of their demands reasonable.

In closing, let me urge you once again to do your duty cheerfully and to place your faith in those venerable institutions which have always guaranteed Roman justice in the past.

Your loving father

Quintus fingered the letter, looked at it again, and put it aside with a wry smile. It had been a mistake to write his father in such bitter tones. The old man could have been expected to answer just as he had, invoking the name of duty and ancient heritage.

He meant well, Quintus knew, and when the Roman Senator had told that delegation of Jews that he felt sympathetic, he had meant that, too. But Quintus could not help asking himself what good "the respect and sympathy of many in the Roman world" had done for the Jews. He wondered how he would feel if he were a Jew living in Judea and asked to content himself with such "respect and sympathy." The pose was hard for the Roman, for he could not quite imagine himself that interested in the wishes of any god, but still, in the end, he had to admit that he would probably feel as the Jews now seemed to feel. He would be angry, Quintus decided, at what appeared to be hypocrisy on the part of such patricians as his father. The fact was, Quintus was well aware, that it was not hypocrisy—that his father really meant it—but the Jews could not be expected to know that.

Quintus was sitting in his room and thinking thus when he received an urgent summons to appear before the procurator.

Rufus told him that he was being reassigned at once to the main force of the X Legion. "It seems your friends, the Jews, have begun some trouble in the south. An entire cohort has disappeared."

"Disappeared?" Quintus asked.

"Disappeared," repeated Rufus. "Along with a tribune whom the legion commander asks to have replaced. So I conceded, with some reluctance, to sending you. You will be missed here, no doubt, but it will only be a temporary assignment until the present difficulty is resolved."

"Have you any idea what the present difficulty is?"

Rufus sighed. "The Jews in some small dunghill of a town killed five Roman soldiers, so we sent a cohort there to punish the place, and the cohort never returned. A patrol sent out after them also disappeared. That's all I can tell you."

"It sounds inconceivable," mused Quintus.

"I'm quite aware of what it sounds like," Rufus said sharply. "Really, Quintus, you have an exceptional talent for stating the obvious."

"I beg your pardon," said the tribune icily.

Rufus made a waving motion with his hand, a gesture that was at once imperious and impudent. "In any case, I would appreciate your leaving soon, tonight if possible, to join the legion. The commander's request was most urgent. The entire Fretensis will march tomorrow in the steps of the missing cohort."

Quintus nodded his head and left the room. Later he bade a hurried farewell to Cornelia and rode out of the city.

Quintus Arminius Caro, tribune of the X Legion, rode beside the legion commander up the slopes of the hills of Judah and wondered just how much hotter it could get. The sun had turned his plumed helmet and armor into ovens that threatened to cook him alive. He removed the helmet for a moment as he rode and thought he could physically feel the slight breeze caused by the motion of his horse blowing steam away from the top of his head. But he soon replaced the helmet, for to ride bareheaded in such sunlight was foolhardy.

"This must be the way the cohort went," the legion commander said. "We are very near Tur Malka now and should soon find out what happened."

The legion continued its march up the hills, looking like some slow-moving, multicolored serpent. In all, counting the auxiliary and cavalry but subtracting the missing cohort and the 1,000-odd men normally stationed in Caesarea, there were more than 6,000 men in that column.

Nathan Bar Deroma, watching their approach from the heights, made this quick calculation. It was a formidable force. To oppose this force, the rebel had with him the Third Judean Battalion of 5,000 men. The odds were not far apart, he knew, and the Jews had the advantage of surprise. He barked out an order to his second in command and returned to watch the legion's progress.

"I think we are making a mistake," said Quintus suddenly.
"What?" asked the commander.

"I don't know," said the tribune, "but this has all the mark-
ings of a trap. We are going farther and farther up a road that
gets narrower and narrower. Wouldn't it be wiser to send up
an advance party?"

The commander smiled. "I've learned," he said, "that if a
battle has to be fought, the best tactic is to go forward and fight
it. I don't know what could have happened to the cohort, but
with the entire legion behind us I'm not especially worried."

Quintus was silent. There it was again, he noted, the same
underestimation of the Jews he had seen so often in Rufus.
Well, he thought, perhaps he was wrong and the procurator
and the commander were right.

The vanguard of the legion turned a bend and came upon a
pass in the hills leading to Tur Malka. What Quintus saw there
came close to turning his stomach. Covering the ground like so
much grass and strewn across the rocks were the broken bodies
of 600 Roman soldiers, some without heads and other transfixed by arrows, and all lying in the awkward, even peaceful
postures of death. The arms and armor had been removed
from the bodies, and the vultures had begun to do their grisly
work on the flesh. A horrid smell rose up from the pass and
poisoned the air of the peaceful hills.

"By the gods," exclaimed Quintus. It was all he could think
to say.

The legion commander spat upon the ground in loathing
and anger. "Those dirty bastards. Those whoresons. I swear
by Jupiter I will crucify every one of them."

The commander, with Quintus beside him, rode to the end
of the pass and dismounted. He ordered the legion to halt and
delegated the fortifiers to bury the dead. It was a noble gesture,
Quintus thought, but foolish. It was just possible that the killers
of the cohort were still about. The commander had much the
same thought and sent about 100 men to scour the hills above
the pass to see if they could find anything.

An hour later the 100 men had not returned. There had
been no sound, but they were never seen again. The commander ordered a like number into the hills to look for them,
but these too simply disappeared.

"Is this some sort of magic?" asked the commander, a frightened puzzlement on his Italian peasant's face. Quintus didn't know, but for the first time in a long while he sensed the cold touch of fear.

The commander mounted his horse. "We must leave this pass," he said. "Let us ride on to Tur Malka and see if we can meet this enemy face to face."

Quintus joined the commander in riding forward, but somewhere inside of him he felt the same strange sensation he had felt before, that they were only riding deeper into a trap set by an enemy far more dangerous than the commander knew.

At length the legion came to a valley, and rising above it was the green and inviting visage of Tur Malka, the Hill of the King. The commander stayed but a moment looking at the lush hill, and then he spurred his horse forward up the road leading to the village. With the forces of the legion behind them, the two officers rode at a walk into the village itself. And there, standing insolently in the square, were about 1,000 Jewish warriors.

A volley of arrows greeted the arrival of the two officers. Quintus jumped from his horse to avoid being hit, and both he and the commander fell back to the protection of the troops.

"Form your lines," shouted the commander, but the order was unnecessary. The men of the line had already begun to assemble in the traditional formations, in an automatic movement. The archers in front let loose a flight of arrows, and a few of the figures in the Jewish group could be seen dropping.

The Roman swordsmen unsheathed their weapons and began moving forward with the cry *"Mors Judaeis"*—"Death to the Jews."

"L'herut Yisrael," shouted the rebels as the opposing forces clashed in the square. The war cries in the two languages blended with the loud clanging of swords into a single indistinct sound that was simply the sound of all battle, any battle. Quintus reflected, even in the heat of it, that the sound was most like a wail.

Now the Jews began to give way and retreated to the very end of the little village, leaving their dead behind them to mix their blood with the dead of the legion. With a roar of triumph the Romans moved after the retreating enemy, the entire legion advancing as one man determined to quench the fires of their hatred with blood.

And then, suddenly, from behind them there came new sounds—the war cries of a multitude. Quintus looked back and saw a large Judean force of several thousand men riding and running toward the massed Roman legion. In a flash the tribune realized that it had all been a trick to draw them into the village so they could be cut off and surrounded.

Within moments the rebels were everywhere, screaming their guttural battle cry and giving individual combat to the Roman troops. Quintus Arminius Caro, the philosopher and man of peace, grasped his sword and plunged it into the stomach of a youthful Jew, drawing it out together with the man's entrails. He ran about like a man who had lost all reason, swinging his sword without thinking, hacking with it through bone and sinew, lunging at the throats of men and at their bowels, and ringing in his ears was a scream of battle so horrible that it was no longer human. It was his own voice.

Until, at last, a sudden oblivion enveloped the tribune, and for Quintus Arminius Caro, the battle was over.

In all, fewer than 3,000 men of Legion X Fretensis survived to make the long march to Caesarea and the comparative safety of the Roman capital. It was a march of retreat through hostile territory which claimed yet another 500 Roman lives.

And as for Tur Malka, the Hill of the King that had stood untouched in the Judean sunshine since the beginning of days, it was left after that single day a mound of broken terraces and ravaged fields and crushed vineyards.

19

There was at that time a distinguished visitor to the Minaean community in Bethar, being a man by the name of Antigonos, who was a representative of the Church of the Nazarene in the province of Syria. And he sat eating the afternoon meal in the home of the hegemon of the Judean Minaeans, Marcus, and after having finished the roast, he asked for a glass of milk.

"I beg your indulgence," said Marcus with some embarrassment. "We do not serve milk with meat."

The Nazarene burst out laughing, and then, just as suddenly, he grew serious and asked his Minaean host, "How long will you continue to compromise our Master?"

"What do you mean?" asked Marcus, who had been born Mordechai Ben-Joshua.

"In the words of our Savior," responded Antigonos, " 'he who is not with Me is against Me.' How long will you hesitate between two opinions? If you wish to be Jews, be Jews. But if you truly seek to follow the Christ, then reject these outmoded practices."

"We in Judea do not consider them outmoded, for ourselves," said Marcus. "We do not ask you to keep the Jewish laws. That was the agreement reached by Peter and Paul. We do not ask you to keep the dietary regulations or the rest of it. But for us, the Law of Moses is still binding."

"Is it?" demanded the Nazarene. "Did not our Master come to fulfill the very Law of which you speak?"

"But did not our Master say that 'heaven and earth shall pass away, but not one jot or tittle of this Law shall be changed'?" countered Marcus. "But enough of this, my friend. You know my views, and I know yours. You did not come here from Antioch to discuss the drinking of milk with meat."

"No," Antigonos conceded, "you are quite right. But there is a connection between what I have come to discuss and these small matters. Therefore, I pray you, bear with me a moment."

"Of course," said Marcus. "The words of the great Antigonos will always find favor in this house."

The Nazarene nodded his head in graceful acceptance of the compliment before continuing. "After the Master returned to His Father in heaven, Peter became the apostle to you, the Jews, and Paul brought the Word to us, the Gentiles. Both spoke the truth, though in slightly different ways, and the two separate groups were nurtured by it, each in its own fashion, yet in brotherhood. But increasingly, the faithful outside of Judea have been thinking, as I do, that the Master brought one Word to all, to Jew and Gentile alike, and that that Word is not confined by national boundaries or age-old prejudices. We seek a catholic, a universal church that will take in all men equally and on equal terms. Do you not agree?"

"Of course," said Marcus.

"Yet you Minaeans insist on remaining Jews and, therefore, on separating yourself from the rest of the Christian community."

"Not at all," Marcus protested. "There is not the slightest conflict between the Word the Master brought and the very Law He himself kept."

"No," said Antigonos, "perhaps not yet. But there can be."

"How so?"

"If you support a Jewish revolt."

Marcus did not hide his surprise. So this is what the visit was about. The rumors had made their way as far as Syria.

"Yes, my dear Marcus," said the Nazarene in answer to the unspoken question. "We have heard much that has troubled us. We have heard that the rabbis have named a leader, and we have heard—with some disbelief—that you are personally supporting this leader."

"It is true," said the Minaean, wondering who had been misguided enough to send the letter.

"But do you not see that, no matter what comes of this revolt, it can lead only to adversity for our faith?"

"No," said Marcus, "I do not see that."

"Well, then, consider that if your rebel loses his battle against the Romans, all of the world's Christians will be persecuted for your having supported him. And if he wins, why, it could be even worse. I have heard that this leader blasphemously considers himself the Christ."

Marcus shook his head. "No, he does not think of himself as the Messiah. He is but a leader of the people. And he has assured me that, in the event of his victory, the Minaeans will be treated with tolerance."

"But it is not your fight," argued Antigonos. "You can lose but cannot win."

"It most certainly is our fight. We are Jews."

"Then you are not Christians," said Antigonos, rising.

"It pains me to disagree with the wise Antigonos," said Marcus, trying to hide the anger he felt, "but I hope he will permit me to remind him that the Master was born among the Jews, as well as all of his early followers, including Paul and the fisherman Peter. The Word they brought was based upon our Law. I fail to see, therefore, how the Christians outside of Judea can remain insensitive to a plight of the Jews, who are their brothers in every way."

"Yet they have not accepted the Master," snapped Antigonos.

"Some have. I am one of them."

"And for that you are blessed. But the others are cursed, and justly so. It is for this that they lost their Temple. For this that they have suffered. And for this will they lose their coming war."

Marcus, also called Mordechai Ben-Joshua, looked incredulously at his guest. It seemed inconceivable. Before Paul had come and preached among them, some of the Gentiles in the Hellenistic world, pagans that they were, had nursed a certain enmity against his people. But could it be? Was it possible for a Christian to hate the Jews?

Marcus sat thinking thus when a young member of his congregation burst in among them with great excitement.

"The Tenth Legion has been defeated at Tur Malka," he announced. "There was a great battle. Thousands were slain. The standards of the legion have been captured."

"A disaster," said Rufus when the bedraggled remnant of the X Fretensis marched into Caesarea and its commander appeared before him. "No cost must be spared. We must put this thing down before it spreads."

"It has already spread," the commander informed him. "Every town on our route here was hostile to us, their people gone or locked up in their houses and arrows raining down on us. We were forced to march through the settled places in haste, like thieves, not even halting to bury our dead."

"How many have you lost?"

"Nearly two thousand men of the line and cavalry, and of the *auxilium* a like number. And the standards of the legion were captured, to our everlasting shame."

"A disaster," Rufus repeated. "But we shall retrieve the standards and avenge the slain, I assure you. I have already sent word to the Legion VI Ferrata to march here from Galilee and assemble with your men to march on the region of Judah and end this thing once and for all."

"And the Tribune Quintus Arminius Caro," continued the commander in chronicling his losses. He did not note the sudden look of pain on the face of the procurator's wife, nor the brief flash of pleasure that crossed Rufus' countenance.

The Legion VI Ferrata, the Iron Legion, did not arrive in Caesarea that night, as requested. Nor did it arrive the following day. Only on the day after that did some 3,000 infantrymen and a smaller number of auxiliaries begin filtering, in disorganized groups, into the city. Their report merely confirmed what their appearance had already made clear—that Galilee and the entire north had risen in open rebellion against the imperial power.

When Quintus opened his eyes in the semidarkness, the thought crossed his mind that, for all of his lifelong atheism, he was in Hades, the "underworld kingdom of the dead dead." But then he saw the flickering oil lamp not far from his head, and by its light he perceived that he was in some sort of cave. And then he felt pain, pain radiating from somewhere on his right side through the entire lower part of his body, and he knew that he was alive.

He looked down and saw that he was lying on a mat of cloth, stuffed with straw to make it soft. He tried to raise his head and felt a sudden surge of nausea and weakness overcome him. He moved his right hand and then his left. Well, he noted with some relief, they were still there. Next came the left leg. But when he tried to move his right leg, even a little, a bolt of pain shot through his body so intense that Quintus thought he might faint. Clearly, he decided, that was where he had been wounded. He managed, despite almost unbearable agony, to move the toes of his right foot to convince himself that the leg was still there. And then, having been reassured on that score, he lay back on the mat and tried to figure out what had happened and where he was.

At length he heard some movement elsewhere in the cave and watched a tall man enter. The armor he wore was of Ro-

man design, but the man was bearded, and on the back of the
Roman-style cape that flowed from his broad shoulders was a
six-pointed Star of David, the Jewish symbol.

"I see that you have awakened at last," said the man in a
Greek laden with the heavy sound of a Semitic accent.

"Where am I?" asked Quintus. "And who are you?"

"I am Simon Bar Kochba, Prince of Israel," said the man
with not the slightest trace of pompousness in his voice, "and
you are in my camp after having been captured in the fighting
at Tur Malka. You were found with your right leg half sliced
off. You have lost much blood, but our physicians have dressed
your wound, and the leg will heal, although you may always
have a slight limp."

Quintus looked into the face of the man standing before
him. It was an open face, as open as the answer he had just
given. It was an honest face. It was the kind of face that, not-
withstanding the circumstances, Quintus had learned to like.
"Bar Kochba," he said, speaking the name slowly. "Son of a
Star. A rather good pseudonym. So you are the leader of the
Jewish rebels, the man responsible for the slaughter at Tur
Malka."

"I am," said Simon, sitting down on a stool beside the
wounded man. "And you, Tribune. How are you called?"

"I am Quintus Arminius Caro. Where exactly are we?"

"We are in the hills of Judah not far from where you fell.
This has been our headquarters for some months now. Soon,
though, I think we shall be able to move from these caves."

Quintus smiled weakly. "If Rufus had listened to me, we
would have sent the legion into these hills some time ago."

Simon's face darkened. "You are a friend of Rufus'?"

"Hardly," said Quintus. "Tell me, what do you plan to do
with me?"

"I'm not sure. You see, you are the first prisoner we've ever
had. Most of my men think we should have let you die. Some
would like to see you crucified, as their own loved ones were
crucified. As for my wife, she thinks I should let you go."

"And what about you, rebel, what do you think?"

"I think," said Simon, "that I have not yet made up my
mind. Fear not, you will not be crucified. We are not barbarians like you Romans. When we kill, we do it swiftly."

"Like stoning," Quintus suggested. "I believe that was your traditional mode of execution."

"It was a long time ago," Simon said. "At any rate, you must stay with us until you heal. After that, we shall see. As I said, my wife believes you should be permitted to return to your own people. She has lived among you Romans and says there are decent people among you who would not oppose our cause if they understood it. For myself, I must confess, I am not so sure." Simon rose to go. "Your physician says you must have rest. I will return to speak with you another time."

"Rebel," Quintus shouted after him. "You have been honest with me, and for that I thank you. But now I am honor-bound to tell you that should I get out of here, and if I am ever given the chance, I will kill you."

Simon smiled. "You will not be given the chance."

The flame of rebellion kindled at Tur Malka spread through Judea like fire through dry grass. Town after town declared openly for Bar Kochba, recognizing Akiba's Son of a Star as Prince of Israel. In Judah, the cradle of revolt, Rimmon and Michmash and Ramah and Givon and Mozah and Kiryath Ye'arim and Bethar declared for the rebels. In the south, on the shores of the Dead Sea, the city of En-Gedi expelled a Roman garrison. And the great centers of learning, B'nei B'rak, Lydda and Yavneh, proclaimed their allegiance. And all of Samaria and all of Galilee. And on the seacoast, Jaffa and Ashdod, though there was a sizable non-Jewish minority in them, closed their harbors to Roman ships. And many, many more.

A Roman patrol ventured forth from Caesarea and was never heard from again . . . A cohort of the VI Legion, on its way to aid the garrison at En-Gedi, was intercepted before it had gone halfway and cut to pieces . . . Two of the remaining cohorts of the X Fretensis suffered heavy losses while going through what had been thought to be peaceful towns on a routine patrol of the coastal plain area. . . .

"The entire nation is armed and fighting against us," the commander of the X Legion told Rufus.

"I categorically refuse to send more men from the city without reinforcements," declared the commander of the VI Ferrata after the slaughter of his cohort.

At length, while the procurator debated with himself how best to save the situation from a political point of view, the survivors of two of Rome's strongest legions sat behind the city walls of Caesarea and waited. Each night they locked the gates of the city against an enemy they could not see, led by a man whose very name was not known to them.

It was several days before Quintus was able to sit up, and when he was, some of the Jewish rebels, with undisguised hatred in their eyes, carried him forth from the cave and into the warm Judean sunlight, which the physician had said would be good for him.

There, while Quintus sweated and groaned and protested that the physician was a blasted fool, Simon Bar Kochba came to him often and laughed at him without malice, and sometimes with him, and at other times he would point out people and places of interest from their vantage point high up on a hill. There was a newly built forge where weapons were being manufactured on a large scale, and there was Rabbi Eleazar Ha-Modai teaching the Law to a group of Talmudic students who were now spending most of their time learning to kill, and over there, that young man was drawing maps and charts for use by the Army of Liberation.

"Why are you telling me all of this?" Quintus once asked.

Simon had shrugged. "It can do us no harm for you to know it, and it might do us some good. We shall see."

Yet for all of his apparent friendliness, Simon would not permit the Roman to send word from the camp that he was alive, nor even to use writing materials so that he could compose a letter to his father to send at some later time.

"Remember," he would remind the tribune, "I still haven't made up my mind what to do with you."

And then, one day, when Quintus was just beginning to hobble around painfully with the aid of a crutch, he was visited by a highly attractive young woman.

"Good morning," said the woman in flawless Latin.

"Good morning," said Quintus. He hopped over to his stool and sat down. "Now surely you are the prettiest rebel I have ever seen. And you speak Latin, too. What are you in this strange army, a commander?"

The woman laughed heartily and with a lack of reserve Quintus liked. "I am no commander," she said. "I am merely the wife of Simon. My name is Mariamne." She stretched forth her hand, and Quintus took it, knowing while he did so that most Jewish women would not shake hands with a strange man. But, of course, most Jewish women did not speak Latin.

"I thank you," said Quintus to the woman. "I understand I owe you my life—although the thanks may be a bit premature. Your husband regularly reminds me that he has not yet made up his mind."

"Oh," said Mariamne, "don't worry. Simon will let you go. He'll think about it for a while, but in the end he'll let you go."

Quintus couldn't quite hold back a smile. "You're rather sure of him, aren't you?"

"No," Mariamne shook her head, "not in the way you mean. But I am sure he'll do the right thing. Because, you see, he always has."

"I see," said Quintus. "I envy him your devotion. But if you don't mind my asking you, what makes you think that letting me go will be the right thing? I mean, for all you know, I could be quite a villain."

Mariamne leaned back slightly and made a show of looking at the Roman. "No," she said at last. "I have a feeling about you. It's hard to describe, but I sense that you are not in the same class as, let us say, Tinius Rufus."

"Well I will agree with you on that," said Quintus.

"But I would still like to know who you are."

"You have my name, and you know that I am a tribune of the legion."

"Yes," said Mariamne, "but that still doesn't tell us very much. It doesn't tell us nearly as much, for instance, as your way of speech and mannerisms, which mark you clearly as of patrician birth."

"You are quite perceptive."

"Nor," Mariamne continued, "does it explain what you were doing at the home of Rabbi Akiba last Passover."

Quintus snapped his fingers. "Of course. I knew you looked

familiar. That means Akiba is in on all of this, too. I suppose that was to be expected."

"I didn't say that," protested Mariamne, but the slight flush on her face betrayed her.

"Don't worry," the tribune said. "I am not an informer, and I have a good deal of respect for the old man. That's what I was doing at his home. He asked me to come to see the Seder, I believe you call it, and I was interested, so I went. Now tell me, who are you?"

"I am Simon's wife."

"That doesn't tell me very much, either."

Mariamne smiled. "You are impudent," she said. "But to tell you what I think you want to know, I am a Jew who was raised in Alexandria and who returned here and married Simon. It was in Alexandria that I learned Latin, as well as Greek."

"If you are as intelligent as I think you are," said Quintus, "tell your husband to call off his revolt while there is still time."

"Time for what?"

"Time to gain some concessions from Rome, like a general amnesty for him and his men."

"I'm afraid I don't have that kind of influence over my husband," said Mariamne. "But, if you don't mind my asking, why should you care?"

"Come now," Quintus said. "You Jews are not the only ones who care about human life, you know. War is senseless, stupid. At best, it solves nothing. At worst, it reduces man to the level of the beasts."

"I was right about you," Mariamne said softly. "You think. You are not an animal."

"Well, thank you," said Quintus with a short, sarcastic laugh. "What did you suppose, that all Romans were out to oppress your people, that none of us had sympathy for you—that is, until you began killing us? We are not men without culture, you know, nor poor in philosophers. Please remember, and tell your husband, that we have attained the highest civilization in history. Rufus, let me remind you, is not Rome."

"No?" asked a voice. "Then who is?"

Quintus turned and saw Simon moving toward them. "Who

is Rome, if not Rufus?" Simon asked. "Is it the men who flogged an old storyteller to death? Or is it the men who crucified the father of my friend and brought sorrow to our village, or is it the Emperor Trajan in whose reign all this took place? Or is it Hadrian, who now chooses to trample our most sacred traditions for the sake of his own vanity? I have heard much of this high civilization you mention, but I have seen none of it. All I have seen is Rufus, so to me Rufus is Rome."

"But he isn't," protested the tribune. "You must believe me. Rome is Vergil and Horace and Juvenal. Rome is Augustus, who brought peace to a war-weary world. Rome is Cincinnatus and the Gracchi. Rome is . . . Rome is my father."

"Yes," Quintus nodded his head to both of them. "My father, Senator Caius Arminius, a man of honor whom you could trust in your quest for justice, along with other men like him."

"You see?" said Mariamne to Simon. "I told you he was a patrician."

"My birth has nothing to do with it," Quintus said. "What matters is Rome, from which radiates a light that has illuminated the world."

"The Rome you speak of," said Simon, "must be dead."

20

To Caius Publius Marcellus, Legatus Syriae, from Tinius Rufus, Procurator Judeae:

Hail and greeting.

After lengthy consideration, I write to you with the utmost urgency to request immediate aid from you and the legions of Rome under your command to quell an uprising in Judea that has assumed major proportions and threatens, I fear, the tranquillity of the entire area.

I had hoped to be able to put down this disturbance before it became a full-scale rising, which explains my hesitation in calling upon you. However, due to inexcus-

assistance. Our decision in this matter is still indefinite, for which reason I ask that you treat it as confidential and not discuss it with the men of the city at this time.

Be well,
Simon

From Simon Bar Kosiba
To the men of Samaria and to Ephraim Ben-Abraham, peace.

May the Lord Whom we both worship grant you good fortune, long life and full flocks.

I have heard of the courage you and your people showed in expelling the Roman garrison from your midst. Know that it shall be remembered in the time to come when the Lord grants us the victory and peace we so earnestly desire.

In answer to your question sent to me by the hand of your messenger, it is my wish that your forces now remain where they are, and they will be augmented by a full Judean battalion that I will dispatch under the command of one Judah Ha-Cohen. It is not to be expected that the Romans will quietly accept this first defeat, and it is both proper and wise that homes be defended by the very people who live in them. A tree grows best in its own soil. Thus, I seek, wherever possible, not to dislodge men from their ancestral homes but to have areas threatened by the Romans augmented by additional warriors.

I have sent a similar letter to the men of Galilee, and they, together with you and with the highly trained troops that I am sending, should be able to meet any threat from the north, from the direction of the province of Syria. It is my expectation that it is from there that the next Roman threat will come.

Be strong,
Simon

From Simon Bar Kosiba, Prince of Israel
To the Gentiles of Acco, Apollonia and Ashkelon, peace.
Why do you stand idly by in the struggle of your brothers, the Jews, against the Roman power which op-

presses you as well? Why do you sit in safety behind your walls while others fight the battle that is your battle?

Have the Romans not taxed you unfairly? Have they not taken from you whatever they desired? Have they not treated your sons as servants and your daughters as harlots? Have they not dealt brutally with those of you who dared to protest?

Though you be few in number in our land, know that in the new Judea we shall create there will be no division between Jew and Gentile, between those who believe as we do and those who seek to keep their own traditions, but all who stand with us now will later share in the same freedom.

I call upon you, therefore, to join with us. Arm yourselves and rise. Expel the Romans in your midst. Strive with us to free the land for ourselves and our children.

(It should be noted here that Simon signed the above letter but that it was written in Greek by his wife and at her suggestion.)

From Akiba Ben-Joseph
To Simon Bar Kochba, Prince of Israel, peace.

I congratulate you on the successes which you have wrought with the aid of the Almighty, and I pray for the swift victory of our righteous cause and an early end to the bloodshed on both sides.

I thank you for the invitation to join you at your headquarters, but it is an invitation I feel I must decline. When I named you as the prince, I did so in the belief that you would act with wisdom and justice. You have not thus far disappointed me in this, and I fear that my presence by your side would tend to inhibit you and would, in effect, negate the very decision that I made some months ago and have had no reason to regret.

Even more important I feel that my place is here, in B'nei B'rak, expounding the Law which Moses gave us, while you, in your place, affirm our right to practice that Law.

Nevertheless, know that my prayers are with you at all times and that I stand ready to provide any specific assistance or advice that you may require.

Please convey my warmest regards to Miriam. I look forward to the day when we may all meet in peace. May it be His will.

Akiba

From Cornelia Ruffina to the Lady Julia, wife of Lucius Artorius:

Hail and greeting.

My dear friend Julia, I write you with the utmost sadness and ask you to receive patiently these outpourings of my heart, for there is no one else in whom I can confide now. Quintus, the object of so much thinking and wondering in my previous letters to you, is missing in a military encounter and most certainly dead. O immortal gods, what shall I do now?

Why, O Julia, did I delay as long as I did? What evil spirit kept me from divorcing Rufus, whatever the cost, and joining my life to that of Quintus while there was yet time? Is there a feeling more bitter than that of remorse over what might have been but for our own folly? For myself, I am filled with a remorse so deep that I have given serious thought to ending my life. To what can I look forward now that Quintus is dead?

Rufus came to my bed the other night, and I thought I would be sick. But fortunately he had his usual trouble and departed in haste after some fumbling attempts. I hate him now more than ever. Rufus is actually pleased at Quintus' death and makes no secret of it. However, I might add that my husband's pleasure is being marred by some serious difficulties in this province.

It appears that the populace has rebelled against Rufus' gentle rule and has somehow managed to defeat the two legions stationed here. The legions are now crowded into Caesarea and, according to rumor, refuse to venture from the city.

The entire situation spells a serious setback to Rufus'

ambitions, and I hope you will not consider it treasonable
of me to find in this some small solace.

My regards to your family, Julia. Wish me strength for
the days that lie ahead.

Cornelia

From C. Publius Marcellus, Legatus Syriae, to Tinius
Rufus, Procurator Judeae:

Hail and greeting.

I regret that you waited as long as you did to inform me
of the troubles in your province and of your inability to
cope with them.

To avoid still further delay, I am at once dispatching the
following troops from Syria, with myself at their head: a
portion of the III Gallica, IV Scythica and V Macedonica,
together with cavalry, comprising a total of 12,000 men.
These are to meet with the X Fretensis and the VI Ferrata,
which you will be good enough to dispatch to Acco, and together will move against the rebels from the northwest.

Additionally I have ordered the immediate dispatch of
Legion III Cyrenaica from the province of Arabia, and I
have requested the legatus of Egypt to send up the II
Traiana and the renowned XXII Deitoriana. These three
legions are to join forces in the south and attack the Jewish
outposts in the vicinity of the Dead Sea, following which
they are to move north and meet with our legions for a concerted drive on the troublesome region of Judah.

Combined with your remaining troops, this will give us
a force of more than 35,000 men to launch against the
rebels in both north and south. I thus hope to bring this
disturbing incident to a swift close.

Marcellus

21

One day late in the month of August Simon came to his Roman prisoner and calmly informed him that "We are leaving now."

"Where to?" asked Quintus.

"South," said Bar Kochba.

Quintus paused for a moment, then said, "Do you mind if I ask why?"

Simon shrugged. "Your people are sending three legions against us. I will meet them in the wilderness around the Sea of Salt." He smiled and looked into the distance. "I know the area well. That's where it all began. A year ago at this time I was right where we are going now. Only then I was leading less than fifty men."

"And that's where it will end," said Quintus.

"Perhaps."

"In a way," said the Roman, "I'm almost sorry."

Simon looked at him in a quizzical way.

"Does that surprise you?" asked Quintus.

"Very much. When we first met, you said you would kill me if given the chance."

"And so I would still, my friend," Quintus assured him. "There is no inconsistency there. So long as you are Rome's enemy, you are my enemy."

Simon chuckled and shook his head.

"But duty does not keep me from admiring you," Quintus continued. "And I do. I admit it. There's something about you Jews, the way you willingly take on the whole world, time and again, that excites one's admiration. But that does not change the fact that you must lose. You cannot be permitted to win."

"Why?"

Quintus sighed. "It's a complicated business, my friend. But

you see, ultimately, it's either you or the empire, you or the
rest of the world. You are the unconquered, the people who
will neither submit nor change, and there is a nobility in that;
but at the same time you are the greatest enemy on earth, because you menace the way things are."

Simon smiled at the Roman. "You are a very strange man,"
he said.

Now here is the log of the Legions III Gallica, IV Scythica
and V Macedonica, which entered Judea from the province
of Syria under the command of Legatus C. Publius Marcellus:

Almost immediately after crossing the border at a point
in the northeast, the legions were ambushed in the small
village of Achbarah. The losses were minor, and Marcellus
ordered the village razed. . . .

The troops marched into the hills, in view of the Sea of
Galilee, and hour after hour as they marched, arrows
rained down upon them from the heights, causing small
but persistent losses among men, officers and horses. Several times the *legatus* sent men into the hills to search for
the source of the arrows, but no rebels could be found. And
on one occasion such a patrol itself failed to return. So the
Roman force moved on. . . .

On the first night of march the legions came to the town
of Migdal in Galilee and found it deserted. Marcellus ordered the troops to make camp outside of the town, surrounding it with the traditional barricade and posting sentries at every fifty paces. And yet, during the night, the
sentries were slain and the camp infested with rebels, so
that nearly 1,000 legionaries lost their lives in a violent
pitch-dark battle, and about half the horses of the cavalry
were taken or killed. But with the dawn the rebels had
disappeared, apparently taking their dead with them, and
though Marcellus spent a good part of the day looking for
them, he turned up not a trace. . . .

The legions marched on in the direction of Acco and
encamped that night near the town of Netupah, which was

also deserted. And again that second night, despite all precautions, the camp was invaded and heavy losses incurred. . . .

It should be noted that man to man, in orthodox battle,
the legions feared no enemy on earth. But this was a kind
of fighting the legions were unprepared for. No battle formations were possible against this enemy, who was neither
in front of them nor behind them but seemed to be everywhere and nowhere at once.

And so, by the following day, the morale of the troops
was exceedingly low, and the Syrians who made up the majority of the force had begun to fill the heads of their
comrades with talk of demons and evil spirits who creep
by night and the vengeful God of the Jews. Marcellus was
forced to order 50 of the worst offenders to be severely
flogged as an example to the others, but the talk of an
enemy who was beyond natural laws continued. . . .

As the troops came down from the hills of Galilee toward
the Valley of Rimmon, they ran into the worst ambush yet.
Arrows came down on them, while a contingent of the
rebels—this time in plain view—blocked the road ahead
and loosed their arrows straight into the advancing column.
But when, at length, driven on by desperation, a group of
legionaries stormed the barricade, they found that the
enemy had somehow disappeared. . . .

The legions encamped that night in the Valley of Rimmon. Because it was a valley, they surrounded the camp
with a trench, in addition to the barricade and the sentries.
Yet, in some unknown fashion, the trench was crossed, the
barricade passed through, the sentries slain and the camp
attacked again. And again there was no sign of the enemy
by the morning light.

The troops pressed on, this time by forced march. They
were ambushed at Yadfath and again at Shaav and again at
Beth Hakerem, and they moved now toward Acco with the
desperation of fleeing men.

Thus, on the fourth day, they arrived at the port city and
joined forces with what remained of the X Fretensis and
the VI Ferrata. Together they formed less than 15,000 men,

Marcellus having lost more than a third of the troops he
had set out with earlier that week.

The legions encamped around Acco for two nights, giving the soldiers a chance to refresh themselves, and their
officers an opportunity to map plans. The area from Acco to
Caesarea formed a narrow coastal strip which had remained
loyal to Rome, and there were no attacks during those two
nights. . . .

On the third of September the five decimated legions set
out from Acco and marched southeast, planning to join up
at the Dead Sea with the legions from Egypt and Arabia
and thus form a massive force that would sweep away all
resistance. Passing through the town of Zippori, the Romans found every house a fortress against them. They
fought their way through and marched due south, en-
camping that night in the Valley of Jezreel.

There were no rebel attacks during the night, but the
troops awoke to find themselves surrounded. They fought
half the day and managed, with heavy losses, to break
through the rebel ring. No prisoners were taken, because
none could be found, and the remaining legionaries moved
by forced march to the town of Beth Yannai. There, in the
mountains of Samaria, they found a rebel army of 10,000
armed, rested and confident men blocking their path. . . .

Marcellus was later to write that it was not cowardice which
influenced him to avoid a clash with that army and order a
retreat due west to Caesarea.

We were in no condition to continue a march through
mountainous territory which seemed united in hostility
against us and which afforded the rebels a chance to fight
on their own terms. It seemed more prudent, from a military point of view, to keep our legions as intact as possible
while awaiting the outcome of the southern expedition at
the Dead Sea. There, in the desert plains, the enemy would
be forced to fight on our terms, and far different results
could be expected.

Consequently, it seemed wise to conserve my strength

until such time as the rebel force had been smashed in the south, after which it was my plan to join forces with the three victorious legions at some midpoint in the province and together subjugate the remaining pockets of resistance. . . .

The two legions from Egypt and the third from Arabia met in the arid stretches of the Arava plain and marched through the wilderness without incident to the area of the Dead Sea. And they encamped themselves on a broad plain facing the cliffs where they knew the main rebel force would be located, and they waited. They waited for Marcellus, not knowing he would not come. And they waited for the rebels to come down and offer battle. Or if the rebels did not want to fight, then the Romans waited for their food to run out so that they would be forced to come down. It didn't matter which. The legions had time. This was their kind of war, and they were past masters at waiting.

The soldiers in Legions III Cyrenaica, II Traiana and XXII Deitoriana were quite different from the men Marcellus had led down from Syria. For the most part these were men of Roman blood, the descendants and heirs of those soldiers who had defeated Antony and had conquered this area of the world for Octavius Caesar. And all of them, but most especially the elite XXII Deitoriana, were crack troops who had never been permitted to become weakened by the soft ways of garrison life. These were Rome's shock forces in the East, and she had placed them in the field now to end quickly what had broken out on Tur Malka.

Simon, standing on a cliff above the Roman camp, looked out upon them. Beside him was Quintus. Neither man spoke, but both had the same thought: This was the best Rome had.

The camp Simon saw below was arranged in the form of a rough inverted triangle. The III Cyrenaica formed one leg of it, and the II Traiana formed the other, while at its base in the distance was the XXII Deitoriana. The idea behind this formation was simple and obvious. Whichever side of the triangle might be attacked, the other two would close in and surround the enemy. The Romans were making no secret of their tactics. That was not their way. Strategy had never been the Roman genius. Patience, discipline, perseverance—these were the iron qualities of the legions, so that Rome had lost many battles but had always won wars.

What Simon faced in that desolate plain was the most efficient machine of war the world had ever seen. It was Rome's invincible arm, the mighty instrument with which she had carved out her empire and maintained her suzerainty over most of the known world. This was the legion—immutable, immovable, fighting in ways that had been so well tested in so many places that there was no possibility of improvement. Its discipline was rigid, its traditions sacred, its organization legend.

There were at this time some 6,000 men in each legion, and under the legion commander the tribunes, and under the tribunes centurions, and under the centurions decurions, and under the decurions the men of the line who formed the maniples. The *auxilium,* foreign troops under their own commanders who helped the legion, varied in number and were, in any case, of secondary importance. So, for that matter, was the cavalry, which Rome, in her rockbound conservatism, had left comparatively undeveloped, along with her navy. What mattered to Rome was the legion, because what conquered was the legion.

And if there were no surprises in the way a legion fought, it was because that, too, had been tested and tried over hundreds of years and more battles until it had been developed to a fine science. The maniples, each man in them a master with the deadly short sword, would fight for only ten minutes each and then would fall back to let the next maniple take over. The Romans had deduced some time ago that a man could fight at the peak of his efficiency for only ten minutes.

Similar, much-tested traditions also governed the setting up of a Roman camp, the building of siege machines, the leveling of terrain, the order of march, the deployment of archers and slingers and the exhaustive training of each individual legionary.

The legions had conquered all Italy for Rome; they had destroyed Carthage; they had smashed the Greek phalanx and had fallen heir to the Hellenistic Empire; they had subjugated Britannia and Gaul and Germania and Hispania and Egypt and Arabia and Syria and Judea and nations and peoples whose names have long been forgotten.

Now they stood and waited—Legions III Cyrenaica, II Traiana, XXII Deitoriana—the armed representatives of might with five centuries of glory already behind them, facing an uneven band of Jewish rebels hiding in the cliffs around the Sea of Salt and led by a man who was called Son of a Star. . . .

Simon looked upon them once more, and he knew that this was to be the crucial test of his struggle, that here, in the open combat in which the legions excelled, the legions would have to be defeated if Judea's cause was ever to triumph. The battle could be avoided for a day or a week or even a month, until the rebels' food ran out, but inevitably it would have to be fought, and there was nothing to be gained by putting it off. He turned, leaving Quintus standing on the cliff, and joined Jonathan Bar Ba'ayah in their makeshift headquarters.

Simon had made Jonathan military chief of this sector, and the two of them now sat through the night making and revising their plan of combat. The local troops had been augmented by heavy reinforcements from the hills of Judah, and together they formed an army of about 20,000 men. Of these the bulk was placed under Jonathan's direct command, Simon retaining some 7,000 of them as a reserve force. The odds were about even: the choice of time to attack on the side of the Jews, but the terrain on the side of the Romans; the possibilities of strategy were severely limited. The decisive question now would be which was the stronger army. And beyond that, Simon reflected, the question really would be which side wanted more to win.

With the sunrise the other officers of the rebels came into the headquarters and were told to assemble their men. Then, alone again, the two old friends turned to each other, and Simon put his hand on Jonathan's shoulder. "We may never meet again, my friend," he said, speaking the Hebrew words with a solemn heaviness. "If I have offended you in anger or through ignorance, forgive me, I pray you, and let me be quit of sin."

"I forgive you freely," said Jonathan, "though I can remember no offense. Now if I have offended you in anger or through ignorance, forgive me, I pray you, and let me be quit of sin."

"I forgive you freely, though I can remember no offense," said Simon, and he turned away so that Jonathan would not see the tears in his eyes.

As the sun crept over the wilderness, there was a blast of ram's horns, and Jonathan's forces came down from the heights into the plain below.

The brass trumpets of the legions answered, their metallic harshness echoing across the cliffs.

From above, Simon could watch the drama begin. Jonathan's troops stood in formation, the cavalry in front and the foot soldiers behind. They stood with their backs to the cliffs to avoid being surrounded by the Roman triangle and forcing the legions to launch the actual attack. But at the same time there was no possibility of retreat.

Now the two legs of the triangle were welded into one large block, and the block moved forward slowly, methodically, like an approaching wall of flesh and iron. Behind the wall, unmoving, stood the XXII Deitoriana in formation—to prevent the two advancing legions being cut off from the rear, Simon deduced, and also to be ready to move in for the kill.

Beside the Jewish leader, Quintus stood watching. And he thought, What a waste. What a stupid, dreadful, criminal, incredible waste.

Now the maniple in the front rank of the advancing Roman formation was within bowshot of Jonathan's men. Suddenly Jonathan gave the signal, and with a fury that surprised even Simon, the rebel cavalry rode forward and smashed into the front ranks of the legions, cutting, stabbing, slicing, destroying. But the formation stood firm and did not give way until ordered to do so. Then they withdrew slowly, in order, and Simon could not help but marvel at it.

Now the Roman cavalry rode forward and met the Judean horsemen in the center of the desolate plain, and the screams of dying animals mingled with the shouts and cries of men into a single sound of horror that rose up to heaven. And still Simon waited with his fresh troops. And the XXII Deitoriana waited.

Behind the horsemen came the foot soldiers of both sides, and these now joined battle with sword and lance, lunging at

one another over the bodies of the slain and slipping in their
blood and rising to die or kill again, as the sun stood at midday
watching and the vultures perched on the cliffs in the noonday
heat, waiting for the feast that was to come.

Several times the sides retired, only to return again and again
with renewed fury. Yet neither side budged from its position
until it appeared there would be no end to the battle and the
killing in that valley of death.

And then Simon noticed a stirring in the ranks of the XXII
Deitoriana in the distance. Yes, they were moving forward to
join the fighting. With the waning day the Romans had sensed
what he had sensed—that it would now take only a nudge to
decide the battle one way or the other. Well, Simon decided,
he would let the Romans nudge first.

The fresh troops of the XXII Deitoriana poured forward
into that valley with shouts of victory on their lips. Cavalry
and foot soldiers together, they smashed into the battle-weary
Judean line, causing terrible losses. But the line would not
give and fought back with an unexpected violence.

At length, when all three Roman legions had joined the
battle and Jonathan's outnumbered troops stood fighting for
their lives, Bar Kochba drew his sword from its scabbard, raised
it on high and shouted in a voice that echoed across the empty
cliffs, "L'herut Yisrael."

He spurred his horse forward, and behind him, into the
ranks of the XXII Deitoriana, rode and ran 7,000 fresh Jewish
troops. The men of the XXII Legion managed to hold their
ground in the face of the surprise onslaught, but Jonathan's
forces were now able to push the other two legions back, farther and farther back on the desert plain, leaving the rebel reinforcements to fight the XXII alone.

Bar Kochba led attack after attack into the ranks of the
Deitoriana, fighting without thinking, without anger and without any feeling at all but the single, senseless will to battle that
had seized and transformed all of the men in that carnage-filled
valley, so that they were no longer men at all. There was a great
sound of shouting in that valley, but no man knew that he was
shouting; there was blood everywhere, but no man was aware
that he was bleeding; there was death wherever one's eyes fell,
but no man realized that he was dying. There was no time,

no opportunity for any of that, for that would have been thinking, and there could be no more thinking in that valley.

And then, in the midst of it all, something happened.

It happened suddenly, so suddenly that no one appreciated the significance of it at the time, although—in point of fact—it had not happened for 350 years, not since Hannibal had crossed into Italy itself. A Roman legion broke ranks and fled.

It happened without warning and with no special reason—that is, no reason that had not existed five minutes before or would not exist five minutes later. A soldier in the front line of the XXII Deitoriana just turned around and ran. And his maniple ran with him. And his cohort ran with him. A centurion who tried to stop them was trampled. A tribune who ordered them to return was dragged from his horse and broken into pieces.

A panic as senseless as the battle itself seized the men of the XXII Deitoriana, and they fled in disorder from the field, with the victorious rebels behind them, cutting them down as they fled.

The panic infected the other two legions, and their men, too, began to run, although in more orderly fashion. Jonathan's men, flushed with their triumph, followed them for a time as the Romans made desperately for the border of the Sinai—the province they call Arabia. But there was no way for an army to follow a group of men who had become fleeing individuals and had ceased to be an army, so Jonathan's troops gave up the chase after only a few miles and returned in victory to the Dead Sea plain.

And as for the XXII Deitoriana, the cream of the Roman Army in the East, it was surrounded by Bar Kochba's force and slain to the last man, so that its number and name would be removed from the roster of legions for all time. . . .

As the sun began to disappear from the plain and as the realization settled upon the Jews that they had won, Bar Kochba rose up, and in a voice made unnaturally loud by the heady emotion of triumph, he shouted seven times, as on the Day of Atonement:

"The Lord, He is God. The Lord, He is God. The Lord, He is God. The Lord, He is God. The Lord, He is God. The Lord, He is God. The Lord, He is God."

And the Jews who had survived the battle shouted it after him, seven times, so that the valley and the cliffs above shook with the hoarse sound of their voices.

Then Bar Kochba ordered that the Roman tribune Quintus be brought forward, and in his hearing he proclaimed, "Thus, with Rosh Hashanah, the New Year that approaches with the first day of the next month, begins the first year of our freedom. This year here, next year in Jerusalem!"

And his men answered with a shout, "Next year in Jerusalem!"

Then, turning to the Roman, Bar Kochba said, "In the hearing of all present, I hereby declare that this man, Quintus Arminius Caro, is free. Let him be permitted to pass from the camp in peace and to be given safe conduct to his own people.

"You, Roman," he said, putting his hand on Quintus' shoulder, "tell them that we are coming. Tell them that from here we march on Caesarea and the northern cities of the coast to free the entire land from the oppressor. Tell them to flee in their ships so that we may not soil our hands with more of their blood. Tell them, Roman, that we are masters again in our own land and that by our lives we have sworn that it shall remain thus forever."

The shouts of the rebels drowned out Quintus' voice as he calmly answered, "I will tell them."

Book Three
ALEXANDRIA AND JERUSALEM

Others may more skillfully form breathing life from bronze and create living faces from the marble; they may plead causes better, and sketch the wanderings of the sky with a rod, and explain about the rising of the stars.

But as for you, Roman, remember that these are your arts: to rule peoples with authority, to impose the way of peace, to spare the humble and to conquer the proud.

—VERGIL, *The Aeneid*

If I forget you, O Jerusalem, may my right hand forget her cunning.

—Psalm 137:5

22

WHILE Legatus C. Publius Marcellus declaimed at great length about the insurrection in Judea, the Emperor of Rome, Caesar Publius Aelius Hadrianus, *princeps, pater patriae, dominus ac deus,* gazed absentmindedly out the window of the palace in Alexandria, out at the unnaturally pure blue waters of the bay, to the island of Pharos with its famed lighthouse beyond. And he thought, What a beautiful sight.

The man sitting in the large chair on the elevated platform in the palace's great hall was a strikingly handsome figure. He had the kind of face that was strong without being insensitive, and his eyes were deep-set and penetrating. The Emperor Hadrian wore a beard, being the first Roman head of state in history to do so, and had thus begun to set a new fashion among his countrymen; until Hadrian, the Romans had generally shunned any growth of hair on the face. But the Hellenistic monarchs had worn beards, and Hadrian's adoption of the fashion afforded a strong hint to the personality behind the bearded face. It was, to a large extent, the personality of a Hellenist— cultured, worldly, stoic, humanitarian. But like the toga that the emperor wore in the traditional style with every fold and knot carefully arranged, it was also a Roman personality, for every trait was orderly and in its proper place.

The emperor's penchant for practical good sense was a decidedly Roman characteristic; it had been demonstrated in almost everything the Romans had ever done, from building roads to expanding their empire, and it could be seen even in the titles they gave their rulers.

It is interesting that of all the titles the emperor bore, one conspicuously missing was the title of *rex*—king. It is interesting but by no means accidental.

Early in the Roman era, more than six centuries before Hadrian, the virtuous citizens of the Eternal City had expelled their last king and had set up a republic in his stead. Consequently, to this day, the very idea of a king was odious to free Romans, and the emperors to whom they had surrendered so many of their ancient rights and who now had more power than any king had dreamed of, would never be so unmindful of tradition as to assume the title of *rex*.

But there were several other titles that they did assume, all of them for perfectly logical, practical reasons.

Hadrian was called Caesar to establish his direct link with the first Caesar, Julius, with whom—in point of fact—he had no link at all.

In Rome he was *princeps*—chief and first citizen of the republic. The fiction was maintained, for theoretically Rome was still a republic, still "a thing of the people." Hadrian just happened to be *optimus*—the best—in that republic, chosen to rule because he was the best fitted to rule; and the fact that he had been handpicked by his predecessor was more often used as an argument in favor of this claim than against it. In fairness it must be said that unlike some who had come before him, Hadrian scrupulously upheld the ancient dignity of the Senate and consulted it on all major issues. But it must also be said that the Senate had not been known to disagree with him.

As *pater patriae*—father of the fatherland—Hadrian (who was born in Hispania) was expected to take special interest in the welfare of Italy. And his admirers pointed often to his well-organized public works projects, his carefully administered grants of aid to the poor of Italy, his trust funds for the children of the poor. These were hailed as landmarks of humanitarianism, and they were that, for Hadrian was very much a systematic humanitarian.

On the other hand, there were those who cynically noted that the *pater patriae* had spent eight of the first fifteen years of his reign outside of Italy, traveling to the far reaches of the empire. These detractors called Hadrian an incurable tourist who gained only the most superficial kind of knowledge from his wide travels; but this was neither kind nor fair. The truth was that Hadrian considered himself less a citizen of Rome than a citizen of the Roman world, and he sought, by his occasional presence, to give each part of that world a sense of loyalty to the whole.

In many countries of the empire, principally in the East, the populace had long confused power with divinity and had, since the beginning of things, been accustomed to worshiping their monarchs as gods. When their own powerful kings had been conquered and displaced by the Emperor of Rome, it seemed only natural for these peoples to begin the worship of the mightier god. Thus the emperor also became *dominus ac deus* —lord and god—but this title was used only rarely in Rome itself while the *princeps* yet lived.

No one in the entire world knew more surely that Publius Aelius Hadrianus was not a god than Publius Aelius Hadrianus. Even had he believed in any of the gods—which he most certainly did not—Hadrian was far too much of a civilized and sensible man to believe any such nonsense about himself.

What he did believe in was the Roman-Hellenistic culture, which in his eyes had become one culture. And he believed in that culture's ability to civilize and unify a world that was largely barbaric and divided. This, in fact, was Hadrian's great passion, and it was a passion that he indulged with the utmost consistency. It was of this that he dreamed, for this that he traveled, because of this that he permitted himself to be worshiped as a god and for this that he had caused new Greco-Roman cities to rise in many provinces of his empire.

Hadrian had visited Judea, among other provinces, some six years before. At that time his humanitarian instincts had been aroused by the ravaged condition of that once rich land and by the ruins of its once beautiful capital. He had given voice to his feelings and had promised to permit, in time, the rebuilding of the Judean capital and of the Temple that had been its singular pride. The promise had been a grave error on Hadrian's part, but he could not have been expected to know it.

Of course the emperor had meant what he said, and when he had returned to Rome, he gave the matter much thought and consulted with his advisers on it. The humanitarian Hadrian wanted very much to rebuild Jerusalem. But the Hellenizer

Hadrian had realized, on thinking it over, that rebuilding the ancient Jewish Temple would only perpetuate the anachronistic separation of the Jews from their neighbors. And that, the rationalist Hadrian had decided, would ultimately be harmful both to the empire and to the Jews.

But the emperor had hit on a compromise. He would rebuild the Judean capital, along with a magnificent temple—but the temple would be to Jupiter, the god universally worshiped throughout the empire, instead of to the obscure invisible god whose service was peculiar to the Jews alone. And as a further compromise and to satisfy those fanatics among the Jews who would insist on clinging to the old ways, he would not only guarantee continued freedom of worship in the province but would permit the building of a new Jewish Temple at any other spot they chose.

The compromise had seemed a brilliant stroke to the emperor, and it was a hint of the fatal flaw in the entire imperial structure that not one of his close advisers had thought to warn him against it.

Hadrian listened to a brief snatch of what the Legatus of Syria was saying:

". . . our legions were attacked before there was any real opportunity. . . ."

By the gods, thought Hadrian, would the man never finish? The emperor found few things more dreary than military affairs, and he was faced now with an afternoon of speeches on the Judean revolt by men who had prepared them in advance, carefully and at length. Hadrian was a man of peace, not so much on principle as by nature and because he found war an annoyance that interfered with his programs. Marcellus spoke to him now in Greek, for the Roman Emperor's predilection for that language's musical sound, in preference to the cut-and-dried, businesslike Latin, was well known.

"And if I may be permitted, therefore, I would like to outline a few proposals in regard to the crushing of this insurrection with the most immediate . . ." Marcellus droned on. Hadrian permitted his eyes to wander again toward the window.

To understand what had brought the Emperor of Rome to Alexandria in response to news of a fresh Judean revolt, one had to look upon that small country not with the patriotic fervor of the Judeans, nor with the mystical reverence with which the Jews outside The Land regarded it, but through the eyes of a citizen of the world.

As a revenue-bearing province, Judea was of little value to Rome. It was not worth even a fraction of what had already been spent there for military needs. Judea's priceless value, which made it indispensable to the empire—any empire—was simply that it was where it was. As far as Rome was concerned, it stood directly in the heart of her provincial network in Asia. To the northeast of that network was the empire of the Parthians, Rome's rival in the area. So long as Rome's complex of Asian provinces remained intact, the traditional balance of power remained intact. But a hostile Judea in the middle of that complex would be like a cancer eating away at the Roman East, breaking up the monolithic structure that had stood as a bulwark against the Parthians since the days of Augustus.

A citizen of the world like Hadrian understood this. He knew that the Jewish rebellions of seventeen years before throughout the East had been carefully incited by the Parthians in an effort to ease the military pressure that the Emperor Trajan was exerting against them. And it was because the Jews had swallowed the bait and had inadvertently helped the Parthian cause that their rising was followed by the bloody vengeance Simon and his generation so well remembered.

But Hadrian, ascending the throne after Trajan's death, had tried another policy. As part of a worldwide attempt at conciliation, he withdrew from Parthia and ended the repressions in Judea. Yet now the Jews were rebelling again; Hadrian felt the sting of ingratitude. But whatever he felt, the Judean rebellion would simply have to be crushed as soon as possible. Hadrian had come to Alexandria to listen to the various ideas for crushing it and to decide on one of them. He now turned his attention back to Marcellus and listened as the Legatus of Syria concluded his long talk.

"Consequently, considering the fact that Judea has no navy, it is my suggestion that we blockade its coast and launch a concerted invasion either from the north or perhaps from the sea. Let me repeat my contention that our error thus far has been in not concentrating our forces. In the face of an undivided, major offensive by the legions, this revolt will crumble as swiftly as it began."

He bowed to the man sitting in the large chair on the raised platform. Anyone but a Roman would have called it a throne. Hadrian inclined his head in courteous response. Marcellus withdrew and took his seat in the great hall.

The Legatus of Egypt, Hadrian's host, now stepped forward, bowed to the emperor and announced the Tribune Quintus Arminius Caro.

Quintus limped forward and bowed stiffly. The emperor, noticing the limp, immediately ordered that a chair be brought so that the tribune could sit while delivering his talk. Quintus thanked him and sat down.

"I am especially interested in your views," said Hadrian, "for I understand you have actually met the Judean rebel leader."

"That is true," said Quintus. "I was his prisoner for more than a month."

"And what are your thoughts?" asked the emperor.

Quintus sighed, fidgeted uneasily in his chair and began. "I have listened well to what the Legatus Publius Marcellus has said. For many years I have had the highest opinion of him in every way, as an administrator, as a soldier and as a man. My high opinion of him and my personal regard for him remain as they were. Thus, I pray he will not be offended if I suggest that what he has said here today is nonsense."

There was a loud murmur in the hall. Quintus waited for it to subside.

"Nonsense," he repeated. "Well-meaning nonsense based upon past nonsense and upon reports he has received from others and has accepted at face value and in all honesty. If the emperor will forgive me, I fear our Judean policy has always been based on such nonsense as this, and consequently that policy has never made any sense to anyone, not to the Jews and not to ourselves. I would now like, with your permission, to inject some rational observations into what we have been discussing, on the admittedly immodest premise that it is just possible that I am right and that the traditional Roman policy in Judea is wrong."

Quintus ignored the undisguised laughter in the back of the great hall. Hadrian smiled.

"The Legatus Marcellus, with the best intentions in the world, speaks of the Judean revolt as an ordinary armed rebellion which can be stamped out quickly by the legions. That is nonsense. This is not an ordinary rebellion, and ordinary measures will not crush it. A blockade of the long Judean coastline would be almost impossible to manage, and, in any case, even a successful blockade would be largely ineffective because the Jews would still have access eastward across the Jordan River and via the Dead Sea. And if we simply pour more legions into Judea, I fear they will meet the same fate as their predecessors.

"What we face now in Judea," Quintus continued, "is a rising of an entire people, backed by the most respected persons among this people and led by a man of exceptional ability. This I saw with my own eyes while I was their prisoner. Thus, the information I give you is firsthand, not, as in the case of my friend Marcellus, largely obtained from Tinius Rufus, who is a scoundrel and personally responsible for much of the present situation."

A roar of shock went through the hall, and Rufus rose to his feet. "I demand to answer that on a point of personal honor."

Quintus rose to face him. "You are without honor, sir," he shouted angrily.

"Gentlemen," Hadrian admonished them. "I order you both to sit. Procurator Rufus, you will have an opportunity to speak after the tribune has finished. Tribune, please continue."

"I do not speak of these matters lightly," Quintus went on, the anger still in his voice. "But we have already lost too many men to mince words now, and I will therefore speak my mind whatever the cost. Fire does not burn in the rocks, and rebellions do not erupt without cause. We have always been surprised by the sudden acts of the Jews because we have never understood the Jews. And we have never understood the Jews because men like Rufus—greedy for power and open to every sort of corruption—never gave us proper information about them. And lacking the proper information, Rome has consistently sent men like Rufus to govern the province in her name.

I speak now not to harm Rufus—whatever my opinion of him
—nor for the sake of the Jews, but for the sake of Rome."

Quintus stood up and, leaning on the back of the chair, addressed the emperor in measured tones.

"As a result of this consistent lack of understanding, Rome
has had more trouble more often and at greater cost with Judea
than with any other province in the entire empire. For their
part, the Jews cannot understand what appears to them a total
lack of sensitivity to their needs and rights on the part of Rome.
This rebellion which appears to have broken out so suddenly
has been a long time in preparation. It could have been foreseen six months ago or even more had anyone in authority
taken the trouble to understand what was happening and to
transmit this information to Rome.

"The Jews have suffered a long series of insults, injuries and
injustices; they have been cheated and betrayed by corrupt ad-
ministrators; their land has been taken from them, often without just cause or the right of redress under Roman law; they
have been taxed heavily and have been forced, in addition, to
pay bribes in order to secure rights that are the due of every
imperial subject; their age-old traditions have been trampled
senselessly, without due consideration as to the consequences.
Is it any wonder that they have rebelled? Why are we so surprised? There is nothing sudden about any of this."

Quintus paused and looked about him. No one was laughing
now.

"Now, then," he continued, "as to the facts of our present
situation. The insurrection is led by a man called Simon. The
rabbis have recognized him as Prince of Israel and have given
him the name Bar Kochba—Son of a Star. Thus the man and
his cause have assumed a pseudoreligious character—and this
among a people whose religion and national loyalty are hopelessly entangled into one fanatic faith. Outside of the Jews,
this Bar Kochba has managed to enlist the Samaritans and some
Gentiles in his movement. But the great bulk of his fighting
force are Jews, and he has fired them with the idea of independence from Rome and renewed Judean statehood, an idea
they now hold with the kind of dangerously hysterical fervor
of which only the Jews are capable. That is why Marcellus

never really met the enemy army; the enemy was—and is—
the entire people. And beyond all of this, Bar Kochba has
carefully studied the kind of tactics the legions use, and he appears to be an excellent strategist in his own right—as we have
learned to our sorrow."

Quintus took a deep breath. "I have told you that the Judean rebellion will not be easy to put down. Now let me be
more specific. The insurrection can be crushed, but only if
Rome is willing to pay a price that is beyond anything Marcellus dreams of. The temper of the Jews now is such that they
will fight to the death before surrendering; they have fortified
every city, every town, every village against us; they will make
us pay with blood for every farmhouse we capture, and they
will force a drain of men and treasure from us that will leave
us sorry victors indeed."

The tribune looked directly at Hadrian, into the dark, piercing eyes. "And I submit," he said, "that none of this is necessary."

"What do you mean?" asked the emperor.

"I ask you, before more blood is spilled, to consider what it
is we really seek from Judea and the Jews. Let us, for one moment, forget the past with its mistakes and prejudices and consider the matter rationally. It seems to me that all we really
seek is a loyal and friendly Judea that will permit Roman legions to pass through—perhaps even agree to the garrisoning
of such troops on her soil—in the event of a threat from the
East."

Hadrian nodded his head, ever so slightly.

"While I was his prisoner," Quintus went on, "I came to
know this man Simon. He is a man of passion, but he is not a
fool. I suspect he knows that Rome, if she throws all her re-
sources into the battle, can defeat him and his movement. But
he is counting on the probability that Rome will underestimate the Jews—as she always has. And he is counting further
on the probability that Rome will not sacrifice as terribly much
as would be needed to regain the small province of Judea. I
submit, *Princeps,* that this is a man with whom Rome could
talk. I therefore recommend to you most highly that you send
a representative to him to open such talks. I myself would be

willing to undertake such a mission if you would so desire it."

"You suggest that we negotiate with this rebel, is that it?" Hadrian asked.

"I suggest," said Quintus, "that we seek a perfectly honorable understanding that would benefit both sides. Let us give the Jews what they want—a free hand in Judea and the right to practice their strange customs in any way they like. Let them build their Temple where they choose; it cannot harm Rome. In exchange, let them give us what we need—their loyalty to the empire in peace and war and the right of access across Judea for the legions.

"I submit, sir, that looked at coolly and without prejudice, this is the only thing that we have ever really wanted from Judea. I believe we can get it in one stroke, without further bloodshed, swiftly and without shame."

Quintus had finished. "I thank you," said Hadrian. "Your words will be carefully considered." The tribune bowed and withdrew.

There was only one man left to be heard, and the Legatus of Egypt introduced him. Tinius Rufus, Procurator of Judea, stepped forward and bowed low. He was smiling slightly, having already overcome the fit of temper that had seized him when Quintus had made his charge, and he appeared the soul of mature calm as he began.

"I will not answer insult for insult. The Tribune Quintus Arminius Caro obviously said what he said in all honesty, though I can only wish that he had consulted with some of his more experienced colleagues before speaking. But he is still a young man, and young men must be permitted their passions, regardless of how intemperate . . . or dangerously wrong.

"I do not know under what influence the tribune fell while a prisoner of the rebels, but I fear it seriously beclouded a mind which—if I may say so—was somewhat muddled and a bit too ready to make hasty judgments on scant information even before the revolt. One would think, judging by the certainty with which Quintus offered his advice and by his attack on the worthy Marcellus, that he had made up his mind to speak after being silent during many long and hard years of military service in Judea. Well, the service may have been hard for Quintus, since he came to us after spending most of his life as a student contemplating the philosophies; but as for its length, it was a little more than half a year—even counting the time he spent as a prisoner."

There was a small titter of sympathetic laughter. Rufus caught its significance at once and continued in the same condescending vein.

"Quintus suggests that the Jews do not understand us. Well, I must agree with him in this, but I fear my reasons in explanation of this phenomenon are not quite the same. It is not that we procurators have been scoundrels, Quintus, though I'm sure that appeals to you as an easy answer. It's rather that the Jews do not and have never understood anyone but themselves, and the reason for this is that they just don't want to. They have sought understanding for their ways, but they have given none to others. Let someone try to interfere with their religion, and they will scream all the way to Rome about it. But let the emperor seek to erect a temple to Jupiter so that all who seek to worship our gods can do so freely, and they rebel. They whine about taxation as if they were the only people in the empire to be taxed; they mourn the destruction of their capital, but they conveniently forget the costly war they started which led up to that destruction; they whimper that they are being oppressed, but they conveniently forget their own treacherous acts that made repressive measures necessary.

"Indeed, if I have erred at all, it has been in seeking too energetically to understand the Jews, in trying too hard, in being too lenient with them when harsh measures were called for; and so, some of the blame for the current situation must, in truth, fall upon me. To this charge of trying too hard for peace and conciliatory ways, Caesar, I would have to plead guilty."

Rufus paused to give the emperor an opportunity to say something. But Hadrian said nothing, so the procurator continued.

"Quintus suggests that we negotiate with the rebels, that we—in effect—sue for peace. He says he wishes to avoid further bloodshed, and that is a noble thought. If I, too, were willing to make a hasty judgment based on my sensitivities

alone and ignoring the empire, I might agree with him. But"
—and here Rufus' look of good-natured calm disappeared and
was replaced by a grim mask—"I am not. I am not willing to
sacrifice the welfare of the entire empire for a handful of
Jewish fanatics. And even if I were willing to sacrifice the empire's welfare, I would not be willing to sacrifice its honor.

"What the tribune suggests, Caesar, is surrender. And that
would not only be ignoble; it would be stupid. To give the
Jews what they want now would be like placing a bounty on
rebellion everywhere. How long before other provinces rebelled to gain their own selfish ends? Perhaps Syria would like
something special, or Egypt, or Gaul, or Britannia? We would
be telling them all, 'Rebel, and you can have anything you
may desire; kill our soldiers, and we will simply walk away.'
The tribune speaks of the cost of putting the Judean insurrection down. Has he any concept, or has he even considered, the
potential cost of not putting it down? I suspect not.

"I will not go on further with this because I think the point
is obvious, and to belabor it further would, if I may borrow a
word from Quintus, be nonsense indeed. Suffice it to say that
I heartily support the recommendations of the eminent Legatus Caius Publius Marcellus—a man of experience, whose
record is filled with honor and service to the empire. I commend his proposals to the emperor as our next course of action."

Rufus' speech ended the session, and shortly thereafter the
emperor retired to his private chambers in the palace. Some of
the officials who had gathered in the great hall lingered in
small groups for a time, discussing the day's events. But there
was really nothing further to be said. The final decision—Hadrian's decision—would be forthcoming in a few days.

Rufus walked past Quintus on his way out. He did not speak
to him, nor even look at him. He passed the tribune without
slackening his pace, and Quintus knew that despite the casual
air the procurator had affected in his speech, he would never
forget what had been said that day. Rufus had opposed him
and what he stood for from the first, but Quintus knew that
now, and from now on, he would be a bitter, unrelenting enemy. . . .

*   *   *

Cornelia stood on the balcony of her suite in the Alexandria palace and reflected how much bigger and more varied and alive was the sprawling, ancient city before her than the provincial city of Caesarea. And she wondered, also, what had gone wrong.

Quintus had been dead and had come to life again. It was almost a miracle, but the joy and wonder of the miracle had been absorbed, accepted and had passed, leaving Cornelia without anything but a certain emptiness she could neither understand nor cope with. What had changed? When Quintus had been dead, she had been sure, so terribly sure of her feelings for him. If only Quintus were alive, she had told herself again and again and again. And then her impossible wish had come true, and Quintus had arrived limping into her chamber one glorious day—wounded, a little older, but much the same as ever. She had thought she would die from the shock of her happiness. But she hadn't. She lived, and she had to go on living still. What now?

There was a soft knock at the door. That would be Quintus, Cornelia reflected. She left the balcony and moved toward the door.

23

From the chronicle of Mariamne:

I am with child.

I am with child, and Simon does not yet know. Should I be offended that he has not noted it? I am not, and I have not yet told him. Perhaps it is selfishness, for in this way, for a little while, the child is mine alone. But I do not think it is selfishness. Simon has had so much to absorb, so much to do, so quickly, that I think I will wait a little before I tell him. He will be pleased, I know. He wants a son, as all men do.

There has been a great deal for us all to absorb. And for me perhaps more even than for the others. Have I absorbed it? Do I understand what has happened to us, to me? I do not know, and I find that I do not care. I am Simon's wife, and I am more than content.

Simon has led our people to do the impossible. The land is free, free as no other land in the world today is free. Perhaps it will not last. Perhaps it is madness, as I once thought, and as I fear still when I think of it. But it does not matter. Everyone around me is happy, and I am happy. I am Simon's wife, his lady, his concubine, his property, and I have never been happier. This, it appears, is my freedom.

It is only when I think of the child that I sometimes begin to be afraid. He or she will come into the world helpless and innocent, yet bearing the burden and the glory of what we have done. I do not want to think thus, for it frightens me. It will be Simon's child, too, and so I am not afraid.

I will tell him soon. I want him to be especially pleased, and so I will wait for a time when he is not unduly occupied. I pray I can give him a son.

Winter came to Judea. The High Holy Days had passed, and the Festival of Booths, and the first rains began to fall, cold rains that seemed to penetrate flesh as well as soil and that filled the dry riverbeds and washed away the blood of the previous summer.

Some there were who had not survived to see this season, men like Samuel of Ashkelon and Amram Ben-David, who had fallen in the fighting. But for those who remained, it was a winter of cautious hope, hope that something was beginning which would last through many winters.

And it was a time of problems, but problems of a new and different kind. Throughout Judea men were awakening to the realization that they were their own masters for the first time in a hundred years, and the farmer who watched the rain fall upon the parched land began to realize, slowly, that the land was his. For the past century most of the arable land in the country had gradually become the property of Rome. Now that land had to be parceled out to the farmers who had previously worked it as tenants. For the most part these parcels were given under contract, and this involved a host of minute details and judgments.

And there were local officials to be appointed, and courts of law to be organized, and disputes to be settled, and boundaries to be fixed, and taxes to be set and collected, and coins to be minted.

For the Jews the setting up of all this administrative machinery in the first months after the victory at the Dead Sea was made a great deal easier by the fact that the stored-up decisions of the rabbis provided a full body of law ready for immediate application. And the grand council—or Sanhedrin, as it was once again beginning to be called—was there to interpret the laws. But still it was one thing to run a country in theory, as the rabbis of the grand council had done, and quite another to run it in fact. And as Bar Kochba soon learned, it was one thing to overthrow a government and quite another to replace it.

No one seemed to know just what the permanent government of Judea would be, so it was run on a day-to-day basis by improvisation, by discussion and by trial and error; and anyone who had a mind to do so could and did help in running the country. That was the major problem of those early months—and perhaps the major glory as well.

Faced with military as well as civil needs, Bar Kochba organized Judea into four major districts with a military and a civil administration for each. His friend Jonathan Bar Ba'ayah was separated from him now. He was military commander of the Dead Sea district, with headquarters at En-Gedi, while Masabala Bar Simon was civil administrator.

In the district of Judah, Nathan Bar Deroma was military commander, and civil affairs were handled by a group of men. In Samaria, both the military commander and administrator were Samaritans—an appointment which had angered some but which Bar Kochba had insisted on, saying these were the men best qualified. And in the fertile region of Galilee, which bordered on the Roman province of Syria, Judah Ha-Cohen was military commander, while civil affairs were in the hands of a representative committee.

As for Bar Kochba, he seemed to be everywhere at once, turning up suddenly at this village or that city. Wherever he was, there was the capital. And wherever he went, large crowds turned out to greet him, waving bundles of palm leaves and shouting *"Hosha' Na"* and holding their children above their heads so that they, too, might see the man who had led Israel to freedom.

Many were the legends that grew up about the orphan from Kosiba. One had it that he had been born far away and had come to Jerusalem riding a lion; another held that he was a direct descendant of King David and that a star had heralded his birth. His heroic deeds were magnified as only folklore can magnify them, and it was said that when the Romans had fired catapult stones at his men, Bar Kochba had bounced them back off his knees onto the enemy.

Simon laughed at the stories, and whenever he spoke to the throngs that all but worshiped him, he would remind them that the victory was theirs, not his. He would make it a point to speak to them only in Hebrew, and he urged all his people to shun the more common Aramaic in favor of the High Tongue that was theirs and theirs alone. In line with this, Bar Kochba ordered that ancient place-names, some of them all but forgotten, be revived, so that even Caesarea became Migdal Sharshan, after the tiny fishing village that had once stood there.

New coins were struck, most of them bronze and of relatively little value so that they would get into circulation quickly. On one side the coins had a palm tree and Simon's name, along with his title—*Nasi Yisrael*—Prince, or Leader, of Israel. On the other side was a vine leaf and the legend, "The Year One of the Liberation of Israel."

Now, if the writing on the coins seemed too expansive, too premature and optimistic, it was in keeping with the heady spirit of the time, a spirit that flowed from the leader himself as he rode proudly on his horse from village to town proclaiming the new era and a spirit that soon infected the entire land.

It infected the wandering minstrels who sang of Bar Kochba's deeds; it infected the simple people, so that they believed all; it infected the youth, so that they swelled Bar Kochba's army to more than 100,000 men, and it infected the old rebels themselves, who now believed that the fighting might truly one day be over. With this spirit upon the Jews there seemed no problem that could not be solved, no end and no limit to what a free people could do.

In Jerusalem, on the first day of the eight-day observance of Hanukkah that marked the freeing of the land and the rededication of the Temple by the Maccabees in an earlier age, Bar Kochba's troops tore up the foundations that the Romans had laid for their new city. And on an altar set up on the Temple grounds, near the charred Western Wall, Rabbi Eleazar Ha-Modai—a Cohen from Modin as the Maccabees had been —offered the first priestly sacrifice to the Lord in more than sixty years.

There, beneath the open sky, a peace offering of thanksgiving was made by Rabbi Eleazar, as the Law provides, while the leading men of Judea stood by and watched the historic event, a prelude to the rebuilding of the Temple and the reinstitution of the ancient service. The offering was a bullock without blemish, and it was slaughtered there, and the priest sprinkled its blood upon the altar and burned its fat. And the meat of the bullock was roasted on the altar and portioned out in small pieces to the spectators and to the priestly caste of Cohanim as a holy feast.

Mariamne watched the sacrificial ceremony from a distance, and she grew physically ill. The slaughter of the animal, the blood and the gore—was this primitive service part of the beautiful religion of love her father had taught her? She could not quite bring herself to believe it, and when she later told Simon so, even suggested that the Jews had outgrown these ancient rites, he snapped at her with a vehemence she felt was unjustified. . . .

So it went in those early months, and as the Minaean community prepared to usher in the New Year 133, Bar Kochba continued training new troops while acting as supreme commander of the entire country. But in actuality the country was being run by many men in many places, and although all were ultimately responsible to him, there was at that time nothing yet fixed or very systematic about any of it. The Sanhedrin— whose own powers and duties had not been clearly stated— felt this a rather impermanent state of affairs. And so it summoned Simon to its meeting one day and offered to anoint him king over Israel.

"I do not wish to be a king," said Simon.

There was a silence in the large meeting chamber, until at last Rabbi Eleazar Ben-Azariah broke it to ask, "Well, what do you propose, then, now that the fighting is over?"

"The fighting is not over," said Simon. "It has only begun. The time is not yet."

"It is for ourselves to choose the time," suggested Rabbi Hanania Ben-Teradyon. "Peace, like freedom, does not come of itself. A nation must be ready for peace, for the ways of peace, and the time to begin is now."

"Yes," said Rabbi Tarphon. "We must think of the rebuilding. We must think of the Temple. We must make plans."

Bar Kochba sighed. "For a long time, my masters, you required men like me to be patient. I do not question the rightness of this, for I recognize that in most matters your wisdom is far superior to my own. But I ask you now, humbly, to be patient with me for a little. For the time being, until the Roman threat is truly over, let us leave things as they are. And bear with me. And trust me."

Later, when Rabbi Akiba Ben-Joseph was walking with Another, the atheist turned to him and said, "Your rebel didn't really answer the rabbis, you know. He wouldn't accept the title of king, but he gave no inkling as to what his plans are."

"You must give him time," Akiba said. "We are all new to this business of independence. And, after all, it would not be wise to act hastily."

Aher smiled and shook his head. "You don't understand, Akiba, or else you don't want to. Your rebel cannot stop. He will never be able to stop fighting."

In the land of Egypt, in the city of Alexandria, the Emperor of Rome summoned his officers and counselors and addressed them in these words:

"Gentlemen. For the past several days I have been considering the various recommendations for coping with the insurrection in Judea. This has been a painful task for me, for I dislike the ways of war. But it has been necessary, and I have made the necessary decision.

"I wish to thank those of you who submitted your suggestions to me. I regard them all as having been made without thought of personal gain or malice. I specifically wish to thank the Tribune Quintus Arminius Caro for reporting his observations, for his well-thought-out proposals and for the very heat with which he delivered them. Indeed, the passion for peace shown by the tribune—and by his distinguished father in Rome—is not unlike my own feeling in the matter."

Hadrian paused for a moment, and in that moment Quintus knew for certain that he had lost.

"However," the emperor continued, "I see only too well the potential pitfalls in trying to make peace with a people who hate everything that all other peoples hold sacred, who have struck ruthlessly against the authority of Rome and have butchered our soldiers without mercy. Consequently I have decided to adopt the recommendations of the Legatus Caius Publius Marcellus, as supported by the Procurator Tinius Rufus, and to impose a sea blockade on Judea. Further, I have sent word to Commander Lucius Urbanicus to proceed here from Germania with his five legions and German cavalry. . . ."

24

As Quintus had foreseen, the Roman sea blockade brought little hardship to Judea. The produce needed by the people could be grown on their own farms; their own flocks provided them with meat, and there was even commerce of a sort—with the East and to an extent also with the West, since Rome's sea power had never been vast and ships whose home port was Alexandria regularly ran the blockade.

There was, in fact, little change in Judea as the winter began giving way to spring. The army continued to grow, mostly now with volunteers from other lands, Jews who had never seen Judea before but had elected to return to it and fight for it; farmers continued to plant; the academies of learning, though deprived of many of their students, continued to function; the Sanhedrin continued to meet; Bar Kochba continued moving from place to place, bringing advice and encouragement.

But there were two events that are worthy of note: the prince quietly ordered the extensive fortification of the mountain city of Bethar; and Mariamne Bath-Menashe Ben-David began to grow big with child. . . .

The two of them lay one night in a bed in the palace in Caesarea—or Migdal Sharshan—the very bed, as it happened, in which a tribune of the legion and the wife of the hated Roman procurator had often made love. Bar Kochba had come to the coastal city to meet with some sea captains who had run the blockade, and Mariamne, her womb visibly filling, had accompanied him.

They lay now with their arms about each other and their faces nearly touching, but not yet asleep. "Simon," Mariamne whispered. "Did you feel that? Can you feel the child?"

Simon looked up sleepily and put his hand on Mariamne's belly. He held it there for a few moments, then said, "No, I can't feel him."

"He's stopped now," said Mariamne. "Or she has."

Simon rolled over to go to sleep.

"You want it very much to be a he, don't you?" asked Mariamne. "I wonder why men always want sons. Do you suppose my father would have been happier if I had been a boy?"

Simon lay back and smiled. "Maybe. But I wouldn't have been. Although then, I suppose, I might have gotten some sleep."

Mariamne laughed softly, though they were the only ones spending the night in the huge palace. "Please," she cajoled. "I feel like talking a little."

"Well," said Simon, "I suppose with a boy a man feels he has a chance to go on. He may love a girl as much, or even more, but a son gives him the hope that, in a way, he won't die."

"Then I hope it's a boy, too," said Mariamne, "because I don't want you to die." She was silent for a time. "Simon, have you considered that if there is a boy inside of me, he will not only be your son but will have a legitimate claim to the throne of David?"

"I have thought about it. But I'm surprised that you have. Haven't you told me often enough that the whole idea of royalty is foolish?"

"And so it is," she said, smiling, "but not when my son is concerned."

Simon chuckled. "Of course . . . And I have thought about it, Mariamne, more than you know, but . . ." He sat up and turned to her. "In all seriousness, Mariamne, if I am a good man and a wise leader, is that any surety that my son will not be a fool, even if he is your son as well?"

"No," said Mariamne. "Not really."

"And if he is a wise ruler, how about his son, and his, and his? Sooner or later you will come up with a tyrant."

She leaned over and kissed him playfully on the cheek. "You've become quite a rationalist under my tutelage. And I suppose that is the fatal flaw in all monarchies, the primitive idea that a good man's son will be equally good."

"Well, there you are," said Simon.

"Then my son will not be a king?"

"I don't know," he said soberly. "I swear to you, I don't know anymore what to do. The other day when Akiba came to me, he asked me the same kind of thing, and I didn't know what to tell him, either. And really, it's difficult to tell Akiba anything now, he's such a saintly, impractical man. He acts as if the Romans had ceased to exist, and he wants me to act that way, too. He wants me to begin the rebuilding of Jerusalem and the Temple right away, but how can I? Can I release soldiers now to start building? And what would be the point of it? It will take years to rebuild Jerusalem, and I don't believe we will have years before the next Roman attack. We would be putting ourselves into the impossible position of having to defend an unfinished Holy City. By my life, it all seems so obvious to me. Am I insane, or can't anyone else see that the fighting is not ended?"

"I think they can see it," said Mariamne gently, "but I think that, well . . . I think they want you to begin building something permanent . . . something more than just defenses against attack, no matter how inevitable that attack may be."

"Are you going to start on me, too?"

Mariamne kissed him again. "No. I'm convinced that my husband is the wisest man in all Judea."

No one knew the exact age of the city of Bethar, but it was thought to be nearly as old as Jerusalem. It was also very near to Jerusalem, perhaps an hour's ride by fast horse, and thus was overshadowed—one reason few people outside of Judea had ever heard of the place. Another reason was that Bethar was situated literally on the top of a mountain, so that the road up was rocky and tortuous and slow. And why would a traveler want to lodge in Bethar when the high road led straight to Jerusalem?

Yet for all of this, the city had thrived from ancient times, serving as a commercial center for the fertile farms in the hills around it. In the old days the farmers of Tur Malka, for instance, had often brought their produce to Bethar instead of to Jerusalem; they could sometimes get a better price for it there than in the capital, which was flooded with goods from all over the country. And of course, once in Bethar, the farmers would buy their needs there, even if they had to pay a bit more, rather than make the journey down from the mountain and around the rolling hills of Judah to Jerusalem.

Later, with the destruction of the Holy City, Bethar had prospered greatly, growing to nearly twice its previous size. But when one mentioned this fact, the pious residents of the city would mutter a quick prayer and, raising their eyes to heaven, loudly state that far rather would they be poor beggars than to have benefited from so great a calamity.

The people of Bethar were being honest when they grieved Jerusalem's fall; but so long as the capital had stood, Bethar had done everything possible to compete with Jerusalem. In those days it had been an uneven contest, for Bethar could not hope to compete with Jerusalem's place in the hearts and minds of the Jews. The Temple had been in Jerusalem, and the royal palaces, and the seat of wisdom and learning. Jerusalem was a cosmopolitan city, while Bethar remained essentially a large town. And Jerusalem was much more accessible; every ruler since David had improved the roads leading to the capital.

But Bethar had one thing that Jerusalem had always lacked

—a constant and independent water supply. Jerusalem, ideally situated as it was, with a superb climate (which is why there had been a city there even before Abraham's time), was dependent for its water upon the collected winter rains or upon man-made aqueducts which piped in water from afar and could be cut off by a besieging army. Bethar, on the other hand, received a steady flow of fresh water directly from several underground brooks. The source of the subterranean brooks was the large Tzalmon Stream which ran through the mountains some distance away, a fact not widely known, especially to outsiders.

Also, the very drawbacks that had hobbled Bethar as a commercial center made it especially attractive to a military man. The mountain on which Bethar was perched was steep, and it sloped in such a way that the city could be approached from only one side; the road leading up that side had to wend its way around terrain that grew increasingly more uneven as one neared the city, and at one point the road moved directly beneath the city. No hostile army could pass that point without risking a lethal shower from above; and even if an attacking army did make it up the road, there was no flat area before the city where it could encamp and lay siege.

To Bar Kochba, the place seemed as impregnable as any place could be, and so he quietly gave orders to add a second wall to its defenses and to prepare Bethar for eventual use as his headquarters and capital. . . .

Bar Kochba was lodging in the coastal city of Jaffa when word came to him through an emissary sent by certain persons in Alexandria that a force of some 30,000 crack Roman troops would invade Judea within the next few months. And on the same day the prince received another visit from Rabbi Akiba Ben-Joseph.

"Peace be with you, Rabbi Akiba," said Simon in welcome.

"And with you, Bar Kochba, peace," answered the rabbi.

The two men sat down at a table in the modest house where the prince was staying. A servant brought wine, and they broke bread and refreshed themselves before speaking, as convention required.

Akiba drank his cup of wine and courteously declined when Simon offered to refill it. "How is Miriam?" he asked.

"In good health, blessed be the Name. She expects to be delivered of our child in late spring or early summer."

Akiba nodded his head. "Good. Good," he said. "I pray all will go well."

"May it be His will."

The two men sat quietly for several moments, fingering their cups. "I suppose," said Simon, "that you have some message for me from the Sanhedrin."

"No," said the rabbi. "Not this time. I have come of my own accord. I wanted to speak to you privately."

"Say on," said Bar Kochba.

Akiba examined the cup again, then put it down and moved it away from him. "About a year ago a young man came to me in B'nei B'rak and asked, 'What does it mean to be a Jew?' I answered him as best I could, and that answer eventually forced upon me certain actions that I had not before contemplated. The Lord favored our cause, and so today, a year later, I return to the young man and ask him a question of my own: What did we fight for?"

Simon looked away from the rabbi. "You know very well what we fought for," he said. "It was to free the land."

"Wasn't there something else?"

"I suppose," said Simon, standing up, "that you've come to talk to me about Jerusalem again."

"You suppose correctly," said Akiba.

"I just spoke to you about it two weeks ago, and I thought you understood that the matter would have to be delayed for some little time."

"Two weeks ago," said Akiba calmly, "you told me the situation had not solidified sufficiently for you to consider rebuilding the capital. I was not really satisfied with the answer then either, but I thought, He is the leader I named. I must leave it to him."

"And now?"

"Now I have learned that you are planning to make your capital in Bethar, that you are building and fortifying another city while Jerusalem lies in ruins."

Simon sighed in exasperation. "Rabbi," he said, "in the Law you are supreme, but in military matters I fear you do not quite understand."

"This is not purely a military matter," said Akiba evenly.

"Right now it is," answered Simon, his voice rising. "Look, I've just today learned that the Romans are preparing to send a massive force against us. They will probably be here before the summer. And you ask me to proceed as if there were no threat at all."

"Perhaps if you proceeded as if there were no threat, the threat would disappear."

"Please, Rabbi," said Simon, turning to the window, "you sound absurd."

Akiba rose and stood beside the prince, putting his hand on Bar Kochba's shoulder. "Simon, my son, I may sound absurd to you, and my demands may appear unreasonable, but try to understand that they are not. In military affairs and in running the country as you saw fit, I and the other members of the Sanhedrin have deferred to you time and again. But try to understand that this request to get on with the rebuilding of Jerusalem and to make it your capital at once is neither absurd nor unreasonable. It is not only your duty; it is practical in the highest sense. A people fights with weapons, but it also fights with its soul. You made that very point when you spoke to me shortly before I named you Bar Kochba. What has changed?"

"Nothing has changed," said Simon. "But it hasn't been a year since you named me, and it hasn't been six months since we drove the Romans out of the land, and they are even now preparing to attack us again. Why won't you understand any of this? Right now I need Bethar, and I don't need Jerusalem."

Akiba looked straight into Simon's eyes. "I understand. I understand that right now you don't need Jerusalem the city, that Bethar is more strategic. But I understand also that you desperately need Jerusalem the Idea, and that, my dear Simon, is something you don't understand at all."

Simon was about to speak, but Akiba lifted his hand slightly to stop him and continued. "One moment. You seem to think that I and the other rabbis are a group of well-meaning but other-worldly fools completely out of touch with practical necessities. But you are wrong, and it is a serious error. If you will study past events, you will find that the right course is most often the practical course as well. The young man I spoke to not long ago understood that. He spoke of the Idea and the people as one; he spoke of building even while we might be forced to destroy; he spoke of a people living their faith on a day-to-day basis and defending it if necessary. But now, Simon, you've turned the whole thing upside down, and the most frightening thing about it is that you don't seem to see what you have done. All that you consider are the needs of war and defense. But what are you defending?"

"I am trying to defend the land," said Simon angrily. "And with it I'm trying to defend its people and the faith they hold and the opportunity they will have to rebuild."

"When?" demanded Akiba.

"When conditions are more favorable."

"And when do you suppose that will be?"

"When we are secure."

"And what is security?"

Simon turned away. "I will not play your Talmudic games."

"Remember," said Akiba, "that your victory was from God. And if you expect God to keep helping you, you must prove yourself worthy. That is the only real security."

Simon turned to him in a fury. "Leave me alone with that kind of talk. Our freedom was not handed to us. We fought for it, and we bled for it. All I ask of God now is that He not help the Romans. Ourselves, we can take care of ourselves."

Akiba turned white. "I'm sorry," said the prince hastily. "I didn't mean it like that. I lost my temper. Forgive me."

"Beware," said Akiba, softly but in a voice shaking with emotion. "Beware." The rabbi walked across the room, preparing to leave. At the door he turned to the prince again and said, "Your own deeds have brought you very near. Beware now, lest your deeds take you very far away."

25

From Simon Bar Kosiba

To Iakimos, the brother, peace.

Information has come to us regarding plans of the Romans to invade our land once again in the near future, possibly from the sea. Know that I have full faith in the loyalty of the men of Acco, as well as the loyalty of our other Gentile neighbors. This loyalty has been well demonstrated in the fight for our freedom.

I now call upon you to do three things without delay to safeguard that freedom.

First, intensify your efforts to learn what you can from the crews of ships that pass through the Roman blockade and dock at Acco. Transmit such information swiftly and directly to me, regardless of how unimportant it may seem, for thus we may hope to gain some foreknowledge of the exact Roman plans.

Second, I am sending you some officers to survey the situation in Acco and the surrounding area regarding defenses, supplies and so forth. Prepare for them a place, and aid them in any way that you can.

Third, place the men of Acco on alert that they may soon have to fight again to defend their homes and rights. Should this, in fact, become necessary, you may tell them in my name that they will have ample help from their brothers, the Jews.

Be strong,
Simon

From Cornelia Ruffina to the Lady Julia, wife of Lucius Artorius:

Hail and greeting.

Thank you, dear Julia, for the warm letter in which you

expressed your pleasure at Quintus' safe return. Our prayers have been answered indeed, but—life is strange.

Do the gods make sport with us, Julia? Sometimes I wonder if they do not toy with us halfheartedly, the way we used to play with dolls when we were children together. For I find now that Quintus is with me again that I am no more capable of action than I had been before. Indeed, I am more confused than ever as to what course to take, and that despite the deep feelings I was so certain of—when was it?

Am I acting like a foolish little girl? Perhaps, but I am truly confused. If Quintus would beat me, force me to his will, it would be easier. But he does not. He is kind and considerate with me, more now even than before. He has asked me directly to divorce Rufus and marry him. I think I love him, Julia, yet I hesitate. Why? Somehow I just don't seem capable of taking the step. I have, in my thinking, even considered a reconciliation with Rufus. After all, he is my husband, and perhaps if I gave him a chance . . . but I don't know.

Despite the unfortunate circumstances that brought us here, I find Alexandria a delightful change from the somberness of Judea. Here there is life night and day, and noise, and activity. People seem more relaxed and don't take things so seriously. And, of course, the city is crowded with foreigners now, including many soldiers from far-off lands, and the rumor is that we shall soon launch an assault on Judea. Which means, alas, that I shall be back in Caesarea before long. The shops here are many and full of a large variety of excellent goods. The linen here is especially fine, and I am having several dresses made. Yet I begin to miss Rome.

My love to Lucius and the children.

Cornelia

From Jonathan Bar Ba'ayah
To Simon, Prince of Israel, peace.

I am sending you, before the new moon, the two battalions of men that you requested to aid in the defense of the coastal area. They will proceed from here to Migdal Sharshan, where they will place themselves under your direct command.

Would God that I could join with you as well. It is a bitter price for our success that we must be separated like this, especially as you are to become a father. May the Almighty grant Mariamne a good and speedy delivery, and may the child be blessed with health.

All here is well, and the troops I shall be left with should be more than sufficient for our defense needs. We find ourselves in the fortunate position here of being surrounded by friends on all sides, with even the Nabataeans to the East showing open sympathy to our cause. Ruth, though she misses Mariamne and you, is acclimating to the life here, and Emanuel is growing at such a rate that one of these days he will be taller than I am.

Be well,
Jonathan

From Mordechai Ben-Joshua, hegemon of the Minaean community

To the Minaean congregations of Judea, peace.

May this letter find you all in good health.

Regarding several queries that have been sent to me, it is by all means permissible and wholesome to utter in our congregations the prayer authorized by the Sanhedrin which thanks God for the beginning of Israel's redemption. It should not be thought that there is any conflict here, for the redemption spoken of by the rabbis is not meant by them in the same sense as the salvation of which we speak. Indeed, it is thought by some that the full redemption of Israel is a necessary prelude to the Second Coming of the Messiah.

Thus, though each congregation is free to act in this matter as it sees fit, the prayer should be highly considered for inclusion in our services.

May you all have a happy Easter season.

Blessings,
Mordechai

To my father, Senator Caius Arminius:

Hail and greeting.

As you have doubtless heard, the emperor has decided to reject our counsel and make a concerted drive to reconquer Judea. I need not tell you of my misgivings about this. I can only hope now that time will prove us both to have been wrong.

Of the military action being contemplated, I cannot write you for the obvious reasons of security. However, should it be successful, I urge you to do all in your power to see to it that a new procurator is named for Judea. This is a matter of the utmost importance, for I cannot begin to tell you of the kind of bestialities of which Rufus would be capable. If restored to his post and power, he will take a revenge on Judea the forms of which would frighten a civilized man.

In this connection let me tell you a little of Rufus' conduct here. We have become open enemies, a development that could no longer be avoided. He was never my friend, of course, but he now hates me with an intensity he dare not show but even whose most casual signs suggest a fire of great heat. For what Rufus hates is not only me but, through me, all that he imagines I represent. This hatred is most flattering, for by way of my far from perfect image he hates all those noble values and virtues which we and our kind hold up as an ideal. Yet he is cleverer than we had given him credit for, and he has managed to mask these feelings from the court and even, I fear, from the emperor himself. He acts the very soul of patient moderation, and the pose, to those who do not know him well, is most convincing. The Senate must see to it that he is not given an opportunity to take out his hatred on any people, not even a people which has rebelled against Rome.

Unless directly ordered to do so, I do not plan to take any part in the reconquest of Judea, nor do I ever plan to see that land again. I am well, and as I wrote you before, my wounds have healed, leaving me with only a slight limp. But, frankly, I have had my fill of Judea and of the Jews and of our attempts to handle them. I am emotionally sapped, and I feel I deserve a little rest.

Alexandria is a pleasant city, and I would as soon remain here until this business is finished with and I am reassigned somewhere else. I would most of all prefer to return to Rome, which I find myself missing more from day to day. Caesarea was so different from the city that it was a novelty, and one could not feel homesick there. But Alexandria, with all the differences, is like an imitation Rome, and an imitation only brings up the memory of the original without really fulfilling it. How well I now understand Ovid's pathetic pleas to be permitted to return to the city from which he had been exiled for life. You would think I had been gone much longer than a year and some months. It seems so much more.

I see Cornelia from time to time when Rufus is not about. He almost never is now, so busy is he with his intrigues. She sends her love and asks to be remembered to our friends.

Quintus

From Akiba Ben-Joseph

To Simon Bar Kochba, Prince of Israel, and to Mariamne, his wife, peace.

May this letter find you both in good health.

I am writing to request the honor of your presence three weeks hence at my home in B'nei B'rak to celebrate the Festival of the Passover with me and my guests.

If it is at all possible, I look forward to having you both with me for the Festival of our Freedom.

Be well,
Akiba

26

Planned by the emperor himself, the banquet to honor Commander Lucius Urbanicus on his arrival to the East was held in the great hall of the Alexandria palace amid considerable pomp. The guests, all men of high rank and their ladies, numbered less than one hundred, and they reclined on couches, in the Roman-Hellenistic fashion, while more than twice as many slaves laid course after course on the low tables before them.

The wiser ones among the guests ate slowly and sparingly, for they knew that the banquet would last a long time and that the courses would be many. But some others would leave the hall from time to time and repair to a small chamber beyond, where a slave would tickle their palates with a feather until they threw up the previous courses and could return to their laughing companions ready for more.

The chefs of the Egyptian capital had spared no effort in procuring and preparing a vast variety of delicacies: There were sparrows' eggs boiled in brine and the roe of fish seasoned with spices from India; there were deviled crabs and marinated lobster claws and eels served in a wine sauce and whale meat and starfish and a purée made from the fins of sharks; there was chicken and goose and pork and beef and lamb, but all cooked in ways that were new and surprising to the taste; there were jellied eagles' feet and candied lizard and the tongues of birds and cuts of meat from wild animals and sauté of unborn pig. And to wash all this down there was wine in great quantity, of every type and shade, brought from all parts of the world. Each new dish was greeted with small squeals of pleasure by some of the ladies, while the more sophisticated among the diners would knowingly compare the taste of this delicacy or that with something they had eaten before and, after chewing it slowly, would nod their heads approvingly to the waiting slave.

Quintus reclined next to Cornelia, while Rufus was across the hall not far from the guest of honor. As the evening wore on and as the tribune drank more than usual, all of the new tastes began, for him, to blend into two categories—spicy or sweet—and beyond that into two more—slippery or dry; and he marveled at how limited was the range of taste sensations.

Across the hall Lucius Urbanicus lay between the emperor and his lieutenant and "friend," a young man in his twenties. For this occasion the commander had chosen to doff his armor and to wear instead the *toga virilis* of a Roman knight. From time to time he would lean over and whisper something to his lieutenant, something that would invariably bring on a fit of giggling from the young man; and he would welcome each delicacy with a great show of delight, clapping his hands or smiling broadly; and once when his friend whispered something in his ear, Lucius Urbanicus laughingly twitted the young man's cheek.

Quintus considered the commander through senses at once dulled and sharpened by wine. He estimated that Urbanicus must be in his late forties, but he didn't look it. The fair hair underneath the wreath the commander now wore showed no trace of gray; Quintus wondered idly if Urbanicus dyed it. He leaned over to Cornelia. "That's a *toga virilis* our commander is wearing," he said. Cornelia nodded. "Don't you think that's funny?" suggested Quintus.

"No," said Cornelia, somewhat sharply. "A man needn't be a bull."

Quintus smiled sardonically and turned his gaze back to Urbanicus, reclining between the emperor and his friend, and to Rufus not far from them. And then he rose suddenly and made for the small chamber beyond the great hall; but he had no need for the services of the slave and his feather.

The entertainment for the banquet, also arranged by Hadrian, opened with a reading of Greek poetry by a well-known Alexandrian actor, and that had been a mistake; most of the guests resented the silence the poetry reading imposed upon them, and the actor, of course, did not cut it short. But after an interminable time, it ended, to be followed by a small orchestra which played Greek music; the music was loud, but the guests were able to shout above it, and so it provided no great disturbance.

And then, as the last courses were served, the toasts began. Hadrian offered the first one, to Urbanicus and his five legions. Rufus offered the second, to the reconquest of Judea, and he was followed by many others. Quintus joined them all, drinking to anything at all and reflecting that he was now so drunk that he could drink with impunity. The final toast was proposed by Urbanicus; it was a long toast but well-spoken in clean and clear, almost theatrical tones, to the glory of Roman arms; it was also an invitation to all in the great hall to join in the Judean campaign. Quintus drank to that, too, although he had already indicated to Urbanicus privately and quite pointedly that he had no intention of joining in the campaign.

Later Cornelia good-humoredly led Quintus into the palace garden; it was far larger but not terribly unlike the garden at the university in B'nei B'rak where they had attended another banquet a year before. Quintus followed her quietly until they had reached a secluded spot, and then, suddenly, he began reciting.

"*Arma virumque cano, Troiae qui primus ab oris* . . ."—"I sing of arms and the man who first came from Troy to Italy and the Lavinian shores. Much tossed by the gods was he, both on land and sea, because of the lasting wrath of harsh Juno."

"Shh," said Cornelia. "They'll hear you."

"And he suffered also many things in war," continued Quintus, "until he might found a city and bring his gods to Latium; whence is the Latin race, and the Alban fathers, and the walls of lofty Rome."

Quintus turned to the woman. "That's Vergil," he said.

"I know," said Cornelia with a smile.

"It was not these youths, sprung from such parents, who stained the deep with Carthaginian blood," Quintus shouted, "nor did they crush Pyrrhus and the mighty Antiochus and the fierce Hannibal; but manly offspring of rustic soldiers—"

"Quiet," whispered Cornelia.

"What has wasting time not impaired?" Quintus continued. "The generation of our fathers, worse than our grandfathers, has created us more wicked still, and we are destined to produce a yet more degraded offspring."

"Will you be still?" demanded Cornelia.

"It's not I who said that," protested Quintus. "It was Horace. Would you like to hear some more?"

"No," said Cornelia.

"*O tempora, O mores,*" sighed Quintus, stumbling down to
sit upon a rock. "That's Cicero."

"I know," Cornelia chuckled.

Quintus looked up at her standing before him, and he shook
his head slowly. "So what if they heard? They would not understand. This is Latin poetry I'm quoting—Latin, Latin,
Latin. Not that effeminate, musical, syrupy Greek."

Cornelia said nothing.

Quintus looked at her again and shook his head again. "Ah,
Cornelia; ah, fair daughter of the gods; ah, lover sweeter than
death, I do not belong here."

"Where?"

"Here. Here in Alexandria. Here tonight. Here now. Here
with Urbanicus."

"You're talking nonsense," said Cornelia. "Why does it upset you so if Urbanicus likes boys? There is nothing wrong in
that if that's what he prefers. He harms no one by it. Don't be
so intolerant."

"*Virtus,*" mumbled Quintus looking down at the ground.
"*Virtus.*"

"What?" asked Cornelia. "I can't hear you."

But Quintus did not answer. He sprang up and ran to the
bushes and was sick.

"Why is this night different from all other nights?" asked
the boy. It was the same boy, but a year older.

And Rabbi Akiba Ben-Joseph answered him as he had a
year before. "We were slaves unto Pharaoh in the land of
Egypt . . ."

It was the annual Seder at the university in B'nei B'rak, and,
at least as far as the order of the ceremony was concerned, nothing had changed. But some of the guests who had been there a
year before were absent now; a few were no longer alive, and
two of the former guests were this year attending another ban

quet, in Alexandria. Still, Simon was there, reclining beside
the rabbi as the guest of honor; and next to Simon was a young
woman, now big with child, who last year had been sitting opposite him.

Akiba looked briefly at the prince as he intoned from the
Haggadah: "And what happened to our fathers happened to us
as well—not only in one instance—but in every age and generation, whenever tyrants rose up against us to destroy us, the
Holy One, blessed be He, saved us from their hands."

And unconsciously, almost imperceptibly, in a movement
caught only by a few, Simon nodded.

The Seder seemed shorter to Simon than it had been the year
before. Last year he had been an outlaw sitting unknown
among the honored guests and glancing furtively at a coldly
beautiful girl who had seemed so out of reach and wondering
nervously what it was the great Akiba had in mind, while this
year . . . well, this year was far different.

And so the Seder ended, and again Akiba arose and offered
his toast. "This year here; next year in Jerusalem."

Simon, as did all the other guests, joined him in the toast.
Why, wondered the prince, did it seem to him now like a
rebuke?

Mariamne had been tired and went to bed early, but Bar
Kochba found himself unable to sleep. And he wandered, with
a sadly sweet nostalgia, through the university garden, coming
at last to an olive tree where he stood a long time, just looking
and thinking to himself that if he looked hard enough he
would see a girl there, a slim girl with flashing eyes and with
her knees drawn up in the manner of a child.

"It has been only a year," said a voice.

Simon started.

"Forgive me," said Rabbi Akiba. "I did not mean to intrude
upon you so rudely. But I saw you standing here, and I thought,
Surely he must be thinking how different it was only last year."

"You are right," said Simon.

The two men began walking aimlessly through the garden.
"Time is a fiction," said the rabbi, "a convenient fiction de-
signed by men, but it is an imperfect way to measure the course
of events. A year can be a thousand years, and two thousand
years can be a day. The truly wise have always understood this,

and therefore they teach the virtue of patience, of ignoring the passage of time."

"And yet," said Simon, not without some malice, "it was you who said, 'Next year in Jerusalem.' "

Akiba nodded good-naturedly. "A good point," he said. "Perhaps I am not as patient as the truly wise. Or perhaps I feel that this next year will be thousands of years long in its effect. And, of course, when we have the opportunity to do with our own hands that which we know should be done, we have no right to be patient."

The rabbi halted suddenly and turned to look at Bar Kochba. "I will tell you a secret now, young man. No, I will tell you two secrets. They may confuse you, but they will help you to understand."

They started to walk again. "I am old enough to remember Jerusalem, and that is my first secret. It was not nearly so splendid a city as we make out. Rome, for one, is more magnificent, and they say Damascus is older and Alexandria is larger. Jerusalem was the most beautiful city in Judea, to be sure, but it did not approach in beauty Jerusalem the memory. Even the Temple—glorious as it was—was only a building of wood and stone; and when I last saw it, it was in need of some minor repairs. The memory, of course, never is."

"That's interesting for you to say," said Simon. "I had imagined Jerusalem to have been the most wonderful city in the world."

"Well, it is now," said Akiba, "and that is the point. That is what I want you to understand, so that you may understand me and the Sanhedrin and our demands, which may seem to you at times intolerant. We are not pagans; we do not worship cities, or a city, any more than we worship idols. What we do worship is an idea—the Idea of the One True Living God—and we revere the ideas surrounding that Idea. The Law is one such idea. Jerusalem is another. We could easily abandon Jerusalem the city for Bethar, or Lydda, or B'nei B'rak or anyplace else, since, in reality, all ground is holy. But to abandon the idea of Jerusalem, the idea of our ancestral Holy City—the place where Abraham offered up his son Isaac, the city where David brought the Ark of the Covenant, the site of Solomon's Temple—that would be to abandon a great deal indeed."

"But if what you say is true," argued Simon, "then the worst thing I could do would be to rebuild Jerusalem. The reality could never come up to the dream, and so it would destroy the dream."

"Not so. Not unless you are willing to say that the reality of your victory has destroyed the dream of a new Judea. I certainly don't think that, and I'm sure you don't. Dreams are powerful because they can mold realities, and a reality based upon a dream can, in turn, enhance that dream and give it new vigor. A Jerusalem rebuilt for the right reasons will give the dream a life it never had before."

"This is getting a bit involved," said Simon, "but I will think about it. What is your second secret?"

"That it doesn't really matter if we rebuild Jerusalem at all."

Simon couldn't hold back a laugh. "Well, now," he said, "you've succeeded in really confusing me. First you say that we must rebuild Jerusalem at all costs, and then you say that it doesn't really matter."

"What matters," said Akiba, "is that we try. And if you think about that, you will see there is no confusion. A rebuilt Jerusalem would be a wonderful thing, but what counts far more is the very act of rebuilding. That is why we have urged you again and again to begin. For if we should try to rebuild the city and fail at the present time for one reason or another, it would matter comparatively little—remember, time is not essential, and Jerusalem will surely be rebuilt sooner or later, since that is the revealed will of God. But if we do not try, Simon, why, we have already failed."

"I shall try," said Bar Kochba. "Believe me, I have every intention of trying. Only give me a little of that time you hold so unimportant."

"It's not time we're concerned about but direction. The direction in which a movement begins is the way it will ultimately go and the way it will inevitably end. I could prove that to you by history, but you may take my word for it."

"And my direction?"

"Basically good, but dangerously misguided at times. You are a good man, Simon, and that is of the utmost importance. You will always be good, because people don't change that radically.

But you have faults, as we all have, only in your case your im-
mense power magnifies those faults so that they can cause damage beyond repair."

"I did not seek the power. Did I not turn down the title of
king?"

"Yes, and there too you meant well, but there too you may
have been misguided. For in rejecting the kingdom, you perpetuate a dangerous situation in which you have more power
and less counsel than you would as a king."

"But it is all only temporary," protested Simon.

"So is life," said Akiba. "So is everything except God and
Israel. Think about it."

27

Quintus awoke to find Cornelia with her eyes wide open,
looking at him. "What is it?" he asked.

"It's morning."

Quintus sat up in the bed, stretched, yawned and kissed the
woman beside him. "What were you thinking about?"

"Nothing," she said.

"Come on," he put his hand in her long auburn hair, playing
with it. "What's going on underneath all of that?"

Cornelia moved her head away and pushed her hair back.
"Quintus," she sighed, "you talk a lot about the old morality.
But has it ever occurred to you that what we are doing could be
morally wrong?"

"No," he said. "We're not hurting anyone by it, and we're
pleasing ourselves. What's immoral about that?"

"We're hurting Rufus."

"Are you crazy?" Quintus exclaimed.

"It seems to me that when you look at it dispassionately,
we're really being unfair to him."

"First of all," said Quintus, "it would be impossible to be
unfair to Rufus whatever one did to him, but let's not talk
about that. You say we're hurting Rufus, but that would assume

that Rufus cares; the fact is, and you know it, that he doesn't
care one bit, because if he did care, he'd be here in bed with
you, and I couldn't be here. I've been able to come to you, night
after night, because Rufus doesn't give a damn about you and
because he prefers other nocturnal amusements. So much for
hurting Rufus. And as far as being unfair to him, I don't see
that at all; he doesn't own you, and even if he did, he isn't using
you."

"That's a rather crass way to put it."

"Well, you know what I mean."

"It's not a matter of ownership in any case," said Cornelia.
"It's a matter of a vow. When we were married, Rufus and I
vowed to love each other, and only each other."

"And has he kept that vow? By the gods, I think he's already
broken it with every boy in Alexandria."

"But that doesn't really release me from the vow."

Quintus glared at her angrily. "Are you trying to get rid of
me, is that it? Because if you are, I would prefer that you told
me so instead of playing the vestal virgin."

Cornelia put her hand on his arm and gave it a little squeeze.
"Don't be silly. It's just that . . ."

"What?"

"Nothing."

"No," said Quintus, "say what you have to say."

"Well, I don't know . . . I can't quite explain it . . . I love
you as much as I ever did, and I enjoy you, but . . . somehow
. . . recently I've been feeling guilty."

"About what?"

"What I said before."

"But how, why?" Quintus cried. "It's the stupidest thing I've
ever heard. It's like that stuff the Jews are always preaching,
all kinds of rigid rules and prohibitions that have no connection with morality at all."

"I know it's not logical," said Cornelia. "Don't worry about
it. It will pass. Nothing will change."

Quintus got up and washed his face in the bowl beside the
bed. "As a matter of fact," he said, dabbing at his face with a
towel, "I want things to change. I think it's time you came to a
decision and divorced Rufus and married me. Then you'd have
nothing to feel guilty about."

"Not yet," said Cornelia. "Later I will. But not now. Not when he's right in the middle of things. That really wouldn't be fair."

"Well, all right," said Quintus in exasperation. "Urbanicus should be landing in Judea soon, so maybe in a few weeks all of it really will be over. And then we can do it at long last."

"Yes," said Cornelia. "Maybe then."

That same morning, in Judea, in the city of En-Gedi on the shores of the Dead Sea, Jonathan Bar Ba'ayah awoke to find that his bed was empty. He looked up and saw that his wife was standing by the window. He said nothing, but Ruth seemed to sense that he was awake, and without turning to him, she asked, "Jonathan, when will the fighting end?"

"I don't know," he said. "What brings that up?"

Ruth shrugged. "I was just in to look at Emanuel, and suddenly it struck me that he has never known a time of peace."

Jonathan was silent for a time. "Nor have I," he said sadly. "Nor, I suppose, did my father—may he be at peace now."

Ruth sat down on the bed, facing her husband, and she took his hand. "Will it ever come? Real peace, I mean, not just victory. Simon has achieved independence and freedom, but will he ever achieve peace?"

"I think so," he said. "I think it will come soon."

"I want it," said Ruth, with an intensity of which Jonathan had not thought her capable.

In the town of Usha in Galilee the learned Rabbi Meir sat in the study of his home with his teacher and mentor of former times, Elisha Ben-Abuyah. And, as on other occasions, the pious rabbi urged *aher* to return to the faith he had shunned.

"Tell me," said Elisha with a smile as Rabbi Meir began again, "why are you the only one of the rabbis who tries to move me from my chosen path? Even Akiba does not argue with me. Why do you?"

"You are my teacher," said Rabbi Meir.

"You mean were."

"No, you still are. I can accept the kernel of your learning while rejecting the husk."

Aher laughed. "You have learned well," he said.

"From you, my master. That is why I cannot understand how one so wise as you could reject the idea of God."

"And I," said Another, "find it hard to understand how one so wise as you can continue to accept the idea."

Rabbi Meir ignored the retort. "How was it possible," he went on, "for you to have lost your faith, a man like you who was steeped in the tradition and so very learned in the ways of the Law?"

"You've heard the story," said Elisha. "About how one day while returning from the house of study I heard a father tell his son to fetch him some pigeons from the top of a tower. The boy went up without hesitating—thus fulfilling the commandment to honor one's father 'that your days may be long . . .' And once at the nest, the boy took all the pigeons except the mother bird—letting her go, as the Law commands, 'that your days may be long.' And yet, despite the fact that he had fulfilled these two positive commandments, the boy fell from the tower on his way down and was killed."

"I have heard the story," said Rabbi Meir, "along with many others. Is it true? Is that how you lost your faith?"

"No," said Elisha, "but it's a good story."

"But what is the truth?"

"Ah, my dear Meir," Elisha sighed, "can't you understand that all the stories are true?"

"Even the ones that conflict?"

"Especially the ones that conflict. That's really what truth is, a lot of different things, some of them lies, that are thoroughly opposed to one another. Truth is consistent only in the Talmud, and it was when I found I could no longer accept that narrow view of life that I rejected the whole business. This is where I differ with you and the other rabbis and with this new prince of yours who doesn't even realize that he started out to do one thing and is now doing another. But that is what life is—conflict and inconsistency."

"And that is your new version of truth, a pack of confusing untruths?"

"Partly. Life is made up of confusion, untruth and absurdity, mostly the latter. In this, at least, I agree with the Gnostics —and never mind telling me that that's heresy, because I've already committed every heresy there is. I think that if there is any God at all, He is merely having his little joke with us, and understanding that is the only way to arrive at any semblance of truth."

Rabbi Meir shook his head. "Yes, that sounds like the Gnostic teaching. I'm glad to say it's made little headway among the Jews."

"Of course," snapped Another. "The Jews are the butt of the joke. They fall for it every time."

In Bethar Mordechai Ben-Joshua, returning from the morning service at the Minaean synagogue, stood for a time watching the men who were adding another wall to his city. The men were few today, for most of them had been dispatched far away, to the coast, to Bar Kochba.

Some of those who had remained as a skeleton force were taking a short break for the morning meal, eating it beside the rising wall, and they were listening as they ate to Rabbi Eleazar Ha-Modai telling them, "Whoever has enough to eat today and worries about tomorrow is a man of little faith."

It was a good homily, thought Mordechai, as he moved away toward his home.

In B'nei B'rak Rabbi Akiba sat with a group of young disciples who were on leave from the army, at the rabbi's request, to continue their study of the Law. They were discussing a fine point regarding the finding of lost property, and Akiba listened especially to the questions being proposed by Joshua Ha-Garsi and Simeon Ben-Yohai, two young men the rabbi felt showed great promise.

In Alexandria Publius Aelius Hadrianus slept late, having spent a good part of the previous night discussing the Greek tragedies with some gifted actors who had been specially invited to the palace.

In Hebron, where she was staying with friends and with a midwife in constant attendance, Mariamne Bath-Menashe Ben-David felt the stirrings of life strong within her.

*   *   *

And in a tent on the coast just south of Acco Simon Bar Kochba was informed that the ships of Commander Lucius Urbanicus had been sighted in the distance making for the Judean shore. . . .

It was late spring, the seventeenth day of the month of Iyyar, in the Year One of the Liberation of Israel.

28

The coast of Judea was clearly visible in the early morning sunlight, and as Urbanicus and his officers scanned it from their ships, few could suppress a small smile of relief and admiration. This had been a brilliant stroke, this invasion from the sea, a bold tactic that the Jews could not have expected. It brought up memories of Scipio Africanus' surprise landing in Africa more than three centuries before—the decisive blow against Carthage. The allusion had not escaped Urbanicus, and as the large fleet of transport vessels made for a natural harbor by the deserted shore south of Acco, he regretted only that the glory of his victory over the rebellious Jews would be minor by comparison.

Not far from that empty shore, hidden from view by the dunes that rose steeply behind it, Bar Kochba watched the Roman ships approach, and he too smiled. His Alexandrian informants had been right, even about the number of the Roman troops. From the size of the fleet the prince estimated there would be just about 30,000 men aboard—five legions with perhaps some cavalry. Behind him Bar Kochba had nearly twice as many warriors. Every advantage was his.

The first ship moored in the harbor and then the second and the third. Now began the tedious operation of landing the men and animals on the shore. Bar Kochba estimated it would take about half the day. He would wait. He had time.

Longboats appeared in the water, and a short while later the first Roman troops in eight months set foot on the soil of

Judea. They disembarked quickly, in orderly fashion, and the boats returned for their next load. Not far from them, barges spewed out their first load of cavalry.

Urbanicus and his lieutenant arrived in the third wave of landings, setting up their command headquarters on the broad beach and supervising the further unloading of the ships. Bar Kochba watched them, watched the purple banner being implanted in the soft sand and gradually surrounded by the standards of the five legions, and he felt again the burning hatred he had first felt in Kosiba many years before.

It was late in the day by the time all the troops had left the ships and taken up their casual positions on the beach. Urbanicus and his lieutenant were studying maps; the legionaries, set at their ease, were gathered in small groups; the German cavalry, tall, blond men who spoke in a harsh language, were feeding their horses.

Suddenly a sharp cry split the air like lightning, and the thunder of a thousand cries and more, and arrows rained down from the Judean sky.

Automatically the legionaries began to group in their traditional formations, but this only provided the Judean archers with a larger target, and Urbanicus shouted for the men to break their ranks. The commanders of the separate legions took up the shout, and the tribunes, and the centurions, and the decurions; but by the time the soldiers had obeyed the order and scattered on the blood-soaked beach, thousands had been slain.

And no sooner had the troops broken ranks than a massive force poured down upon the disorganized men with sword and spear. Then, like a spent wave, the attackers withdrew quickly to the shelter of the dunes before the legionaries could regroup, as the Roman archers and slingers fired wildly after them.

"Press forward," shouted the leader of the German cavalry, and without a moment's hesitation the horsemen rode from the beach, upward into the dunes, waving their battle-axes and crying out the names of their Teutonic gods.

The Jews met the cavalry amid the hills of sand; they had been ready for the attack, and the ground they were fighting on was their own. They surrounded the German horsemen and cut them down.

The crews of the Roman ships, seeing the plight of the legionaries, directed a hail of missiles toward the heights beyond the shore; but the catapult stones could not always be cast with accuracy, and they took as large a toll among the Roman troops as among their enemies until Urbanicus hastily signaled that the bombardment be stopped.

Repeatedly the Romans tried to push forward into the dunes, where they might gain a foothold, but the Jews met each attack by setting up a wall of arrows that the invaders could not penetrate, whatever price they were willing to pay. And as the sun set, a feeling of elation gradually came upon the defenders, for they knew already that they would not be overcome; while the Romans sensed with a deadly finality that they were beaten, that they could neither advance nor retreat but would be forced to stand there, on the beach, until they were slain.

But although the battle had in fact been thus decided in the early hours of the evening, the men on both sides continued fighting with a desperate fury; their realization could not save them, nor could their reason, for—as in all battles—there was no reason involved, and the fighting and dying went on long after all reason for it had passed.

It was only in the morning, when the beach was already so covered with the slain that their corpses hid the sand, that Urbanicus issued the order to retreat to the ships that would take the broken legions to Alexandria, the very ships that had brought them to Judea filled with confidence only a day before.

At a signal the longboats and the barges set out once again from the vessels anchored offshore. The first contingent of Romans scampered into them, and the boats hastily moved off toward the waiting ships. But they were no sooner in the deep waters of the harbor than flaming arrows began hissing at them from the Jewish ranks. The arrows imbedded themselves in the wood of the longboats and of the barges, turning them into pyres for the soldiers aboard or else sending the legionaries screaming to the bottom of the harbor in their heavy armor.

And, almost simultaneously, the Jews launched an attack against the distracted Roman forces onshore who were watching in horror the death of their comrades. It was the most violent attack of all, and before it subsided many more of the

Romans had been slain, including Urbanicus' friend and lieutenant. The casualties on the Judean side were not heavy, but
among them was the oldest of the rebel chieftains, a man who
had become a legend in his own right, Nathan Bar Deroma, the
hero of Tur Malka.

The commander of Legion XI Claudia now stepped forward
and told Urbanicus that his men had elected to remain behind
and cover the retreat of the other legions. It was no empty gesture. The XI Claudia, drawn from Europe, was made up of
warriors of the old Roman school. It had covered itself with
glory many times, and if death was now required to add to that
record of glory, the men of the legion were ready to accept it.

Urbanicus, overcome by desperation, accepted the offer and
ordered the remainder of his soldiers to strip off their armor
and swim out to the ships. Those who could not swim joined
the lines of the XI Claudia and stood calmly awaiting their
doom.

It soon became apparent to Bar Kochba what was happening,
and as he watched the XI Claudia move together in formation,
ready to sacrifice itself for the comrades who were already beginning their short swim to the moored ships, he felt a surge
of admiration. And he raised his hand, and suddenly the rain
of arrows stopped. And he stood up, unprotected, on a mound
overlooking the beach and the XI Claudia, and he addressed
the legion in Latin, in these words:

"I am Bar Kochba, Prince of Israel. You have fought on the
side of oppression, but you have fought well and with honor.
We Jews are not insensitive to bravery. We grant you, therefore, your lives. Swim out to your comrades on your ships and
depart in peace. We shall not attempt to stop you. We ask of
you only one thing: Do not return. For if you do return, we
shall surely take of you that which we have now spared."

Bar Kochba disappeared again behind the mound, and an
unaccustomed stillness descended over the beach and the dunes
beyond. The commander of the XI Claudia nodded, and the
first group of legionaries began slipping out of their armor
and, with a slowness born of suspicion, moved into the water.
No arrows fell, and so another group joined them, and then
another. They swam out thus in turns, leaving their armor be-

hind them and helping along those who were unable to swim, until at the end the last Roman soldier had once again departed from Judea. Except the dead. . . .

Lucius Urbanicus was not seen on deck throughout the voyage back to Alexandria. He remained in his cabin, mourning his friend. And it was, whatever his detractors were to say, an act of love.

And on the coast of Judea, only minutes after the last Roman ship had disappeared from view, a messenger came and told Bar Kochba that Mariamne had given birth to a son.

29

Lucius Urbanicus returned to Alexandria in disgrace and with less than 10,000 of his men. As word of the disaster moved across the city, a kind of panic gripped the inhabitants of the poorer sections, and it spread upward, so that by the second day there was a rumor throughout the city that Egypt itself was in danger of invasion by the victorious Judeans. The Jews of Alexandria, who had been concerned for their own safety, found themselves suddenly befriended by neighbors who had spit at them on the street only a week before. But some of the Jews believed the rumor, too, and those among them who had long ceased to be Jews, who had even undergone the painful operation to remove the signs of circumcision in an effort to become Gentiles in body as well as spirit, now underwent a second operation—even more painful—to restore the mark of the Covenant of Abraham.

All of this took perhaps a week to subside. When it was over, Urbanicus had left the city and retired to private life; the people who had spit upon the Jews before began to do so again; prices that had been suddenly inflated returned to normal; the citizens of Alexandria began to talk once again of what kind of summer it would be, and the Romans found themselves faced with the sobering question of what to do next.

Again the emperor summoned his officers and advisers to the palace. Again Rufus and others argued for war, calling for more legions and better stratagems to defeat the Jews; but their arguments this time seemed to many less convincing than before.

Again Quintus pleaded for a peace based on reason, and he was joined now by some who had previously chosen to remain silent; and this time Hadrian appeared more inclined to listen to the pacifist proposals, especially as they were now abetted by strong pressure from Rome—not only from various senators but from the imperial treasury, which had to finance the warfare.

This latter consideration was, in the eyes of many, the most decisive argument for an end to the conflict. And it was the kind of argument that could be expected to weigh heavily in the mind of the First Citizen of the Republic. . . .

Jonathan Bar Ba'ayah, the child's godfather, carried it into the main room of the house in Hebron; the guests rose and said to the eight-day-old infant, "Welcome."

Simon then stepped forward and pronounced the traditional declaration.

"I am here ready to perform the precept to circumcise my son, even as the Creator, blessed be He, has commanded us, as it is written in the Law."

Rabbi Eleazar Ha-Modai took the child and said a blessing over it. Then placing the infant on Jonathan's knees—and while Mariamne stood in the rear of the room trying not to look—he performed the ancient operation quickly and with skilled hands, so that the child let out but one short whimper.

Rabbi Eleazar daubed at the cut with a piece of cloth and intoned the words that welcomed the child into the brith— the Covenant of Abraham and the Brotherhood of Israel.

"Our God and God of our fathers, preserve this child to his father and his mother, and let his name be called in Israel— Menashe the son of Simon. . . ."

The name had been that of Mariamne's father, and she had chosen it to perpetuate his memory.

"With the sanction of the awe-inspiring and revered God, Who is a refuge in time of trouble, the God girt with strength, the Lord mighty on high, we will give thanks to Your Name in the midst of the faithful," intoned Rabbi Eleazar. Then turning to the guests, "Blessed are you all of the Lord.

"With the sanction of the Holy Law, pure and clear, which Moses the servant of the Lord commanded us as a heritage, we will give thanks to Your Name in the midst of the faithful; blessed are you all of the Lord.

"With the sanction of the priests and the Levites, I will call upon the God of the Hebrews; I will declare His glory in every region; I will bless the Lord. We will give thanks to Your Name in the midst of the faithful; blessed are you all of the Lord.

"With the sanction of those present, I will open my lips with song, and my very bones will declare: Blessed is he who comes in the name of the Lord. We will give thanks to Your Name in the midst of the faithful; blessed are you all of the Lord."

And the guests answered, "We will give thanks to Your Name in the midst of the faithful; blessed are you all of the Lord."

Menashe was returned to his cradle, and the guests sat down to celebrate his acceptance into the Covenant with a festive meal. There were toasts to the child, to his parents, to the god-father, to the man who had performed the circumcision.

It remained for Rabbi Akiba Ben-Joseph, who had journeyed from B'nei B'rak to attend the brith, to utter the traditional hope that the child would go on to "the Law, to the marriage canopy and to good works." And then he sat down, and smilingly taking the hand of the father, he told him, "Now you have someone to build for."

"Now," said Simon soberly, "I have someone to fight for."

To my son, Quintus Arminius Caro:
Warm greeting.
It is at times a terribly bitter thing to have been right. Commander Lucius Urbanicus, leader of that ill-fated expedition which we both tried so hard to prevent, has returned to the city, a broken man. The Senate gave him an

official reception, and we surely did our best to persuade
him that he had been but a victim of the inscrutable fates,
but Urbanicus answered our attempts with a patient smile
that all but told us we were a bunch of old fools. I had met
him only once before, years ago following a triumph, and I
was not at that time very much impressed with him. How
ironic that he should seem such a likable figure now, in disgrace.

Yet whatever any of us may think of Urbanicus, the
naked facts speak their melancholy piece. Five legions decimated and an entire contingent of cavalry destroyed without even being given a chance to defend themselves
properly. And indeed it could have been far worse. The XI
Claudia would not be in existence today were it not for the
chivalry of the Jew. What a debacle! I can think of only
one even vaguely similar instance, and that was many
years ago. The revolt of the Britons at that time caught us
off balance and resulted in heavy losses. But at least we were
able, after the first crushing blows had fallen, to regain our
posture. And Faustus Julius Severus, that great general, was
able to reconquer Britannia without too much bloodshed.
But, alas, our current situation is worse. And Severus is an
old man now, as I am, and in retirement. And the new age
brings us no new Severus.

But why am I telling you all this? Surely you know our
plight better than I. It is now incumbent upon us to bend
all our efforts toward preventing further bloodshed. I am
happy to report that more and more of my colleagues are
coming around to our way of thinking, that nobility need
not be proved on the battlefield, and that the cause of the
empire can be advanced at times better by means of peace
than war.

I think that, provided your Jew will be reasonable, we
should soon be able to conclude a peace with Judea that
will be just to both sides. Surely the protracted warfare has
been hard on that little land, and an end to the conflict
should be most welcome to the Jews.

The summer has only begun, but Rome is already a
steam bath. I cannot remember a worse. The Senate is due

to conclude its deliberations soon, whereupon I plan to take refuge at our country villa. I shall in all probability write to you next from there.

Your loving father

It was the month of Tammuz and summer in Judea. The days had grown uncomfortably warm, and in the low-lying plains the hot air settled and lay still.

It was the month of Tammuz, nearing the end of the Year One of the Liberation of Israel, and the farmers beginning the summer harvest went to the fields girt with sword; and every third man assigned to the fortification of Bethar spent the day in training; and as the fishermen cast their nets in the Sea of Galilee, their eyes wandered watchfully over the mountains of Syria in the distance.

It was the month of Tammuz, and the rabbis and the scholars and the disciples of the academies prepared solemnly for the next month, which was Ab—the time of mourning; for the capital remained still in ruins.

In Lydda Simon Bar Kochba, Prince of Israel, lay in bed alone, in the well-guarded house of his local officer, with the heat heavy upon him, and he could not sleep. It was the month of Tammuz, and the land yearned for peace, and the prince lay awake, thinking and wondering what it was that he could do.

Mariamne and their son were in Bethar; for Bethar was the best-guarded city in the entire country, and it had become, in everything but name, the capital of Judea. With them now was Jonathan Bar Ba'ayah, who had left the Dead Sea district to replace the slain Bar Deroma in the strategic region of Judah.

Simon was in Lydda to attend the meeting of the Sanhedrin the following day at the urgent summons of that body. The Sanhedrin, to be precise, had invited the prince, for it had no authority to summon him. In truth, none in the whole land had final authority save Simon Bar Kochba. And yet the prince felt that the Sanhedrin had summoned him—even more, had commanded his presence. And for all of his power and the Sanhedrin's lack of it, Bar Kochba was not entirely wrong; for the Sanhedrin had an authority that was beyond power.

And as Simon lay there, wondering what it was that he could tell the old men of the Sanhedrin, he felt a certain helplessness despite his great power. He felt more like Simon Bar Kosiba than Bar Kochba, and the thoughts that ran now through his active mind were more the thoughts of the obscure rebel than of the mighty prince.

In the old days, Simon reflected, it would have been easier. There was a time when he could have dazzled the old men with the brilliance of his dream, but that time had passed. There was a time when he, the angry warrior, could have demonstrated to the calm wise men the need for patience, but that time, too, had passed.

Where was he now? What was his position, and how could he state it? He felt certain that he was right, that the course he favored was the only correct one for Judea, but how could he make the old men see it?

Tortured by his dilemma and unable to sleep, he thought back to the beginning, to another old man, the one they had called the Zealot.

"Ten measures of beauty came into the world," the old man, the Zealot, had once intoned, "and of these nine were taken by Jerusalem."

Simon the boy had heard these words from the lips of the old man, the Zealot. Simon the rebel had fought for these words. Yet Simon the prince had not rebuilt Jerusalem, had not yet even begun. Could he explain to the Sanhedrin why? Could he have explained it to the old man, the Zealot?

Certainly he had found it increasingly difficult to explain things to Akiba. A wall seemed to have risen between him and the old sage, and Akiba stood behind it with his paradoxes and his unreasonable insistence that certain things must be tried even if it were a foregone conclusion that they would fail.

And worse yet for his personal peace of mind, a similar wall had begun to rise between him and Mariamne since the birth of their child. Increasingly she, too, demanded to know when peace would come. "Why can't you accept the fact that we have won?" she had asked him, and the question, coming from his wife, seemed to Simon a bitter accusation. As if it were his fault that the country was not yet at peace in this month of

Tammuz; as if he were to blame for the way things were in the world.

Why wouldn't anybody let him conduct matters as he saw fit? Simon asked himself. Why couldn't they simply trust him? He had surely earned their trust. Why wouldn't Mariamne understand that victory was not yet, that this was only a respite? Why did the Sanhedrin not understand that so long as the Romans remained in the lands around them, surrounding them with hostile power, so long would Judea not be truly free?

Why, in his dreams, would the old man, the Zealot, refuse to understand that he couldn't rebuild Jerusalem? Not yet. Not until full victory.

In his mind Simon rehearsed the facts as he saw them and as he would present them to the Sanhedrin the following day.

True, the Romans had been expelled from Judea, but Rome still dominated this area of the world. In such a situation Judean independence could be only a temporary affair; it might last a year, perhaps even a decade or two. But sooner or later the Roman circle would close in on Judea again, exactly as it had in the first place.

Why was it that no one else seemed able to see this obvious fact of geography? For the moment the only thing to do was to keep Judea in complete readiness against the possibility of still another Roman offensive. Beyond that, if the Jews were to have any hope of securing their independence, they would have to spearhead an assault on the entire Eastern Empire. That was why Bar Kochba could not rebuild Jerusalem yet; that was why he could not think yet of disarming the nation; that was why he was, even now, seeking alliances with the enemies of Rome.

30

The members of the Sanhedrin entered the meeting hall singly or in pairs, each of them nodding courteously to their guest, the Prince of Israel, before taking their seats.

The seats were in tiers arranged in a semicircle, with the youngest and newest members of the council sitting in the highest-placed seats farthest removed from the center, while the venerable sages sat in the front row at floor level. A large chair had been placed in the middle of the hall facing the assemblage, and Simon, trying not to look as uncomfortable as he felt, took his place in it.

When all of the members had been seated, with none absent on this occasion, Rabbi Eleazar Ben-Azariah, who with Akiba shared the leadership of the Sanhedrin, arose and solemnly announced, "With the permission of Heaven and the sanction of those present, we hereby open this meeting of the Sanhedrin, on the fifth day of the month of Tammuz in the year 3893, the Year One of the Liberation of Israel."

He sat down, and Akiba arose to introduce the council's guest:

"Simon Bar Kochba, Prince of Israel, who has graciously consented to accept our invitation."

Now Simon rose and, as custom dictated, bowed to "my masters in wisdom" and asked, "how might I be of service to this most noble body?" Then he, too, sat down.

Rabbi Tarphon, who had been chosen to convey the Sanhedrin's sentiments, rose from his seat in the front row and began.

"I have the honor, first of all, to convey the official congratulations of my colleagues to you for your great military success in defending the land, and to acknowledge your courage as a leader and your wisdom as a ruler."

Rabbi Tarphon paused, and Simon, now prepared for the worst, nodded in appreciation to him and to the conclave.

"What you have done will surely go down in the annals of our people," continued Rabbi Tarphon. "Surely the Almighty has taken cognizance of it, and may He continue to bless the work of your hands and the meditation of your heart. For ourselves, our brother Simon, we are well pleased with what you have done thus far. But we feel constrained to ask what you plan to do henceforth and to offer our counsel to you regarding this."

"I will gratefully hear whatever counsel is proposed by the wise men of Israel," responded Simon.

Rabbi Tarphon took a deep breath. "It is now nearly a year since the land has been freed from the Romans, and it is already nearly two months since the Lord delivered us from their renewed threat. Today the might of Rome sits in Alexandria of Egypt; the empire is caught off balance; it wonders what to do; while wondering, it does nothing. This has given us an opportunity that we, the vast majority of the Sanhedrin, feel you should not ignore or let pass. It is therefore our counsel that you take advantage of this situation and send representatives to Alexandria without delay to conclude a peace with Rome. We feel that we are currently in the best possible position to do so."

Tarphon stopped for some sort of response from Simon. The prince's brow wrinkled up in thought. A negotiated peace? He had expected the Sanhedrin to ask him to begin rebuilding Jerusalem, to release men from the army, to set up a more permanent form of government, even to ignore the Roman threat perhaps. But to dicker for a treaty of peace? To come to terms with the hated oppressor? He had not expected that. "What sort of peace do you have in mind?" he asked, making no attempt to hide his coolness.

"A peace that would cost us nothing yet might well satisfy Rome," said Rabbi Tarphon. "We have won what we fought for; we have our independence; we have our freedom; we have the beginnings of our own government again; we have the site of Jerusalem and of the Temple. We lack nothing now but peace.

"As for Rome, she has lost much: She has lost this province;

she has lost legions; perhaps most important of all, she has lost prestige. But it is our belief that Rome would be willing to sustain these losses in exchange for one concession. Let Judea offer to Rome a treaty of peace that would grant her the right to move men and supplies across our land should she need this to guarantee her own safety. Such a right could be limited by whatever safeguards you feel are necessary. And it would give Rome the one thing we of the Sanhedrin believe she now seeks —security for herself. Thus both sides could achieve their aims at once without further loss of life or of honor to either side."

The aged Rabbi Tarphon sat down, and Simon looked across at the assembled sages, teachers, scholars and scribes before rising. "My masters," he said, "Rome has been our enemy for a hundred years. I do not believe that a piece of paper will change that. Only force can change it."

"But force has changed it," said Rabbi Hanania Ben-Tera-dyon. "Now let us be strong and complete the task, even as it is said, 'Who is mighty? He who turns an enemy into a friend.' "

"Do you imagine," cried Simon, "that the Romans will ever be our friends? Why do you refuse to come to terms with reality? Have you forgotten what the Romans did while they were here? Don't you understand that they are our bitter enemies and always will be?"

"No," said a voice, and Simon turned to see Rabbi Akiba rising from his seat. "Rome is not our eternal enemy any more than the Hellenistic Empire was, or Babylon, or Assyria, or Philistia. The rule of brute force is the enemy, and ignorance, and the sickness of soul that comes from not understanding God's plan, and fear of what is not understood, and the blind hatred that is the result of all of this. These have always been our enemies, and these will always be our enemies until, in the fullness of time, man rises above them."

"I will not argue philosophy with you," said Simon. "That is your province. As for me, I am a realist."

"I beg your pardon," said Akiba, "but you are not. You have merely become a practical man of late, and like most practical men you are far less realistic than the dreamers. You now see only a small part of the reality, the part you want to see. You have chosen to ignore the fact that our very victory over the might of the Roman Empire was—in purely practical terms—quite impossible. We achieved it because, like dreamers, we fought for the right despite the certainty of practical men that we were doomed. But, of course, the way of right ultimately prospers, and the man who showed me that best of all now stands before me and argues that it is not so."

The old sage and the young prince stood facing each other in the hushed chamber, and all eyes were upon them. These two, each in his own way, had moved together to move the world, but with victory they had noticeably drifted further and further apart. Now would come the clash and the resolution that could no longer be put off, and there was not a man in that hall who did not sense it, nor a man who did not feel with it a certain sadness; yes, and with it a sense of shame as well at being spectators to what, perhaps, should have been a private moment for the two.

"You want me to beg," said Simon angrily. "You want me to ask for peace at the very height of our victory."

"You must," said Akiba. "That is the time to ask. Now is the time when we can gain the most from Rome."

"We cannot gain more than our freedom, and that we have already gained in the only way a nation can ever gain it from Rome—by force of arms."

"You can gain peace."

"The price is too high. The price is our independence."

"You know not the price," said Akiba. "Approach the Romans. Find out the price. Try it."

"I will not," said Simon, turning away. "I will not haggle with the butchers."

Rabbi Tarphon, who had watched with increasing pain the conflict between the two men, now stepped forward and suggested, "Perhaps Bar Kochba has a plan of his own, Akiba."

"I do," said Simon.

"Then if you would be good enough to let us know it," said Tarphon, "we may find that there is nothing to argue about."

Akiba sat down uneasily as Simon faced the conclave and began.

"My masters, I yearn for peace as much as you. I have a son now—may the Lord keep him well. Do you think I do not seek peace for him? But I want a peace that will be real, will be permanent, and will not cost us what we have won.

"I said before that I am a realist"—Simon glanced for an instant at Akiba. "Now permit me to explain what I meant. If you will but look at a map, my masters, you will see that there is far more involved in the events of the past year than just Judea. To the north of us is the Roman province of Syria, to the south is the Roman province of Arabia, and to the southwest the Roman province of Egypt; to the east are the Nabataeans, also subject to Rome. Only beyond that, in the northeast, is there an area free of Roman domination, the Empire of the Parthians.

"If we were to make peace with Rome now, under these conditions, how long do you imagine that this island of independence of ours would last? Is it not clear what would inevitably happen? When we grew weak enough in our sloth, the Romans would simply move in again. And that would, once again, be the end of Judean freedom."

Simon paused for a long moment and watched the faces of the rabbis, noting with quiet satisfaction that several looked at each other and nodded.

"I therefore seek more than a treaty with Rome could ever bring. I seek a freedom that will not be temporary and a peace that will not be temporary. And for this, I am willing to sacrifice the immediate peace we all desire—yes, and more than that if it should become necessary."

Bar Kochba took a deep breath. Now would come his final touch, some confidential information that might shock the elders but would move them to realize that his plans were far-reaching.

"To this end," he began, "I have taken steps toward ousting the Roman power from this entire area. I have sent representatives to the Parthians to ask for their aid. There should also be no difficulty in enlisting the help of the Nabataeans, who have long smoldered under Roman domination. Thus, with a concerted effort, I seek to ensure that what we have won we shall be able to pass on to our children, and their children after them."

Simon had finished, and many voices suddenly broke the silence.

"But that will mean more war," said one of the rabbis.

"If what you plan comes to pass," asked a second rabbi, "what will prevent the Parthians from conquering us after the Romans are gone?"

"Is there to be no end of fighting?" asked a third.

"What about Jerusalem?" asked a fourth.

At length Akiba raised his arm in a bid to speak, and the tumult died down. "I have only one question to ask of the prince," he said. "I have asked it of him before, but it remains still the only real question: What was our rebellion for?"

"As I have told you," answered Simon, "to gain freedom for Judea, to drive out the oppressor."

Akiba shook his head sadly. "But those are only words," he said. "Once—it seems now like a thousand years ago—a rebel came to me and asked for my help. I tried to turn him away with words, but he would not let me. He forced me to see the realities that lay behind certain words—the specific suffering of specific individuals—and his words moved me. They moved me so that in time I put aside my lifelong conviction that all war was wrong and actually helped him to begin a struggle in which tens of thousands have already perished.

"But in the very beginning," Akiba continued, "I offered that rebel an important piece of advice. I urged him to understand, and to bear in mind, that hatred blinds one's eyes to the truth. Remember, Simon? That first day in B'nei B'rak? Now, I ask you, what in your eyes is the truth? What is it that we fought for? What have we won? Why must we keep fighting?"

Simon sighed in exasperation. "You know as well as I do why we fought. To rid ourselves of the Romans, once and for all."

"Wrong," said Akiba. "We fought for much more than that. We fought for Jerusalem and the Temple and for what they represent to us. We fought for the right of every individual Judean to fear nothing and no one but God; to plant his field without being afraid that others will eat of it; to raise children without being afraid that they will grow up to be slaves. And to be free—truly free—in his mind and his soul as well as his body. In short, we fought for a series of bold dreams."

"Of course," said Simon. "It is obvious that we fought for all those things."

"But these things can come about only through peace. Understand, Simon, that the struggle was not so much against the Romans as for our dreams. We were forced to fight the Romans only because they made it impossible for our dreams to become realities. Now that the Romans are gone, they have ceased, in effect, to be enemies."

"But there is so much more involved," protested Simon. "Your view is hopelessly narrow."

"It is your view that is narrow," said Akiba. "You see us as merely a small nation in the midst of a mighty empire, while I see us as the only power on earth capable of toppling what Rome stands for, for we alone in all the world present an alternative to the rule of brute force. And I care not whether that rule be exercised by Rome or by Parthia or by any tyranny that may follow."

"I am sorry," said Simon with finality, "but in such matters, Rabbi, I must ask that you defer to my judgment."

Akiba sighed. "Very well," he said. He rose and began making for the door.

"Where are you going, my master?" asked Rabbi Eleazar Ben-Azariah.

"I am returning to B'nei B'rak," said Akiba sadly. "I shall remain there henceforth. I want no hand in this."

As the sage stood at the door, Bar Kochba went to him, and in a whisper so that no one else could hear it he said, "I beg your forgiveness. On my life, I did not mean to offend you."

"You did not offend me, Simon, my son. It is not that. God be with you." And the rabbi made again as if to go, but Simon took hold of his cloak, as once—a millenium before—King Saul had taken hold of the garment of the prophet Samuel. "I beg you, don't go," said Bar Kochba, a hint of terror in his voice. "I need you."

Akiba smiled and put his hand on the prince's shoulder. "You don't need me, my son. Once, long ago, when you were a rebel against injustice, I was able to help you. But you are a rebel no longer. You have become a conqueror, and I cannot help you anymore."

And with that, Akiba turned and went to his home in B'nei B'rak.

And, as it is written of the prophet Samuel, "He grieved for Saul."

31

An understanding of what the Judeans were doing came upon the Romans suddenly after weeks of official lethargy and confusion. One summer's afternoon, while Alexandrians sought relief from the heat in a midday nap, word came to the Emperor Hadrian of unusual activity among the long-dormant Parthians.

It took not many more days to piece together what was happening. A stiff note of warning was sent to the Parthian king, and the garrison troops in the territory of the Nabataeans were put on special alert. And on the same day the Emperor Hadrian came to an important decision; he decided on total, unrelenting war against the former province of Judea.

The decision was not generally announced, but word of it soon leaked out among the Romans in the Egyptian city. The substance of the decision, as well as its import, was contained in a single name, and that name was enough: Severus. . . .

Faustus Julius Severus—that name sufficed to begin a spirited discussion among almost any group of Romans. Severus, the conqueror of Britannia; Severus, the brooding, moody, laconic Severus.

There were few Romans in Alexandria who had ever met Severus, but there were fewer still who liked him. The man's reputation was shrouded in mystery, but it suggested boorishness, stubbornness, a lust for personal power.

Which is why when the name of Severus leaked out to the Romans, it told everything. It told of the kind of war Hadrian had in mind, and it told of the seriousness of the situation for the emperor to have recalled Severus to active duty.

Nearly twenty years had passed since Faustus Julius Severus, then renowned as the conqueror of Germania, had been called upon to crush a revolt that posed a dangerous threat to the security of Rome. The Britons—large blond savages who practiced human sacrifice and who painted themselves blue when they went into battle—had rebelled and had destroyed the IX Legion in an infamous massacre.

With the early success of the Britons all of Northern Europe was on the brink of rising against the empire when Severus took the field. With unquestioned bravery and by means of a series of brilliant military strokes he defeated the barbarians on their own ground. News of the victory made Severus immensely popular with the Roman masses, and the Senate prepared to grant him the triumphal insignia.

But the general had no sooner returned to Rome than he began issuing a long list of charges and demands. He dared to state—before the Senate itself—that its own lethargy was largely at fault in having failed to prevent the British insurrection; he named many, including the scions of some of the leading families in the empire, as having been guilty of negligence or corruption, and he demanded their immediate dismissal and even the trial of three on charges of treason.

Where the Roman administration of the northern provinces was not openly criminal, Severus had gone on to say, it was antiquated, rigid, hopelessly inefficient. That, he argued, was why those provinces had been so ready to consider joining in the British revolt. He demanded radically new policies for Britannia, for Germania and for Gaul, and he demanded new governors for them as well.

As has been noted many times since, had Severus the diplomatic tact to soften his words, he might well have gained some of the objectives he sought. But as his detractors pointed out, he had acted like a peasant and spoken to the Senate in rough, blunt tones. Instead of politely suggesting errors, he had charged stupidity and corruption; and instead of making recommendations, he had presented demands.

Under these circumstances he had left the Senate no choice but to uphold its much vaunted dignity. All of Severus' proposals were rejected.

The great general left the *curia* as abruptly as he had come and—like a pouting child—had laid down his commission. No one had tried to stop him, and Severus never sought to return to the military career he had left at its very height; nor, for that matter, did he seek or accept any sort of public office. Instead he had contented himself for two decades with living on his comfortable estate in northern Italy, surrounded by his family and a few close friends who would come to visit from time to time. Nothing was known of his private life, and, so it was said, that was exactly the way Severus wanted it.

Now he had been recalled to duty in the closing years of his life by the emperor himself. This enigmatic man would be coming to the court in Alexandria to prepare a war of reconquest against the entrenched Judean rebels. . . .

"It's all over," said Quintus. "All our hopes for a peaceful solution."

"Well, don't brood about it," said Cornelia. "There's nothing more you could have done. And, frankly, I never believed that Rome would give up Judea, under any conditions."

"Perhaps. Yet I still believe that a peaceful arrangement would have been preferable. In any event, I think the emperor exaggerates the Parthian threat. And we certainly cannot blame the Jew for seeking their aid, given the circumstances."

"But you cannot blame the emperor for reacting as he did, either," offered Cornelia.

Quintus sighed. "That's the worst of it. Everyone seems to have acted reasonably, but the result is that the hands of reasonable men are tied." He looked up at her. "So, as you have said, there is nothing further that I can do here, and I will probably be leaving Alexandria before long. Which is what I wanted to talk to you about. I think it's time you made a decision."

Cornelia turned away. "Why do you always force this thing on me? Why must everything we talk about always end up in this?"

"Because it always does," said Quintus simply. "Look, Cornelia, this time I'm not going to shout and storm. I've thought it out, and perhaps I'm a bit older and—yes, even cooler—than I was when it started, and I've decided to stop torturing myself. So you've got to make up your mind one way or the other, because I will not permit it to continue this way."

"That sounds . . . very much like an ultimatum."

"Yes."

Cornelia turned to him with an impudent smile. "And supposing I decide not to divorce Rufus, what then?"

"Then," said Quintus with finality, "you will be divorcing yourself from me forever."

"But I can't make the decision now," said Cornelia furiously, smashing her little fists in her lap. "I can't. I can't. I can't."

"Why?"

"Because I'm not ready. Everything's up in the air now. You yourself said as much."

Quintus rose and took his plumed helmet in his hand. "Everything will always be up in the air for you, Cornelia. It's always been that way. I don't know what keeps you from making the move that reason and your own passions so clearly dictate, but I don't intend to be part of your confusion any longer."

"Don't go," Cornelia pleaded. "Stay with me tonight."

"Ask your husband to stay with you," snapped Quintus.

"All right, then, go," said Cornelia angrily. "It's easy for you, isn't it? You can just step away from me and this whole thing with your precious *virtus* intact. Only I don't know how you could ever have said that you loved me."

"You know I love you," said Quintus. "I'm not going to tell you again."

"Give me just a little more time," Cornelia begged. "Just a little more."

"All right," he said, standing at the door. "I will give you until the final plans are made for the Judean campaign. That should be at least a month. I will come to you then."

"And tonight?"

"No," said Quintus. "I will come to you then."

"*Teki'ah,*" intoned Rabbi Akiba, and the blower of the shophar, the traditional ram's horn, responded with a long blast that reverberated through the synagogue at the university in B'nei B'rak.

"*Shevarim, Teru'ah.*" Three rising notes and nine short ones.

"*Teki'ah Gedolah.*" A long, drawn-out, wailing blast. The sound of alarm. The call to repentance. The call to remembrance of sins. The signal heralding the judgment of the Just Judge.

The synagogues of Judea, and those in all the lands of the dispersion, were filled to overflowing on this day, as Jews everywhere repeated the ancient prayers, the ancient affirmations.

"You remember all that has been done since the beginning of Eternity . . .

"This day, on which Your work was begun, is a monument to the first day of Creation; it is a statute for Israel, a decree of the God of Jacob. And on the nations is sentence pronounced— which to the sword and which to peace; which to hunger and which to plenty. And each separate creature is visited on this day and marked for life or for death . . ."

"And therefore, O Lord," chanted the reader in the Bethar synagogue where Bar Kochba and his wife worshiped, "give glory to Your people, praise to them that fear You, hope to them that seek You, free speech to them that wait for You, joy to Your land, gladness to Your city, a flourishing horn to David, Your servant, and a clear shining light to the son of Jesse, Your anointed, speedily in our days."

Many in the Bethar synagogue looked guardedly toward Bar Kochba and toward his wife sitting in the gallery of the women, for it was well known to them that the child of this couple was of the seed of David, as well as the son of their liberator. . . .

"But on account of our sins we were exiled from our land and removed far from our country, and we are unable to go up in order to appear and prostrate ourselves before You," intoned the reader in the great synagogue in Alexandria. "May it be Your will, O Lord our God and God of our fathers, merciful King, that You may again in Your abundant compassion have mercy upon us and upon Your Temple and may speedily rebuild it and magnify its glory . . ."

"Our God and God of our fathers," prayed the Jews everywhere, "let us be remembered by You for good; grant us a visitation of salvation and mercy from Your heavens . . ."

And in every synagogue the sound of the shophar waxing loud, as it had been heard at the foot of Mount Sinai proclaiming the approach of the Eternal God and by its piercing sound welding twelve primitive tribes into the people of Israel.

"Teki'ah." A long blast.

"Shevarim, Teru'ah." Three rising notes and nine short ones.

"Teki'ah Gedolah." A long, drawn-out, wailing blast. The sound of alarm. The call to repentance. The call to remembrance of sins. The signal heralding the judgment of the Just Judge.

It was Rosh Hashanah, the beginning of the New Year 3894 and of the Year Two of the Liberation of Israel.

32

Faustus Julius Severus arrived at the imperial court in Alexandria without fanfare. In contrast to the banquet that had greeted Lucius Urbanicus, there was merely a gathering in the great hall of the palace consisting of the emperor's major officials and advisers and several other interested parties, Quintus among them.

They were clustered in small groups, whispering, when through a side door came a bald old man wearing simple armor that had been out of fashion for decades and limping heavily on one leg. As if by a command, the hall grew still.

The man limped forward until he stood before the emperor's seat. Then, in a gesture so archaic that it was filled with drama, he drew his sword from its scabbard and raised it in salute.

"Hail Caesar Publius Aelius Hadrianus, *princeps,* first citizen of the republic," he said in Latin.

Hadrian, smiling courteously, raised his own right hand and answered in Latin.

"Hail General Faustus Julius Severus, conqueror of Germania, conqueror of Britannia."

Quintus was deeply moved by the exchange. It was like something out of a play about the bygone days.

At a signal from the emperor, a chair was brought forward

for Severus, who sat down in it heavily. "How may I serve you?" he asked.

"I call upon you," said Hadrian, still speaking the Latin that his general had imposed upon him, "to put down the rebellion in Judea and to restore the purple banner to that province."

"Upon mine honor, I accept the charge," responded Severus, "and by the immortal gods I will attempt the task, and if the fates so decree, I shall conquer for Rome."

Few in the great hall could suppress a smile at the repetition of the ancient vow. It was all so quaint. Was this Severus serious? Why, next he would ask for augury by the priests.

But Severus said nothing more, and so Hadrian asked him, "What is your plan for the campaign?"

"I have, as yet, no plan," said the general, "and if I did, *Princeps,* with your permission, I would not announce it at this large gathering."

A murmur went through the hall. Indeed, this Severus was as much of a boor as people said. Did the old fool dare to question their loyalty? Hadrian felt it necessary to express his confidence. "We have no secrets here," he said.

"Perhaps that is why," suggested Severus quietly, "when Urbanicus' five legions landed in Judea, the Jews were ready for them."

The murmur in the hall grew to a roar of protest, but the noise was broken by the sound of a hearty laugh from the emperor. "You are indeed a straightforward man," he said. "You do not mince your words."

"I am honest," said Severus, with not the trace of a smile on his face. "But for the moment, as I have said, I have no plan. When I do have one, I shall tell you privately.

"First," he continued, "I wish to study the situation in detail so that I may make an intelligent plan. For this purpose I seek the counsel of one who, I was informed in Rome, was a prisoner of the Judean rebels. I request as my aide the Tribune Quintus Arminius Caro."

The emperor looked to Quintus. "What say you, Tribune?"

Quintus arose. "It would be an honor to serve under the distinguished Severus."

Severus also arose. "Then, with the emperor's permission, I would begin at once."

Hadrian nodded, and the two men limped from the hall. Rufus watched them go, and he muttered, "What a peasant that Severus is."

"I want you to tell me everything you know about the Jews," said Severus when the two were alone. "Begin at the beginning, and leave out nothing."

"Well," said Quintus, "you know the Jews."

"I know nothing," said Severus. "Tell me."

Quintus sighed. "Then, as a start, let me say that their revolt was not completely unjustified. You understand, my purpose now is not to condemn anyone, or . . ."

"By the gods," Severus cut him off, "no diplomacy, I beg you. We cannot afford it. With me, at least, say exactly what you think."

"All right. In that case, to be blunt, the Jews rebelled because they were forced to it. Had they instead meekly submitted to what was becoming open oppression, I—as a man who cherishes honor—would have had a great deal less respect for them than I do."

"Good," Severus nodded his head. "Good."

"Tinius Rufus, procurator of the province, robbed them blind. All kinds of injustices took place, and if the Jews sought the protection of Roman law, they had to pay Rufus for it."

"I see," said Severus. "And this was the basic reason for their revolt."

"No," said Quintus, "and that is the devil of it. All of this made them angry, readied them for war against Rome, if you will. But what really touched it off—and this must be unintelligible to you—was the emperor's decision to rebuild their capital."

"I'm listening," said Severus.

"You must understand that the Jews are not like us, nor like anyone else, either. They are unique, and that is something we Romans have never fully appreciated. Among all other nations religion is a means by which the common people learn to accept the way things are. The priests of this god or that guide them in this way or that, tell them to follow this ritual or that, and the people do what the priests tell them, or they don't. It's a part of living for most people in the world—religion—and sometimes a government—including our own—uses the gods to make people do what they might otherwise not want to do but what is basically in their interest or in the interest of the state. Thus, invariably and among all peoples, the gods support war when war is called for in the national interest; and the gods invariably promise victory, and when it does not come, why, the conquered feel that the gods of the conqueror were stronger."

"Of course," said Severus. "Now, tell me, how is it different with the Jews?"

"Well, for one thing, in the case of the Jews their God sometimes calls on them to do things that are obviously not in their interest; yet they will do it, because for them religion far outweighs any other consideration. But that is only one difference. The Jews have no Temple anymore, and no priests, but they have their Law, and they have wise men who expound it. Now this Law is not merely ritual; it covers everything that a Jew might possibly do, from the way that he prays to what he may or may not eat, from his responsibilities to his neighbor to the precise maximum distance that he is permitted to walk on the Jewish holy day. And to the Jews this Law with all its major and minor provisions is supreme over princes, over empires, over life and over death. So you see, when the emperor decided to build his city and a temple to Jupiter on the site of Jerusalem, the Jews did not look upon it as other people would. They did not see the plan as something that would benefit them economically, nor as a move that would enhance their national prestige, nor as anything in fact but a desecration of their holy ground."

"If what you say is true," commented Severus, "and I'm sure that it is, then the decision to build Aelia Capitolina was certainly ill-advised."

"It was worse," said Quintus. "It was stupid. The rising of the Jews could have been predicted."

"Hmm," Severus mused. "Yes. The rising could have been predicted. But not the rest of it. Tell me, Quintus, do you believe in any of the gods?"

"No, of course not."

"Good. Then, without resorting to gods or fables, explain to me the secret of the Jews."

"Secret? What secret?"

"This leader," said Severus, "what is his name? Barekokeba?"

"Bar Kochba," Quintus corrected him. "It means Son of a Star."

Severus smiled. "I'm afraid Barekokeba is about the closest this old Italian tongue of mine can get. He may very well be a natural military genius, this man; all signs point to it. But still he is only one man. He is not a god or a magician. Yet the fact remains that under his leadership the twice-decimated populace of a minor province, a people we have twice defeated and thought to be thoroughly subjugated, has risen to become a more serious threat to us than ever before. Consider, Quintus, what it is the Jews have done without a standing army, with no navy, with no real government, with no capital, with no allies, with no arms or matériel from abroad. They have thrown us out of Judea and have thus far kept us out; they have smashed two separate Roman armies; they have wiped one legion out; they have caused us some forty thousand casualties; they have single-handedly shaken the mightiest empire in the history of man and now actually menace its continued existence. I would call this miraculous, if I believed in miracles. But I don't, and neither do you. So now I ask you to try to explain to me, in the natural terms we both respect, how have they managed to do this?"

"Sometimes a single, outstanding man can be a powerful force."

"Not that powerful. There must be something besides. Try to think what it is. Try to think and tell me, what is the secret of the Jews?"

Quintus sat back, perplexed, and he thought, and although a conclusion continued to elude him, he began to tell the general about his experiences in Judea, about what he had observed in the rebel camp, about Simon, about his meetings with Akiba, about the Seder in B'nei B'rak.

Severus listened without interrupting, for days on end. And he spoke to others as well, to the Legatus Marcellus and to centurions and simple men of the line, and even to Rufus. And then he closeted himself for some days with his maps and with his thoughts, and only after that did he finally send word to the emperor that he was ready to see him and outline his plans. . . .

The audience with Hadrian was held this time in a smaller room of the Alexandria palace, for only those directly concerned with the Judean campaign were admitted, in accordance with Severus' wishes. These were the Procurator Rufus, the Legatus Marcellus, who was in overall charge of the area, and the Tribune Quintus Arminius, who, it was quietly understood, was to be the general's second in command.

Severus greeted the emperor with the same archaic salute he had used on his arrival, and then he handed Hadrian a list of the troops and supplies he was requesting.

Hadrian glanced at the list, then looked up at Severus in disbelief. "There are thirteen full legions with full auxiliary and cavalry on this list," he exclaimed. "Why, put together that's about one hundred fifty thousand men, nearly twice as many as the total of all the troops we have used in Judea to date."

"That's right," said Severus. "I will need that many right at the start. And I will be honest with you; I cannot promise, with the military situation being what it is, that I will not need more men before we are through."

"But every one of these legions is from Europe," Hadrian protested, "from the Danube area and Britannia. The cost of bringing them and their auxiliary here will be tremendous. Why can't we use some of the local troops?"

"Two reasons. First of all, the Danube and British legions are better fighters, more hardened and less prone to Eastern superstition; they are, in fact, our best troops in the whole world, and our best troops now belong in Judea. Second, what with this Barekokeba's overtures to the Parthians and Nabataeans, if we should lose a battle or two, we might need the local legions to deal with other disturbances in the area."

"I trust," interjected Rufus, "that the general is not going into the campaign with the expectation of losing."

Severus turned to the procurator. "The general is going into the campaign with his eyes open. The Jews are far stronger than anyone has thus far given them credit for, and this has been one of their greatest military advantages. It will be no easy victory."

"But you do foresee victory?" asked Hadrian.

"Yes, if my conditions are met."

"Very well. Your request is granted. You shall have your legions from Europe."

"I want more," said Severus.

"More? What? More legions?"

"No," Severus shook his head. "The legions are to defeat Barekokeba's army, and we will do that. But I promised you victory, and for that I will need more than the legions. What I seek in addition is full authority over the province, civil as well as military, at least until the threat is over. I ask this so that I may institute the beginnings of a new policy in Judea, one that has not heretofore been attempted. From the very day that we reenter the province, I seek to try conciliation and persuasion where before only force and suppression have been used. And I want no interference."

"But that is unheard of," exclaimed Rufus. "Rome rests on the cooperation of civil and military authority."

"Rome is not resting now," observed Severus.

"Perhaps," offered Marcellus, "if the general would explain the reason for his unusual request."

Severus limped forward until he stood directly in front of the emperor's seat. "Consider this," he said. "The legions defeated a Jewish army more than sixty years ago, and another grew up after it. The legions defeated that as well, but now a third Jewish army threatens the empire. Give me the legions I request and we can defeat this army, too, although it is far stronger than the previous armies the Jews have raised against us. But if that is all we do, what will we have gained? Clearly, there is something in the Jews that the legions have never defeated, because the legions alone are not enough to defeat it."

"Well, what do you suggest?" asked Rufus, not even trying to mask his impatience.

Severus ignored him. "Again and again," he continued, "before I left Rome and since, I have sought to solve the puzzle of the Jews, to learn their special secret. What impels them to

raise army after army against us? What gives them the strength
—or the desire—to refuse to bow to the gods and the values
adored by the rest of mankind? What enables them to assert
and reassert their own strange ways in a world which, essentially, is hostile to those ways?

"I think I now know this secret. I believe it lies in the memory of the Jews, a memory that each individual Jew shares with
every other Jew in the world; a memory of their brief brush
with glory long ago that is kept alive from generation to generation, that is stored up in their books and taught to their
children and spoken of in their synagogues and sung about in
their poetry and discussed in their councils and celebrated at
their festivals and woven into their clothing and cooked into
the special foods that they eat. It is this long memory of what
they once were that goads them to strive continuously to revive
a past which, in reality, is dead. But it is never dead for them,
because they remember it. If we want to conquer the Jews—
not just defeat them—we must destroy this memory.

"Yet consider, I ask you, how carefully this must be done,
and you will understand why I seek extraordinary authority.
The legions are a great force, but I cannot use force to root
out a memory. Fear does not make people forget; it helps them
to remember. No, *Princeps,* for true victory the fabric which
makes up this memory must be unraveled carefully, even gently. The Jews must be shown not that their ideas are dangerous, but that they are foolish; not that their legends are unique,
but that basically, with a few minor changes, they would be
like everyone else's; not that their ways are hard—for there is
something noble in that—but that they are unpleasant, need-
lessly rigorous, unnecessary. Once this false notion of theirs is
removed, this notion that they are something select and special, why, then, the Jews will have the same ideals as all the
other subjects of the empire, and they will cause us no further
trouble.

"This, then, is the sort of war I plan to fight. First, with the
legions, I will defeat this Jewish rebel. Then, with your authority, I will embark on the greater task. I will blot out for
all time the memory of the Jews."

Book Four
BETHAR

And I will bring the land into desolation; and your enemies that dwell therein shall be astonished at it. And I will scatter you among the heathen and will draw out a sword after you; and your land shall be desolate, and your cities waste.

—Leviticus 26:32–33

And you shall become an astonishment, a proverb and a byword among all nations whither the Lord shall lead you.

—Deuteronomy 28:37

33

A FRESH ROMAN OFFENSIVE against Judea was launched on two fronts late in the winter, toward the end of the month of January. In the north an auxiliary force from Syria crossed the border and was fought to a standstill by the farmer-soldiers of Galilee. In the south Arabian cavalry made several raids on outlying settlements.

It became clear quite early that in neither sector was the Roman commitment very heavy. Yet Bar Kochba would not authorize a counterattack in the north by the regular army, nor did he order a punitive expedition against the Arab raiders.

Instead the prince and a large part of his army quietly encamped themselves in and around the ancient city of Jaffa, on the central coast, far from the scenes of fighting. . . .

It was early in the morning, on the twenty-third day of the month of Shevat, in the Year Two of the Liberation of Israel, that Simon Bar Kochba scanned the city of Jaffa from a hilltop that overlooked it and watched a large Roman fleet as it made directly and at full sail for the harbor.

So his information had been correct, Simon reflected. The Romans had been unable to resist another invasion from the sea, the only boundary the Judeans could not adequately patrol. But this time they had been more prudent and had preceded their major move with diversionary attacks north and south in an attempt to draw the Judean army elsewhere while they landed the bulk of their troops here in Jaffa.

Very clever, mused Simon. Much cleverer than they had been in their last invasion some nine months before. But still not clever enough. He was ready for them again. Jaffa had been evacuated of all but fighting men, and a large Judean force was deployed out of sight in the upper city and the rambling heights beyond. Bar Kochba had left a token force in the lower city, near the port, to offer the first of the invaders a show of resistance. These would flee after a brief skirmish, and the Romans would be permitted to land the remainder of their troops and to occupy the lower city. But they would get no farther than that.

Now the first Roman ship approached the harbor. Soon, thought Bar Kochba, it would begin again. Soon the longboats would appear, and the barges. Soon the legions would disembark and would occupy the port area and would try to move forward to the upper city. They would be met with arrows and catapult stones and an army ready to destroy them. And this time, as he had warned, there would be no mercy.

The lead ship sailed into the harbor, moving toward the port. And then, suddenly, it made a quick turn of its bow back toward the open sea. And at the same moment the ship's catapults let loose a barrage of fire upon the lower city. The barrage consisted of pitch and bitumen-soaked wood pieces set ablaze and hurled from the ship the short distance into the port area. There was no accuracy possible in scattering the fiery missiles, but none was needed. The few that found their way through open windows or onto the roofs of wooden structures started fires that quickly began to spread.

The first ship sailed from the harbor; a second moved in to take its place, and just as systematically, it too unloaded its cargo of firebrands.

The small group of defenders stationed in the lower city tried for a time to extinguish the blazes, but they soon despaired of this and ran from the flaming buildings—to be picked off as they fled by archers on the Roman vessels.

Judean catapults began heaving boulders at the ships from the upper city. Most of the missiles fell into the sea, but one found its mark. It smashed against the deck of a ship, splitting it in two and pitching its occupants into the waters of the harbor.

A roar of triumph rose up from the Judean ranks, but it was short-lived. Other vessels picked up the survivors, and with comparatively little delay the bombardment continued.

From his post on the hilltop outside the city, Bar Kochba noted with a start that the occupants of the smashed ship appeared to have been surprisingly few, not many more than the number of the crew. The prince stood at some distance from the harbor, and he quickly assured himself that he would not have been able to see many of the survivors, while the legionaries belowdecks might well have sunk in their heavy armor. Yet still he wondered, with a growing uneasiness, if and why there might have been an empty ship in that Roman fleet.

The land catapults bravely went on heaving their stones at the vessels, but they were at a serious disadvantage, since the targets they aimed at were relatively small, while the Romans could heave their fiery missiles anywhere and know they were striking at enemy ground. And as the fire spread, the Judean catapult men were forced to withdraw from their most strategic positions at the edge of the upper city to still higher ground, and more and more of their missiles went wild.

The blaze could be kept from spreading to the heights, but as for the port area, it would have been senseless suicide for any of the defenders to move into it and attempt to put out the flames. So there was little they could do but watch helplessly as the port of Jaffa, the port from which the prophet Jonah had set out, burned to the ground.

Bar Kochba watched the scene in angry frustration, and he vowed that he would make the Romans pay for this act of destruction. And he thought. And he made plans and mental notes. And he passed the word for his troops to be ready for the eventual enemy landing. And he waited. And as the flames in the port area began to die out, he wondered what it was the Romans were waiting for. Until, finally, Jonathan ran to him, white and trembling in fury, and blurted out the news.

"The Romans have landed at Caesarea. They've tricked us. They're back."

Quintus Arminius Caro stood for a long moment in a room of the palace at Caesarea and looked about it sadly. The room had not changed. The walls had not changed. The hangings on the windows had not changed. The bed had not changed. In the year and a half since he had been in this room with Cornelia, the world had changed; but for the room, for Cornelia and for himself, nothing had really changed at all.

Quintus walked from the room to the large hall of the palace, which, as of an hour before, had become the Roman high command in Judea. Severus was in the hall alone, studying his ever present charts. He looked tired, strangely disconsolate, and in that moment he seemed to Quintus a lonely old man.

"Hail General Severus," said Quintus on entering.

"Hail Quintus," said Severus without looking up. "How does it look outside?"

"Everything is in order. The city has been pacified. Three legions and auxiliary have been landed so far. The rest should be onshore by nightfall."

"Casualties?"

"We lost about a hundred men in the first wave of landings during the actual fight for the city. The Jews seem to have lost about the same number."

"You have taken the necessary precautions?"

"The walls are manned, and sentries are patrolling the streets. Outside, the British cavalry and auxiliary units have sealed off the city from the surrounding area, as you ordered."

"Good. It appears we shall be here for several days."

"Do you expect the Jews to attack the city?"

"I wish they would," said Severus, "but I doubt it. Why attack us here and lose the advantage of fighting on their own terms and their own ground? No, if I were this Barekokeba I would wait for us to leave Caesarea, and I suspect that is what he will do."

"If I may say so, sir," offered Quintus, "this landing here during the diversions at Jaffa and at the borders was a brilliant move."

"Not really," said Severus absently. "The border diversions were not effective, and we were lucky in Jaffa. And as for the landing by sea, it was a rather obvious tactic. The Jews have no navy. But let us not forget that they do have an army—a very good one—and from here on in that is what we will be facing. Let's keep that in mind. It has been an auspicious start, but I'm far more concerned about the end."

Quintus nodded. "Oh, yes," he said, almost as an afterthought, "we have taken prisoners. They seem to be residents of the city. Outside of the women and children, there are nearly a thousand men. All of them were armed."

The general looked up at him. "What do you think we should do with them?" he asked.

Quintus turned away.

Severus walked up to the tribune. "Do not be disturbed," he said. "I am not Rufus. Order the prisoners to be assembled in the city square."

Quintus saluted and walked from the hall.

When his command had been carried out, Severus folded up his charts, put on his plumed helmet and limped outside to the steps of the palace facing the city square. There, surrounded by legionaries, were the men who had been captured that morning in the brief but violent fight for Caesarea. Severus considered them. They seemed a defiant lot. He could see no fear in their faces; the general noted that with some astonishment and with admiration as well. He noticed also that there were few Jews among the prisoners. Most appeared to be of mixed Hellenistic blood. Severus wondered idly why they had joined in the revolt, but he imagined they had had their reasons. He spoke to them now in a loud voice that boomed across the square.

"You all know the penalty for rebellion against Rome. That penalty is death by crucifixion, a penalty which you have all incurred. However, by the authority vested in me by the Senate and the Roman People, I lift that penalty and order your immediate release."

The prisoners in the square, each of whom had resigned himself to the inevitable horror, looked at one another in stunned disbelief.

"From this day forth," Severus continued, "you are all once again free citizens of this city and of this province, entitled to the full protection of Roman law. I call upon you all to go back to your homes and to your shops. The war, for you, is over. Live your daily lives as normally as you can, and you shall have nothing to fear; worship any or all or none of the gods, as you wish, and there will be no interference. As of today, there is no cause for rebellion nor anything further to be gained by it, for I promise you a new order of justice. I promise this in the name of Rome."

Severus motioned to the officer in charge of the prisoners. "Centurion," he said, "tell your men to make room for the citizens of Caesarea to depart the square."

The centurion, as stunned as the prisoners themselves, barked out the command, and the legionaries broke their ranks while the men who had been trying to kill them only hours before moved from the square slowly, suspiciously, still unable to believe what had happened.

Severus turned and, with his aide behind him, reentered the palace.

Quintus could barely control the throbbing in his voice as he congratulated the general.

Severus took off his helmet and slumped down in a chair. "Tribune, I want you to issue the following directives in my name: Henceforth, crucifixions will be forbidden; any atrocity committed by our troops will be severely punished; the penalty for rape and looting will be death; and unless orders are issued to the contrary, today's procedure will be followed with prisoners—all will be released."

Quintus looked up from the papyrus on which he was noting the orders. "You know, sir, that some of the men we release in this way may eventually join in fighting us elsewhere."

"I expect some of them may," said Severus, "at least in the beginning. In that case, I fear, we will have to defeat such men more than once. That would be unfortunate, but it can be done. Remember, Quintus, that we are trying to do a much harder thing. We are trying to defeat an idea."

34

On the twenty-fifth of Shevat, the Roman fleet that had served as a decoy at Jaffa bombarded the coastal fishing communities of Yavneh-Yam and Ashdod-Yam while on its way back to Egypt. The fleet encountered no effective resistance. But the following morning the ships, still sailing south, moved into a carefully laid trap in the harbor of Ashkelon. Oil had been poured into the waters of the harbor, and as the Roman vessels hove into it, the defenders ignited the oil and turned much of the harbor into a sea of flame. As the trapped ships tried to get away, catapult stones rained on them from shore. In all, nine Roman ships were thus sunk in the harbor of Ashkelon, dealing Rome her first blow of the new campaign.

On the same day, however, Rome achieved an important land objective. Five legions that the Judeans did not realize were there suddenly smashed across the border from Syria, marched swiftly south to the stronghold of Migdal near the Sea of Galilee and overwhelmed it.

The Roman strategy at this point was not very difficult to make out. It would have been understood perfectly well by Pharaoh Thutmose III, who, 1,500 years before, had sought exactly the same objective that the Romans were now seeking. That objective was what the Romans called the Via Maris, what the Jews called Derech Ha-Yam and what the Egyptians, the Canaanites and the Philistines had each called after their own tongue. It was the natural highway leading from Egypt in the south, across Judea, to Syria in the north.

Both Via Maris and Derech Ha-Yam mean Way of the Sea, since, for the most part, the road follows the coastline of Judea. In making directly for Damascus, however, the road branches off sharply at Caesarea to the east and then to the northeast in a natural path toward its destination that leads across Galilee. Significantly the last major Judean city on the Via Maris before the Syrian border is Migdal.

From the moment the five legions took Migdal, following the capture of Caesarea, the Roman plan became evident to anyone who knew the map of Judea. If the two bodies of invading troops, north and south, could join forces along the inland section of the Via Maris, they would not only control that important stretch of road and assure their supply lines, but they would, by their presence, effectively cut off the north of Judea from the rest of the country.

But it is a long distance from Caesarea to Migdal, and after cutting across the coastal plain, the road from Caesarea begins wending its way around the foot of the mountains of Samaria toward the ancient city of Megiddo and the broad Valley of Jezreel beyond it. And for a distance of some eight miles before Megiddo the road is hemmed in by the Carmel Hills on the left and the mountains of Samaria on the right. This is the Megiddo Pass, the meeting place of opposing armies since before history. . . .

Before long the two Roman forces, north and south, began their predictable movements along the Via Maris. But because these movements were predictable, the Romans knew from the start that they could expect heavy resistance.

In the north this resistance came almost at once. The five legions that had entered the country from Syria had moved only a short distance southward from Migdal when they found themselves bogged down at a spot on the Via Maris controlled by the cliff top citadel of Arbel. Their attempts to take the citadel by storm were repulsed, and only after weeks of savage fighting were they able to overcome the heavily outnumbered garrison and move on. And still ahead of the northern troops, as they were aware, was the most treacherous part of their march, the part that would take them through the hill country of lower Galilee. . . .

By contrast the eight legions under Severus' direct command at first met no resistance as they marched from Caesarea on the Via Maris in the general direction of Megiddo. In point of fact, they met no Jews at all in moving across a section of the flat coastal plain, but the scenes of destruction that they passed attested to the fact that their movement along this road had not been unexpected. Farm after farm had been left deserted, its wells stopped up, its crops burned so that the Romans could not eat of them, its house and sheds smashed so that the Romans could not find shelter.

"Observe, Quintus," said Severus as they passed such a farm, "the strength of an idea. There is not a farmer in all of Italy who would do this to his land."

The progress of Severus' troops was thus unhindered until they came to the small village of Narbatha, a collection of mud huts on the Via Maris. The residents of the village had remained in their homes, and they resisted with a violence that caught the Romans off guard, so that it took the better part of a morning to subdue the little place. The prisoners taken in the fighting, who in this case numbered less than 100 men, were released.

The legions marched from Narbatha and on the following day reached the stronghold of Beth Yannai just off the Via Maris and commanding the entrance to the foothills of Samaria. They arrived to a hail of arrows and missiles. And as the Romans were setting up their camp outside the city under this bombardment, there was a surprise attack by warriors who sallied forth and invaded the Roman position, cutting down men and animals before retreating to the protection of the city wall.

With methodical persistence the Romans laid siege to Beth Yannai, surrounding it with earthen ramparts and setting up their catapults and stone throwers to bombard the wall and the city beyond.

The Jews, scorning repeated offers to surrender, continued making sorties when they were least expected and inflicted heavy casualties. But each time, more and more of the raiders themselves were slain, and as the days of the siege turned into weeks and the weeks into a month and more, the Roman grip around Beth Yannai tightened, and the sorties grew fewer and more feeble, and battering rams began to resound against the wall of the stronghold.

Yet the fight for the city continued, and even the coming of the Jewish Festival of the Passover did not diminish it, for the Law held that self-defense was permitted at all times. And so the Jews of Beth Yannai defended themselves and their city as best they could, despite overwhelming odds.

But ultimately, of course, those odds triumphed, and the stronghold of Beth Yannai fell to the Roman forces on the nineteenth day of the month of Nisan, following a siege of one month, two weeks and two days.

When it was over, Severus ordered the city razed. And this time the several thousand Jewish prisoners captured in the fighting were not released. Instead they were ordered taken back under guard to Caesarea.

Later, in the Roman camp near the ruins of Beth Yannai, Quintus asked if this move represented a change of policy.

"Maybe," said Severus wearily. "I don't know. I just can't risk it anymore."

"I see," said Quintus.

But Severus looked up at the tribune as if he had been accused, and he asked, "Quintus, do you know how many men we have lost here in a fight for a small city that Rome has never heard of?"

"I'm afraid that I do."

"Well, then, I ask you, how can I keep releasing prisoners to fight us again? It had seemed like a good idea, but I just can't risk it any longer."

Severus sat back and put his hand over his eyes. "Have you seen these prisoners, Quintus? I looked them over today. They included a lad who can't be more than fourteen and an old graybeard who must be in his seventies. He was manning a stone thrower on the wall when he was captured." Severus laughed, a short, bitter laugh. "Can you imagine that, Quintus? By the gods, with all my talk about not underestimating the Jews, I'm afraid I have done so as well."

Quintus was silent.

Severus took his hand away from his eyes and looked directly at the tribune. "At any rate," he said, "I have no intention of abandoning the policy of conciliation. If anything, the frenzy with which the Jews fight has made me realize all the more how vital such a policy is. It's just that, for the time being, we will no longer release prisoners."

"What do you plan to do with them?" asked Quintus. "Will you have them kept under guard in Caesarea?"

"No," said Severus. "That would be unfeasible. No, I have another plan. The prisoners we have taken here will be put on a ship in Caesarea and transported to the slave markets of Alexandria, where they will be sold to pay for some small part of this campaign. But that," he sighed, "is not really the point. They will not be slaves for long. Their brethren in Egypt will buy them up and free them, whatever the cost. It appears this is also a feature of their Law. But that is not really the point, either. The point is, it will get them out of Judea."

"A wise plan," offered Quintus, "and just."

"In any event," said Severus, "it will get them out of Judea. . . ."

*   *   *

From Simon Bar Kosiba

To Judah Ha-Cohen, military commander of Galilee, peace.

The Roman force that landed at Caesarea has overcome the valiant defenders of Beth Yannai and is even now preparing to continue moving northward on Derech Ha-Yam, toward the Megiddo Pass. It is in the pass that I plan to meet them with the major part of our army. It is there that we shall strive to halt the enemy advance and to drive the Romans back to the sea.

For your part, it is imperative that you keep the legions that invaded from Syria bogged down in the hills of Galilee, preventing their farther progress. These troops must remain separated from the main Roman force that came by sea.

We are ready to meet the main force in the Megiddo Pass and to defeat it in what may well be the decisive battle of the war. If, however, the legions from the north should manage to break through to Megiddo, they would, together with the main force, surround our own troops and form a massive army that we could not overcome in open battle. It is vital, therefore, that you hold back the northern legions, whatever the cost.

Know that after we have achieved victory over the main body of the enemy, we shall move from Megiddo at once to come to your aid.

Be strong,
Simon

To my father, Senator Caius Arminius:

Hail and greeting.

I take pen in hand tonight with extreme distaste, for I am so weary that I can hardly form the characters of the alphabet. Yet I feel I must write to let you know that I am unharmed and perhaps also to form some sort of chronicle of events that, if taken separately, would make no sense at all.

A shockingly high number of Romans and a great many Jews have perished within the past two months in a struggle for control of a small stretch of road that I could ride over at leisure in an hour or so. Most of the struggle was centered around a minor city that I might not even notice on my ride, yet the city took us a month and a half to capture. The importance of the city, except for the fact that it is near the road, is nil. The importance of the road itself is not clear to me at the present moment, though somewhere in my mind I know it well, for nothing is clear to me now except that I am tired.

Severus told the emperor he foresaw no easy victory over the Jews, but I fear even he did not fully appreciate the quality of the foe we would be facing. The entire population is united against us, and if a place is not fiercely defended by the Jews, then it is destroyed by them before we arrive. And I share with Severus the painful realization that the worst is still somewhere ahead of us. For we have not yet met the bulk of the regular Judean army, and the resistance we have encountered to date seems to have been mostly on the part of armed citizens rather than seasoned soldiers.

As for Severus himself, I have nothing but admiration for him. He is a Roman in every sense of the word, and if there is a man alive who can defeat these people, he is that man. Despite everything, he has consistently refused to permit even a single prisoner to be slain as an example, and until recently he released every rebel who fell into our hands. Now he has decided to begin deporting those we capture, but even so he will not suffer any prisoner to be harmed, saying that he wants to demonstrate to the population that they have nothing to fear from Roman rule. There has been open grumbling by the troops against this policy of Severus, but it is a mark of the man that he simply ignores it.

Our current objective is to meet those legions which crossed into Judea from Syria. In doing so we will have to capture a very long stretch of this road leading all the way to the Syrian border, but if we succeed in this, we will cut off the north of Judea from the rest of the country. You may be surprised at the forthright manner in which I state this fact of military strategy, but it is quite clear from their actions that the Jews see all too well what we are trying to do.

The worst of our present situation is that we have lost contact with the legions in the north, and for all we know, they are no longer in existence. It seems absurd to suggest that five legions with auxiliary and cavalry could be obliterated, but in this country nothing is impossible.

I will write you again as soon as my duties allow, but please try not to be concerned if there is a lapse of time, as it may happen that there will be no way for me to get letters to you. In any case I trust my next letter will be more heartening.

Your loving son

On a pleasant spring day less than a week after their costly victory at Beth Yannai, the troops commanded by Faustus Julius Severus entered the Megiddo Pass.

The change of terrain was sudden. As the Romans marched forward, the gently rolling country along their route sprang up to form steep hills and rises on both sides of the Via Maris. And just as suddenly the Romans found themselves under attack.

The attack began with a flight of arrows. Then, as the legionaries took cover beneath their long shields, a large body of men poured down from the surrounding hills and smashed itself against the invading column.

Thus, on the twenty-fifth of Nisan, in the Year Two of the Liberation of Israel, corresponding to the year 134 in the calendar of the Minaeans, began the battle of the Megiddo Pass.

The Romans repelled that first attack and the second and the third, and they fought their way through again and again, in more than two weeks of painfully slow progress and sudden death, until they came at last to the narrowest part of the pass, not far from the city of Megiddo. There, behind a wall of barricades that blocked the Via Maris, stood the massed army of Simon Bar Kochba.

A bombardment of catapult stones, lances, arrows and rocks greeted the Roman approach, followed by a violent assault in which the Jews—screaming their battle cry—leaped across the barricades and hurled themselves upon the invaders.

Here, by the city of Megiddo, the battle assumed its full fury, as the Jews fought with all their might to drive the Romans back through the pass. But the Romans, having come this far, were not to be driven back, and they answered the Jewish on-slaughts with attacks of their own, aimed at smashing through the barricades. Yet, despite the most savage assaults, the Jews would not yield, so that after a time the battle settled down into a bloody stalemate in which both sides stood firm and fought and died in that pass, separated only by the barricades and by their mutual determination.

Severus sent legion after legion to try and break through the Judean line, and the soldiers in them went forward with a sense of duty that blocked out fear; but each time, the legion-aries were forced to withdraw, leaving their dead to add to the barriers that blocked the pass.

Bar Kochba, too, sought by assaults and stratagems to dis-lodge the enemy; but in this his warriors had no success, and though many perished, they achieved not the slightest change in the position of the opposing force.

Yet both sides continued striving for a change day after day for week after week, hoping that if the enemy could not be routed, he could at least be worn down. . . .

From the chronicle of Mariamne:

Today was Menashe's first birthday. He is a beautiful little boy, if I may be excused for thinking this. He has Simon's deep-blue eyes and a deadly serious little manner, yet for all of this he seems to take after my father. He has a certain humor in him which is neither from Simon nor from me, but which gives me a start whenever I recognize it.

Simon is not here, of course, and I try not to think at all of where he is or what he may be doing. It is a trick, and it sometimes works. Here, in Bethar, we are comfortable enough. We have a house of our own, and I see Ruth and her son every day. It was from her that I learned the trick of not thinking, for I could see how she had mastered it.

It occurs to me that Simon was also away on the day that Menashe was born. I pray that in future years we shall all be together. But I must not think thus. I must make no

demands of the future, for that way lies the fear I am trying
so hard to avoid. There is no cause for fear. Everything will
be well, for Menashe, for Simon and even for me.

On the twenty-ninth day of the battle of the Megiddo Pass
a Judean force that had made a raid across the lines was surrounded before it could return to the safety of the barricades
and killed to the last man.

On the thirtieth day the crack British cavalry lured the Judean horsemen into a pitched battle in the hills above the pass.
The battle cost the defenders nearly half of their cavalry, but
the survivors managed to ride back to their own lines, and the
pursuing Britons were unable to penetrate the Judean position.

On the thirty-first day a cohort of Dacian auxiliaries strayed
too close to the barricades and was wiped out in a sudden assault.

On the evening of the thirty-second day the Tribune Quintus Arminius Caro sat down in his tent and wrote the following
letter:

> From Quintus Arminius Caro to the Lady Cornelia:
> Hail and greeting.
> I hereby break my vow and write to you again, because I
> am weak, and because I still love you, and because I am
> convinced that I will soon be dead. Thus, I offer this letter
> as my final testament to you, who have made my last years
> senselessly happy and just as senselessly sad.
> I have loved only three things in my life—Rome, my
> father and you. I could explain my first two loves, but the
> third would not fit into any system of logic that I have
> learned. I have loved you, Cornelia, for what you are, yet
> I have loved you also despite everything that you are.
> You have caused me much pain, and at our parting you
> still made yourself unable to come to the decision I so
> urgently begged for. But I suppose, now that I think of it
> in the cool approach of night, that this at least followed

logically from the first. From the beginning you gave me everything but yourself. You never gave me that, not in all our days and nights together. And perhaps I was wrong to demand it of you. Perhaps, Cornelia, it is the one thing you cannot give.

Yet for all of this, as a tribute to the sweet insanity we call love, know that I would not have given up any of it, not even the pain.

Ave atque vale
Quintus

At the end of the thirty-fifth day of the battle, under cover of a moonless night, the Romans attempted to cut across a section of the surrounding hills and attack the city of Megiddo from the rear. But the expedition, led by the Tribune Quintus Arminius Caro, was itself surprised and set upon by Judean warriors posted in the hills to guard against just such a move.

"Withdraw," Quintus shouted as he realized that his own force was in danger of being encircled. "Withdraw," he shouted again, drawing the attention of one of the Judean archers. . . .

When the survivors of the unsuccessful foray made it back to the shelter of the Roman camp, they carried the tribune, who had been wounded with an arrow in the side.

At dawn on the thirty-seventh day the Judeans launched a concentrated offensive against the Roman forces. The powerful assault caught the Romans off balance, and they sustained heavy casualties; but there was nothing like the general break in the line that Bar Kochba had hoped for, and as the day's fighting ended, the position of the Roman forces remained, basically, what it had been before.

By the fortieth day of that battle the living on both sides were dulled into a delirium of death and killing. Night brought no surcease to the fighting, and each morning saw a new assault by one side or the other. There seemed no end to the battle and no prospect of it, and there was no longer a man on either side—including Severus and Bar Kochba—who seriously expected to leave that pass alive.

The dead were now piled up high before the barricades,

bloated and decaying and poisoning the air of the pass with their stench and coloring red the beautiful green ground of the fertile hills. Vultures came daily to eat of the bodies before the eyes of their living comrades on both sides, but neither the invaders nor the defenders could risk moving into the thin strip of land between them only in order to chase the birds of prey away. And so the vultures would remain and eat until, inevitably, the battle was renewed and frightened them into flight.

It was on the forty-sixth day of the battle, being the eleventh of the month of Sivan, that Bar Kochba looked across the Valley of Jezreel and saw the approach of a fresh Roman force from the northeast. They were, clearly, troops of the five legions that had crossed over from Syria. Judah Ha-Cohen had reduced their numbers, but he had not been able to hold them, although, as the prince would learn, he had given his life in the attempt.

Bar Kochba looked at Jonathan, and Jonathan turned away.

There was no choice, and both men knew it. The Judeans could not let themselves be trapped in the pass between two Roman forces. Simon gave the necessary orders. The city of Megiddo was burned to the ground, and what was left of the mighty army that had gone with Bar Kochba to Jaffa the previous winter retreated at the end of spring from the Megiddo Pass, moving through Samaria to the south, to Bethar. . . .

Later that same day the two Roman forces met and became one. They now controlled the entire interior section of the Via Maris, and with it much of the north of Judea. But the toll throughout had been frightful. Nearly 50,000 Roman troops had perished, most of them in the fight for the Megiddo Pass.

The horror of the battle impressed itself heavily upon both the Romans and the Judeans, and through them upon the minds of men, so that in time the very name "Megiddo" brought up visions of war and slaughter.

In Hebrew the mound which the city had become was called Har Megiddo—the Hill of Megiddo. But in the Greek and Latin tongues the name was corrupted into a single word, a word that came to denote the ultimate in destruction. That word was "Armageddon."

35

To Caesar Publius Aelius Hadrianus, *princeps,* from General Faustus Julius Severus:

Hail and greeting.

It is my unpleasant duty to call upon you now for reinforcements to replace men lost in the fight to reconquer the Via Maris, along with the towns and cities on its route from Caesarea to Migdal. These losses, I am sorry to say, were heavier than had been anticipated, the Jews having thrown up resistance that was beyond my worst expectations. Nevertheless, we have succeeded in our major objectives so far, and as I told you in Alexandria, I have full confidence in our ability to subjugate the entire province.

For this task, however, I will need an additional three legions, together with auxiliary, which I request again to be drawn from Europe.

Please let me know as soon as possible when these troops can be expected.

With respects,
Severus

The Roman victory at the Megiddo Pass did not end the Judean resistance in the north. If anything, the inhabitants of Galilee now fought for their homes and their freedom with increased fervor, throwing up fierce opposition at Ramah, at Shaav, at Bethlehem of Galilee, at Acco and at many other places all across the region.

At times a force of the defenders would appear in the field and offer the Romans open battle. But Severus, with the fury of Megiddo still fresh in his mind, avoided this wherever possible. Instead he pursued a policy of siege, of cutting off communications among the Judean strongholds, of blocking roads and sealing off supply lines. It was, perhaps, not a glorious sort

of war, but it was the sort of war in which the rigid discipline
of the legions counted for more than the desperate courage of
their enemies.

With the Via Maris in Roman hands Bar Kochba could promise no early help to the defenders of Galilee, while the sizable
Samaritan army charged with the defense of the region directly
to the south was itself in no position to attempt smashing
through the Roman line separating it from the beleaguered
area. And within Galilee the Romans soon controlled all the
routes, so that every separate stronghold and village and town
invested by the various legions found itself alone, isolated and
surrounded.

Yet every place thus besieged held out longer than could have
been foreseen, surrendering in the end to hunger and thirst
more than to the Romans. And when the Jews were able to retreat in the face of an overwhelming enemy force, they left a
trail of devastation behind them, wreaking more havoc on their
own ground than the invader had done. And when, as sometimes happened, the Jews refused either to retreat or to surrender a stronghold, they fought to the last man with a violence
that astounded their enemies.

Throughout the months of the fight for Galilee Severus continued trying to persuade the Jews to lay down their arms. But
in this he was one man fighting vainly against an unhappy
memory and a glorious dream—the memory of three generations of Roman tyranny and the dream of an end to all tyranny.

Severus set up checkpoints at Hammath on the Sea of Galilee,
at Bethlehem of Galilee and at several other sites, and he urged
Jews to come to any of these points and surrender, placing
their trust in Roman honor. A few did, but very few. For the
most part, the Jews of Galilee stood on their ground until they
were pushed from it or dragged from it or slain on it.

And indeed, a few small towns in the hills of Galilee—along
with the stronghold of Safed high up in the mountains—would
never be overcome by the Romans, and the unconquered Jews
within would remain in their homes through the ages to bear
witness that this was the land God had given them.

But the other strongholds did fall, singly, violently, at great
cost to both conqueror and conquered. In some areas of Galilee
the defeated Jews managed to flee before the advancing legions

and make it across the border with their families to find refuge in neighboring lands. Those who fell into Roman hands were, as a matter of policy now, deported to the slave markets of Alexandria; but there was a limit to what these markets could sell, and many of the prisoners were transported still farther, to the countries of Europe. Wherever they were taken, there were other Jews to buy them and release them at once, as a religious obligation, so that all Jews who had survived the war were soon free, although in exile.

And what they all had in common, those Jews who fled and those who were forcibly deported, was a strangely mystical determination to return to the land in which they had suffered so much. It was a determination they taught their children, together with a firm though patently groundless belief that they would be back, soon, if not this year then the next, or the next. . . .

By midsummer the Romans had subdued the effective resistance in Galilee. They found themselves rulers of an area that had been all but depopulated, masters of cities razed, of villages smashed, of farms destroyed, of age-old forests that had been burned in a day, of fruit trees that had been chopped down to make battering rams, of groves trampled, of vineyards turned into mounds of stones, of hillsides laid bare, of once green valleys plowed into dust by marching feet. And they looked upon it all in wonder.

At about the same time the additional troops Severus had requested arrived in Caesarea. With them was the procurator of the province.

Quintus stood before the smiling fat man in the Caesarea palace, and he asked him pointedly, "What are you doing here, Rufus?"

"Now, now," said the procurator, "is that the way for old friends to greet each other? Are you not concerned for my welfare? I am concerned for yours. I understand you were wounded again, though ever so slightly this time. How are you, Quintus?"

The tribune sighed. "Rufus, I have spent the last seven months in the lowest pit of Hades. I have killed men whom I have had no particular desire to kill. Now I ask you once again, what are you doing here?"

Rufus shook his head in a show of hurt. "I have been sent

by the emperor himself," he said, "in order to cooperate with
General Severus in restoring Roman rule to this province and
in assuring that there is no repetition of what has happened."

"I thought it had been agreed there would be no interference
with Severus."

"I said cooperate, not interfere. This province needs some
sort of government while Severus is still busy subjugating
the greater part of it, don't you agree? Someone will have to
launch the very policy Severus proposed, of removing the Jews
as a threat to the empire. Someone will have to govern the areas
already reconquered and to arrange for their resettlement."

"Their resettlement?"

"Of course," said Rufus. "No Jew who has left this province,
by deportation or in any other way, will be permitted to return. So we will settle others here, from Syria and elsewhere.
That is the best guarantee that what happened will not happen
again. It is the emperor's own idea."

"You won't get many to settle in Galilee," Quintus said.
"Most of it is a wasteland now. It will take a generation of hard
work to make it livable again. And I suspect the same will be
true of much of the rest of the province before we are through."

"That's not my problem," said Rufus. "The emperor is offering a generous bounty to those who do come, and that should
draw some. We don't need many."

"A Judea without Jews," mused Quintus. "An interesting
thought."

"That's another thing," said Rufus. "It's not Judea anymore.
We want to divorce this place from the Jews entirely. Henceforth, the province is to be called Palaestina."

"Palaestina? Where did you ever find that name?"

"The emperor created it. It's taken from the Philistines, a
people who once shared this area with the Jews."

"But there are no such people anymore," observed Quintus
sarcastically. "With all respect to the emperor, the name 'Palaestina' will never be accepted."

"That," said Rufus, "is also not my problem. What is my
problem is to aid Severus in . . . blotting out the memory of
the Jews, I believe he termed it."

"That's right," said Quintus. "And I ask you to remember
that Severus is still in overall charge of this area, no matter how

close you have managed to get to the emperor in recent months. I have been told to inform you that no atrocities are permitted, that you are not to exact vengeance on anyone for having taken part in the revolt, that you are not here to punish."

"I understand," said Rufus coldly.

"Very good," said Quintus. He turned his back on the procurator and strode from the room.

Quintus spent that night in the Caesarea palace. He spent it with Cornelia, who had accompanied her husband on his return to the province.

They lay together, and they made love, and they exchanged words, but they did not really speak. Cornelia had meant to say so many things, but somehow she did not. Quintus, too, had planned to talk to Cornelia again, to repeat the pleas and the arguments that he had used before, but somehow he could not begin. And as the tribune rode from Caesarea in the morning with the three new legions behind him, he reflected that he had not said anything at all.

36

The three fresh legions led up from Caesarea by Quintus joined forces with Severus' battle-hardened troops at a spot along the Via Maris. From there, while Quintus remained with the general, the new legions and three others were dispatched to the east, to the old Roman garrison town of Geresh across the Jordan. Their orders were to strike back from Geresh toward the west and thus attack the region of Samaria from an unexpected quarter.

The more than 70,000 men remaining with Severus began marching south along the coastal plain, headed for the region of Judah. They fought many skirmishes along the way, but no major battles, for the Jews had apparently decided to cede the coastal plain for the time being and make a concerted stand amid the hills of Judah, where the revolt had broken out.

Thus, as the Romans moved southward, the towns along
their route fell to them in quick succession, often without resistance. Kfar Sava fell, and Migdal Afek, and Antipatris, and
the area from Lydda to the sea, which included Tz'rifin and
Beth Dagan, and the little university town of B'nei B'rak. . . .

The conquering Roman general and his tribune arrived at
the university of B'nei B'rak shortly before sundown. They
were alone and rode quietly to the main gate, where the steward
of the house ushered them in respectfully, brought them wine
and asked them to be kind enough to wait a few moments. A
little while later Rabbi Akiba Ben-Joseph joined them. Quintus noted with a start how much the rabbi had aged since they
had last met; the old man's back was stooped now, and his hands
shook a bit and his eyes seemed to be looking at some point
far away. Only his voice remained unchanged.

"Forgive me for having kept you waiting," said Akiba. "It
was the time of the evening prayer."

"We understand," said Quintus.

The rabbi looked at him absently. "You are the Tribune
Quintus. We were together last, as I recall, under more auspicious circumstances. For me, at least."

"It was the Passover ceremony," said Quintus. "More than
two years ago now."

"Yes, yes. I remember it well."

"I have come," Quintus went on, "to introduce my commander who wanted very much to meet you. This is General Faustus Julius Severus."

Severus rose before the rabbi and bowed his head slightly.
"I am honored."

Akiba shook the general's hand and courteously motioned
him back to his seat. "I have heard of you," he said. "I have
heard many good things. You are a fair man. It is a pity we are
on opposite sides."

"We need not remain so," said Severus. "Henceforth we can
be on the same side, Rabbi, the side of justice and of reason."

Akiba shook his head sadly. "Alas," he said, "we cannot."

"But why?" asked Severus. "If you believe me to be fair, you
must trust me."

"I trust you. But there are things beyond your control, as

there are things beyond mine. Sometimes, when we think we control things the most, we control them the least."

"What do you mean?" asked Severus.

"It was all correct," the rabbi said, "all the prophecies of consolation I gleaned from my studies—the redemption of Israel, the restoration of a free Jewish state, the rebuilding of Jerusalem, the beginning of a new era. I was only off on the timing, perhaps by a millennium or two. That is all."

Severus glanced at Quintus quizzically. Akiba caught the look and smiled a sad smile. "Everything is foreseen," he said, "but freedom of choice is given. A paradox, I know. But then, so much of the truth is paradoxical, isn't it, Tribune?"

"The general can do very much to ease the plight of your people," offered Quintus. "And you can help him."

"It is a thing beyond our control," said Akiba. "I realize that now. The general does not realize it yet. A force has been set in motion, and its course is inevitable, I fear. I helped to set one part of it in motion myself, but that doesn't matter because—being the man I am—my action was inevitable as well. The freedom of choice was mine, but it was foreseen by the Almighty before I was born. All that will happen now is likewise foreseen, though the freedom of choice to do right or wrong remains with each individual man to affect his own individual destiny; but you see, his choice is also foreseen. Some of what has been foreseen for my people as a whole has been revealed to us in our Holy Books, and I fear I understand the nature of it."

"Come, now," said Quintus, "you have not just looked into your Holy Books for the first time. Did you not see this before? And if not, what makes you so certain that you see it correctly now?"

"I saw it before," said Akiba, "but I and many of the other rabbis hoped that the misfortunes prophesied for Israel referred to events already past, though there were some who warned against such an interpretation. Alas, they were right, and much evil still awaits my people, for thus it has come up in the mind of God and thus it is written. But you see, God is good, and nothing that He does or permits to be done is for evil. And so the redemption we sought too early will come in its time, for that too is written, in clear, unmistakable terms."

Severus arose. "I'm afraid we must press on," he said. "Perhaps later we shall meet again."

"Yes," said Akiba.

The general and his aide moved toward the door. "Peace," said Severus.

"You are a good man," said Akiba. "It is unfortunate that you were born so late, and so early."

The Romans walked from the room and from the house. Outside, Quintus turned to the general and said, "I fear the old man has grown senile."

But Severus was silent.

From Simon Bar Kosiba

To the men of Safed, peace.

You stand today as the last outpost of Israel in Galilee.

Despite the most valiant resistance, the enemy has succeeded in breaching our strongholds, in slaying thousands of our brothers, in exiling many thousands more, in occupying the north of our country.

Yet for all of this, Galilee remains unconquered, for you remain unconquered.

Would God that we, your brothers in the south, could come to your swift aid. But we cannot, for we must look now to our own defense. Therefore, we call upon you, while knowing how much it is that we ask, to maintain yourselves in Safed. Survive, my brothers, and fight on that you may survive to the day when we shall be able, all of us, to retake Galilee for Israel.

Be strong,
Simon

From Simon Bar Kochba

To the men of Samaria and to Ephraim Ben-Abraham, peace.

We have received information that the Romans have marched a large force across the Jordan to Geresh. It seems probable that this force will now attempt to recross the Jordan at some point in the vicinity of Beth-Shean and invade the territory of Samaria.

Since a still larger enemy force is even now headed for the region of Judah, it will be impossible for us to send you any help at this time. We have, however, full faith in the courage and might of the warriors of Samaria.

Be strong,
Simon

From Simon Bar Kosiba

To Yehonatan Bar Mahanaim and to Masabala at En-Gedi, peace.

I hereby order that all the men of Tekoa and of Tel Arazin be mobilized at once, by force if necessary. I am informed that the men of Tekoa are presently engaged in the repair of their houses, as if we were at peace instead of threatened with destruction. I order that such activity be stopped at once on pain of severe punishment and that the men in your area ready themselves to fight for their lives.

Simon

Simon finished the last letter and showed it to his second in command, Jonathan Bar Ba'ayah. Jonathan read it and put it down.

"Do you think it too stern?" asked Simon.

"No," said Jonathan. "I suppose not."

"Well, then, tell me. You were military commander of the Sea of Salt district for more than half a year. What is the matter with the people in Tekoa?"

"I understand them," said Jonathan softly. "They are weary of war. The fighting is far from them now, and for the moment they seek to forget it. So they repair their houses, even while knowing that the houses may be destroyed before long. But they refuse to think about that, at least until they are forced to. I understand them. But," he added, "they are brave men. Fear not, they will carry out your orders."

Simon nodded, rolled up the letters and put his seal upon them. The seal seemed especially appropriate now. It showed a man wrestling with a lion.

"What do you think will happen now?" asked Mariamne as the two of them ate the evening meal in their home in Bethar.

Simon took a piece of the flat Judean bread and broke off a chunk. "I wish I knew," he said. He ate the bread slowly. "I know what we must do, but only God knows what will come of it."

"What about the Parthians?" asked Mariamne hopefully.

Simon laughed a short bitter laugh. "I am informed that we can count on the Parthians if we win, in which case, of course, we will not need the Parthians. Old Akiba was right. I suppose he was always right. By the Name, I hope he is well."

"B'nei B'rak has been taken, hasn't it?"

"Yes," said Simon softly, "along with the whole coastal region. I simply could not defend it. We need the best of our army here in Judah. But you know," he looked at her earnestly, "up in the north Safed still stands. Do you see what that means, Mariamne? In the middle of a large area conquered by Rome's mightiest legions led by her finest general, there lives on a major community of Jews who will not surrender; who will not bow; who will not leave the land of their fathers.

"And perhaps," he continued, "perhaps Safed has now set the pattern; I don't know. If we can hold Samaria and Judah, we have beaten the Romans; if we can hold just Judah, still we will not be defeated; and if out of the entire country we can hold only a few places like Safed and Bethar and En-Gedi—if we have nothing else—yet we will have assured our ultimate victory. Time is on our side, Mariamne. I sense that. And perhaps one day, if we can just manage to hold out, we will be able to get back all that we have lost."

"It is true," said Mariamne. "I sense it, too. If the worse comes to the worst, simple survival could bring us victory."

There was a long pause as the two of them continued eating. And then, suddenly, Simon pushed the food away from him with a violent gesture and pressed his hands to his eyes. "Tell me, Mariamne. Tell me bluntly. Is it my fault? Have I, through my vanity, brought all this upon our people?"

Mariamne reached across the table and put her hand on his arm. "No," she said softly. "You mustn't think that. I swear to you, there is not a man in Judea who thinks that. Whatever has happened and whatever may happen now, you will always be remembered as one of the great heroes of Israel."

"One hundred and fifty thousand Jews have died here since we began," Simon groaned, "and countless others have been dragged away to far-off lands. Men, women and even little children. People who followed me, who trusted me. And who knows how many more will die and how many more will be exiled before it is over? And it is all on my head, all those deaths and all that suffering. There is no possible atonement for such a sin, Mariamne, no atonement."

"Stop it," Mariamne shouted, springing up from her seat. "If you lose heart now, we are truly finished."

Simon looked up at her.

"You are the Prince of Israel," she said, her voice throbbing yet surprisingly firm. "And your son is a Ben-David. His is a line of great men, of whom you are perhaps the greatest. Yes, greater even than David, for you have fought not for the kingdom but for the right. The Jews who died and those who have been exiled fought for the right with you. You led that fight as you lead it now, and there is no shame in that. There is only honor in that, no matter what the end of it may be."

Simon stared at his wife in amazement. "Thank you," he said at last.

From their encampment at Lydda the Roman legions with Severus marched southeastward, into the region of Judah and into what they knew would be the most violent stage of the war.

And behind the legions, occupying the territory that they had conquered, there marched a smaller army. It was made up of a nucleus of Romans, surrounded by a much larger group of adventurers and drifters of mixed ancestry, most of whom did not know exactly what that ancestry was. This was the civilian administration and the police force of Procurator Tinius Rufus.

At first, there was nothing special to mark the fact that the area had come under Rufus' authority, and those who remained in the towns and villages of the coastal plain continued living their daily lives much as they had before.

In B'nei B'rak, for instance, Rabbi Akiba went on expounding the Law to such students as were still left to him. Perhaps the only difference was that the rabbi now seemed less inclined to get involved in long theological discussions. Almost as if he were in a hurry.

The first noticeable sign that Rufus was back came to the university in the form of an unexpected visit to Rabbi Akiba by the procurator's wife.

"I am glad to see that you are well," said Cornelia, trying without much success to hide her shock at the rabbi's changed appearance.

"We live," said Akiba simply.

"I have come to ask you a question," said Cornelia.

"Ask, and I shall answer it if I can."

"I know you Jews consider yourselves the chosen people. But is it true that you look upon this as a burden as well as an honor?"

"It is true," said Akiba, wondering as always what the procurator's wife was getting at. "The Law is a burden that our ancestors chose freely to accept upon themselves, and each generation of Jews renews that acceptance. This is the Covenant between ourselves and God. By accepting the Law, we become the Almighty's people, His witnesses on earth and the caretakers of His basic truths. But you see, this Covenant also imposes upon us a great many obligations. For you to be considered a righteous person in the eyes of God, Cornelia, you must keep only seven basic moral laws. I, for my part, am obliged to keep six hundred and thirteen separate commandments."

"I thought you Jews were good bargainers," said Cornelia. "That doesn't sound like much of a bargain, this Covenant of yours."

The rabbi smiled, and for a fleeting moment Cornelia thought she saw in the old man the Akiba of former days. "Perhaps not, but then it is no more and no less of a bargain than love. Indeed, that is a perfect analogy and one made in the Song of Songs. The Covenant is not merely a bargain; it is a marriage contract between God and Israel. And just as you would not weigh the demands of a lover against his gifts, so we do not weigh God's demands against what we receive from Him. Of course, we cannot carry the analogy to its human extreme, because God loves all peoples."

"But Israel most of all," Cornelia suggested.

Akiba shook his head. "Let us say He loves Israel with a special kind of love, because Israel is his firstborn, as it were. But for the same reason, He expects more of Israel, because

He has given Israel more than to all of His other sons. And if such a firstborn son rebels against the precepts of his Father, will not the Father be more angry at him than at any of His other children who does wrong?"

"I don't know," said Cornelia. "I don't see what you get out of it all."

"It is very complex," said Akiba. "But primarily we receive the opportunity to serve Him best of all, because we understand Him best of all. And it is our special mission to spread this understanding throughout the earth."

"Yet you discourage converts."

"Because we do not ask that all men be as we are. It is not necessary. It is only necessary for men to be righteous, to love one another. If they do that, by whatever name they call themselves, they will speed the advent of the Kingdom of God, when all evil will cease and men will live in everlasting happiness through accepting the Divine Will."

Cornelia thought for a moment, and then she rose. "I will come to see you again," she said.

"As you wish," said Akiba.

She did come back several times after that, each time with a fresh question for the rabbi to answer.

"What is the name of God?" she asked.

"We never call Him by name," Akiba explained. "We call him *Adonai,* which means my Lord. Or we call Him God or simply the Name. While the Temple still stood, the high priest would pronounce the name of God once a year, within the Holy of Holies, on our Day of Atonement, while asking forgiveness for our sins. And even then, he would do so in terror, for if the high priest was unworthy of his office, God would know it, and when he pronounced the ineffable name, God would slay him on the spot."

"Yet you know the name."

"Yes, we do. But it is a name no Jewish tongue would presume to pronounce."

"But why?"

"Because we are unworthy. We are unclean on account of our sins. And also because to call God by any one name, even the one that has been revealed to us, is to limit Him. He cannot be limited. He is infinite. He is beyond any one word or collection of words, beyond the dream of any artist or sculptor, beyond human conception, beyond the earth, beyond eternity."

Cornelia grew thoughtful. "It makes sense," she said at last.

"Now I have one question to ask of you," said Akiba. "I need not tell you that you are welcome here. But if you will forgive me, I am most curious to know what is behind this great interest of yours."

Cornelia smiled. "I want to find out all I can about you Jews before you become extinct," she said somewhat maliciously.

But Akiba answered seriously, "It is your world that will become extinct."

"Perhaps," said Cornelia, getting up to leave. At the door she turned to Akiba again, and this time her expression was grave. "Rabbi," she said haltingly, "I hope you are aware that my husband is determined to kill you."

"I know," said Akiba. "I'm surprised at his forbearance."

"His hands have been tied so far," Cornelia explained. "Severus will permit no reprisals for the revolt. But, Rabbi, please be careful."

"I appreciate your concern," said Akiba warmly.

On the nineteenth of Elul the legions under Severus overcame the stronghold of Beth Guvrin at the entrance to the hills of Judah. The furious fight for the city had cost the Romans more than 3,000 men. There were few Jewish prisoners. Most of the men of Beth Guvrin had fought to the death. Some had managed to retreat from the city and move across the hills to the citadel of Bethar.

Severus ordered Beth Guvrin razed and the Jewish prisoners transported to the port of Gaza and from there into exile. He reconstituted his troops in the face of the Roman losses and then split his forces again. Three legions and a supporting contingent of auxiliary were sent under the command of the Tribune Quintus Arminius Caro to take the city of Hebron and thereby cut the lines of supply from En-Gedi to Bethar.

As for Severus, he and the soldiers remaining with him began a perilous march northeast, a march that would lead them across the deadly hills of Judah to the den of the lion, to Bethar.

37

The two bodies of Roman troops marching through the hills of Judah moved toward their separate destinations slowly. The distances from Beth Guvrin to Hebron and from Beth Guvrin to Bethar were short, less than a day's march under normal circumstances. But the circumstances now were far from normal, and each of the two Roman forces found itself repeatedly set upon in hit-and-run raids that took a steady toll. The Jews had left not a pass undefended, not a rise above the road without archers behind it, not a single opportunity for ambush neglected; and the small mountain villages in the path of the Romans put up the kind of resistance that surprised even the seasoned legionaries.

But while the Roman progress could be slowed, it could not be halted; and by the beginning of Rosh Hashanah 3895, the Third Year of the Liberation of Israel, Severus' troops were no longer far from Bethar, while Quintus' forces had already fought off three major attacks and were encamped in the area around the city of Hebron.

With the subjugation of the greater part of their homeland by the Romans the Jewish war for survival developed into two separate struggles. In one the ultimate stronghold was Bethar; in the other it was the synagogue. In one struggle the Jews faced Faustus Julius Severus, the greatest general of the age; in the other they faced a far more bitter enemy, the Procurator Tinius Rufus.

Yet while Severus approached the stronghold of Bethar with his tough legions, Rufus seemed to be doing nothing. His single overt act at this point was to station spies in the various synagogues in Roman-controlled Palaestina. The spies made no attempt to hide their identity, but they did not flaunt it. They did not take part in the service, but neither did they interfere with it. They merely sat in the back and listened to the poetic Hebrew words of the service, words quite close to the vernacular Aramaic which they all spoke.

The presence of the spies caused a certain amount of nervousness in the congregations of the Jews. There was, after all, always the possibility that some age-old prayer meant only for the ears of God might be misunderstood by Rufus' police. Specifically concern was centered around a single line that was said at both the morning and the evening service. The line, which came immediately after the *Shema*—the ancient declaration of the unity of God—was: "Blessed be the name of His glorious Kingdom for all eternity."

The kingdom referred to, of course, was the Kingdom of God, but Rufus' police might well think the line meant something else. There was no point in endangering the decimated congregations of occupied Judea, the rabbis decided, and they prudently advised the Jews to begin uttering this line softly, instead of loudly as in former days.

This advice was in keeping with the Law, which taught that a Jew might not risk his life without purpose. Indeed it was incumbent upon him to remain alive so that he might bear witness to the Word of God. It was only when the alternative was to betray that Word by surrendering his spirit to the forces of evil that a Jew was actually obligated to die, *Al Kiddush Ha-Shem*—for the sanctification of the Name.

But there was nothing so momentous involved in saying a few words softly; God would hear them in any case. Consequently the Jews would continue to say aloud the Shema—"Hear, O Israel, the Lord is our God, the Lord is One." And then they would add in a whisper, "Blessed be the name of His glorious Kingdom for all eternity."

And so is the custom to this day.

From all over Judea, men streamed daily into the mountain city of Bethar. These were the unvanquished survivors of a thousand fallen places who had made their way across the hills, destroying everything that had stood in their path and ravaging the land behind them so that the enemy could gain no benefit from it. Such men would inevitably end up in Bethar, entering the city through the main gate or through one of the secret underground passages that led to it from various spots farther down the mountain.

Until the outbreak of the war, Bethar had been a sizable

city of some 20,000 inhabitants. Later, when Bar Kochba decided to turn the city into his major stronghold, its population gradually swelled to 50,000. Now there were more than 70,000 men crowded within its two concentric walls, plus about 1,000 women and children.

The overwhelming preponderance of men was strange for a Judean city, but Bethar was no longer an ordinary city. Many of the original inhabitants had gradually left to ply their trades elsewhere as Bethar became increasingly a military stronghold. Others had been evacuated during the past six months to make room for inhabitants of a different kind.

Those who now comprised the population of Bethar did not, for the most part, want their families with them. Some had no families left, while those who had been able to do so had led their wives and little ones across the border to the safety of other lands before crossing back to come to the stronghold; each of these men had promised his family that he would send for them soon when the fighting was over, and in his heart each of them sensed that it had been a pious lie. They did not speak about it among themselves, but they all knew that from Bethar there could be no retreat.

Here were gathered the old rebels who had survived the long years of warfare; here were the men who had once fought the Romans in small groups before Bar Kochba had risen to unite them; here was the remnant of the original battalions formed before the revolt began; here were the heroes of Tur Malka; here were the conquerors of the Dead Sea plain, the destroyers of the XXII Deitoriana; here were the warriors who had driven Urbanicus back; here were the survivors of the Megiddo Pass and of fifty strongholds and 985 separate towns and villages that had been overrun by the invader.

Here were former disciples of Rabbi Akiba who were students no longer; here was Rabbi Eleazar Ha-Modai, the priest and gentle teacher who did not cease to pray for a miracle to save his people; here was Mordechai Ben-Joshua, the follower of Yeshu.

They had come from many places; they had fought in many battles; they had tasted victory more than once. But more than once in the past eight months they had been forced to yield, to withdraw, to give ground, to retreat. Here, in Bethar, they were resolved to make a united stand against a world to which they would not bow. And they vowed that, come what might, so long as one of them lived, this ultimate stronghold of a free Judea would never surrender.

They had made this vow quietly, not to Bar Kochba, nor even to God, but to themselves.

On the sixth of Tishri the legions with Faustus Julius Severus came within view of the walls of Bethar and began moving up the mountain road to the city. But the road was so fiercely defended that after two days of heavy fighting, the Romans were obliged to withdraw and make their camp farther down the mountain. There was little they could do from that vantage point, while waiting for the other Roman forces to complete their tasks and join them, but watch the city of Bethar high above, standing strong and secure in the Judean sunlight.

From an observation post on the outer wall of that city, Bar Kochba looked out at the Roman encampment, and he came to a decision. He estimated that he had nearly twice as many warriors within Bethar as there were in that camp. The prince wondered if, perhaps, he had not been given another chance. . . .

From the evening of the ninth to the evening of the tenth of Tishri is Yom Kippur—the Day of Atonement—the holiest of all days for Jews, a day of fasting and prayer and self-examination. The season of penitence begins with Rosh Hashanah, but its climax comes ten days later with Yom Kippur, the day when Jews believe God seals the fate of men and nations for the coming year. It is a day when Jews are permitted, briefly, to kneel, and this in itself is a matter of some moment to them, for they are normally forbidden to bend the knee to anyone— even to God. It is, in all, a day when Jews feel closer to God than at any other time and when, perhaps because of this closeness, they sense without being told that the fear of man is a vain and foolish thing.

In Palaestina, which was now most of Judea, it was a mournful Yom Kippur, for there was not a congregation in all the land that was not diminished. And where were so many of the Judean congregations which in years past had sent up their prayers to Heaven? Alas, they were not. Of those that remained, a disproportionate number of the worshipers were old men and children. They filed into the synagogues dressed in white. And Rufus' spies filed in with them.

In every synagogue the evening service began with the traditional proclamation by the elders of the congregation.

"With the knowledge of the Almighty and with the knowledge of the congregation, by the authority of the Heavenly Tribunal and by the authority of the earthly tribunal, we hereby declare it lawful to pray with transgressors."

Thus were the gates of prayer flung open to all, to the most grievous sinner as to the righteous. For who was man to judge?

The congregations then chanted the Kol Nidre, the public declaration by which all vows obtained by force are annulled; for man is free, and oaths uttered under compulsion can have no binding value in the eyes of God. Afterward there came the time for the recitation of the Shema.

And at this point a strange thing happened. There had been no advance consultation or planning, yet it happened spontaneously in every synagogue that remained across the conquered land.

"Hear, O Israel," proclaimed the Jews, "the Lord is our God, the Lord is One."

And then they paused and turned to the spies in their midst. And as if declaring their defiance to those spies, to Rufus, to the emperor, to Rome, to every earthly tyranny that sought to enslave the spirit of man, they burst their restraint and without fear they shouted at the top of their voices, "Blessed be the name of His glorious Kingdom for all eternity."

And so is the custom on Yom Kippur to this day.

38

On the twelfth of Tishri, only three days before the Feast of Booths, the warriors of Bethar burst forth from the city and poured out on the hillside, attacking the Roman camp with sword and bow.

The assault was so massive and well-planned that Severus, the erstwhile besieger, found himself suddenly in danger of being encircled by the Judean forces. He did the only thing possible under the circumstances and ordered a retreat along the route that he had come.

The Jews, flushed with the swift reversal, pressed their advantage. They attacked again, and again they attempted to encircle the Romans, and again they forced Severus to retreat. The tactic was repeated day after day as the Jews took the offensive for the first time since Severus had landed at Caesarea.

"For the freedom of Jerusalem," they shouted as in former days.

"For the freedom of Israel," they screamed as they released the fury they had carried with them for so many months.

They drove the Romans from the area of Bethar; they drove them past the village of Beth Zecheriah; they drove them from the hills of Judah; they drove them back to the ruins of Beth Guvrin, and they threatened to drive them all the way to the sea.

In answer to an urgent summons the Tribune Quintus Arminius Caro lifted the siege of Hebron and moved with his troops to Severus' aid. But the sizable garrison of Hebron moved out behind them to reinforce the warriors of Bethar in pushing the offensive against the enlarged Roman force.

By the end of the month of Tishri everything had been turned upside down, and it seemed, despite all that had happened, that victory for the Jews was still possible, that there might yet be a repetition of the Dead Sea triumph, that the Romans might yet be defeated, that the land might yet be freed. Men who only a month before had resigned themselves to death now revived old dreams and permitted themselves the absurd hope that the remnant of Jews left in their ancestral homeland might still, somehow, prevail over the mightiest empire on earth.

But it was to be the last charge of the lion.

Even as he prepared to carry the battle into the coastal plain, Bar Kochba received word that Samaria had surrendered. The Samaritans had fought long and hard by the side of the Jews, but in the end, faced with the overwhelming might of Rome, they had chosen to submit. Simon reflected sadly that in this, too, Akiba had been right. While the other rabbis had objected to the Samaritans on religious grounds, Akiba had only warned that their hearts would never be as fully in the war as the hearts of the Jews, that the Samaritans had a long history of submission to conquerors. Yet even now Simon could not really condemn them. They had not had as much to lose.

The message from Samaria was a warning that the six legions and auxiliary which had accepted the surrender of the region were now free to march on Bethar. But it was more. All at once it summed up the tragic fact of the Jewish situation, a fact that had not been essentially changed by the victories of the past three weeks. It brought home to Simon that there would always be new enemy troops on the way, drawn by Rome from a world that was eager to destroy the Jews. And it meant that Bethar and the small area around it was all that was left of Judea. The rest, with but a few valiant and isolated exceptions, had become Palaestina in fact as well as in name, a strange new country in which Jews had little part.

The burden of the message broke suddenly through the dream that Simon had permitted himself, and in that moment he knew that the dream, at least for his time, was over. The realization was ironic, for he had just won a major battle; he had beaten Severus himself. But it was too late. The Roman had been too thorough. Where were the Jews who would replenish his army of liberation? Where were the farms which would feed it and the villages that would give it shelter? Where were the strongholds that would resist the invader? In all the land there was only one left. Mournfully, but with a desperate resolve, Bar Kochba ordered his army to move back into Bethar.

Immediately following the Feast of Booths, Procurator Tinius Rufus issued a historic edict to the Jews of Palaestina. The edict had the full approval of the Emperor of Rome, since it appeared to be nothing more than an implementation of General Severus' stated policy to blot out the memory of the Jews.

The edict made no mention of the revolt or of the hand that the rabbis had had in it. It threatened no reprisals, but in fact guaranteed to the remaining Jews of Palaestina their full rights as citizens of a Roman province. The heart of the edict was contained in a single paragraph which outlawed the practice of what it called "certain primitive superstitions."

These included the circumcision, the keeping of the Sabbath and the study or teaching of the Jewish Law. . . .

A few days after the promulgation of the new edict, the rabbis gathered together secretly in the town of Lydda to discuss how to meet its threat.

Basically the conclave was split into two groups. One held that the edict had to be defied in its entirety—whatever the consequences. Such a course, it was conceded, would result in many deaths, but it would insure the survival of the Jewish people as a whole. The second group took a diametrically opposed view. Quoting the Bible to show that God had given the Law so that "man should live by it," this group argued that survival was in itself a commandment of the Law, for how could a dead man live by its precepts? Faced with the threat of death, these rabbis said, a Jew was permitted to suspend the keeping of the entire Law for a time in order to survive until the danger had passed.

At length a third alternative was offered. It was the proposal not of a group but of a single man who in former years had cut sharply through many an impasse of the grand council.

Rabbi Akiba Ben-Joseph had taken no part in the council's deliberations since his break with Bar Kochba, and those who had not seen him since had been struck by the change in his appearance. Quite suddenly, Akiba looked his ninety-five years, and some whispered that his legendary intellectual powers had been weakened by time and by the crushing blows of the past year. But he spoke now in a clear voice, and he struck quickly to the heart of the current dilemma with the vigor of former times.

Akiba at once discounted both extremist views as self-defeating. To openly practice every minor precept of the Law in the face of the Roman edict would, he argued, be tantamount to mass suicide—which in itself was forbidden by the Law. On the other hand, to save life by sacrificing the Law in its entirety, even if only for a time, would be survival without meaning, "for there are precepts so basic to life under the Law that survival without them would be a contradiction."

Akiba took a deep breath before continuing. "We speak this

day to a tragically diminished community of Jews in Judea. What we say will guide them, but we have no way of knowing that the force of our words will end there. A new and terrible period has begun for our people, and its duration has not been revealed to us. Rufus is not our first enemy, and he will not be our last. The current threat will pass in its time, but the way we meet it may well serve as a model for future generations of Jews. Thus, we have the awesome responsibility of speaking not only for here and now, but across the ages.

"It is clear that the Law requires personal survival. We are here to serve God on earth and to bear witness to His eternal truths before the nations; we must remain alive if for no other reason than to fulfill this mission, and the Law already permits us to bear arms on the Sabbath, for instance, and to breach certain of its other ordinances if this is required for self-preservation. In a case like the present, where the very keeping of the Divine Commandments places us in mortal danger, I believe that even certain of the major ordinances of the Law may be temporarily set aside until the danger passes. It is my view that a Jew may desecrate the Sabbaths and the festivals if his life depends on it, that he may eat forbidden food, that he may pray alone and in secret—or perhaps not pray at all—if these things are required for his survival. But before we say that the entire Law may be suspended for the sake of survival, let us ask ourselves, 'survival as what?' We have always had the opportunity to safeguard our physical survival by abandoning our Law and adopting the ways of the heathens. Indeed it is that very opportunity which is now being offered to us. Clearly we seek something more. We seek survival—but with the Law. We may thus permit that Law to be breached, but only if its very essence is not destroyed in the process.

"I believe the essence of the Law consists of three basic teachings: that God is One, Just, Infinite and Eternal; that the home is God's ultimate temple and must be kept holy; that every human life is sacred to God. These three tenets must be accepted unconditionally by every Jew at all times and under all conditions. There can be no compromise on any one of them, not even on pain of death.

"It is therefore my view that a Jew may, if his life is at stake, set aside all of the commandments of the Law save those which forbid idolatry, immorality and murder. Before he breaches a single one of them, he must willingly lay down his life for the sanctification of the Name.

"A Jew may not, even on pain of death, deny the existence of the Only God; he may not, even on pain of death, defile his or any other home; he may not, even on pain of death, kill his fellowman in cold blood. To say that he might be permitted to do any of these things for the sake of his survival under the Law is an absurdity.

"And there is a fourth requirement which lies especially heavily upon us, the rabbis and scholars. It is a no less basic tenet of our faith, for it is a commandment on which all of the others depend; indeed, it is the key to our survival. The study of the Law may never be set aside or suspended or interrupted —whatever the personal risks it may entail. For without study there can be no transmission of knowledge. And without knowledge there can be no observance of the Law, even after the danger has passed."

Akiba sat down, and the hall grew silent as each of the rabbis considered the old sage's words. It was clear to them all that, despite the sweeping mitigations, what Akiba proposed was a resistance to tyranny as stubborn—and as dangerous—as that other resistance he had supported two and a half years before.

Some of the rabbis had their misgivings about accepting Akiba's counsel. They were human; they understood the risks such a course would involve; they feared for their lives. But in their hearts they had known from the start that the old man was right again, that there was no real choice. So in the end they approved and ratified and made into Law the opinion of Rabbi Akiba Ben-Joseph on the principles for which a Jew must stand even if his life be required of him.

And so it is to this day.

From a window in his headquarters Simon looked out and watched the last of the still loyal Samaritans filter into Bethar. In all there were less than 1,000.

"They might have held out longer," said Jonathan.

Simon shrugged.

"What is your plan now?" asked Jonathan.

"My plan," said Simon, "is to survive. Even if we have to die for it."

Jonathan smiled. "Day by day you sound more like Akiba."

"Well," said Bar Kochba, "I am getting older. And I am getting wearier, and I wish sometimes that I could sleep for a long time. The whole world is against us, my friend. Can you conceive of that? In all the earth there is not a single nation which will help us."

"It has always been thus."

"And yet," Simon continued, "we did it. We did the impossible. We united as a people into one great moving force that shook the world. We drove the Romans out of the land, and we kept them out for more than a year. We destroyed an entire legion, and we swept away a dozen more. That has never been done before, not by any other people. And we did it ourselves, by God, alone and without help. What we have done can never be changed. And what we have become in doing it, that can never be changed either, even if . . ."

"Do not despair," Jonathan urged. "It is not over. We may yet snatch victory from them."

"Perhaps," said Simon. "But I am more concerned now with something else, something more lasting than victory. I want to defend Bethar as no place anywhere has even been defended, not even Jerusalem. For if we can hold Bethar, Jonathan, we hold Judea. The Romans understand this. That is why they will fight with all their strength to take this last stronghold from us. Bethar is the symbol of our freedom now, and so long as it stands, Jews can think upon it wherever they are scattered and know that the land will be theirs again. Yet, I suppose, in the worst event, if . . ."

Jonathan stopped him. "There is no if. We will hold Bethar."

"Still," Simon persisted, "if—Heaven forfend—the massed might of all the world manages to overcome Bethar, I swear by my life that the city will fall with a crash so loud no Jew will ever forget it."

The siege of Bethar began late in the fall, in the month of Heshvan, as more than 100,000 Roman troops gathered in a wide circle around the foot of the mountain on which the city stood. They gradually narrowed the circle, in slow steps, at a cost that mounted steadily the closer they drew to the stronghold.

At the beginning of the battle for Bethar there were 75,000 men within the city, almost all of them Jews, including nearly 2,000 members of the Minaean sect. Each had his daily task, and sometimes a man would go to perform such a task and would never return. But for the most part the inhabitants of Bethar lived lives that were almost normal. They thought and spoke and laughed at bad jokes and complained about the strictness of the discipline and told the same stories more than once and argued over the merits of different wines and mended their sandals and cursed the rain or the wind or the heat; they wrote letters to their loved ones, ignoring the fact that there was no way of sending them; they argued heatedly over the most petty matters with comrades for whom they had an hour before risked their lives; they dreamed of women they had had and of women they never would have; they ate and they slept; and sometimes they would catch themselves planning for the future. In short, they indulged in all those little mental tricks that all men use to stay alive.

At regular intervals a corps of these men would sally forth from the city through a hidden tunnel and would appear suddenly in the midst of a Roman contingent. They would strike quickly, killing as many as they could, and then they would disappear, together with the bodies of their dead. On any of these occasions the men in such a raiding party could have used their opportunity to escape from the beleaguered city, to make their way through a tunnel to behind the Roman lines and to safety. Yet not one man ever did so, though not one of them would ever have thought of himself as a hero.

There were at this time nine tunnels leading from Bethar to various spots below the city. All were carefully patrolled night and day and had been so constructed that they could be quickly collapsed in case of enemy discovery by pulling away a few key beams. Only eight of the tunnels were used for the hit-and-run attacks against the Romans. The ninth, which led to a small cave at the very bottom of the mountainside, was kept in reserve, as an emergency passage.

The existence of the tunnels soon became obvious to the besiegers, but despite steady attempts they had no success in finding any of them. The mouths of the tunnels had been cleverly camouflaged, and the Jewish raiders who would issue forth from them took great pains to insure that no Roman witness survived. Thus, as the winter rains began, the location of the hidden passages remained unknown to the Romans.

The rains swelled the flow of the subterranean brooks that supplied Bethar with water, and Bar Kochba ordered that some of this be collected and stored in large barrels. It was the kind of extreme precaution that had lately become typical of the prince, extreme because the underground brooks had not been known to dry up even in the hottest of summers.

Yet Bar Kochba ordered the water collected, and the full supply of food within the city was strictly rationed, and when anyone questioned any of this, Simon would always answer, "Who knows how long we will have to hold out?"

39

In Palaestina, the country that surrounded Bethar, it was a savage winter. It was the time that came to be known as the Hadrianic Persecution, and it had, up to that time, no parallel in the long history of the Jews.

The edict forbidding the practice of the Jewish Law was enforced with rigor, as Rufus' police patrolled the closed synagogues and his spies watched all gatherings of Jews and informers were paid a reward if they turned in a Jewish neighbor who might have uttered a quiet prayer or affixed a mezuzah to his doorpost. Punishments for all such infringements of the edict were unusually severe, most often death.

A contemporary writer, Nathan the Babylonian, who journeyed to the Holy Land to see for himself if the brutal stories were true, decribed the conditions in these words:

"The expression in the Ten Commandments 'those who love Me and keep My commandments' applies to the people who live in Palaestina and offer their lives for the Law.

" 'Why are you being taken to execution?'

" 'Because I circumcised my son.'

" 'Why are you being taken to crucifixion?'

" 'Because I read the Bible or ate matzoth.'

" 'Why are you being beaten a hundred blows?'

" 'Because I waved a palm branch.' "

Yet the harsh edict which the Emperor Hadrian approved and which came to be called by his name was in force only in Palaestina, and the Jews were free to leave; indeed, that was one of the edict's major purposes, to clear the land still further of its troublesome natives.

And many did leave now. They left behind the borders of their land and the land of their fathers with weeping and rending of clothes, but they left, because they felt they owed it to their children to remain alive.

Nevertheless, others stayed despite the risks, despite the daily arrests, despite the public executions that took place regularly. They stayed because they felt they owed it to their children to stay and because they believed, as Akiba did, that it was better for a Jew to die in the Holy Land and be buried in it than to live on elsewhere. And they stayed because they believed, as Akiba did, that it was their duty as Jews not to flee from tyranny but to resist it.

And many of them died bravely for their faith, so many and so bravely that the memory of their martyrdom was to echo across the ages.

"May the Father of Mercies who dwells on high remember in His mighty compassion those pious, righteous and innocent ones, the holy congregations, who laid down their lives for the sanctification of the Name," begins a prayer still recited by Jews every Sabbath. "Beloved and pleasant were they in their lives, and in their deaths they were not divided. . . ."

And there is another prayer which commemorates not the multitudes of the "holy congregations" but rather the Ten Just Men who were their leaders. The story of the Just Men is recited by Jews on their holiest day, on Yom Kippur, for they know that in pleading for God's mercy on that day they can bring up no better example of the fidelity of their ancestors than this.

"Now it happened in the reign of a certain emperor," begins the story, "that no remedy was found for the Ten Just Men doomed to death by his command . . ."

The story has survived as it was written, in parables and poetic symbols and with hidden meanings understood only by the faithful, so as to disguise it from the Roman spies who might be about. Yet the names of the martyred ten are clearly inscribed it it.

Rabbi Ishmael and Rabbi Simeon, sages of known nationalist views who were the first to be executed at Rufus' command.

Rabbi Hanania Ben-Teradyon, who was arrested by the Romans on the charge of teaching the Jewish Law. He was condemned to be enwrapped in a scroll of that Law and to be burned alive in it while wet layers of wool were placed about his body to slow his death. Yet Rabbi Hanania bore the agony calmly, and he proclaimed aloud the Shema in his final moments as his students wept at his feet. And then, as he and the scroll were being consumed, he looked above him at the rising smoke, and he saw not as other men see, and his last words to his students were these, spoken in a tone of great joy: "The words. Behold, the words of the Law ascend to Heaven."

Rabbi Hutzpith, the interpreter, whose tongue was torn out and cast to the dogs before he was slain.

And Rabbi Eleazar Ben-Shamua.

And Rabbi Hanina Ben-Hachinai.

And Rabbi Yeshevav, the scribe.

And Rabbi Judah Ben-Damah.

And Rabbi Judah Ben-Baba.

And one other sage, the greatest of them all, whose name was to head the list. . . .

Despite the persecution Rabbi Akiba Ben-Joseph continued teaching the Law at his university in B'nei B'rak. He expounded it to those few who were left of his old disciples, and to those whose former teachers had been slain or imprisoned, and to such colleagues as Rabbi Meir, who had fled to B'nei B'rak from Galilee and who now sat at the master's feet taking in his words.

Akiba would teach and lecture and render decisions on questions brought to him without any attempt at secrecy, as if he were oblivious to his place and time; on occasions when weather permitted, he would seat himself beneath a tree in his garden and lecture there.

When some of his more prudent colleagues suggested that he be more cautious, Akiba would answer that it was beneath the dignity of the Torah to hide it as if it were some ugly thing; no, he had always taught thus, in the open, and he would continue to do so; and if it was ordained that he should suffer for it, then he would suffer for it.

Once a colleague whose views were traditionally opposed to Akiba's came to him and asked him bluntly, "Akiba, aren't you afraid?"

"I will tell you a parable," said Akiba, answering him thus:

"One day a fox stood by the water's edge and watched as the fish fled from place to place in terror to avoid the nets of the fishermen. 'Why don't you come up on the dry land?' suggested the fox. The fish laughed bitterly and answered, 'They say you are wise. You are not at all wise but foolish. If we have reason to fear in the water which gives us life, how much more so on the dry land, where we will surely perish?'

"The Torah is our life," Akiba said. "If we have reason to fear while studying it, how much more so if we abandon its study."

Some days later the colleague who had so confronted Akiba was himself arrested for a minor infringement of the Roman edict. But Akiba remained conspicuously unharmed. . . .

Cornelia Ruffina had become a regular visitor to B'nei B'rak, but she had been absent from the university for several weeks. Akiba did not question her absence any more than he had questioned her presence. The woman had never revealed much about herself or her motives, and Akiba had more pressing matters to occupy his attention, and so after a time, he had begun simply to accept her occasional visits as he accepted most matters in life over which he had little or no control.

And then one day Cornelia appeared again, suddenly as always. Only this time she was much agitated, and she made no effort to conceal it. She asked to see the rabbi urgently and at once.

Akiba met her in his study. Cornelia was standing by the window, gazing out at the garden. "Won't you sit down?" asked the rabbi.

Cornelia turned to him. "Do you want to die?" she asked heatedly.

"No," answered Akiba calmly. "I am not mad. And no sane man wants to die."

"Then stop this study of yours. Don't be so stubborn."

"I'm afraid this kind of stubbornness is required of us."

"Don't you know what Rufus is doing?" asked Cornelia. "Don't you know that the seashore is lined with crosses? Don't you know that he's burned a rabbi alive for doing in secret what you dare to do in the open? Don't you know about these things, or don't you care?"

"I know," said Akiba, "and I care most deeply. I am grieved because of a man like Rabbi Hanania Ben-Teradyon—may his memory be for a blessing. But I grieve not for him; he is assured of paradise by virtue of his martyr's death. I grieve, rather, for myself, because I have lost the wisdom of his teaching and the pleasure of his friendship. God will surely repay those who lay down their lives for His Name. And He will repay Rufus as well, in time."

"But don't you understand," said Cornelia pleadingly, "that it is you Rufus is after? That it has always been you? That it is primarily because of you that he went to all the trouble of dreaming up this new edict and getting the emperor to approve it? Don't you see that he's killing the others now as a prelude, that he's saving you for last as the final and greatest example of all? And you're helping him every step of the way."

Akiba walked over to Cornelia and gently guided her into a chair. "But if that is so," he said, "do you imagine that I could escape his vengeance, seeing that he has the might of the entire empire behind him?"

"At least you could try," said Cornelia bitterly, "instead of playing into his hands."

Akiba sighed. He was genuinely touched by the woman's concern, and so he tried now, patiently, to explain. "Try to understand that what I am doing is merely following the dic-

tates of my faith. One cannot compromise with evil. Not only
is such a course morally wrong, but it is doomed to failure—
as in the present case, where if Rufus is blocked in killing me
one way, he will do it in another. If a man truly loves the Lord
with all his heart and with all his soul and with all his might
—as I teach that he should—then it follows that he must fight
evil with all his heart and with all his soul and with all his
might, even though his own life be required of him. Shall I
abandon this teaching now, in my ninety-sixth year?"

"But you tried to fight," protested Cornelia. "You tried and
you failed. Why can't you accept that?"

"Time will tell if we have failed," said Akiba. "I am content
to leave the judgment to time."

Suddenly Cornelia burst out crying. She lay her head down
on the table before her and sobbed bitterly and loudly and
without control. Akiba tried to calm her, but he didn't know
how, and so she cried thus for a long time, letting out all that
was within her unrestrained, as a peasant woman might, until
at last she raised her head and through the tears still streaming
down said to Akiba in a shaking voice, "Rabbi, there is a life
within me."

"What?" asked Akiba, still distressed by the scene.

"I am pregnant. It is my fourth month. Soon it will begin to
show."

"So Rufus is to have a child," said the rabbi.

"Not Rufus."

Akiba looked at her quizzically.

Cornelia drew out a handkerchief and dabbed at her eyes.
"Rufus is not the father of the child," she said. "There is so
much I have to tell you, and I wish I could tell it slowly and
gently, because you are such a holy man. But there is no time,
and so I must tell it all now. Please don't be shocked."

"I do not shock easily," said Akiba.

"I'm sure you have suspected for some time that Rufus and
I are not particularly close," Cornelia began. "What you do
not know is that except for a few brief months after our marriage when I was still dreaming the foolish dreams of a little
girl, I have hated him all these years. You see, Rabbi, you know
Rufus as a cruel tyrant, but I know him as a man. And he is
not a man at all, not in any sense of the word."

"I am not surprised," said Akiba. "If he were whole, why would he be a tyrant?"

"Be that as it may," Cornelia went on, "I have not denied myself the pleasures of the marriage bed all these years. I did what any other Roman woman in my position would do; I took lovers. Those who knew me well felt sorry for me, and I suppose I enjoyed that, too, although, as I only recently came to realize, the situation was a very comfortable one for me."

"Comfortable?"

"Yes. I owed nothing to anyone. Rufus had tricked me, and so I could do with him whatever I liked, and no one would blame me, and he was in no position to condemn me. And as for my lovers, if any of them became too possessive or troublesome, well, I could just walk away. After all, I was married."

Akiba smiled despite himself. "You are quite honest," he said, "to admit all that to yourself."

Cornelia let the remark pass. "I had several lovers in the course of the past ten years. The most recent affair, and the longest, has been with a tribune of my own class. For some reason I didn't take the necessary precautions with him the last time. Perhaps I didn't want to. I don't know. In any case, he is the father of the child."

"I suppose you mean the Tribune Quintus Arminius Caro."

"Yes," said Cornelia with a start. "Of course," she reminded herself, "you know him and have seen us together. But that isn't important. What I'm getting at is, I plan to leave Rufus and Judea as soon as feasible and go to Rome or somewhere else far away to have my child and to raise it."

"I see," said Akiba. "You plan to marry Quintus."

"No," said Cornelia. "I will leave and never see Quintus again. You see, Rabbi, he doesn't know about the child. And I don't want him to know, ever."

"But why?"

"Because I don't love Quintus. I never loved him, though I thought for a time I did. I know now that I never loved anyone in all my life, not even myself. It was Quintus who inadvertently made me realize this because I came so close to loving him that I discovered how far away I really was. And so I couldn't possibly marry Quintus. It wouldn't be fair to him. And it wouldn't be fair to me, either, because it would tie me to the old life, one way or the other. So, inevitably, it would be unfair to the child. No, what I plan to do is to go away and have this child and try to love it and so, somehow, make something of life for both of us."

Cornelia stopped and looked up at Akiba as if she were expecting some kind of response, and so the rabbi said, "I must be frank with you, Cornelia. I cannot condone what you plan."

"I do not ask for your approval," said Cornelia brusquely. "Let God judge me; I am not afraid. But I do ask you for something else."

"What?"

"I wish to become one of you. I wish you to make me a Jew, to convert me or whatever you call it."

"What!" exclaimed Akiba. "Now, in the midst of all this persecution, you wish to become a Jew?"

"Yes," said Cornelia. "Now. Here. Today."

Akiba shook his head. "Well," he said, "you have finally managed to shock me."

"Try to understand, Rabbi, that I ask this not so much for myself. For the first time in my life I care more for somebody else, and that in itself is a wonder. I care for this child. I want to give it life, and I want to give it love, and I want to give it truth. All those times I came here during the past few years I have really been listening, although I know it didn't always look that way, and now I have finally become convinced that your people are the only ones who fully understand the whole truth about the way things are. That is why you are so willing to die, because you have something to live for. That is something I never had, and I want it now so that I can give it to my child."

"I understand about the child," said Akiba, "but I don't understand about you. If you had come to me and asked for this a year ago, I would have understood it better. But why now, in the darkest hour of my people's history, do you want to join your lot to ours? Frankly, Cornelia, in your position, it just doesn't make sense."

"But it does," said Cornelia. "Look, you must know that from the very beginning I was attracted to your teachings. That's why I kept coming here. But there was always one thing that disturbed me, one point that made me doubt the truth of it all, and that was your casually stated but constantly recurring insistence that you Jews are the chosen people. Everything else about you and your Law was different, but that one claim made you sound like every other people on earth. I used to think to myself, It is just another cult; deeper than the Isis-Serapis worship; more interesting than the Mysteries; but otherwise, they are just like us Romans, because we also think that the gods have chosen us to rule. When your rebellion seemed to be succeeding, I was not impressed. Politics has always bored me, and I couldn't have cared less who controlled this little province. But now, now that you have been beaten and are being persecuted more than any other people has ever been persecuted and yet insist on clinging to your beliefs, now I sense that perhaps you really have been chosen for something special. And now that I see how all of you, from the most humble to men like yourself, are willing to die for a single provision of your Law, why, I realize that you really are different from any other people on earth. And with the realization of this one thing everything else falls into place, so that I see that all of your teachings must really be true. This is something people like me could never have seen if you had won."

Akiba chuckled to himself. "How diverse are Your paths, O Lord," he muttered, lapsing into Hebrew.

"What did you say?" asked Cornelia.

"Just an observation," said Akiba. "It is interesting how you have come to understand something quite basic. But I must tell you that you still understand only one small part of one truth. There are a great many more truths that you should understand before even considering such a major step. Conversion is a rather long process with us. We are not so concerned with the number as with the quality of our adherents."

"I know all that," said Cornelia. "I told you that I have been listening. I may not understand as much about your Law as some, but I understand as much as most of your own people do. I know about the six hundred and thirteen commandments. I know about keeping the Sabbath. I know the stories from your Holy Book. I even know that it is your duty as a rabbi to try to talk me out of converting. But I also know that you have no right to keep me from converting if I am really set on it. And I am."

Akiba sat back. "Very well," he said. "Come back in a week, and we will talk about it again."

"No," said Cornelia. "I cannot take the chance. You may not be alive in a week. I must be selfish now so that I may be unselfish for the first time in my life."

"Nevertheless," said Akiba firmly, "I will not convert you now. I cannot take the chance that this is some passing mood of yours. The Law is too holy to be given or accepted on a whim. I make no promises for next week, but we can talk about it some more then."

Cornelia arose and began making for the door. "What if you are dead in a week's time?" she asked.

"That," said Akiba, "is a chance we shall both have to take."

40

To my father, Senator Caius Arminius:

Hail and greeting.

The siege of the last Jewish stronghold is progressing, though with frustrating slowness.

About a week ago we had succeeded in narrowing the circle around the stronghold to the point where it became necessary for some of our men to march up the single road leading directly to the city. We had every reason to expect that this would be a difficult task, but it turned out to be impossible.

From the moment they set foot on the road our soldiers found themselves under heavy bombardment. The worst of it, however, came at a spot where the narrow road twists directly beneath the city's outer wall. Men passing this point were subjected to a deluge of boiling oil, and those who managed to get through were repeatedly set upon by attackers both from the city and from behind, as the Jews apparently made use again of one of their hidden passages.

We were thus forced to retreat from the vicinity of the

city several times, and while security requirements do not permit me to give you our exact casualty figures, they were dreadfully high. It became clear to Severus that the situation required extreme action, and he finally ordered that the rocky and uneven terrain of the area surrounding the city be leveled so that a proper siege can be conducted. Our troops began this work today with the building of a series of protective screens and barriers to ward off the hail of missiles anticipated from the city walls while the actual leveling is in progress. The terrain is such that this promises to be a massive engineering feat, but there is simply no other way of encircling the city, though, frankly, even when the work is completed I do not see our way clear. Our camp surrounding the stronghold will still be at some distance and somewhat below the walls, an inescapable natural disadvantage that will hamper the effectiveness of our artillery and make a direct assault on the walls extremely dangerous. As for starving the Jews out, there seems no early prospect of this, since it is apparent that they have stored up a considerable quantity of supplies within, and they seem to have water as well. Furthermore, the defenders of this stronghold are obviously the cream of the Judean Army, and the manner in which they fight would make one think that this was the first stage of the war, not the last.

I must now confess to an honest confusion as to the Jewish motives. We are all well past the point where we underestimate these people, but what they are doing now appears to me to be nothing short of mass insanity. Daily Severus has had couriers calling out to them in their own tongue promising life and even freedom to any Jew who will surrender. By this time, surely, they must know that Severus' word is good, and it is evident that they have nothing further to gain from this war, yet not one of them has come forward to accept the offer. It would appear that they are determined to die, even if that death is pointless.

Severus seems to understand them better than I do. In fact, he does not appear at all surprised that his daily pleas are ignored and predicts a long siege. At times, I must admit, Severus' ideas are almost as obscure to me as those of the Jews. His stubborn insistence that this last stronghold be taken at any and all costs seems, on the face of it, to be unjustified, since practically the whole country is now ours, and the comparatively few Jews left in it cannot be expected to pose any serious threat to us in the future. Yet Severus maintains that if the Jews manage to hold onto this one city on top of a mountain in the middle of nowhere— even if they never leave the city—they will have beaten us and won the war. I'm afraid I don't quite follow his reasoning in this, but I have come to trust Severus' judgment without reservation, so I expect he is right in this as well.

I was saddened to hear of the death of our old friend Justinius. He will be sorely missed in the Senate, especially in these trying times. Please convey my condolences to his family.

Your loving son

"Why do you want to become a Jew?" asked Akiba.

"I explained it to you last week," said Cornelia.

"Tell me again."

Cornelia sighed. "I accept the truth of your teachings. It is that simple."

"You could accept the truth of our teachings without becoming a Jew," suggested Akiba. "You could even follow the Law. You could go so far as to keep the Sabbath and other of our rituals, and your virtue for doing so would be higher than if you became a Jew."

Cornelia shook her head. "I'm through with halfway measures," she said. "That's the sort of thing I've been doing all my life. No, if I am to be a Jew, then I want to be a Jew."

Akiba looked at her for some moments before speaking. "Are you aware," he said at last, "that if you once take this step, there is no way back?" Cornelia made as if to say something, but Akiba stopped her. "I must tell you this first of all," he said. "It is one thing to be born into the Covenant, to be raised in it and so forth. A person who has been a Jew all his life, even if he knows less about the Law than you, cannot have any illusions about where he stands. This Covenant of ours, you can hide it from the whole world, but you can never hide it from God. The Covenant cannot be dissolved, and from the moment you were to enter into it everything you did would be judged in the light of your new standing. You understand if—for example—you were to become a Jew today, then tomorrow you might do some perfectly ordinary thing that you did yesterday, but tomorrow that same thing would suddenly be a grave sin for you, while yesterday it was of no moment in the eyes of God."

"I'm through with yesterday," said Cornelia. "It is tomorrow I'm interested in."

Akiba arose and stood by the window. "I don't know what to do," he said. "I will tell you frankly that I am confused as to the proper course to take with you. Under normal circumstances I would ask you to wait some more months, to learn some more, to understand more, to consider more. But . . ." he turned to the woman. "You were quite right the other day when you said I had no real authority to keep you from entering into the Covenant if you are determined to do so, but I fear, Cornelia, that you do not fully appreciate what it entails."

"I appreciate it at least as well as a Jewish child who may have been born today."

"Yes," said Akiba, "but you see that child was fated to be a Jew for reasons that we accept as being beyond our knowledge and control, whereas you . . ."

"Perhaps," offered Cornelia, "I was fated to become a Jew."

"But you have free will in the matter. There is the ultimate difference. Otherwise, the analogy of birth is a good one, for if you were to convert, you would, in the eyes of God, be reborn. You would even be given a new name—Sarah—after Abraham's wife, the first woman convert. And in everything else, too, your previous life would end, and you would start anew."

"That is precisely what I want," said Cornelia. "Precisely."

Akiba sat down again facing the woman. "Your child," he said. "By converting, you would deprive him of any choice. Being born of a Jewish mother, he would automatically be born into the Covenant."

"I am aware of that," said Cornelia. "And I will raise him so that he would not want it otherwise."

The rabbi turned away and fidgeted with the skullcap on his hairless head. "You know that of all the religions we alone do not seek converts, for we do not need to have our faith bolstered by having others agree with us."

Cornelia nodded her head.

"You know that it is my duty as a rabbi to try to talk you out of taking this step, to point out all the obvious and not so obvious disadvantages, since it is only thus that we can be sure that people come to us of their own free will and for the right reasons."

Cornelia nodded again.

"You can see that a cloud has descended over all Israel," Akiba went on. "But what you do not know is that I think the cloud may hover over us for some time. Now I ask you, Cornelia, why would you want your child born under such a cloud?"

"The cloud will pass. I believe that."

"But it may not pass in your lifetime, or in the lifetime of your child, or of your grandchild, or your great-grandchild. Yet you seek, of your own free will, to place them all under that cloud. Why?"

Cornelia sighed and looked away into the distance. "Rabbi," she said, "have you ever in all your long years lived for nothing beyond yourself?"

Akiba thought for a moment, and then he shook his head. "No, I loved my parents. And I loved my wife, very deeply."

"And when these people died?" Cornelia persisted. "Did you live for just yourself then?"

"No," said Akiba, grudgingly, understanding perfectly well what the woman was driving at.

"Why?"

"It's hard to explain. I could tell you that it was because the Law commands us to love our fellowman, but that isn't the real reason. People don't follow the Law because it tells them to. I suppose they follow it because they sense that there is a truth in it."

"Well, then, try to understand," cried Cornelia, "that I have this sense now. All my life has been sleeping and getting up and eating good food and smelling pleasant scents and wearing nice clothes and making as if I love. There was never anything more between being born and dying for me, or for people like me. Only now, somehow, I feel the lack of something else, and I know that if I cannot have it, then from now on all life, no matter how pleasant, will be meaningless to me. And if I cannot transmit it to my child, then I know that I will doom him to a life as meaningless as mine."

Akiba looked at her in silence for a long time. "Come back tomorrow," he said finally. "And if you still feel this way . . ."

"Please do not make me wait beyond tomorrow," Cornelia implored. "Please, Rabbi."

Akiba escorted her to the door. "I will see you tomorrow," he said.

Menashe Ben-Simon had just begun to talk, and his father played with him now, in their home in Bethar, with the cold wind and the wrath of the world kept outside.

The Prince of Israel played thus with his son a long time, teaching him new, simple words and listening in quiet delight as the child repeated them, pronouncing the Hebrew in the clean, crisp tones that Simon used. Until at last the boy's mother came to take him to bed. The child protested, and Simon good-naturedly helped him, and together they wheedled another half hour or so out of her. But then Mariamne did put him to sleep, and when she returned, she found her husband no longer smiling.

"I want him to grow up knowing what it was all about," he said without looking at her. "I don't care what he knows about me, but I want him to know what it is to be a Jew and to be a man. I want you to teach him this, Mariamne. I entrust you with it, no matter what."

"Don't be silly," said Mariamne. "You will teach him yourself."

Cornelia returned to the university in B'nei B'rak the following day, and when she expressed herself as being still determined on her course, Akiba instructed her in some of the minor as well as the more important precepts of the Law, together with the penalties attached to their transgression. Cornelia listened, and she was not deterred, and so, for the first time, Akiba began to tell her of the rewards awaiting the righteous, of the beauty of the Law, of the majesty of God, of the glory of Israel's election. Cornelia listened, and she nodded her acceptance of the whole, of the burden as of the splendor.

So at length Akiba called for the wife of one of the rabbis, and she escorted the Roman lady to the bathhouse of the women. There, Cornelia Ruffina, daughter of Senator Caecilius, undressed and immersed herself in the lukewarm water in an act of purification, which also symbolized the washing away of her old life.

And when she had dressed and returned to Akiba's study, she found him there with Rabbi Meir and the young Joshua Ha-Garsi, and Cornelia knew that these were the witnesses required by the Law. Akiba motioned her into a seat and began asking the customary questions.

"Is it of your own free will that you seek the fellowship of Israel?"

"It is," answered Cornelia.

"Are you aware that before taking this step you partook of forbidden food and profaned the Sabbath without incurring punishment, but henceforth if you do these things penalties will befall you?"

"I know and accept the responsibility willingly," answered Cornelia.

"Do you not know," asked Akiba, "that Israel is now afflicted, persecuted, humbled, distracted and suffering chastisements?"

"I know," answered Cornelia, "and am unworthy to share their hardships."

Akiba looked at the witnesses, and they nodded. The three men arose, and Cornelia did likewise.

"Repeat after me," said Akiba, *"Shema Yisrael, Adonai Elohenu, Adonai Ehad"*—"Hear, O Israel, the Lord is our God, the Lord is One."

"Shema Yisrael, Adonai Elohenu, Adonai Ehad," repeated Cornelia.

"Blessed be the name of His glorious Kingdom for all eternity," intoned the witnesses.

"And you shall love the Lord your God with all your heart and with all your soul and with all your might," quoted Akiba from the holiest of Books. "And these words which I command you this day shall be upon your heart, and you shall teach them diligently to your children and shall talk of them when you sit in your house and when you walk on the way and when you lie down and when you rise up. . . ."

Akiba placed his hands upon the woman's head, and he blessed her with the ancient blessing of the Cohanim:

"May the Lord bless you and keep you;

"May the Lord cause His Face to shine upon you and be gracious to you;

"May the Lord lift up His Face to you and grant you peace."

"Amen and amen," answered the witnesses.

Akiba removed his hands and said to Cornelia, "Welcome, Sarah, our sister in Israel."

"Welcome," said Rabbi Meir.

"Welcome," said Joshua Ha-Garsi.

Cornelia, overcome by the drama of the ceremony, fell on her knees before Akiba and sought to kiss the old man's hand in thankfulness.

But Akiba drew his hand away, and gently but firmly he raised the woman and told her, "That is one of the things you may never do again, not you nor all your line. You may never bow to anyone or to anything upon this earth."

41

The month of Tevet passed, and the month of Shevat, and then it was the month of Adar, toward the end of winter, early in the year 135 in the calendar of the Minaeans.

The Romans had gradually leveled the land around Bethar, and they now ringed the city with their might like a third wall more solid than the walls of stone; but the walls of stone still stood as well. The besiegers had found five of the tunnels leading from the beleaguered city, and these had been destroyed by the Jews before their enemies could use them; but there remained other passages that had not been found, and the Romans were not unaware of it. The couriers still went out daily to call upon the defenders of the stronghold to surrender; but no one in the Roman camp entertained hopes anymore that the pleas would ever be heeded.

And daily there was the bombardment from the Roman catapults and stone throwers and quick loaders that stood at intervals around the walls of Bethar; and daily there was the return bombardment from the walls directed at the Roman artillery positions and at their camp beyond. And there were the battles. They would be fought by the outer wall when the Romans tried to scale it; or farther back when the Jews took the offensive; or even behind the Roman lines when a corps of Jews suddenly appeared there from one of their tunnels. But they would be fought, daily, so that it became not so much a siege as a constant series of major and minor battles in which men died seemingly without end and to a purpose that had long since sunk into obscurity.

Many perished in those battles. In the four months since the Romans had invested the stronghold 25,000 Jewish warriors had been slain. Yet, with their heavy losses in the first part of the siege, the total Roman toll was even higher, and the three legions that had spearheaded the early assaults had been reduced below minimum strength. Reluctantly Severus had been obliged to ask the emperor for troops to join to these legions, and he was told that he would have to content himself this time with auxiliary units and with forces drafted from the navy, from the ships that lay anchored off the coast. Hadrian was no longer willing to go to more expense than was absolutely necessary; he had tired of the drawn-out warfare.

For the troops on the line the weariness was a great deal more real but a great deal less apparent. Most of the Roman soldiers now arrayed around Bethar had been fighting almost continuously for more than a year, while the Jews within had been at war for two and a half years. The strain was there on both sides, and sometimes it showed, but only in between the battles; for neither the legionaries drawn from the frontier areas of Europe nor the defenders of Bethar were the kinds of men who would permit it to affect the way they fought.

The strain showed on Bar Kochba as well. He was only thirty-three years old, yet his hair and his beard had become streaked with gray. And it showed on him in other ways, too,

in ways strange for strain to show, for he grew angry less easily
now, and he seemed more patient with his officers and men,
and with his family most of all he was especially tender. He
would be with his son now as much of the time as his duties
allowed, and from time to time he would take the boy around
the city and the fortifications with him, and show him things,
and explain matters to him, and in general speak to the child
as to an equal. And when the prince's wife would appear, people could not help but notice the way he would smile at her,
or touch her hand, or give over their son.

Yet there was one man in Bethar on whom no strain showed,
and that was Rabbi Eleazar Ha-Modai, who still acted as if victory for the Jews was only a matter of time, patience and
prayer. Being of the priestly tribe of Cohanim, Rabbi Eleazar
was not permitted by the Law to approach the dead and could
not, therefore, officiate at burials. But he would often stand
beyond the cemetery precincts and pray for the fallen, though
never with grief on his countenance; nor would he utter the
prayer for the dead on behalf of the slain, for to Rabbi Eleazar
Ha-Modai the men who had lain down their lives for the Jewish homeland were not really dead. Indeed, he would explain,
they had ascended directly to paradise by virtue of their selfless
sacrifice, and while their comrades had good reason to miss
these heroes, to mourn for them would be unfair, for they were
blessed.

The Law made all this clear to Rabbi Eleazar Ha-Modai,
for to him the Law and the land and justice and right were so
inextricably bound that it was impossible to separate one from
the other. He was a learned man, but he was not primarily a
scholar. He saw a beauty in the Law, and therefore he ac-
knowledged it as true, rather than the other way around; nor
would the distinction have concerned Rabbi Eleazar.

Every day the elderly teacher from the town of Modin would
rise early and, after conducting the morning service, would
make his rounds. First he would go to visit the wounded, and
then he would make a circuit of the walls surrounding the city,
chatting with the men at their posts, bringing them words of
encouragement and telling them parables and sometimes even
joking with them. And if one section of wall was damaged or
perilous, yet Rabbi Eleazar would not think of leaving it out

on his tour, lest—heaven forbid—he offend any of the warriors by his absence.

The warriors, of course, would not have been offended, but truth to tell they had grown accustomed to the sight of the old man trudging toward them, and had he not come one day they would surely have missed him. And so Rabbi Eleazar was thorough and circumspect in his rounds, which usually occupied him until late in the evening.

At that time, his duties finished, the rabbi would retire to the little synagogue behind his home and would converse there with the Almighty. He would approach Him always with a smiling face, for the rabbi did not believe that the Lord liked to see men in tears, and in any case it was unseemly to approach the Giver of Good with complaints. Rabbi Eleazar believed with perfect faith that everything the Lord did was good in its time, and the one thing he would ask in his nightly talks with Him was that the time be soon, although the rabbi would quickly add that the time would, of course, be best when He thought best.

The defenders of Bethar were not, by and large, unbelieving men, but they had long ago ceased to expect a miracle that would save them. Yet they all now shared one common belief; they believed it senselessly, and on those rare occasions when one of them expressed it, he would do so with a smile, so that his comrades might think perhaps that he was not wholly serious. But the belief, for all its obvious irrationality, was quite serious. It was generally held by the defenders that so long as Rabbi Eleazar was there to intercede for them, the city of Bethar would never fall. . . .

As the winter rains slackened and as the wind began to blow the early scents of approaching spring, the university in B'nei B'rak remained still a haven in a country that had become a cruel place for Jews. Regularly now refugees would come to the university and would blurt out terrible tales of the atrocities being perpetrated by Rufus' police. They were distraught people, these Jews who had fled their homes after holding out for so long, and they told their tales in disorganized fashion; but as the tales told by them all were essentially much the same, the small band which had remained with Rabbi Akiba

Ben-Joseph at the university grew quite adept at picking out any new details and at calming these visitors.

From all the tales it became clear that of the rabbis who had once held a leading position on the Sanhedrin in Judea, Akiba now remained the only one alive and in Palaestina. The old sage knew, of course, that this state of affairs would not last; he had known it for some time; and he supposed, as did so many of the people who came to caution him, that Rufus was saving him for something special.

Outwardly this knowledge and this suspicion were not at all in evidence, for Akiba continued acting and teaching much as he had always done. But it would be unfair to the man Akiba to say that he was not inwardly moved by his realization.

So, more and more in these last days of winter, Akiba would just sit and think to himself. He thought about life as most living men do not think to think of it; he thought of the young trees in his garden that he would not see blossom; he smelled the newborn air, and he thought how good it was to smell the air; he stretched forth his arm to wind his tephillin around it, and he thought how good it was to feel that old peasant's arm. But against such earthbound thoughts Akiba had others that far outweighed them. He thought of what awaited him beyond the vestibule of this world; he thought how pleasant it would be to take up his discourse with so many old colleagues; and above all, he thought of the joy of his reunion with his wife Rachel, and he almost looked forward to it.

Yet there was one thought that did disturb Akiba. He wondered how it would be in those last hours and moments before the weak but stubborn link that tied him to this earth was actually severed. It would be severed in pain, he knew, for he knew Rufus, and in contemplating his death Akiba felt the same sense of inadequacy that had plagued him all his life. He knew what he had to do, and he was determined to do it, but still, he wondered if he could depart with the calm nobility that so many of his colleagues had shown. It was not at all vanity that made Akiba wonder thus, yet it was the one thought in which he permitted himself a certain element of fear.

It was early in the spring, in the beginning of the month of Nisan, that Another came to warn Akiba that the threat of death was very near.

"You speak with urgency," observed Akiba as the two old men walked through the university garden as they had so often before.

"I have reason to believe that your arrest can be expected at any time now," said Elisha Ben-Abuyah. "I have been informed that relations between Rufus and the emperor have never been better, what with Bethar holding out as long as it has. And it has been months since Rufus has had a suitable spectacle for the mob in Caesarea. And there is no one left now but you. That is why I have come to warn you to act before it is too late: Disband your university at once; tell your disciples to go away; hide your books. Play the game, Akiba, just for a little while."

"Do you really expect me to?" asked the rabbi.

"I expect you to be reasonable at long last," said Another.

"Do you really expect me to?" repeated Akiba.

Aher shook his head sadly. "No," he sighed. "Not really. Reason tells me that you are too old to change."

Akiba smiled. "Yet you came," he said, "while knowing that it would be a useless errand. How very kind you can be, Elisha, when you are not so reasonable."

Elisha turned away, and when Akiba looked at him again, there were tears in the apostate's eyes. "I will tell you the truth, Akiba," he said. "I miss the rabbis. I miss all those old fools I grew up with and studied with and argued with most of my life. In my own way, I suppose, I loved them, God help me . . ."

Elisha tried to choke the words back, but Akiba had caught them. "You speak of love and of God today," he said. "Beware, Elisha, you are getting perilously close to faith."

"I have never been farther," snapped Elisha. "Even if I had believed before all of this, how could I possibly believe now?"

"If you ask me to answer that rationally, I cannot. But as I have told you so many times before, there are things beyond reason."

"You are as obstinate as ever," said Elisha. "If you had only listened to me before, your own life would not be in danger now."

"And what then?" asked Akiba. "Would I then have continued my existence on this earth forever? And to what purpose? There is the major flaw in your reasoning, Elisha, and there it has always been. If there is nothing worth dedicating our lives to, then our lives become nothing."

"And so they are," said Another. "And so they have always been. There is the flaw in your faith."

The two men moved on in silence. They had reached the point of difference. They had reached it thousands of times before from thousands of different angles, but ultimately they had reached it and had then gone on to speak of other things.

Only this time, *aher* said, "Akiba, did I ever tell you how I lost my faith?"

"No," said Akiba.

"And you never asked me."

"No."

"You've heard the stories, I suppose."

"Yes, I have."

"I'm curious; which one do you think is true?"

"None of them," replied Akiba evenly.

"Really?" Another laughed. "Why?"

"Because none of the stories is about you, Elisha. Not one of them fits. All of the stories tell of something you saw or something you heard which shook you so deeply that you suddenly decided to renounce God. But you, Elisha, you were always the one who was so adept at finding hidden meanings in things, in viewing events from many vantage points. Had you actually witnessed any of the tragic occurrences that these folktales tell of, why, you would have quickly found some interpretation to reconcile it with the point of view you were holding at the time."

Aher smiled and was silent for a long moment. "You know, you're quite right," he said at last. "The stories are just that, though I must admit I was quite pleased that so many people believed them. It proved my theory about people and their willingness to accept legends in place of truth. But you see, Akiba, I could never tell anyone the truth, because nobody would have believed me. The truth in this case is so strange, so . . . so . . ."

"Unreasonable?" Akiba offered.

"Yes," said Elisha. "You might say that."

"The truth so often is," observed Akiba.

"It just happened one day," Elisha said. "That's really the whole story from beginning to end. It was not an especially bad day. In fact, it was during a period of tranquillity, and I didn't see or hear anything out of the ordinary that day. I was on my way home from the house of study, and suddenly it just hit me that there is no God. The idea simply crept into my head. I suppose I'd been trying to keep it out for a long time, because when it finally got in there, I couldn't seem to get it out. I looked around me on the street, and I thought, All these people here think Somebody is watching them all the time, but they are wrong. There is nobody above them, and nobody below them, but they are afraid to admit it to themselves. They are so afraid that they have created a God so they can be afraid of Him instead of facing their own futility and the senselessness of their lives. I must admit to you, Akiba, that when I first had this thought, it occurred to me that I might be struck dead on the spot for my secret blasphemy. But I wasn't. I wasn't harmed at all. In fact, I felt relieved, as if some heavy weight had suddenly been lifted from me. And I never saw any reason for placing the weight back, so I didn't. That's all there is to it. That's how I lost my faith. But it's an absurd story, isn't it?"

"Not at all," said Akiba. "On the contrary, it sounds most reasonable. I'm quite sure that's just the way it happened, because it had to happen that way with you sooner or later."

"Had to?"

"Of course. You didn't lose your faith that day, Elisha. All you did do was decide at long last to stop playing a game that could never have made much sense to you and had therefore, with time, become like a weight. There was every reason for you to throw off the weight sooner or later. But as for faith, you never had any faith to lose."

"How can you say that?" protested Elisha. "How can you twist things that way? I was the best student at the university in Yavneh. My father had me trained in the Law from earliest childhood."

"That is true," said Akiba, "whereas I—as you used to delight in reminding me in those days—had been an unlettered peasant during all of my youth. But you know, Elisha, there is one thing a man learns on the land, and that is to accept some

things as being quite beyond his control and even his understanding. He works hard; he plants his seed; he mates his cat-
tle. But sometimes the harvest is good, and sometimes the rain
fails him, or the corn is blasted by the wind; sometimes his
calves are hearty, and sometimes they sicken and die. The peasant does all that he can, but he learns to accept, and if one season is bad, then he tries to survive to the next season, hoping
it will be better."

"I never liked you at the university," Elisha interrupted
him. "It's strange, now that I think of it. When we were on
the same side, I despised you. It was only later, when our paths
had parted, that I came to have a fondness for you."

"But I liked you," Akiba said. "And I even understood your
dislike. After all, I was much older, and my mind was slower,
while you always grasped things at once. In those days I was
terribly impressed with you, Elisha. We all were. I would
sometimes come across a line or a passage in our studies that I
frankly did not understand. So would the other students, and
even the great rabbis who taught us would admit that there
were sections of the Torah whose full meaning had eluded
their grasp. But with you, Elisha, that never happened. Somehow or other you would always manage to explain every line
that came to your attention. I must say I didn't always agree
with your interpretations, but I always found them brilliant.
Later, however, I came to realize that you made these interpretations—no matter how farfetched—because you desperately needed them. That is why you could not be tolerant with
me or with anyone else who questioned an opinion you had
stated. It was only when you no longer cared that the tolerance
developed.

"But the point is," Akiba went on, "that you could never
accept anything that you did not understand fully and at once.
So it was only a matter of time before you would turn your
reasoning faculties away from the individual lines and to the
essence of what we believe and, failing to understand it all at
once, would reject it."

The two men walked toward the end of the garden path,
toward the rabbi's house. "And you, Akiba," Elisha asked, "has
your way led you to understanding?"

"I do not understand it all," Akiba said. "Perhaps I don't

even understand most of it. But I have spent a lifetime trying to understand some of it, and I am content."

The two of them had neared Akiba's home when suddenly a voice rang out. The old men looked up to see a squad of Roman police barring their path. "Which one of you is Rabbi Akiba Ben-Joseph?" demanded the officer in charge.

"I am," said Akiba.

Two of the Romans grabbed the rabbi's arms and began leading him away. "What are you doing?" asked Elisha, running alongside them. "You can't just take him like that. Where is your warrant? He has done no harm."

The Romans were amused by the old Jew's protestations, and as he followed them and tried physically to hold them back they simply pushed him off. But after a time he grew tiresome, and so one of the Romans drove a sword into Elisha's stomach and left him on the grass to die. . . .

It was there that the disciples found him, unconscious but still alive, and they carried him gently into Akiba's house, laying him on Akiba's bed, and they summoned the few rabbis remaining at the university to be at the old heretic's side in his final moments.

When Elisha opened his eyes, the first one he saw was Rabbi Meir, his student of former times, and with an effort he said to him, "They've taken Akiba. I couldn't stop them. They've taken him."

"We know," said Meir.

"I wanted so very much to save him," said Elisha. "I would have given anything for it."

"Akiba was not afraid," said Meir. "But I am afraid, my master. I am afraid for you."

"Repent," said one of the other rabbis. "Renounce your apostasy before it is too late. You still have time."

Elisha looked about him with annoyance. "Is God such a fool?" he demanded of the rabbis. "I think I have more respect for Him than you do. He knows I am dying. He would laugh at me now."

"But if you believe that He knows," argued Meir pleadingly, "then you believe that He is. I beg you, call upon His name, for He is merciful."

"It is too late," said Elisha. "For me, it is too late."

"It is not too late," insisted Meir. "God does not see as you or I see. He sees the whole, from beginning to end, a man's deeds and feelings and confusions as well as his words. I beg you, for my sake if not for your own, end your life as you began it—with trust in Him."

"No," Elisha said. "I chose my course in life, and I will face the consequences now. Reason demands that much."

Elisha closed his eyes, and for a moment Rabbi Meir feared that the defiant old man had already died. But Elisha opened his eyes again, and now, in a desperate move born of love, Meir suddenly lifted his hands to Heaven in the dying man's sight and declared, "Lord, if Rabbi Elisha Ben-Abuyah is condemned to die the Death, then I ask to be condemned with him, for he was my master, my guide and my familiar friend."

Elisha burst into tears, and for the first time his face showed the shadow of fear. "Do not condemn yourself," he implored. "God has surely heard you, and He will not relent."

"Then let God hear you," Meir said, "and save us both."

"You do not understand what you are doing," groaned Elisha. "You do not understand God as well as I do. You never did."

"But in my stubbornness I am your true disciple," said Meir calmly. "I will not take back my words. Both our souls are now in your hands."

Elisha looked at his old pupil, and he felt the approach of death, and he knew that now there was no time left for argument. And so he asked the rabbis to sit him up, for he would not face God while flat on his back. And through his tears, but with a dreadful urgency, he began the prayers of the Return.

"I have sinned. I have transgressed. I have committed iniquity. I have spoken falsehood . . ."

The rabbis listened, and they sensed that a path they did not know, a strange path, the path of another, had in the end led to the same conclusion.

"May my death be an atonement for all my sins," intoned Elisha. "Into Your Hand I commend my spirit. *Shema Yisrael, Adonai Elohenu, Adonai Ehad.*"

Thus died *aher,* and the rabbis closed his eyes and covered his face, and they prayed fervently for the man of reason who

had laid down his life in an attempt to save his friend. And
they carried his body into the garden of Rabbi Akiba and buried him there, in the shade of a tree. And on his tombstone
they wrote, "Here lies Rabbi Elisha Ben-Abuyah, another of
the sages of Israel."

42

A state of siege, for all the violence that attends it, is a state
of balance. So long as it is maintained, the force outside cannot
get in, and the force inside cannot drive the attacker away.

From the very start of their stand in Bethar the Jews knew
they could not hope to tip the scales enough to defeat the angry
world outside their walls. But they sought to maintain the balance, and they had managed, by a united act of will, to maintain it for more than five months, and they hoped—those who
still entertained hope—that they might maintain it long
enough for the world to lose heart or interest or for the world
to change so that it no longer posed a threat to the Jews.

But there is a limit to what even the strongest determination
can achieve, and with the advent of the spring, at about the
time of the Festival of the Passover in the month of Nisan, the
balance began to shift, though almost imperceptibly, to the
side of the attackers.

The defenders sensed the shift, and they strove with a yet
heightened effort to move back the scales. But the effort itself
cost lives, and with the arrival of the reinforcements Severus
had requested, the Romans outnumbered the men of Bethar
by nearly two to one. . . .

There were two walls around the city of Bethar. The inner
one, the original wall as strengthened by the defenders, surrounded the city itself with its dwellings and other structures.
Around this wall, however, at a distance of several hundred
feet, Bar Kochba had ordered the construction of a second,

outer wall. It was this outer wall that the defenders of Bethar now manned.

The Romans aimed their stone throwers and quick loaders directly at the men stationed on the outer wall, while with their large catapults they kept up a steady bombardment over the wall. But, of necessity, the Roman catapults were situated at some distance from the beleaguered city, on lower ground, and all their heavy missiles fell in the area between the two walls while the city itself remained untouched.

After a time, the defenders posted on the outer wall became adept at spotting the boulders that would hurtle in their direction toward the heavily fortified strip between the walls. The boulders made a harsh, rushing sound as they sailed through the air, and the first to hear the sound would shout the traditional military warning—"Baby on the way"—so that the men in the missile's path could throw themselves to the ground in time. Thus, while some of the boulders did find their mark, many of them bounced harmlessly off the inner wall and were later gathered up by the defenders for use against the enemy that had hurled them.

But early in the Roman month of March, corps of men from each of the legions began foraging for usable timber in the forests near Bethar. Then, under the supervision of their engineers, they started building a series of movable towers, each of them slightly higher than the outer wall of the city.

From a distance the men of Bethar could see the towers rising in the Roman camp. There appeared to be thirteen of them in all—one per legion. Mounted on each of the high towers was a platform well shielded against the missiles that could be expected to rain upon it, and each of the platforms was wide enough to accommodate a catapult and its crew.

Like their tactics, the Roman genius for building quickly and well afforded few surprises, and by the end of the month of March the towers were completed. They stood high in the distance out of the range of the Jewish artillery, and the defenders wondered with an idle horror when and precisely where they would be used.

The answer came a few days later, as an unusually dense flight of arrows, stones and lances from quick loaders forced the defenders of the outer wall to take cover. While the men on the wall were thus distracted, the Romans rolled the large towers forward on their wheels. There were perhaps fifty legionaries behind every tower, using the massive structures as a shield and at the same time pushing them toward the city.

The towers were concentrated against an area of the city that appeared especially vulnerable, and once in range the artillery on the platforms began spewing missiles beyond the outer wall, over the inner wall and into the heart of Bethar, smashing into buildings, breaking everything and everyone that stood in their path.

The towers had been in position for but a few minutes, and the cries of triumph still rang from the throats of the legionaries behind them when Bar Kochba gave the signal.

Suddenly a large force of Jews, each with a torch in his hand, emerged from the city. In a move so well-planned and swift that the Romans hardly had time to react, the large force became thirteen separate squads, each of which rushed directly for a tower. Then, in nearly simultaneous actions, the men in the squads tossed their torches into the bases of the towers and ran back to the safety of the outer wall—all in a matter of moments.

By the time the legionaries realized what was happening the towers were in flames, and the men stationed on them were in danger of being roasted alive. In their terror they jumped from their high perches, many of them breaking their legs, while their comrades on the ground, having no water or other means of extinguishing the fires, ran about in a mad confusion as the fortifications on the wall opened up with a shower of arrows and missiles.

The legionaries regrouped and began to withdraw, but they had not gotten very far when they found their retreat cut off by a Jewish force behind them. The Jews, who had come through one of their secret tunnels, gave battle to the startled Romans and destroyed the enemy contingent to the last man. Then they moved forward over the bodies of the slain and entered Bethar in triumph through the main gate.

The entire tactic had been witnessed by General Severus and the rest of his men from the Roman camp, but it had been executed so quickly that there had been no time to save the towers or relieve the embattled contingent. In less than an hour the last of the towers had burned to the ground, and the earth around them was littered with Roman corpses.

It was, in all, the greatest stroke the Jews had managed since the Romans had invested Bethar, and it brought great rejoicing to the city. The men within had not tasted victory for a long time, and they drank it now like a heady wine, and they sang and danced in the streets like conquerors.

It was on that day that Bar Kochba knew for certain that Bethar was doomed.

Late at night, as the prince and his wife lay in their bed, the sounds of revelry still reverberated outside.

"I hope they don't wake the child," said Mariamne.

"Let them be," Simon sighed. "It may be their last time."

Mariamne reached over and touched his cheek. "Why so downcast?"

"You can tell a lot," said Simon, "by what men rejoice over. Two years ago at about this time they were rejoicing over the defeat of Urbanicus and thirty thousand Roman troops. Today they rejoice over the destruction of thirteen wooden towers. . . ."

To my father, Senator Caius Arminius:

Hail and greeting.

Before getting on with my dreary chronicle of this endless war, I wish to tell you of some extremely disquieting rumors which have reached us here and to ask for your prompt intercession if they are true.

As you may know, we recently received some troops pressed into service from the ships that lie anchored off the coast of Judea—or is it Palaestina? Will I ever get used to that wretched new name?

In any case, these troops brought word of various atrocities supposedly committed by Rufus' civil administration in those areas of the province which the legions have left behind. The rumors reached Severus' ear as well as my own, and he finally summoned a handful of these reinforcements to give him a firsthand report. Needless to say, these soldiers grew restrained in the presence of their commanding officer, and they promptly withdrew some of their earlier statements as having been exaggerated or based on hearsay.

Nevertheless, from the sum total of their disorganized information it becomes clear that at the very least there have been a large number of crucifixions in Caesarea and along the coast. As for some of the other stories being bandied about by the troops, I can only hope that they are merely fancy. But regarding the crucifixions, about which there appears little doubt, they represent a direct violation of Severus' standing orders. I cannot imagine for what reason such a large body of men was being put to death, but Severus has expressly forbidden crucifixions for any offense whatsoever.

There is a great deal involved here, Father, perhaps more than I understand, but I want to make clear to you that any such act by Rufus undermines everything that Severus has been working for in this province for the past year. He seeks to conciliate the Jews remaining here, to prove to them that rebellion against Rome is not only hopeless but without reason, so that they will never again raise a threat to the empire here or anywhere else. Whether or not this is a wise policy is not for me—or for Rufus—to decide. Severus was promised a free hand by the emperor, and I believe he should be given the chance to conclude this war as he sees fit. I therefore bring this to your attention as a member of the Senate.

Regarding the war itself, we have suffered another unfortunate reverse, although it was subsequently somewhat compensated for.

In a move toward weakening the resistance of the last Jewish stronghold preparatory to a direct assault on the walls Severus ordered the construction of a series of conventional siege towers which would enable us to direct our missiles into the center of the city.

But alas, no sooner were the towers in place than the Jews, showing their customary recklessness, ran forth from the city and put the torch to every one of them. This sounds absurd on paper, I know, but it all happened so suddenly that we simply had no time to do anything to stop it, and before we knew what was about, the Jews had retired and the towers were in flames.

Worse still, the legionaries standing before the city regained their equilibrium only to be set upon by a large force of Jews attacking from the rear—via one of their infernal tunnels. To cut an unpleasant story short, a number of our men were lost, and the Jews achieved an unexpected victory.

There is, however, one bright spot in this otherwise dark picture. The Jewish tactic was clearly observed by us in the camp, and we saw the location of the tunnel they had used. This tunnel was subsequently assaulted by us and had to be destroyed by the enemy. Judging by its position, it was the most strategic tunnel available to the Jews, and at least we have the small comfort of knowing that this particular tactic will not be repeated. There are, unfortunately, probably other tunnels left, although we have by now found and forced the destruction of six of them.

I cannot help but wonder if the Jews realize that they have actually accomplished nothing with this latest tactic —as well as with all the months of furious fighting here at Bethar—other than to delay the inevitable. It seems so very long ago that I was a prisoner of the rebels, then at the dawn of their movement, yet now—in the twilight of the Jews—I find myself thinking often of their leader. It is strange to speculate that this man with whom I talked and ate and sometimes even laughed is now only a short distance away from me. What can he be thinking, I wonder. Why is he so intent upon doom for himself and his people?

Severus has ordered the construction of new towers. These are to be encased in steel, and as an added precaution, soldiers will be permanently stationed around them with no other duty than to watch for any sudden moves toward the structures.

I can see that I am not much of a prophet, for as I wrote you, I had hoped that the war would be over by spring. Yet the Jews fight on and confound all my predictions. But they are only men, Father, and men, faced with such overwhelming odds, must either yield or die. Surely the battle cannot go on much longer.

Your loving son

"I want you to do something," said Simon.

"Whatever you command," said Jonathan.

The prince shook his head. "This is not a command. This is a request from one friend to another."

"Then," said Jonathan with a smile, "the force of it is stronger still."

Simon turned away, and he locked his hands behind him as was his custom, and he said almost casually, "The city is doomed, Jonathan. You know it; I know it; any man in Bethar who does not know it is a fool. For myself, I am content to fall with the city, along with those who would remain with me to fight to the death."

"I am one such," said Jonathan.

"I know," said Simon. "That is why what I will ask you will be especially hard."

Jonathan was silent, and Bar Kochba turned back to him now. "I am not afraid to die," he said. "I have been so close to death so many times since my boyhood that he seems like a constant caller, and perhaps it is proper to let him enter at last. But I don't want to die for nothing, Jonathan. I want my death and all the other deaths that have already been and will soon be to have some meaning. The memory of what has happened here must survive. It must survive with people who will survive and can pass it on so that other generations may learn from it."

Simon paused and sat down. "I have said it in a very roundabout way. Perhaps I don't mean it quite that way. Perhaps all I really want is for my wife and my son to survive. But it doesn't matter. It all comes to the same thing—a reason, Jonathan. A reason for all that we have done, for our lives as for our deaths."

"Say on," said Jonathan softly.

"We have, as you know, three tunnels left that lead from the city. There are still some families of fighting men within Bethar, about sixty women and children who have stubbornly insisted on remaining until now. I have arranged to have them taken out tonight, by force if necessary, and led to safety."

"Good," said Jonathan. "A wise and noble plan."

"But there are four I have not made arrangements for."

Jonathan looked up.

"They are your wife and mine and our children," Simon
said, and for the first time since their childhood, Jonathan saw
tears rolling down his friend's cheeks. "I cannot risk that Mariamne will be taken prisoner, and poor little Menashe would
make too good a prize in Severus' triumphal procession. I want
them taken from the city separately. I want them led to the
coast, and I want them put safely aboard a ship bound for
Rome itself. Mariamne speaks a perfect Latin, and the capital
would probably be the safest place in the world for them."

"And there's a large community of our people in Rome,"
Jonathan offered. "The way from here to the coast would be
somewhat dangerous, but it could be negotiated through the
mountain passes. Yes, it is a good idea, and I am pleased and
relieved that you have thought to include Ruth and Emanuel
in it."

"I have also included you," Simon said.

Jonathan shook his head. "It is out of the question. I do not
care to live on without you. We have been together too long. It
is only fitting that I die with you."

Bar Kochba grasped his friend's arms. "I need you," he said
earnestly. "I need you to take them. Jonathan, in the name of
our friendship I beg you to do as I ask. I cannot trust anyone
else. There is no one who knows the passes as well as you, no
one who can lead them and guard them as well as you. If you
will take them, I will die happy, but if you refuse me and someone else goes with the people I love most in all the world, I
will perish in fear and despair."

Simon would have gone on, but Jonathan stopped him. "I
will do it," he said. "I will do it for the sake of Ruth and
Emanuel and Mariamne and Menashe, but mostly I will do it
for you. And I will come back, Simon. I will put them aboard
a ship as you ask, and then I will return here to fight by your
side."

"No," said Simon. "Go with them. Don't try to come back.
That would be insane."

"I will disobey that one order," said Jonathan. "I will do
what you have asked, and then—if God wills it—I will come
back and fall with you in Bethar."

43

It was a quiet day in the city of Bethar. The Romans had begun the construction of their new towers; there was a lull in the fighting by the outer wall, and within, the Prince of Israel spent the day playing with his son. And when it came time for the child to be put to bed, he retired with his wife to eat the evening meal.

They sat facing each other and ate as on other days, and then, suddenly, Simon looked up and said in a hoarse voice, "I love you, Mariamne. I haven't told you that very much recently. I suppose because I didn't have time or perhaps because I had all the time in the world."

"You didn't have to tell me," said Mariamne softly.

"But I wanted to," said Simon. "Because . . . because I'm going to ask you to do something now that will take all the love you have, for me and for Menashe."

She fixed her eyes upon him, feeling a certain sense of danger, and of pain.

Simon spoke as casually as he could. "In a few more hours, when the night is dark, Jonathan will take Ruth and Emanuel from the city. Everything has been arranged, and the danger has been minimized. I want you and the child to go with them. I want you to go to Rome, where you will be safe, and I will join you there myself in a few months. . . . Fear not, I have made full provision for my own exit from the city. Only I cannot go now because . . ."

"Stop," Mariamne cried. "Do you know me so little? How can you think that I would leave you? Let Ruth take our child with her own. He deserves his chance at life. But for myself, there can be no life without you."

"There must be," said Simon, raising his voice. "You owe it to Menashe, and to his son, and to his. And you owe it to me."

"You are right," she said. "I do owe it to you. I owe you so very much more than I can give. But I cannot give it, Simon. You ask too much."

Simon grew silent, and they continued eating and drinking without talk until, toward the end of the meal, Mariamne began to feel strangely drowsy, and half suspecting what her husband had done, she looked up at him as if to engrave the sight on her memory and said, "You didn't ask me, Simon, but I love you; my love for you is stronger than death . . . There are no words, no . . ."

Simon jumped to his feet and caught his wife as she lapsed into unconsciousness, and as he lay her down and kissed her for the last time, he said through his tears, "You didn't have to tell me."

They had taken Rabbi Akiba Ben-Joseph to Caesarea, and they locked him up in a cell in the prison there to await the judgment of the procurator. Akiba was to spend months in that cell while Rufus balanced his desires against the weight of the authority the emperor had given him, and in that time the rabbi was treated well and even with a certain courtesy. His Roman guards were aware of the standing of their prisoner, and they were in some awe of him and even knew an element of fear. For the Jews were the most mysterious of people, and who could say if this chief of all the rabbis was not able to cast spells?

Consequently Akiba was treated with deference, and he was permitted the daily attendance of his disciple Joshua Ha-Garsi, who cared for him and brought him his food and water. He was even allowed visitors for a time, and one of these was Simeon Ben-Yohai, who had returned from the safety of his exile to be near the old man. Repeatedly he begged Akiba to continue instructing him in the Law, while the rabbi, fearing for the young man's life, put him off. But in the end he yielded, explaining to Simeon in those terms of the earth which had never left him, "My son, more than the calf wants to suck the cow wants to suckle."

Gradually other scholars began to come, one by one, each of them literally risking his life for the privilege of drinking in the great sage's words. Often they brought him questions, pressing questions that only a man of Akiba's standing could answer. And there was no one left in the land of Akiba's standing save Akiba.

What was to be done with the calendar now that the Sanhedrin no longer existed to determine when it was necessary to
correct it by the addition of days? Was it permissible, under
the trying circumstances, to accept the word of a single witness
that a man had been killed so that his wife could remarry?
Could this or that ceremony be suspended for a time? Could
some rite heretofore practiced in public now be validly performed in private?

Akiba rendered his decisions swiftly and in unambiguous
terms. He revised the Jewish calendar, putting it into a precise
form that would keep it accurate automatically from season to
season without the need for special action by any outside
agency. Similarly, in case after case, he made decisions that
would enable the Jews to go on without a Sanhedrin, without a
country, without him.

Thus, in a prison cell, Akiba Ben-Joseph molded the destiny
of the Jews as no single individual had done since Moses. His
actions and judgments would affect the Jews to the end of days,
and the deep-seated love of Zion that shone from his words
would direct the course of a people's yearning for the next
1,813 years. . . .

It was shortly before dawn when Mariamne awoke to find
herself secured tightly on a moving donkey, her face resting
on the animal's neck. With a sigh she slipped her hands out of
the harness that held her in place and sat upright. In front of
her on another donkey were Emanuel and Ruth, who now held
little Menashe in her arms, and leading the small caravan on
foot was Jonathan, dressed in the loose-fitting robes of a merchant.

Menashe sensed at once that his mother was awake, and he
opened his eyes and cried, "I want to go to *Imah*." Ruth handed
the child over with a smile. Mariamne, seating him in front of
her, whispered, "You must speak softly now."

"Where is *Abba?*" asked the child in an exaggerated whisper.

"He will meet us later," she said. "But we must be very careful now. You must speak softly, and you must not speak at all
unless we are alone or with Ruth and Jonathan and Emanuel.
Soon I will teach you a new way of speaking, a way you can use

even when strangers are about." Menashe nodded without understanding and promptly fell back asleep, and Mariamne reflected sadly how quickly she had begun to do exactly what Simon had asked.

They halted with the sunrise and encamped in a wooded area, resting there until nightfall. When it grew dark, they moved on and by morning had come to a small village beyond the hills of Judah, at the entrance to the coastal plain. There, almost without words, they were received at the home of a local family and remained at the home until the following morning. Then, leaving the donkeys behind, they resumed their journey in an oxcart which Jonathan had obtained from their host.

The cart, with the two women and Menashe bundled in the rear of it and Jonathan and his son seated up front, creaked over the high road leading up the coastal plain toward Caesarea. At times groups of Romans would pass the cart, but they would take no notice. It looked very much like a peasant and his household, and about the only thing that struck the Romans was that the cart moved with painful slowness, and whenever a contingent came by, they rode around it as quickly as they could.

For a long while Emanuel and his father sat side by side in silence, but finally the boy turned to Jonathan and asked, "Where exactly are we going?"

Jonathan answered the six-year-old boy without hesitation, as if he were speaking to an adult. "You are going to Rome. A merchant ship sails from Caesarea tomorrow morning, and passage has already been arranged. Since Aunt Mariamne speaks Latin and Greek, she can easily pass for a Roman matron on her way home with her child. In any case she has Roman citizenship through her father, and there should be no problem there. As for you and your mother, I think it will be best for her to pose as Mariamne's maidservant traveling with her own son. The two of you can speak Aramaic, and it will be assumed that you are Syrian provincials. Little Menashe, of course, need not speak at all."

"And you?" asked Emanuel.

Jonathan looked away. "You are a big boy," he said. "You know I cannot go with you."

"I understand," said Emanuel truthfully. . . .

The five of them arrived in Caesarea late that night. Jonathan, seeking to attract as little attention as possible, left the oxcart at an inn not far from the entrance to the city, and they proceeded on foot through the streets, passing some bored-looking police and here and there a knot of revelers and coming at last to the port and the waiting ship. It would sail with the dawn in a few hours. Jonathan presented the necessary documents to the booking agent, who accepted them sleepily and welcomed the passengers, after which he diplomatically withdrew so they could say their farewells.

The little group stood there at the gangplank, and Mariamne, with Menashe in her arms, kissed Jonathan and whispered to him in the High Tongue, "The Lord be with you."

"And with you," he answered in a throbbing voice. "And with the child."

Mariamne walked up the gangplank, and Jonathan watched the woman and her sleeping child disappear around the deck of the ship. "Take care of her," he said to his wife. "She will need your help."

"Mariamne is stronger than you know," said Ruth. "In the end, I suspect, she will take care of us."

They looked at each other then in the flickering port light and, in a single bitter moment, accepted the full meaning of what was happening. And Jonathan took his wife in his arms, and they kissed, and in that kiss they put all the love and the fear and the joy and the pain that they felt and had felt for each other. Yet the kiss, too, lasted only a moment, and then Jonathan caressed Ruth's cheek and said, *"L'hitraot"*—"To our next meeting."

Ruth closed her eyes and nodded her head.

Jonathan smiled sadly, and with a certain wonder. "You have never questioned me. In all these years, not once."

"There is no questioning a blessing," she said, and she squeezed his hand and held it as if to remember its touch. "You must go. It is best for you to leave the city before dawn." And Ruth let go of his hand and moved up the gangplank without looking back.

Jonathan was left alone now with his son, and he embraced the boy and kissed him, trying with all his might to hold back the tears he felt. "You must grow up very quickly now," he told the boy. "You must grow up even sooner than I did."

"I will try," said Emanuel, crying now.

"And you must come back here. Whatever you do, you must always remember who you are and what you are and who your fathers were. And wherever you go, you must remember that this is your home, here, in this land and in no other."

"I will remember," said the boy, wiping his tears away. "And I swear to you and to God that we will come back here one day, all of us." And Emanuel stretched forth his hand like a man, and he shook the hand of his father and walked up the gangplank with a steady gait. And from the deck, in an act of bravado that made Jonathan proud even as he regretted it, the boy shouted in a clear voice the Hebrew word "shalom."

"Shalom," Jonathan answered under his breath, adding a blessing. And then he turned so that the boy might not see his father weeping. . . .

He walked back through the streets of Caesarea alone, toward the inn and the oxcart, toward Bethar, toward death. He walked sadly but also with a sense of relief, for he knew that the worst that could happen to him now was that he would die. And in a way it seemed to Jonathan fitting that he should die, for what else remained to him in this, his thirty-fourth year? He had lived and had loved and had fought for what he believed, and he had taught his son to cherish the things he held dear. Did any man ever accomplish more?

Jonathan came to the oxcart, but as he was about to climb into it, a squad of three policemen approached him.

"Is this yours?" asked the officer in charge, motioning toward the cart.

"Yes," said Jonathan.

"Your papers."

Jonathan handed the policeman his forged travel permit.

"Paulos Bar Alexios," read the officer aloud. "From?"

"The province of Syria. It's all there, on the paper."

"Yes, but now."

"I have been given a farm not far from here."

The officer handed Jonathan back the document. "You should not travel so late at night," he advised. "It is dangerous."

"You are right," said Jonathan. "I had planned to leave much earlier, but," he winked at the policemen, "Caesarea is a difficult city to take leave of."

The men laughed. "Did you have a good crop?" asked the officer good-naturedly.

"Passably fair," answered Jonathan in the manner of peasants. "It's too early to tell about much of it, but it seems passably fair."

"Well, then," said the officer, "seeing as how you are not a niggardly Jew, how about buying a flask of wine and sharing it with us? By the time we drain it, it will be light, and you can leave then. It will be safer."

Jonathan left the cart and accompanied the three policemen into the inn. He had no choice now, and perhaps, he thought, he might even pry some useful information from them.

They sat down at a table, and the innkeeper set a large flask of sour red wine before them. Jonathan filled the cups of the policemen, and then his own. "How goes it with you here in Caesarea?" he asked.

The officer drank his cup down in one gulp and wiped his lips. "It's a rotten job," he said, refilling his glass. "I should have stayed in Antioch. This is the worst assignment I've ever had."

"How so?" asked Jonathan.

"Ah, these rotten Jews—the curse of Ishtar upon them. You can't get any money out of them; you can't control them; you can't frighten them; you can't even kill them properly."

"I don't see why they should be causing you much trouble now," offered Jonathan. "There're only a handful of them here in Caesarea, I understand, and they're unarmed."

"You don't know them," said the officer with a wave of his hand. "You're off on your farm now, and you're used to civilized people, being from Syria. The Jews are crazy barbarians. Look, there's a law here now that they're not supposed to practice their religion. Me, I don't give a damn about their religion or about them, but I've got to enforce that law, and they know it. So what happens? You close their synagogues, so they just go ahead and hold their prayer meetings elsewhere. Now any fool knows you can't keep that sort of thing secret, and sooner or later we get wind of it. So you make a raid; you arrest a few and crucify them, and they die almost happily, praising their invisible God. And the next day, the ones who remain, why they go to another prayer meeting somewhere else."

"I'll tell you the truth," said another of the policemen. "They scare me. They're not human, these people. Look at this fighting in Bethar. By the balls of Zeus, they just don't know what it means to surrender. Sometimes I even think maybe there's something to this God of theirs."

"You're an idiot," said the third man. "If their God were really so powerful, why couldn't he save them?"

"Still," persisted the policeman who had spoken up, "if I could, I would offer sacrifices to their God as well as my own. But with them, it's either their God or all the others put together. And they're like that with everything."

Suddenly, the door of the inn flew open, and a police patrol hauled in a bearded old Jew.

"Well, there's an example for you," said the officer, rising. "He was probably on his way to a morning service when our men grabbed him."

The police who had gathered in the inn, about twenty of them in all, rose up and surrounded the old man. With a cruelty born of boredom and maintained by habit, they poked at the Jew with their lances and dragged him to the floor by his beard and spit on him and kicked him and tore at his earlocks. The Romans—or, rather, the brutalized provincials who made up the Roman police force in Palaestina—laughed as they tormented the old man, laughed as they tried to make him whimper and beg for mercy. But the old man did not, and so with each kick they hated him more, and they feared him more and tried still harder to make him act less like a man; for every moment that he remained silent, the accusation of his humanity rained down upon them like heavy blows.

Jonathan bore it as long as he could. He looked away and tried not to hear and to think instead of other things. He thought of Simon and of Bethar, and he thought of the death that he had vowed himself.

But in the end he could think of nothing but the old man being taunted by the heathen, and so the only Jewish warrior in Caesarea threw back his merchant's robes and drew the sword with which he had fought by the side of Bar Kochba.

"*L'herut Yisrael,*" screamed Jonathan, and he drove the sword into the belly of the police officer with whom he had just shared a flask of wine. He killed eight others in his fury before they managed to subdue him.

There was no trial and no need for one. Jonathan's action had condemned him to death, in the only manner of execution prescribed for such an offense.

Mariamne stood on the deck and looked out at the shoreline of Judea already shrinking in the distance. She did not permit herself to cry, but under her breath she whispered, "Good-bye, Simon."

"What did you say, *Imah?*" asked the child beside her.

"Nothing," said Mariamne hastily. "Go play with Emanuel."

The boy ran off, and Mariamne turned to see a Roman woman looking at her. The woman, heavy with child, was leaning on the rail nearby, and Mariamne realized that she had heard the boy speaking Hebrew.

She smiled at the woman casually and said, in Latin, "They learn so fast. We were here only a few months, and already he picked up some of the local dialect."

"I hope mine learns as fast," said the woman, glancing at her swollen belly. Then she regarded Mariamne more closely. "Have we not met?" she asked.

"I think not," said Mariamne, truthfully but perhaps a trifle too quickly.

"Are you bound for Rome?"

"Yes. And you?"

"I, too," said the woman. "I want to bear my child there, if he—or she—will wait." She stretched forth her hand to Mariamne. "It will be a long voyage, and I am traveling alone. My name is Cornelia."

The wife of Simon Bar Kochba, bound for exile with his son, took the Roman woman's hand. "I am called Mariamne," she said.

Jonathan Bar Ba'ayah watched the ship disappear over the horizon, and he closed his eyes and muttered a prayer of thanksgiving that his father had taught him. A bolt of pain shot up from his left palm to the shoulder, forcing his eyes open again.

He felt the beginnings of a groan rise up in his chest, but he choked it off quickly, for there was a Roman guard seated by the foot of the cross, and Jonathan Bar Ba'ayah had resolved to show him how a Jew could die.

But the pain was insistent, and it spread now like a growing fire across the entire upper half of his body, tearing at his muscles and at his flesh with the ripping action of a dull saw. Instinctively he tried to shrug his shoulders, but of course that was impossible, for all the weight of his body was now centered in his shoulders and supported by the spikes in his hands. Yet Jonathan Bar Ba'ayah let out not a sound.

"Why can't I groan?" he asked himself. "It is but a foolish vanity. Surely the Roman at my feet has heard men cry out in pain before." But still, despite his fevered reasoning, he kept his anguish within, for Jonathan Bar Ba'ayah had an example constantly before his eyes in these final hours, the example of another man who had died on the cross; and he would not betray his father now by dying less valiantly than he had.

Thus Jonathan the son of Ba'ayah had kept silent, even when they had driven the spikes into his hands—the three spikes straight and the fourth bent over across his right palm; the three spikes straight and the fourth bent over across his left palm. And when they had stood the cross upright so that his body hung from the nails in his hands, the pain had seemed beyond endurance. But Jonathan had kept silent, startling his executioners. And perhaps he had even frightened them a little.

The worst part had been the first two or three eternities on the cross when he had still been fully conscious. Then the agony had been sharp and well defined and concentrated in little pools at separate areas of his body—in his right hand and in his left; in his right bicep and in his left; in his right shoulder and in his left; in his neck and in his chest pushed out and in his stomach drawn in.

But later, at about the time that the ship carrying Jonathan's world sailed from view, the pools of pain blended together into one large ocean of agony, and the crucified man could feel everything draining into that ocean—his blood and his pain, his dreams and his memory and his life.

"I am dying," Jonathan reasoned with himself, "so why can't

I groan? I am dying, so why can't I ask for a drink of water?"
Yet he did not. He hung there, suspended by his hands and
feeling the tyrannical weight of his body in his arms and in his
shoulders, licking the sweat that poured past his eyes and toward his lips, listening to his blood trickling, trickling, trickling from his hands to the ground below. And he was silent.

Jonathan Bar Ba'ayah had been crucified by the shore, as
had so many others, and he looked out now at the deep blue
waters, and he watched those waters moving in and retreating
in gentle waves, moving in and retreating. And again he felt
an excruciating awareness of the pain moving through his hands
and his arms and his shoulders.

He forced himself to think, hoping that by looking within he
could keep outside the pressing consciousness of his own body.
He thought how good it was that his wife and son had left Judea, along with Simon's wife and son. He thought of Simon, his
old friend from boyhood, and he felt a sudden surge of pity so
overwhelming that for a long moment it blocked out the pain.
"Poor Simon," he thought. "Poor Simon is all alone now." And
he came close to tears as he brought up a vision of the man
he loved with the silent intensity with which men love one another. And Jonathan Bar Ba'ayah prayed for Simon, silently,
even as he hung on the cross dying in his agony.

He thought of the rebellion that had failed. But had it really
failed? Hanging there by his hands, Jonathan Bar Ba'ayah began to get confused, so that the solid certainties of the life that
he was leaving melted before him like tallow in the sun. Was
death defeat? Was defeat always defeat? Was death truly death?
In the borderland where Jonathan now hovered, the obvious
answers were not at all obvious, and the questions seemed most
reasonable.

He thought of his father and of the irony of fate. It was a long
way from Kosiba to Caesarea, but really not such a long way
after all, and as the last drops of life drained from the man on
the cross, his own individuality drained with it, not away from
him as something to be lost but together with others, so that his
father's being flowed together with his own, and his own being
together with that of his son, all together into a being that
would not end.

And so, at last, a gentle numbness came over the crucified

body, and Jonathan perceived a haze descending like a curtain over his eyes. And as the sense of personal extinction drew near, he leaned back his head on the cross, not out of pain but to cover his head so that he might pronounce to God the final affirmation of his faith in ultimate Right. And he shouted it aloud so that his Roman guard might hear it, *"Shema Yisrael, Adonai Elohenu, Adonai Ehad."*

But a small drop of life still remained, and as the man on the cross looked out at the world again, he thought he saw two small figures crouching at his feet. They were boys, but too big for Emanuel and Menashe. He blinked his eyes and looked again, wondering who the boys were and who he was and where he was bound.

And then, suddenly, the image grew clear, and he saw quite vividly that the figures at his feet were, of course, his young son Jonathan and his son's friend Simon.

The dying man saw them there in a fleeting instant of clarity, and he smiled at them to allay their grief, and with his last strength he said to the boys, "Remember what I taught you. . . ."

44

Two days after the ides of May Severus' steel-encased artillery towers were ready, and the legionaries began rolling them toward the city of Bethar. Now there was no occasion for stratagems by either side, and the towers were pushed forward by naked might, and their course was slowed by naked might, and the ground over which they passed was soaked with the blood of the mighty.

The defenders of the stronghold, knowing that the placement of the towers and their catapults in position would herald the end of Bethar, fought savagely to keep them back from the walls. Unable to burn the high structures, the Jewish warriors sought to topple them, and they did manage to smash two in this way. But eleven towers still remained, and these the defenders strove to stop from moving toward the city, blocking the way to Bethar with their bodies.

The determination of the Jews had become desperation, and they fought now to save Bethar as if their own lives did not matter, as if death had no power over them.

Even their new battle cry reflected the new spirit. No longer did the Jewish warriors shout *"L'herut Yisrael"*—"For the freedom of Israel"—as they charged forward, for they knew that Israel would not be free in their time. Instead, their shout was for the ages: *"Am Yisrael Hai"*—"The people of Israel lives"—and it was not so much a battle cry as a cry of defiance to the world.

But death, though scorned, took its toll, and as the summer approached, there were fewer than 20,000 warriors left in Bethar. And two more of the underground passages leading from the city had been discovered and destroyed. And despite everything, the Roman towers continued inching forward and neared their destination.

Thus, on the fourteenth day of the month of Sivan, Simon Bar Kochba caused the following proclamation to be prominently posted throughout the city of Bethar:

To the warriors of Judea, peace.

We are now approaching the final stage of the battle for Bethar. As your leader, I must tell you that it is a stage which may well end with the fall of the city and all that is therein. For myself, I have resolved to remain in the city and to share its fate, whether for good or for evil. I invite those of you with a like resolve to remain with me and to save Bethar or to fall with it.

But there is a limit to what a commander can order his men to do, and that limit has been reached. I have led you for three years, and all Israel with you, and you have followed me loyally without hesitation or complaint. Together we have achieved many great victories. We fought Rome as no nation has ever fought her. We drove the invader from our midst, and we governed our own land ourselves. Single-handedly, we have risen up against the forces of tyranny, and we have shown the world that tyranny can be broken, that mighty armies can be smashed by the God-given spirit of man. In this way, at least, we have achieved a measure of triumph.

Now I feel the course of events has abrogated my right of authority over you. I cannot order you to die, nor would I do so even if I could.

As of this date, there remains one secret tunnel leading from Bethar. With this knowledge, I hereby release all of you from your vows to me and to the Army of Liberation. You are free to leave the city, those of you who so desire. Inform your officers, and an appropriate occasion will be arranged while there is still time. Let those of you who depart do so in peace and without feelings of guilt or remorse, for you have, each of you, done more than any leader could have demanded, and there is not a man among you who has not many times proven himself a hero. And who knows if it will not take more courage to live in the days that lie ahead than to die.

As for those who elect to remain with me in the city, would that I could promise you victory or even the preservation of your lives. Alas, I cannot. But at the very worst I can promise you one thing, a prize denied to the mass of men.

I promise you death with meaning.

Simon Bar Kochba
Prince of Israel

The trial of Rabbi Akiba Ben-Joseph was held in the great hall of the Caesarea palace. Procurator Tinius Rufus was the judge, as well as the prosecutor, and the hall was thrown open to spectators so that they might see the dispensation of Roman justice. Among them was Joshua Ha-Garsi, the rabbi's disciple, his companion and now his closest friend.

There had originally been a long list of impressive charges against the rabbi, beginning with the charge of high treason against the Roman administration. But Rufus was a clever man, and in the end all of the charges had been reduced to one, with the others being implied rather than stated. The single outstanding indictment against Akiba was that he had taught the Jewish Law in open defiance of the imperial edict.

Akiba did not deny the truth of the accusation, nor did he seek to mitigate it. Indeed he went so far as to elaborate on his action, stating publicly that he had done no more than his duty as a rabbi and that he would do it again if given the chance.

Rufus did not even attempt to hide his delight at the rabbi's candor. He stretched out the trial as long as he could, and then he sentenced Akiba Ben-Joseph to death.

In passing sentence Rufus dwelt in detail on the manner of the rabbi's execution. It was not a completely original mode of killing, for there is no such thing, but at least it was original for Rome, and the procurator had thought of it himself.

Akiba was to be put to death publicly in Caesarea's Roman arena. He was to be flayed alive, the skin and flesh torn from his body until he died, his agony to serve as an example to all who would witness it.

The date of the execution was set at two months hence to afford time for the promulgation of the sentence, so that the new settlers in the various parts of Palaestina could arrange to come and see the spectacle.

Shortly after the posting of his proclamation, two officers came to see Bar Kochba. One was Ephraim Ben-Abraham, the leader of the diminished Samaritan force within Bethar. He informed the prince that the 200-odd men still under his command had elected to leave Bethar and try to make it back to their own mountains. He tried to apologize.

"I beg you," said Simon, "not to feel that you are doing anything ignoble. You have fought with us from the beginning, and we will not forget it."

"We are tired," said Ephraim Ben-Abraham simply, and he walked from the prince's headquarters.

Later in the day Mordechai Ben-Joshua appeared before Bar Kochba.

"Please be seated," said Simon as the Minaean leader stood ill at ease. "How may I serve you?"

Mordechai sat down facing the prince, but he looked away as he spoke. "It is your proclamation. There are some five hundred followers of Yeshu left in Bethar. They would leave the city, as you have offered."

"Depart in peace," said Simon. "The Samaritans are to leave tomorrow night. You may go with them."

Mordechai continued looking away. "It is at my urging that they are going," he said. "They did not wish to leave. I convinced them."

"I understand," said Simon softly.

"No," said Mordechai, rising. "You do not really understand. And I want you very much to understand."

Simon rose and stood beside the Minaean. "I do not condemn you. There is only death here."

Mordechai turned to him. "I told you that it was I who convinced them, and now I will tell you why."

Bar Kochba made as if to speak, but Mordechai raised his hand to stop him. "I want you to know this whether you want to know it or not. The Minaeans do not fear death, for we know that there is no death. My men wanted to remain with you, but I convinced them that they had no right. There are followers of Yeshu all over the world now. Here they are called Minaeans. Elsewhere they are called Nazarenes or Christians. Wherever they are, they stand in constant danger of persecution by hostile Roman authorities. I realized from the start that if it became known that the Minaeans as a group supported the Judean revolt, it would bring down a heavy reprisal on the followers of Yeshu everywhere, whether Jews or Gentiles. Thus far we have been fortunate, because the Romans have not distinguished between one group of Jews in this war and another. And in any event the risk seemed worth taking so long as there was the slightest hope that the cause of Judean freedom might triumph. But now . . ."

"I understand," Simon repeated.

"I told my flock they had no right to go on risking other lives in a cause that—forgive me—is clearly doomed. I convinced them that they should leave here and try to flee across the Jordan to the city of Pella, where there is a large Nazarene community. The decision is mine, not theirs. The fault is mine."

"There is no fault," said the prince. "Have you not been with us all these years? Have you not died alongside of us by the thousands? If the Romans have not been able to distinguish between your flock and mine, it is because there is no real difference."

Mordechai turned away again and grew pensive. "In truth," he said, "there is but one thing about this step which distresses me. The Nazarenes who dwell beyond the Jordan are worthy followers of the Christ, but they are not Jews as we are. Thus, by leaving here, we will for the first time since our Master walked among us be severing our direct ties with the Jewish community. I pray you, forgive us that."

Simon realized that the Minaean was truly upset, and so he took Mordechai's hand, and solemnly he said, "By the God of our fathers, the only God whom we both worship, I swear a bond of everlasting brotherhood between us. We have fought as one for the one truth of the one God. And we and our seed shall remain brothers to the end of time."

"I thank you," said Mordechai, his voice trembling. "May it always be remembered that all who worship Yeshu's God are of the same Covenant."

"So be it," said Simon. "Depart in peace, you and all who go with you."

Mordechai started as if shaken from a trance. "Not I," he said. "I am not going."

"What?"

"Not I," he repeated. "The others will leave, but without me. I thought I had made that clear. I will stay in Bethar with you."

"But why?" asked the prince. "You are a Minaean. You are their leader. Why not go with the members of your flock?"

"No," Mordechai said. "I must stay." And then he smiled sadly, and as if to explain everything by it he added, "My father was a Sadducee."

There was a full moon on the evening of the fifteenth of Sivan, but the men leaving the beleaguered city of Bethar had no choice. Once having made their decision, they could not afford to wait, and it would be two weeks until the new moon Tammuz.

They drew lots and went in shifts, ten men at a time, into the mouth of the last remaining tunnel. Within they lighted torches and proceeded softly through the narrow cavity, the seemingly endless distance that led to the foot of the mountain on which the stronghold stood. Once outside they were to leave the tunnel swiftly and scatter. The Samaritans were to make for their own territory. The Minaeans had decided to assemble later and cross the Jordan in a united group.

Thus they went, ten by ten, ten by ten, in an operation that lasted through the night, mixed groups of Samaritans and Minaeans, leaving certain death for the uncertainties of the life that lay beyond Bethar.

Now there was a certain Samaritan whose name was—but his name is not important. He was a man from the land of Samaria, a follower of the rites of the Samaritans, and he was a brave man, which is to say that he had been a brave man for three years. He had early enlisted in Bar Kochba's brotherhood, and he had helped to expel the Romans from his home ground, and he had kept them out, and he had tried with all his strength to resist the conquering Roman advance organized by Severus.

But this particular Samaritan was even braver and more loyal than most, so that when the bulk of his people had made their peace with the Romans, he had fled along with Ephraim Ben-Abraham to Bethar. Here he had continued his struggle against tyranny by the side of the Jews for seven months. He had stood and fought while many of his brethren perished before his eyes. He had fought valiantly, and he had had every intention of fighting on to the end until Bar Kochba had made his magnanimous offer releasing him from the vow that he had taken.

All of the above is stated to show that the Samaritan in question, contrary to the legends that were to be told about him, was neither a coward nor a traitor. It is only that he was a man, and there is a limit to what even a brave man can bear under the unrelenting pressure of total war.

Thus, the Samaritan had elected to leave Bethar along with the rest of his people. He had done so grudgingly and perhaps even with a little shame, but he missed his wife and children and his farm. And though he had risked death, he did not relish it.

The Samaritan had drawn a lot that relegated him to the final ten who were to leave the city, and he had commented with a wry smile that he had never been lucky in his life. And he waited for hours, with a mounting nervousness greater than the fear of death, while ten after ten went before him into the mouth of the tunnel and disappeared from view.

Ultimately the turn of the Samaritan's ten came, and he plunged into the darkness of the tunnel with the others, and he lighted a torch and carried it over the twisting length of the passage. It was cool and damp within, and he looked about him fearfully, wondering if this was what the underworld of Sheol was like, terrified lest the tunnel cave in and bury him alive.

The Samaritan slipped once in the mud of the tunnel, and the others looked at him accusingly for the noise. But apparently no one had heard, and he picked himself up and moved on.

Toward the end, as the light of the full moon shone through the exit from the underground passage, the torches were extinguished, and again lots were drawn. And again, the Samaritan, who had never been lucky in his life, drew the lot for last.

Now the men in the final ten began to rush forth from the tunnel. They went one by one, each man running as silently as he could to the shelter of the woods beyond; the man who was next waited a few breaths, and then he too rushed out and disappeared into the night; and the next man; and the next; and the next. Finally only the Samaritan remained. He looked out and saw the path that he would have to take, and with a lunge he went forth and ran with all his might.

"Halt," roared a voice.

The Samaritan turned in his flight to see a Roman guard standing not far from him. Seized by panic, he changed direction and continued running until the Roman's lance seared through his side and pinned him to the ground. . . .

The Samaritan's wound was bound, and he was taken before General Severus. He had the distinction of being the only warrior from Bethar to have fallen alive into the hands of the besieging legions, and he was considered most valuable as a potential source of information.

Severus had planned to threaten the man, to hint at the awesome possibility of crucifixion. But it was not necessary. The wear of the years of fighting and fleeing and fearing descended upon him suddenly, and together with the pain of his wound they reduced the Samaritan, so that all the years of his bravery gave way to a single moment of cowardice. That moment was enough. In that moment he blurted out the location of the tunnel that was the last avenue of escape from the beleaguered city.

Far worse, before the moment was over, the Samaritan had disclosed to the Romans the source of the underground brooks which supplied Bethar with water.

45

The day after the capture of the Samaritan, a corps of Roman engineers built a dam to divert the course of Tzalmon Stream so that it no longer fed a series of subterranean tributaries. The stream itself was somewhat removed from Bethar, but the act was not. With it the Romans sealed the fate of the city, and they knew it.

The rains had passed, and with the destruction of the final tunnel leading from Bethar there was no way to fetch water from outside the city, and the supply that had been stored up within could be rationed to last only so long. Bar Kochba cut the ration to a cup a day per man, and then to half a cup, yet the city held out. And ironically, the heavy casualties that the Romans inflicted in the continuing battle for the stronghold insured that it would hold out still longer, for every day there were fewer men to supply with water.

On the twenty-sixth of Sivan, the Romans finally managed to bring their towers into position before the city walls, and the artillery atop them began to pummel the heart of Bethar, so that a hail of death rained steadily from the skies and cut down many of the Jewish warriors as they walked in the streets or rested in preparation for their next shift on the walls or waited in line for water.

Even the weather now seemed to be on the side of the Romans. As the dying spring began to give way to summer, a *sha-*

rav came up out of the desert, afflicting the defenders with its hot dry wind, chapping their skin and parching their thirsty lips and filling their eyes and their nostrils with dust.

Yet the Jews fought on despite the missiles, despite the weather, despite their mounting thirst. They sallied forth from the city and renewed their attacks on the towers; they answered the massive Roman bombardment with an insistent trickle from their own artillery pieces; in the hand-to-hand combat they fought violently and without quarter until they killed or until they died.

But the towers were not destroyed or toppled or moved; the Jewish missiles and showers of boiling oil took their toll, but not nearly so great as the toll exacted by the Roman artillery; many Romans fell in the hand-to-hand combat, but many Jews perished as well, and numbers—like time—now favored the besiegers.

On the fifth of Tammuz the Romans brought up a heavy battering ram and began hammering with it against a section of the outer wall. The ram, suspended by thick ropes from the top of a huge tripod, was moved back and forth in its course by crews of legionaries, and the dull sound of its booming thundered through the city like a peal of doom.

A large screen of wood and metal was mounted on the top of the tripod to protect the Roman batterers from the men on the wall above. But the wall was strong and not easily breached, and the Jewish archers and slingers soon learned to find chinks in the screen and would pick off the Roman crews one by one. But each time a legionary working the ram was killed or wounded, he was quickly replaced, and the battering continued.

On the thirteenth of Tammuz, in a tactic that had become typical but against which there was no real defense, a contingent of Jews suddenly emerged from the city and slew the batterers and their guards and toppled the tripod holding the ram. They were killed almost immediately afterward, but they had achieved their objective. The battering had ceased.

The Romans responded to the setback in their usual meticulous fashion. They stubbornly fought off attempts by the Jews to destroy the ram altogether, and in wave after wave they braved the flight of arrows from the wall and managed, at length, to right the large tripod so that the assault on the outer wall could begin again.

Rabbi Eleazar Ha-Modai heard the sound of the battering renewed as he stood alone in the little synagogue that had become his personal fortress. The rabbi had come to the synagogue for a brief respite to rest before completing his daily rounds and to say the afternoon prayer. He was thirsty, and he was hot, and he was tired, and perhaps he even felt slightly the edge of despair. But, as always, he strove to overcome these human frailties as he approached the Almighty, and he did not ask how or why or when but contented himself with trusting in the Lord's wisdom. For, as always, Rabbi Eleazar sought not so much to know as he sought to practice.

And so he practiced his faith now, reciting the afternoon prayer through a throat so dry that he could hardly utter the words and with the thunder of the battering as a backdrop. And as he stood there trembling with the weight of his years, his body weakened by the heat and his thirst, the Lord heard both the whispered words of the afternoon prayer and also the unspoken prayer of Rabbi Eleazar's heart. And He answered both prayers by showing the old man, as in a clouded vision, all the future that was to be with his people from that day forth until the end of days.

Rabbi Eleazar saw it all before his eyes in a sudden flash of understanding. He saw the horror of the long night that was descending, but beyond that he saw the magnificent radiance of the dawn. And while the beauty of the future redemption was thus before him, the Lord took mercy upon Rabbi Eleazar Ha-Modai so that the old man died there, before the sundown, in the midst of his vision. And those who found him in the little synagogue noted that his face bore a smile, and they wondered what it was he could have seen beyond all the brutality that surrounded them.

They buried Rabbi Eleazar in the cemetery amid the fallen heroes. They did not mourn him—at least not openly—for so he had taught them.

It was on the day following the rabbi's death, being the seventeenth of Tammuz, that the Romans breached the outer wall of Bethar. . . .

The first wave of legionaries who moved through the hole smashed in the outer wall by the battering ram must have known that they were doomed. But such is the hold of discipline and such the fever of battle that they rushed forward to their deaths valiantly and seemingly without hesitation. Only a few Romans survived the second assault into the breach, and a few more lived through the third. But, in the Roman manner, there was a fourth onslaught, and a fifth, and a sixth, and a tenth, each wave of men enlarging the hole in the wall until it became a wide passage, so that after five days of savage fighting, Bar Kochba ordered his soldiers to abandon the defense of the outer wall and retreat to the safety of the second.

With the disputed area in their hands the Romans methodically demolished the entire outer wall that had for so many months resisted their assaults, and sensing the kill, they quickly moved up their siege apparatus and began attacking the last barrier that separated them from their enemies.

Toward the end of Tammuz the legionaries succeeded in setting up their battering ram against the second wall of Bethar. The Jewish warriors still left alive within the city now fought totally without fear, for they were now totally without hope. Desperate men half-maddened with thirst, they sought only to sell their lives at the highest possible cost, and they fell in heaps, surrounded by heaps of the fallen enemy, all alike left unburied as the battle raged on before their sightless eyes.

Where before the Jews had scorned death, they now ignored it completely, seeing that death could not long be put off and could not possibly be avoided. Heedless of the missiles that flew in their direction, the defenders took up their positions atop the remaining wall and showered the Romans below with boulders and lances and arrows and boiling oil and burning pitch and with their own corpses—only to be followed immediately by another group on the battlements.

Screaming *"Am Yisrael Hai"*—"The people of Israel lives" —detachments of Jewish warriors ran forth in a mad eagerness to attack the besiegers and their engines of war. Inevitably they were overwhelmed and killed, but until death overtook them, the force of their frenzy claimed many Roman lives as well.

"Am Yisrael Hai," shouted the Jews as they attacked. *"Shema*

Yisrael," they cried as they fell. *"Mors Judaeis"*—"Death to the
Jews"—screamed the Romans. And the cries, together with the
clash of swords and the twang of bows and the wailing of
the wounded and the crashing of the boulders as they landed
and the thunder of the ram against the wall, filled the hills
with a violence that drove away such animals as still remained
anywhere near the center of the fury.

Throughout the incessant battles the bombardment of Bethar
continued, both from the towers and from artillery on the
ground, for there was now only one wall for the missiles to sur-
mount. And the battering ram continued its assault on that
wall, its crews working day and night, relieved at regular intervals and replaced when they were slain.

Thus, on the second day of the month of Ab, a section of the
inner wall of Bethar was toppled by the attackers. The Romans rushed into the city with shouts of triumph, only to smash
against a final wall—a deadly wall of flesh.

But the determination of the Jews—if not their desperate
resolve—was matched now by the determination of the Romans
themselves. They had been denied victory too long, and they
were determined to seize it now, whatever price they would
have to pay.

And so the Jewish line began to fall back, steadily back in
a circle toward the center of Bethar. It was an ever narrowing
circle, for the men who made it up grew daily and hourly fewer
in number, and by the seventh of Ab the Jews of the city who
still lived were surrounded by an angry enemy that outnumbered them thirty to one.

Yet this shrunken force of defenders refused to yield, and
on the eighth of Ab they fought with a new and heightened
desperation born of a feeling that the Romans could not possibly have understood. Without discussing it among themselves
the surviving Jewish warriors had quietly resolved to hold
Bethar for just one more day. The reason for this was vague yet
real; it was not rational but poetic. The remaining warriors of
Bethar knew that they would soon die, and they knew that with
them the city would fall and with it would fall the last shred
of the Jewish state. They knew they could not change the ending of their drama, and so they sought at least to end it on an
epic note, to hold out for one more day so that Bethar might

fall on the ninth of Ab—the anniversary of the fall of Jerusalem.

And hold out for one more day they did, repelling the most violent Roman attacks and narrowing their circle yet farther, until by dawn on the ninth of Ab only a few hundred of them were left, gathered together on a hill that had once commanded the center of what had once been the mighty stronghold of Bethar. They were all that remained of the Army of Liberation, and they were led still by the man who had led them in their multitudes.

It was shortly after sunrise, and there was a lull in the fighting as the Romans prepared for what both sides knew would be the final assault. The Jews were fasting this day, not because of the tragic anniversary, for the Law would have permitted them food and drink under the circumstances of battle, but because there was no food or drink left.

The man they called Son of a Star arose in the midst of them, and he looked upon their faces. He saw them sitting calmly and without fear, and he thought of others who were not there. He thought of Jonathan, and he was glad that his old friend was not there but, hopefully, safe in exile. He thought of Nathan Bar Deroma and of the other rebel chieftains who had been with him in the beginning, who had laid down their lives in other battles, in other places. He thought of Akiba, and he prayed that the rabbi was unharmed. He thought of Mordechai the Minaean, the son of Joshua the Sadducee, who had been slain three days before. He thought of his own life and of its ending. He thought of Mariamne and of little Menashe, and he thought of the future.

Simon Bar Kochba, Prince of Israel, addressed his army in words carefully chosen and slowly spoken, but uttered in a tone as firm as in former times.

"The day of fighting is at an end. It ends for us, by chance or design, at the same season and even on the same day that it ended for our grandfathers. We are, ourselves, coming to an end this day, but I do not believe that the life of our people will end with our lives. I have, in truth, no concrete reason for my conviction, yet I believe with perfect faith that from this end of ours a new beginning will ultimately grow. We die today, as all men must. But truth remains alive.

"Our people have fought long and hard and valiantly. Many have perished. Many have been forced into exile. Many places have been destroyed. Perhaps something has been gained by all of this. I do not know. Someday others will know, and perhaps that in itself is a sort of victory.

"I know that we are, as a people, weary of war. For my own part, I have no regrets, for it is the only way I knew. And who knows if, in the end, it will still not be the only way for our children to regain this good land. But for now it is over. Now other ways will be tried. I pray they will succeed where I have failed, and . . ."

Bar Kochba's voice was drowned out by the Roman battle cries as the legionaries ran in formation toward the hill where the surviving Jews stood.

The prince drew his sword from its scabbard. *"Am Yisrael Hai,"* he shouted as he went forth against the enemy for the last time.

"Am Yisrael Hai," echoed his men as they joined in the final battle. . . .

The city of Bethar fell to the Romans on the morning of the ninth of Ab in the Jewish year 3895, corresponding to the month of July in the calendar of the Romans and the year 135 in the calendar of the Minaeans. It fell after a siege of nine months, ending a war that had lasted three years, and it fell in the only way the defenders of Bethar had vowed it could ever fall—when there was not a single one of them left to offer resistance.

The brief spurt of Jewish independence wrought by Bar Kochba was crushed exactly 65 years after the destruction of the Second Temple by Titus Flavius Sabinus Vespasianus, and 710 years to the day after the destruction of the First Temple by Nebuchadnezzar, king of Babylon. On the evening of the ninth of Ab General Faustus Julius Severus had every reason to believe that he had dealt the Jews a death blow. Titus and Nebuchadnezzar had felt this certainty before him.

Indeed, the end of Bethar was the end of Judea, and the surviving Jews were now a people without a country, scattered abroad throughout the Roman world. Their ancestral land was largely desolate, and it grew increasingly so; the plan to

settle others in it met with little success, and most of the foreigners who did come to settle soon left, for they found that the
land would not yield up her produce to them. Some Jews remained in the country; some would always remain, but these
were only a remnant holding out in a land that had been taken
from them. And for a very long time after the fall of Bethar
the Jewish state would exist only as a memory and a dream, a
symbol and a legend—like Bar Kochba himself.

Rome made no secret of the fact that her victory over the
Jews had been a formidable feat. For the first and only time
in his reign, the Emperor Hadrian assumed the conqueror's
title of *imperator* on the defeat of Bar Kochba, and his victorious general was subsequently to be honored with the triumphal
insignia. It was, perhaps significantly, to be the last occasion
in Roman history for the conferring of such an insignia.

Even as Rome celebrated her triumph, she had little reason
to rejoice in it. The fabled Roman army had been severely crip-
pled in the costly war, and the bones of legionaries lay strewn
across the conquered land. Hadrian himself alluded to the
unheard-of Roman losses in his victory report to the Senate by
purposely omitting the traditional opening statement: "I and
my army are well." The omission had never been made before,
not in the 887 years since the founding of the city. But there
was sufficient reason for making it now.

In all, 580,000 Romans and Jews had perished in the war.
And in the words of the Greco-Roman historian Dio Cassius,
"There is no end to the victims that fell from hunger, disease
and fire. . . ."

On the morning of the tenth of Ab General Faustus Julius
Severus walked with the Tribune Quintus Arminius Caro
through the wreckage of Bethar, amid the bodies of the slain,
and felt a sense of grudging admiration. For Severus and his
tribune were Romans, and they could appreciate in full the
valor of men who had fought so stubbornly for a lost cause.

They were not walking aimlessly through the city they had
conquered; they were searching. They were searching for the
corpse of the Jew who had for so long held the world at bay.
Severus was not a brutal man, but he was a practical one. He
wanted Bar Kochba's body found and exhibited, so that the

spirit might be killed as well. Quintus accompanied the general in the grisly quest because he was the only Roman alive who had ever seen the Son of a Star face to face.

But there was a sea of bodies in and around Bethar, and it was virtually impossible to tell one from another. In death the defenders had seemingly arranged themselves into a fearful tangle of arms and legs that formed, really, a single united body that defied division. And so Severus finally called off the fruitless search and ordered the city razed, together with its dead.

The stronghold of Bethar thus became a mound of charred stones and bones and ashes. Some days after its destruction, a group of pious Jews braved the danger and went to the scene to bury such bodies as they could find. But none of the Jews remaining in Palaestina ever settled the place again.

In the centuries that followed, weeds grew from the graves of the slain and embraced the ruins. Other peoples eventually wandered into the deserted area, and Arab nomads settled there. But, partly out of respect and partly from fear, they left undisturbed the blocks and stones that lay strewn amid the weeds of the hilltop. These they called *Hirbet al-Yahud*—the Ruins of the Jews. And so it is called to this day.

As for Bar Kochba, the manner of his death was never learned, and for a time many stories abounded among the Jews that he was still alive, still dug in at the Dead Sea or up in Safed, still vowing to continue his fight against tyranny, still determined to restore the land to its rightful owners.

But ultimately the tales also died, and only the legend remained—like light from a dead star.

46

On the second day after the fall of Bethar the legionaries broke camp and prepared to depart the site where they had lived and where so many of them had died during the past nine months. One unit of soldiers was then dispatched to a section of the Dead Sea cliffs where, it was reported, a small group of diehard rebels from the En-Gedi region had holed up with their families in a series of caves. The unit was instructed not to offer these last insurgents combat but to besiege them in the caves and starve them out. It was only a mopping-up action in any case, and enough Roman lives had already been lost.

The rest of the Roman force that had reduced Bethar marched behind Severus to Caesarea. Moving at a leisurely pace, they covered the ground in about two days, and Quintus wondered idly if the distance between Bethar and Caesarea had always been this short.

Much of the area covered by the returning Romans had been wasted, yet here and there a new farmhouse on what was left of a farm dotted the dreary landscape.

"New settlers," Quintus remarked. "Foreigners. I see the emperor's plan has been put into operation."

"Dregs," commented Severus wryly. "Reprieved prisoners. Exiled thugs and their whores. A fine population."

The new settlers grew in numbers as the Romans came to the coastal plain, the area that had offered the least resistance and had therefore been the least ravaged. From these people the returning troops began to get the first shreds of concrete information on what had been happening in Palaestina during the long months they had been encamped around Bethar. The news, often imparted with undisguised relish, shook Severus more than Quintus had seen him shaken in all the months of bitter warfare.

As soon as they arrived in Caesarea, Severus and the tribune made directly for the procurator's palace. They burst in on Rufus as he was eating, and Severus asked him, "How did you dare?"

Rufus pushed his plate away and extended his hand to the general. "Permit me to congratulate you on your glorious victory," he said ceremoniously.

"And permit me to congratulate you on your stupidity," snapped Severus, ignoring the procurator's proffered hand. Quintus reflected that it was the first time he had seen Severus angry.

Rufus withdrew his hand with a sigh. "What seems to be distressing you?" he asked.

"By the immortal gods," shouted Severus, "you know perfectly well. While I have been fighting the rebels in Bethar, you have been fighting me in Caesarea. How did you dare?"

"I have not been fighting you, but the Jews. I have the emperor's authority for that, to aid you, to . . ."

"To aid me? You and your scum have undermined everything I have been trying to do. While I preached conciliation, you were crucifying thousands. While I promised full freedom to all who came under the protection of Rome, you burned a rabbi alive. While I worked to make these people forget their archaic ways, you have been giving them martyrs to remember."

"They broke the law," said Rufus.

"What law?" demanded Severus.

"The emperor's new edict. The law forbidding the practice of the archaic ways you speak of. The law I have been enforcing in conformity with your very aims."

"Only an imbecile or a swine like you could have twisted my words to justify this kind of oppression," declared Severus.

"I am not offended by your words," said Rufus calmly. "I know they are spoken in the heat of anger."

"But I am offended by you," said Severus with a grimace of distaste. "I am offended by your presence. I am offended that you dare to call yourself a Roman. Your very existence offends me and offends the memory of my ancestors."

Rufus managed a little smile. "Nevertheless, we shall have to learn to get along. I am here at the emperor's command."

"There is only one piece of good luck," said the general, disregarding the remark. "At least we have come back before you were able to commit your greatest atrocity and your greatest blunder."

"What are you referring to?" asked Rufus, and for the first time his face clouded.

"Your planned murder of Akiba. That would be the worst thing of all. You will call it off at once."

Rufus met the general's eyes. "I will not call it off," he said. "The execution is set for tomorrow. Word of it has been posted all over the province."

Severus walked to the procurator's seat and gripped the fat man's shoulders with all his strength, and for a moment Quintus thought he would kill Rufus on the spot. Instead Severus spoke to the procurator in a hushed tone which was all the more ominous for its restraint. "You will call it off," he said. "I will not permit you to destroy in one morning all that we have worked and bled three years to achieve."

Rufus rose and in so doing wrenched himself from the general's grasp. "You cannot tell me what to do. This is a civil matter. I have some authority too, you know."

"Do not force me," said Severus evenly, "into a test of strength. I have no political ambitions, and so I am not in the least afraid. But I could ruin you. In fact, the idea delights me, but I don't want to have to use my legions against your police. It would set a bad precedent."

"You would not do that," said Rufus, as if to reassure himself. "Not you with your sense of tradition."

"I would do it with the utmost reluctance. But I am still in overall charge of this province, and if you will not accept that fact peacefully, I have no choice but to impress it upon you by force. Needless to say, the necessity for taking such an extreme step would have serious repercussions in Rome."

Quintus could not suppress a smile, nor did he want to. The old soldier knew whom he was dealing with.

Rufus resumed his seat, and beads of perspiration appeared on his forehead. "Please sit down," he urged the general and his aide.

"Our position here is not as simple as you may think," Rufus began when they were seated. "This new edict, whether wise or not, bears the emperor's signature, and it is law. It specifically forbids the teaching of the Jewish religion. Now if Akiba had sought to get around the edict or had even breached it in secret, it would be easier to spare him. But he flouted the edict openly, and he announced publicly at his trial that if he is released, he will go on teaching as before. If we release him now, after all this, it will seriously damage our standing here, especially in the eyes of the new settlers. And so we must go through with the execution. Akiba himself has forced our hand."

"We must do something," Severus insisted. "I am convinced

that if the old man is put to death in the arena, it will deal us a defeat that could ultimately undo our victory at Bethar."

"I'm afraid I don't follow you," said Rufus in honest bewilderment. "Unless you want me to just release Akiba without a word and let him resume his teaching."

"It could do no real harm," said Severus.

"That I will not permit even if you threaten me with your legions. And I'm sure the emperor would back me up to that extent."

Unfortunately Severus was sure, too. The way Rufus had maneuvered the affair, the old man would have to make some concession, no matter how small, to save his life.

As if he had read the general's thoughts, Rufus said, "Let Akiba go into the arena tomorrow and publicly renounce his faith as a stupid superstition. If he will do that, I will spare him."

"Akiba would never do that, not if threatened with a thousand deaths."

Quintus spoke now for the first time. Directing his words to Rufus, he said softly, "You really are determined to kill him, aren't you? You seem almost desperate to make an end of this old man, who cannot be far from death in any case. I wonder why."

"Leave me alone with your philosophizing," said Rufus. The procurator turned to Severus. "Understand that this is the man responsible for the revolt. Not Bar Kochba. Bar Kochba was only a figurehead. Akiba was the brains behind it all, from the beginning."

"He was not in Bethar," observed Severus. "He did not fight me at Megiddo. The man who did was no figurehead. But Akiba was the soul of the revolt; I know that. And that is exactly why you must not kill him."

"Suppose," suggested Rufus, "that the old man would proclaim publicly only that the rebellion was wrong, that it was a criminal act. It has failed in any case. Let him sign a document to that effect, and I will spare him."

"He would not do that, and you know it." Severus thought for a long moment. "But suppose I go to Akiba myself and get him to sign a document affirming that, in general, all rebellion against legal authority is wrong and ill-advised. We would not need to be specific. Everyone who saw the document would know exactly what was being referred to. In this way we could save both the rabbi's life and our prestige among your precious rabble. And, in exchange, you would quietly stop enforcing the edict and permit him to continue teaching, quietly."

"That would be surrender," Rufus protested.

"It is good sense," said Severus firmly. "His teaching cannot possibly harm us. His execution would."

"I'm afraid the rabbi will not agree," said Quintus.

"He would be a maniac not to agree to this," Rufus cried in frustration. "We are offering him everything in exchange for nothing."

Severus rose and turned to the tribune. "I think Akiba will accept this compromise," he said hopefully. "I will present it to him and explain it. He is, after all, a man of reason."

Quintus shrugged.

The general limped from the chamber, bound for the prison where Akiba was being held. Quintus also arose. He had reached the staircase when Rufus informed him casually that Cornelia was nowhere in the building.

"Where is she?" asked the tribune.

"She seems to have left me."

"What are you talking about?"

"I always felt I was a most understanding husband," said Rufus. "Nevertheless, several months ago she just disappeared. I was not too alarmed at first, thinking she was probably off on one of her . . . errands. I was, at the time, terribly busy with affairs of state, and later . . ."

Rufus was still speaking as Quintus hurried from the room. In a frenzy he rushed from the palace and through the crowded streets of Caesarea. He went to shops she had frequented; he questioned merchants who knew her; he stopped women on the street and whirled them about to look at them. Frantically he moved to the shore; then, more slowly, back again to the forum, and from there returning to the sea, walking without plan, searching.

As the night descended, he stumbled yet again through the heart of the city, now ceded by the populace to revelers and whores. He called her name aloud, without caring who else might hear or what they might think of him.

"Cornelia," he shouted like a drunkard. "Cornelia. . . ."

It was late in the evening when the tribune returned to the palace. Perhaps Rufus was lying, perhaps Cornelia was there after all and it had only been one of the procurator's brutal jokes. Like a madman now, he ran from room to room looking for her, hoping at any moment to come upon her. He came at last to the large hall of the palace and found Severus sitting there with Rufus. One look at their faces told him what had happened.

"I don't suppose you managed to locate my wife," said Rufus drily as the tribune entered.

Quintus did not reply.

"If you had not been in such a hurry to leave," the procurator continued, "I would have told you that my informants believe she lived in Lydda for a time under an assumed name and then left the province altogether. But," he added maliciously, "I'm sure she'll turn up again, now that you're back."

Rufus was in obvious good humor. Quintus ignored him and asked the general, who was sitting dejected and absorbed in his own thoughts, "What happened?" although he knew.

"The old man thanked me warmly for my concern, but he said he couldn't sign any such document. He said he wouldn't betray the noble Jews who fell in the war. He said that he had supported Barekokeba from the beginning to the end and would not now diminish the honor due him, even if only by implication. And he said that, in any event, a Jew was required to rebel against tyranny, that it was a religious duty, and that he couldn't possibly deny this, either publicly or privately."

"You see," said Rufus triumphantly. "There is simply no way to conciliate these people. Now you see what I have been up against."

Severus arose. "Let's get out of here," he said to the tribune. "We can sleep with the men in the camp outside the city."

Rufus escorted the two officers to the door. "I was willing to compromise, don't forget that. But it is impossible. The only way to deal with these people is through force and public example. It is the only way we shall ever get them to abandon their ways and accept Roman civilization."

Severus turned to the procurator. "You will impress Roman civilization upon them tomorrow morning," he said.

As they walked from the palace, Severus continued talking at length and in a rambling manner which was not at all like him. "I asked Rufus at least to change the manner of execution, to make it less brutal. But he would not hear of it. He's determined on his spectacle; he lectured me on the needs of Roman policy—on the 'unpleasant necessities,' I believe he called them. He said an example was essential, that a horrible death was necessary for someone who had purposely flouted an imperial edict. There is something terribly wrong, Quintus, and it is not only with Rufus. We seem determined on our own destruction, just as the Jews were, only with us it is even worse."

Quintus had been listening intently, and suddenly the thought struck him that while Rufus' basic brutality was impelling him to destroy Akiba and Severus' basic *virtus* and concern for Rome impelled him to want to save the old man, neither was really thinking of Akiba himself. Quintus now thought of him not as an example, nor as a martyr, nor as an indication of Rome's moral health, but as a man, as the gentle scholar with whom he had discussed philosophy; as his host in B'nei B'rak; as an elder whose very years should entitle him to special consideration; as a teacher who faced death for the crime of teaching; as a man. And as Quintus thought thus, it came to him that the manner of execution was not an academic consideration, that Akiba the man would feel the most unspeakable agonies as he was being flayed alive, and that any who watched him—unless he were himself less than human— would share in that pain tomorrow and every single day thereafter until the day of his own death. And in that instant of sharing Akiba's humanity, Quintus determined that he would not leave it up to a Rufus or even to Severus, but that he himself had the responsibility to save Akiba from the execution of the brutal sentence. . . .

"It all seems familiar, somehow," Severus said. "Have you ever had that feeling, Quintus, that you have been someplace before, have experienced before what you are experiencing now?"

"Yes," said the tribune. "Everyone has. It is a common phenomenon."

"Well, I have it now, but the sad thing is that I know exactly when and where all this happened before. It was twenty years ago, after the war in Britannia, that our hard-won victory was tossed away by fools and men like Rufus. I tried my best to stop them, and they called me stubborn and rude and a peasant. But all I was trying to do then, as now, was to preserve Rome from what was becoming the only enemy she could not conquer—herself. When I failed, I withdrew from public affairs because I thought if I could not save what Rome was, at least I would not help in the process of disintegration. Yet now I have done it again. I wonder why it was my unhappy destiny to have to repeat this."

Quintus thought to himself, My plans are not so grand. I will not save Rome. I will not even save Akiba. But I will try to save something of his humanity, and perhaps of my own as well.

"At any rate," Severus continued, "we are powerless now. Rufus has been too cunning. Akiba will be killed in the arena tomorrow, in a manner so barbaric that it will forever brand all Romans. And I, the victorious general, and you, the son of Senators, can do nothing whatsoever to stop it."

"Perhaps," said Quintus under his breath, "there is one thing."

47

The heavy door to the cell opened, and Quintus entered. Akiba looked up from the open scroll he had been reading in the quivering light, recognized his visitor and smiled.

"Shalom, Akiba," said Quintus, extending his hand.

Akiba took the hand warmly in both of his own. "It was kind of you to come," he said. "Forgive me for not rising."

Quintus sat down on a low stool facing Akiba. The old man looked bent and tired. "How do you fare?" asked the Roman, knowing even as he posed the question that it was stupid.

"I fare well," answered the rabbi without hesitation. "To-morrow my burdens will be lifted from me."

Quintus avoided the old man's gaze. "Rabbi," he said halt-ingly, "that is why I have come. . . . Sometimes, the role of friend is more difficult than any other. I wish by all the gods in whom I do not believe and whom I would despise now if I did believe, that I could grant you your freedom. . . . But I cannot."

"I know," said Akiba, "and it is not your doing. But the thought does you honor."

"Yet there is one thing I can offer you," Quintus continued, "one true if strange token of friendship and respect." He looked at Akiba and silently cursed himself and cursed his feel-ings and cursed the destiny that had cast him in this role. Then he reached into the folds of his cloak and produced a small vial. "I offer you death, quick and clean," he said, handing the vial to the rabbi. "With this, at least you can cheat Rufus of his spectacle."

Akiba considered the Roman closely in the flickering candle-light, and his eyes sparkled as they once had long ago on that day when Quintus had first met him at the university in B'nei B'rak. "I thank you, my friend," he said with emotion; and he handed the Roman back his vial.

"Take it," said Quintus in an urgent whisper, pushing the vial toward Akiba again.

"No," said the rabbi. "I cannot."

Quintus sprang up from the stool, knocking it over. "Are you insane?" he demanded. "Do you insist on death by torture? Does your warped religion require you to perish in the most ignominious fashion?"

"Sit down," Akiba commanded gently, "and let us talk to-gether as we did in former times, as men of reason."

Quintus righted the stool and grudgingly resumed his seat.

"There are two excellent reasons why I cannot take this poi-son," the rabbi began, "but the trouble is you may not really understand either one of them. First of all, I did not give my-self life, and I have no right to take it. God gave me life; God must take it."

"God will not take it," Quintus interjected. "The execu-tioner will take it in the morning, with or without your God. And he will take it in the midst of your agony and before a mob of howling fools."

"Well," said Akiba, "perhaps that is the second reason."

"You were right," Quintus said in exasperation. "I do not understand."

"What I mean is, if the first reason is for God, then the second reason is for my people. All my life I have sought to serve both God and the needs of my people. By surrendering my life to the will of God, I serve His purpose to my last breath. And as for my people, I suspect that what they need most of all now is my death, and my death in such a fashion that they will remember it. For Quintus, if they remember the manner of my death, they will surely remember what I died for and also what I lived for. Do you see it now?"

Quintus arose and slowly paced the cell for several minutes. Then he looked at Akiba and asked, "Why?"

"Why death?"

"No," said Quintus. "Why life? Why love and hate and war and building? Why live for a cause and why die for it? Why anything? Why?"

"A question for a question," said Akiba.

"Agreed," said Quintus. "But answer mine first, if you can."

"You have begun the answer by asking," said the rabbi.

"I do not understand."

"Then consider, Quintus, that until very recently my people have been the only ones in the world who steadfastly asked, 'Why?' Our entire history has been the asking of this single question, and all our body of knowledge is, admittedly, but a part of the answer. So we have continued asking the question. Mind you, we have not asked it idly, nor as a philosophic exercise, nor as a lament, nor as an excuse. On the contrary, every generation has sought the answer industriously, and the question itself is based on our faith; for Quintus, to ask the question earnestly is to believe that there is an answer. We do believe it, and so we seek by our lives and sometimes by our deaths to uncover as much of the answer as we can and to pass it on to the next generation. We have been seeking the answer now for fifteen hundred years, through prosperity and glory as through troubles and defeats and disasters, and we have been seeking it largely alone. And now you, a noble representative of a mighty power that has utterly overwhelmed us, steps forward and asks, 'Why?' Do you not see an irony in that?"

"I see nothing," said Quintus. "Least of all do I see an answer or a point or a purpose to anything at all."

"The point is man," said Akiba, "and the purpose is his improvement. For you see, Quintus, by the very asking of the question man becomes better."

The Roman shrugged his shoulders and permitted himself a cynical smile.

"Yes," Akiba continued. "In this way man elevates himself higher and higher above the beasts, who never ask, 'Why?' In this way he overcomes the occasional Rufus, who does not care to know 'why' but who glories in the darkness. In this way man rises toward the answer."

"Perhaps," said Quintus.

"You do not believe me now, but it does not matter. If you wish to understand me and my life and my death, understand that in this process of man's elevation, his progress toward full humanity, I believe my people have a unique role. We must survive if for no other reason than to keep posing the question and, by our presence, to help answer it. We must survive, because I firmly believe that without us man cannot survive."

Akiba saw the skepticism in the Roman's face and was silent for a long moment. "In any case," he said at last, "all men die. I have been given the rare opportunity to die for a purpose. Many people will see me die, some of them Jews. They will remember it, and it will help them to survive."

Quintus began pacing the floor again, thinking. Suddenly he turned to Akiba. "My dear Rabbi, at the risk of paining you in these final hours, I must tell you that your people most certainly will not survive. Your army has been crushed, your leaders slain, your cities destroyed, your land laid waste and most of your people cast from it and even its very name changed. No matter how bravely you die now, your people will not survive another generation."

"You are wrong," Akiba said, "very wrong. But that is because you do not understand that we have won this war and you have lost it."

"No," said Quintus, feeling an anger rising within him. "I do not understand that at all, any more than I understand any of the rest of your tortured Oriental logic. My reasoning is not so subtle perhaps, but at least it leads me to understand some simple things. I understand that death is evil and pain is evil and death through pain is the most evil of all things."

"Yet the truth is, Quintus, that we have won, despite our tragedy. Our country has been taken from us and our people scattered, but wherever he is now every Jew carries in his heart the ideals we fought for. And he will pass these ideals on to his children, so that in a way each of them will always carry his own country in his heart. Can you say as much for the Romans?"

Quintus was silent.

"Rome is dying," Akiba continued. "You must know it. Yet you could not prove it with your straightforward Western reasoning, only with my tortured Oriental logic, for the city of Rome still stands in all her might and her people still dwell therein. But for all of this, Quintus, in the depths of your soul you know that the Rome of today is not what your grandfather's Rome was. And the Rome of your grandson will not be what Rome is now.

"You speak of a generation, but we deal in eternity. Go back to Rome in fifty or sixty generations, and you will recognize neither her face nor her soul; speak to her, and she will not understand you; try to raise conquering legions from among her sons, and she will fail you. Then come back here, and you will find us speaking the same language and holding the same ideals and worshiping the same God as when you left us for dead. This, my friend Quintus, I firmly believe. And this is what I am dying for."

"If I believed you," said Quintus, "if I believed anything that you have said, then I would pity your people even more than I pity you. For if they did manage to keep alive their strange ideals and ways under the present circumstances, then wherever they would go they would be singled out as different. They would be outcasts in every country on earth, hounded from place to place, hated everywhere; at best, tolerated; at worst, destroyed. That is the penalty the world exacts for being different."

"Do you know the penalty for being the same as everyone else?" Akiba asked. "It is death—not the simple, empty thing I will experience this morning—but true death, death of the soul, death of all that is noble and godlike in Man."

Quintus rose to go.

"You still owe me the answer to a question," Akiba said.

"Ask," said the Roman.

"You risked everything that you are to come here tonight in a desperate attempt to save an old man a little pain. Why?"

"I can't answer you," said Quintus softly. "I don't really know. I swear I don't know. I would give my life for you, Rabbi. I would willingly take your place in the arena, and I don't know why."

Akiba smiled and placed his hand on the Roman's shoulder. "Well," he said, "there, in your puzzled sympathy, lies your answer. Keep searching, and you will find something more lasting than empire. Keep searching, Roman, and what you will find in time is God."

48

"With what materials may the Sabbath lamp be lighted," asked Rabbi Akiba, "and with what may it not be lighted?"

His disciples, huddled together in the small cell, were silent.

"It may not be lighted with cedar bast," answered Rabbi Akiba, "nor with floss silk, nor with willow fiber, nor with nettle fiber, nor with water weeds—all of these forming imperfect wicks."

It was a lesson like a thousand other lessons that Akiba had taught, on a minor point of Talmudic Law, and the rabbi went on with it now as casually as if the disciples had been seated around him on a calm and pleasant day of peace in the university garden at B'nei B'rak.

"It may also not be lighted with pitch, nor with liquid wax, nor with oil which, having been set apart as a heave offering and having become defiled, is condemned to be destroyed by burning, nor with the fat from the tails of sheep, nor with tallow."

Rabbi Akiba looked up, and he saw that his disciples were not really listening. "Well," he said, "we shall continue the lesson another day." And his disciples wept bitterly.

"Do not doubt it," Akiba said gently. "There will be other days when we shall all meet again, God willing, and continue our discourse. But that is far off for most of you. Yours now is the more difficult duty in this world. You are now the soldiers of Israel. Therefore, remember what you will see this day. That," added Akiba with some hesitation, "is my final wish of you. No, my final command. That you go to the arena and witness my death."

Joshua Ha-Garsi, the rabbi's favorite, was the first of the disciples to find his voice and protest. "Do not ask this of us, my master. We do not have your strength. If I must watch you die by torture before the heathen, I will surely lose my faith as did Rabbi Elisha Ben-Abuyah."

"No," said Akiba loudly and firmly. "You will go, and you will watch it, and you will remember it, and you will not lose your faith. When things go well, when God's justice is evident to all, there is no need for faith. It is now that unquestioning faith in the ultimate wisdom of God will be needed, and it is for you to demonstrate it now, for it may be needed yet by the children of your children's children in the long night that is to come."

The rabbi had issued his final wish. Akiba rose now and blessed them singly, placing his hands upon them and thereby ordaining each of them a rabbi, a teacher of the Way.

He came at last to Joshua Ha-Garsi, and he blessed him, and afterward he lowered his hands to the young man's shoulders and held him as a father holds his son. "I ask you to understand," he said softly. "If I die here today, and you and your fellows do not see it, if I die before the heathen and not before the eyes of my own people, then I die truly for nothing. I am not the first Jewish martyr, and I will not be the last Jew to die for what he believes. There will be others, many others, before our redemption comes. They must have an example to follow. Therefore, I charge you, Joshua, that you witness my death this day and remember it and write it down in a book that others may know of it in a thousand years and more."

The bright morning sunlight streaked in through the cell's

barred window, and as Rabbi Akiba Ben-Joseph completed the act of ordination, the door opened to admit a Roman guard of three men. The Romans stood dumbly at the entrance, half afraid of the rabbi, half embarrassed at the task that was theirs to perform.

Seeing the guards, the disciples raised up their voices and wept.

But Rabbi Akiba smiled.

"What strength is yours," exclaimed Rabbi Joshua Ha-Garsi through his tears. "How can you smile now?"

"I have always taught," said Akiba calmly, "that a man must love God with all his heart and with all his soul and with all his might—even though his own life be required of him. But you know, I often wondered if I could do it. And now I smile, because I see that I can."

Epilogue

The mob seated on the elevated stone benches of Caesarea's Roman amphitheater let out an excited roar as the aged Rabbi Akiba entered the arena.

Akiba blinked as the bright Judean sunlight hit his eyes. Then he saw the multitude that was so hungry for his blood, with Rufus seated in a large enclosure in the midst of them, and he stiffened and moved forward to his destiny with the steady step of a man half his age.

As he neared the center of the arena and the stake that had been driven into the ground there, the rabbi halted, and in a voice loud and clear so that all could hear him, he recited the Alenu—the martyr's prayer.

"It is our duty to praise the Lord of all, to acknowledge the greatness of the Architect of Creation, Who has not made us like the heathens and has not dealt with us as with other peoples of the earth, Who has not assigned us a lot like theirs, nor the destiny of their mobs . . ."

The crowd screamed its fury, drowning out the rest of the defiant prayer. The prayer was in the High Tongue, of course, but the Hebrew was close enough to Aramaic so that every member of that mob could understand it and understand as well that this wretched old man, this condemned Jew, actually had the effrontery to thank his God for having made him different, for having made him one of an outcast and hated people.

Akiba finished his prayer calmly. Then, just as calmly, he walked to the stake and made not the slightest resistance as the executioner chained him to it and bared the upper part of his body so that the skin and flesh might be ripped from it in accordance with the brutal sentence.

The thousands ringing the arena edged forward on their hard seats in eager fascination as the executioner lifted a sharp, rakelike instrument to Akiba's back. He pulled the instrument down hard over the old man's body, making deep and bloody furrows in the white skin. The executioner was openly frightened of the condemned man, and he performed his task efficiently and as quickly as he could, making cut after cut in the rabbi's back, bloodying it, mutilating it so that the figure chained to the stake no longer resembled a human form.

But through it all, Akiba uttered not a sound, and those close enough to see his face realized that he was not only alive but even appeared composed. And as the rabbi's eyes searched among the crowd and found his disciples there, some thought they saw him smile.

"Dig deeper," came an angry voice from the mob. "Kill the Jew."

"Kill the Jew," roared the multitude. "Kill the Jew."

The executioner looked up to the procurator and prayed silently to his own gods that he might end this day's work, but Rufus made no sign, and so the executioner continued as before.

Faustus Julius Severus, seated beside the procurator, heard the violent outcry, and for a fleeting moment he thought how happily he would turn his legions loose upon this mob. The moment passed, and with it passed an age.

Next to the general sat Quintus Arminius Caro, whose ancestors had founded the age.

And now the time came for Rabbi Akiba Ben-Joseph to die, and he looked up at the summer sun for what he knew must be the last time. And suddenly the sky darkened, and a cold and heavy wind came up from nowhere and blew across the bloody sand and the arena and the multitude thronged around it. It is written in the legends of the Jews that at this moment God debated with Himself whether or not to destroy the earth and reduce the universe once more to water, but that a prayer from Akiba, asking patience for man, moved Him from His angry course.

Rufus noted the darkening sky, and for the first time in his life he felt true fear—not the fear of death, for men like Rufus do not fear death, but the horrible, cold, penetrating fear that somehow his entire existence had been a blunder. "Are you a wizard," he cried out to the dying man, "or are you utterly insensitive to pain?"

Akiba looked at him, but he did not answer. Instead, feeling his life slipping away, he shouted with all his heart and with all his soul and with all his might, *"Shema Yisrael, Adonai Elohenu, Adonai Ehad"*—"Hear, O Israel, the Lord is our God, the Lord is One."

And he died upon the last word, *"Ehad"*—"One"—drawing it out long and loud with his final breath so that it came out, *"Eha-a-ad"*—like a clarion call in the midst of battle.

"Eha-a-ad"—like the blast of a shophar waxing long.

"Eha-a-ad"—like a cry of victory.

And to this day, the Jews of the earth, when they repeat the affirmation of their faith, draw out the last word long and loud so that it comes out, *"Eha-a-ad."* They do this in memory of Rabbi Akiba, his life, his ideals, his struggle and his glorious death.

Thus did the Romans blot out for all time the memory of the Jews.

Afterword

In the Jewish year 5720—corresponding to the year 1960 in the calendar of the Minaeans—a team of Israeli archaeologists abetted by soldiers and volunteers undertook an expedition to a series of nearly inaccessible caves in the Dead Sea cliffs near En-Gedi.

With the aid of rope ladders the members of the expedition descended into the canyons and entered the caves. Inside they found a large bundle of letters written in Hebrew script and closed with a seal that showed a man wrestling with a lion. The letters were "From Simon Bar Kosiba to Jonathan Bar Ba'ayah"; "From Simon Bar Kosiba, Prince of Israel, to Jonathan and Masabala"; "From Simon Bar Kosiba to the men of En-Gedi". . . .

They found several letters written in Greek, addressed to Gentile Judeans and referring to them as brothers.

They found deeds and contracts dated by the years "of the Liberation of Israel."

They found coins bearing on one side the name "Simon" and on the other the legend *"L'herut Yerushalayim"*—"For the freedom of Jerusalem."

They found religious objects, including fragments of tephillin and Bible scrolls.

They found personal effects of men, of women and of little children.

And they found something more. . . .

Preserved by the area's dry climate were the skeletal remains of those determined to die in freedom rather than live in slavery.

These had been the last of the Jewish defenders. With the fall of Bethar they had fled from their homes in En-Gedi to the nearby caves, taking with them their wives, their children, their necessary effects and such collected legal records and official correspondence as might once again be needed in a better day.

Learning of their presence in the caves, the Romans had encamped on the plateaus above, giving the defenders the choice of surrendering or of dying of hunger and thirst. They had chosen to die. . . .

The last of the Jewish defenders? But the soldiers on the expedition are of the Army of Israel. And the leader of the group that found the letters and the skeletons is Professor Yigael Yadin, former chief of staff of that army, today a foremost archaeologist and authority on ancient and dead civilizations such as that of the Romans.

The members of the expedition were moved to silence by their discovery. One man expressed what they all felt. Standing amid the ruins of an ancient Roman camp, in a modern encampment with the Star of David flying above it, he uttered the ancient cry, *"Am Yisrael Hai"*—"The people of Israel lives."

I began this work on the ninth day of the month of Ab in the Jewish year 5722—1,827 years to the day that the Roman Empire gained its final victory over the Judean state. It was a costly triumph for Rome but a total one that left her undisputed master of the East. Judea's defeat, equally total, saw her last effective stronghold destroyed, her land ravaged, her army broken beyond hope of repair, the cream of her scholars butchered, the remnant of her people scattered from their ancestral homeland.

The victory was gained by Rome. And yet, on this day, there is none to mourn the many thousands of Roman legionaries who perished in Judea. No poet sings of their valor. No temple of Jupiter stands open to receive their triumph. No priest offers up prayers in their behalf to the many gods of Rome.

The Roman Empire itself lies buried in the dust of history, its language, customs, religion, hopes and dreams relegated to the realm of the scholar.

But the state which the Romans crushed so utterly lives today; its language is spoken by children; its ancient customs are still practiced; its hopes and dreams have infected much of mankind, and its God is worshiped in various ways over an area larger than the Roman Empire ever was.

The reason for this strange paradox lies in the strength of

an idea and of this idea's ability to triumph over defeat, disaster and even death.

There is a lesson in this that has more than passing significance for our own time.

It was an attempt to understand this paradox of survival that first drew me to an interest in the Bar Kochba revolt. For here ends the ancient Jewish state, and here—rising out of the ashes of Bethar—begins the stubborn dream of a renewed Jewish state. The dream persisted for more than 1,800 years, a period representing fully one-third of all recorded human history. During that period, the Jews—scattered, physically weak, subject to systematic oppression, driven from place to place, prey to the whims of princes, the angers of pashas and the opportunism of tyrants—somehow managed to survive as a single people with a common bond. No one, to my knowledge, has ever offered a reasonable explanation for this unique phenomenon.

The Bar Kochba revolt was the final struggle between two giants of the ancient world. Rome's evident power was concentrated in her military and material might. Judea's power was less obvious, for it lay in the shadowy realm of ideas. The clash of these two forces resulted in a synthesis which we call Christianity—a Judean idea that spread across the Roman world. In a sense, antiquity itself ends at this point, while other things —new things—were just beginning.

The long wanderings of the Judeans, or Jews, begin here.

The significant spread of Christianity begins here.

The fall of the Roman Empire begins here.

The Middle Ages, in a real sense, begin here.

And yet, despite the far-reaching consequences of the struggle, there are relatively few references to it in ancient records. The reason for this is best summed up in a simple Roman proverb: History is written by the victors. There were no victors in the Bar Kochba revolt.

For Judea, the war had resulted in a disaster unparalleled until modern times. Although the nation had not been its own master for more than a century, so long as a sizable community of Jews lived in the land there was always the hope and the possibility of regained independence. With the crushing of the revolt and the subsequent exile of the Jews, the possibility faded, and only the hope remained. It was a hope that had to span nearly 2,000 years before the possibility once again presented itself.

For Rome, the war was prolonged and bitter and resulted in unprecedented losses. Hadrian, in omitting the phrase "I and my army are well" from his victory report to the Senate, spoke eloquently of what it had cost the Roman Empire to defeat the Jews.

Not until many years after the revolt did either Roman or Jew take pen in hand to write of it; and even then, when they did write, it was not without bitterness. It is from these sources that I have taken the basic facts around which I weave my story: from the Greco-Roman Dio Cassius, from the Talmud and from the various Jewish legends about the Bar Kochba revolt that were passed on by the survivors to their children, and to their children, until this day.

Before writing this book, I sought to collect as much of the varied data on Bar Kochba and his period as I could find. This included historical, religious and legendary material, along with the evidence of the latest archaeological finds. The search inevitably brought me to the land where the revolt took place, among the people whose ancestors were its heroes.

This book is a novel, not a history, but that doesn't mean the story did not happen. Indeed, all of the main points of the story are historical fact, and all facts known to me have been used. What I have tried to do, to the best of my ability, is to recreate the events as I believe they may have happened and to make assumptions based on the spirit of the period to fill in those gaps where history is silent.

Similarly, most of the characters in this book are historical personalities. In the case of the one or two fictional ones, they represent a composite of people and currents of thought known to have existed in the era.

Some of the characters and their ideas will, I imagine, appear surprisingly modern to the reader. This, too, is not an invention but rather an honest attempt to portray an age of conflicting ideas, of confusion, of uncertainty, of skepticism and atheism side by side with firm faith—an age, in short, strikingly similar to our own. And of course the characters express themselves in modern terms, for the languages they were speaking were then quite modern.

*   *   *

There is a wheel that turns in the world, goes an old rabbinical maxim.

The last of Bar Kochba's warriors waited across the centuries for the wheel to make a single rotation. Left in the Dead Sea caves by the Romans, they lay there without being found as a succession of conquerors came and went. It would almost appear that they were waiting until their descendants could return for them, to the land they themselves had tried so hard to keep.

Those descendants did return, and they removed the bodies from the caves for burial in conformity with Jewish custom.

And in the Jewish year 5721—1961 in the calendar of the Minaeans—the heroes were given an official state funeral and laid to rest with full military honors provided by a new army of a new Israel.

The wheel had made its inevitable turn.

ANDREW MEISELS

Tel Aviv, Israel